YOURS, MINE AND THE TRUTH

BY

ANNETTE J. CORCORAN

Block 4 Harcourt Rd,
Saint Kevin's, Dublin,
D02 HW77, Ireland

ISBN (978-1-80719-063-7)
ISBN (978-1-80719-064-4)

Cover Design by Dublin Book Publishing

For my boys, who have never let me finish a cup of
coffee while it is still hot. And for Steven, who makes
sure I always have one anyway.

Acknowledgements

To Dublin Book Publishing, which helped bring my book to life and guided me throughout the editing process. Ryan McKenzie brought my words to life. From start to finish, I was supported and encouraged. My Project Manager, Jenika Snow, became a lifeline.

Table of Contents

AUG 22ND, 2025 – CHARLOTTE...1

Oct 12th, 2002: Charlotte.................................... 7

Mar 7th, 2008: Clara 13

Sept 5th, 2008. Charlotte 18

22 August 2025: Charlotte........................ 25

5 September 2008: Clara 32

Mar 16th, 2009: Clara 46

June 20th, 2009: Niall...............................60

Aug 22nd, 2025: Charlotte........................68

July 25th, 2009: Clara 86

Aug 22nd, 2009: Niall 94

Aug 22nd, 2009: Clara 103

Jan 27th, 2010: Clara 109

Aug 22nd, 2025: Charlotte.......................116

Feb 3rd, 2010. Conor 136

Aug 22nd, 2025: Charlotte.......................150

Mar 1st, 2010: Clara 155

Mar 1st, 2010: Niall 163

Aug 3rd, 2010: Conor 170

Dec 25th, 2010: Clara 178

25 December 2010: Niall 191

Aug 22nd, 2025: Charlotte 199

June 16th, 2018: Charlotte 220

Aug 23rd, 2025: Charlotte 230

5 January 2020: Clara 239

Jan 7th, 2020: Niall 246

13 January 2020: Clara 251

Aug 23rd, 2025: Charlotte 258

Jan 15th, 2020: Niall 264

Jan 23rd, 2020: Clara 271

23 January 2020: Niall 278

30 January 2020: Clara 283

31 January 2020: Niall 291

1 February 2020: Clara 297

8 February 2020: Niall 305

Aug 23rd, 2025: Charlotte..314

Aug 23rd, 2025: Niall...327

Aug 23rd, 2025: John 335

Aug 23rd, 2025. Reya 342

Aug 24th, 2025: Charlotte 352

6 September 2025: John 360

Epilogue...372

1

AUG 22ND, 2025 – CHARLOTTE

Ok, I found something huge, nobody panic!

The mouthwatering scent of bacon curled through the air like a siren's call, seeping through the crevices of our new home. I pictured it drifting past unpacked boxes, slipping under the hallway door, and climbing the staircase like steam from a boiling pot, nudging the twins from their slumber. Reality, however, was less poetic. I was the one at the stove, not Niall, who had an infuriating knack for getting bacon perfectly crisp without summoning the fire brigade. Me? I was already bracing for the smoke alarm's inevitable shriek. Consistency is my hallmark, for better or worse.

After days of chaos, with cardboard boxes, bubble wrap, and polite yet unnerving chats with strangers who all seemed to recall Niall's childhood escapades, I craved the calm ritual of breakfast. I yearned for the comfort of a sizzling pan under my hand. But my mind refused to stay anchored. It wandered to places I hadn't visited in years.

We had finally settled in County Kildare, the small town where Niall grew up. The move was a nightmare. Who moves on a Thursday, of all days? The roads were gridlocked, and the twins, restless in the van, swore they were being "cardboarded to death." As the sun set, we made awkward small talk with neighbours who still chuckled about Niall's naked sprints through childhood gardens. "There were swimming pools!" he insisted. Beneath my excitement, a quiet dread began to form.

The house still smells faintly of dust and unfamiliar paint. Boxes are stacked in every corner, labelled in hurried Sharpie scrawl, half-unpacked, awaiting a rainy afternoon's motivation. The place is vast, almost too large for us now, yet it hints at the life it could hold with time.

It's three storeys tall, with creaky floorboards and narrow hallways that catch the morning light just right. Five bedrooms, four bathrooms, and a kitchen so spacious it echoes when I speak. The island could seat ten comfortably, and the oversized windows flood the counter with golden light in the afternoons. It already feels like the heart of the house. Still, it's not home yet: not with everything in boxes, not with the silence that settles too quickly after dark. And then there's the attic.

Its entrance hides behind a narrow door off the third-floor hallway, as if trying to stay unnoticed. I ventured up once, just once. The stairs creaked, untouched for years. The air felt heavy, almost alive. Dust clung to old furniture draped in yellowing sheets, and the way the shadows shifted made my skin crawl. There's no need to return. At least, that's what I tell myself.

The rest of the house brims with potential. I can almost see it: warm lights, framed pictures, laughter filling the kitchen. The attic, though? No, thank you. I'll avoid it if I can.

The twins collapsed into bed the previous night, their energy finally spent. I'd shooed them from unpacking like a shepherd with sleepy sheep, promising a fresh start come morning. As they drifted off, cocooned in mismatched blankets and dreams, I returned to the kitchen, desperate to find the right box: the one with utensils, pots, pans, the pieces of normalcy. That's when I found it. A box, marked in black Sharpie: "Kitchen Drawers" on one side and, oddly, "Niall's Office" on the other.

At first, I thought little of it. We'd reused boxes; things got muddled. But its weight and the awkward way it resisted opening sparked my curiosity. Then I saw them: photographs, dozens of them. Not snapshots stuffed into envelopes or shoved in drawers. These were framed, preserved, cherished. And not one had ever hung on our walls.

From the box, I lifted a photo of Niall holding a giddy boy in one arm and a laughing girl in the other, both about three years old. I blinked. Rory and Emily. Before grief settled into their bones, before silence grew between them. Then I saw her, and everything stopped.

Her eyes were familiar, her smile achingly so. That wild, confident energy that once lit up every room was unmistakable. A tidal wave of disbelief swept over me as my mind struggled to grasp the impossible truth.

It was Clara, her arms wrapped around Niall and the children in a wife's pose.

Clara was my childhood best friend. She braided my hair every morning before school because, in her words, I looked "like no one owned me" otherwise. She insisted we apply for jobs at the local coffee shop together. She sat with me for hours, filling out college applications because forms gave me crippling anxiety. Then, one day, she became the girl who fought with me so fiercely it shattered our friendship, leaving a ten-year void until a strange coffee shop reunion just before the world shut down.

And now, she was the woman whose family I had unknowingly taken.

My breath caught, the air thick. For a moment, the kitchen walls seemed to tilt. How had I not known? I sat down, gripping the photograph as if it might vanish. That coffee shop morning flooded back, sharper now, less hazy.

Clara had been frighteningly thin, her bright confidence dimmed into something fragile and panicked. She fidgeted constantly, her fingers dancing nervously along her coffee cup. Her eyes darted to the door, as if expecting someone to burst in. When I asked what was wrong, she shattered like glass. Words spilled out, too fast, too wild: mistakes, regrets, and how she had spiralled after losing our friendship, trapped in something she couldn't escape. Then, abruptly, she shut down, pulling a Jekyll-and-Hyde switch.

"I'm happily married," she said, her words brittle beneath a forced smile. "I love my children. They're everything to me."

Her eyes flicked away too quickly. Then, almost frantically, she added, "This was fun! We should do it again sometime!"

Before I could respond, she was on her feet, grabbing her bag. She ran, actually ran, out of the coffee shop. By the time I reached the door, she was gone. I had never chased anyone, but I chased Clara, desperate for answers. Like a scene in a film, she vanished into the crowd, as if she'd never been there.

Now, here I stood in what might have been Clara's home, raising her children, married to her husband. Was it fate, or something darker? It felt like the plot of a low-budget horror film.

The back door creaked open. I jumped. Bacon sizzled fiercely in the pan, and only then did I notice the smoke alarm blaring for who knows how long.

BEEEEEEP! The alarm wailed, as if neglected and abused.

"God, not again!" I muttered, waving a tea towel beneath it uselessly.

Niall stepped in, grinning like a child caught eavesdropping. "I heard you were cooking bacon."

I scowled, masking panic with playfulness. "Who told you?"

"The fire alarm, Charlotte," he said, reaching effortlessly for the reset button with a broom handle. "Heard it from the shop."

His ease and charm should have soothed me, but they gnawed at me instead. I looked at him and saw pieces that no longer fit. What hadn't he told me? Did he know I was her friend? Did he ever plan to tell me? I forced a smile, tossed my practised "wife glare" his way, and watched him cross the kitchen, whistling as if everything were normal. Nothing felt normal anymore.

I tried to focus on cooking breakfast for the twins or at least salvaging it. I loved these children fiercely, wanting to be their home, their comfort, their warmth, or at the very least, to cook them a decent meal. I never meant to replace their mother, only to honour her memory, even if I hadn't truly known her. Now, I felt like an intruder in my own life. Every touch, laugh, and memory came with a question mark. And I couldn't stop thinking about the journals.

In that same box were leather-bound notebooks. I initially thought they were Niall's, but most were Clara's, filled with looping handwriting and scratched-out thoughts. What secrets did they hold? What truths had been left for me to find? Did she intend for me to discover them, or had I stumbled into something I was never meant to know?

The twins would be downstairs soon. I had bacon to rescue and toast to burn. But something had shifted inside me. A darkness curled at the edges of my life, like smoke around a flame. I didn't know the truth, but I was about to find out. And whatever it was, it would change everything.

2

Oct 12th, 2002: Charlotte

You made a new friend, do not fuck it up.

The smell of disinfectant mixed with cheap floor polish hit me the moment I stepped into the corridors of St. Agnes Catholic Secondary. The double doors shut behind me with a heavy clunk. It felt like a verdict and the sound carried the weight of being sealed into something I already suspected I could not escape. My shoes squeaked across the linoleum, sharp and ridiculous, and for a moment I simply stood there, swallowed by the harsh buzz of fluorescent lighting and the restless hum of teenage chaos. Laughter rose and fell in waves, someone shouted down the hall, and locker doors kept slamming like stray gunshots that made my nerves jolt.

My heart thudded against my ribs, my breath shallow and unsteady. I knew I had two choices. I could head for my locker and risk running straight into her, the girl whose name still made my stomach twist into something sharp, or I could walk into class empty-handed and face the consequences of that instead. Yet after what happened last week, Sonia seeing me alone anywhere felt like dangling meat in front of a lion. Even thinking her name made my skin prickle.

As for my tutor, the woman was little more than a glorified paperweight. She had all the usefulness of a chocolate teapot. The last time I forced myself to ask her for help, she blinked at me with that vacant expression she wore like perfume and said,

"Have you tried just talking to Sonia?"

What on earth was I meant to do with that?

"Why no, Miss," I snapped back,

"Should I do it before or after she kicks the ever living shit out of me?"

Naturally, I ended up with detention. I should have expected nothing less.

So, when the bell finally rang, it was already too late for everything. Too late to get to my locker, too late to gather my things, and far too late to blend quietly into the background where I usually hid. I kept my eyes low as I slipped into the classroom, pulse racing. My friends, my safe harbour, were huddled near the back, yet all the seats around them were filled. The only empty chair sat at the front. Right beside a girl I did not recognise.

That was when I first saw her. Clara. She had a head of wild, untamed hair the colour of burnt copper, strands catching the light like autumn leaves on fire. Her presence was oddly still. Almost serene, as if she existed in the eye of a storm while the rest of us spun frantically around her. Calm. Cool. Entirely unbothered. I hesitated and glanced back at my friends. They offered a smile and a thumbs-up, the universal sign for everything being fine. I was not convinced. I did not know if this girl belonged to Sonia's orbit. I did not know if sitting beside her would make my life easier or far more complicated.

"Sorry," I murmured, hovering awkwardly over the chair.

"Is it okay if I sit here?"

She did not blink. Instead, she replied in a voice that sounded almost theatrical,

"Frankly, my dear, I do not give a damn."

I stared at her.

"I am sorry, what?"

"If you have never seen Gone with the Wind, we are going to have problems," she said with a smirk.

"But seriously, sit. Mr Darcy is coming."

I barely had time to pull the chair under me before collapsing into it.

"I am Clara," she announced as she turned towards me, her smirk refusing to budge.

"I quote films constantly. It might get annoying, but I will not apologise because that would suggest I intend to stop, which I absolutely do not."

Something about her unfiltered honesty cracked open a small door inside me. My nerves, always simmering close to the surface, spilled into my usual defence mechanism: sarcasm.

"I am Charlotte," I blurted, the words tripping over themselves,

"Recently outed bisexual and general social liability. You might get stick for sitting with me, talking to me, or just breathing the same air. Fair warning."

The moment the words left my mouth, my stomach dropped. Why did I say that? Why now? Why her of all people? She paused, her smirk softening for a second, and I braced myself for the expected rejection.

Instead, she shrugged.

"You kissing girls compared to me channelling Clark Gable like a possessed theatre kid? I win the weird card today. You can try again tomorrow."

She smiled, warm and reassuring.

"Charlotte is a lovely name, but I shall call you Lottie."

Then she laughed. Not a polite breath through her nose. A full, unrestrained laugh that lit up her entire face. It was the kind of smile that made you believe the world might not be as cruel as it felt. From that moment on, something shifted between us.

Lunch that day became the first of many shared rituals. My four best friends welcomed Clara as though she had always belonged, and she slipped into our tight-knit circle with surprising ease. She felt like the missing puzzle piece we never realised we had lost. Over the next four years we lived loudly and boldly. We stood up to bullies, fell in and out of love, cried over exam scores and broken hearts, and planned our Debs as if it were a red-carpet event waiting to be televised. We were bright, chaotic, and wonderfully mismatched Barbies in glitter, eyeliner, and worn leather jackets.

Even when adulthood pulled us in separate directions, we remained tethered by something deeper than proximity. College, careers, relationships, the slow unfurling of independence; we tackled it all with a mixture of hope and stubbornness. Three of the girls excelled in academia. The rest of us threw ourselves into the working world, clutching job applications in one hand and pride in the other. No matter how far we drifted, we held the line. Group chats kept buzzing. Late-night calls held us together. Monthly reunions were filled with wine, laughter, and the sort of emotional check-ins that felt like home.

But Clara began to slip. And none of us noticed quickly enough.

At first, it was subtle: a cancelled lunch, a missed call, a vague excuse offered with a laugh that did not quite reach her eyes. Then it became a pattern. Clara stopped picking up the phone. She was always busy, always just out of reach, as if she had slipped into a rhythm none of us could follow. When we did manage to see her, she was still Clara, vibrant, witty, alive, yet there was a shadow in her gaze, something faint and troubling, like a light flickering behind frosted glass. It was easy to pretend nothing was wrong, although a quiet sense of unease sat at the back of my mind.

By 2008, everything worsened. Clara began avoiding even me, and we lived barely ten minutes apart. We had always drifted in and out of each other's homes, dropping by unannounced with tea or gossip, and it was normal for us to keep track of each other's lives. That ordinary closeness began to erode, slow at first, then with startling speed, as if someone had quietly turned a key and locked her away from the world.

Then her mother mentioned something strange. She had not heard from Clara in days, and she suspected Clara might be seeing someone new. The idea felt wrong. Clara always made time for her mum, and she introduced us to her partners early, even the casual ones. She was an enormous true crime enthusiast, and one of her biggest fears was becoming the subject of one of those chilling documentaries where friends described her as the type of girl who lit up a room. Clara would never date secretly. She would never leave us guessing. The secrecy and the ever-growing distance made no sense, and the more I thought about it, the more unsettled I became.

I watched for signs. Wondered. Obsessively replayed conversations. I never found any answers. Then, last night, everything shifted. I found her journals tucked behind a stack of old photo albums, as if she had hidden them yet hoped someone might discover them one day. Could these pages hold the truth we had all missed? Would they explain how we went from being the closest of friends to becoming strangers in the space of one argument that had never felt final?

My heart caught as I recognised Clara's handwriting: loopy, neat, always in black ink, always unmistakably her. My fingers trembled as I opened the cover. A thousand thoughts told me not to do it. It was not right. It was not mine. Yet something deeper, something weighty and insistent, urged me on. I needed to know. I needed to understand what Clara could not bring herself to say. I needed to hear what she had not trusted even me to hear. What I uncovered in that journal could change everything. And perhaps, in a way I did not yet grasp, it already has.

3

Mar 7th, 2008: Clara

You got the interview, now breathe.

First Entry: New Journal

I stared at my reflection this morning as if I were sizing up an opponent. My breath clouded the mirror, and I wiped it clean, almost imagining that I could clear my doubts with the motion.

"You are strong. You are fierce. You bow to no one," I whispered again and again, as if repetition alone could anchor me to something solid.

The truth was far less flattering. My stomach lurched in a way that made me think I might collapse on the cold bathroom floor before I even left the house. Today felt like a turning point, a day that might nudge my entire life in one direction or another.

I always arrive early. Fifteen minutes, at the very least. It is partly professionalism, partly survival. Those quiet moments before anything begins are when I gather myself, when I reclaim my They told me the interview would be a formality. A simple meet and greet. I never believed that for a second. People like me do not walk into places like this with an easy smile and a polished degree. I am a dropout with a patchy CV and a barista job that barely covers rent. Yet somewhere beneath all that, under the chaos and the fear, there is a small fire. It has kept me moving, even when logic said I should stop.

My mother taught me that. She spent years working as a receptionist, the kind of woman who blended into the background until you realised she was the one holding everything together. She never bragged, although she could have. I remember the pride in her posture, subtle yet unwavering, and even now I feel as if I carry a piece of that strength. It is not glamorous, often it is exhausting, but it is mine.

Then there is Mr Donnelly. God help me.

For three months he has walked into the coffee shop with the easy confidence of someone who believes the pavement was designed for him alone. The atmosphere changes when he enters. People straighten up and laugh a little too loudly, as if drawn into an orbit they cannot escape. He is impossible to overlook, not only because of his swimmer's build, his square jaw, or that deep measured voice, but because of the quiet certainty he carries. I can still recall the faint scent of his aftershave, sharp and expensive, clinging to the cuffs of his suit.

I never blushed. I never behaved like the other girls who nearly tripped over themselves to get his order right. I flirted just enough to keep him coming back, just enough to ensure he saw me as more than a girl behind a counter. I convinced myself it was strategy rather than vanity, that if I held his gaze with a smile that suggested confidence rather than eagerness, I might make him notice the ambition beneath the surface.

He never wore a ring, although he carried the kind of aura that whispers of secrets. Married-man energy, I call it. Not the clean sort where love is worn proudly, but the kind shaped by tan lines on fingers and stories kept in shadows. I am not the type waiting to become someone's second choice. Not for attention, and certainly not for a job.

Walking into Donnelly Marketing this morning was like stepping into another world. Glass panels, glossy desks, sharp corners that reflected my image back at me. Each reflection felt like a challenge. I saw the version of myself that I tried so hard to conceal, young and underqualified, pretending to know what I was doing. The receptionist regarded me as if I might pocket her stapler, yet I still smiled, polite and unbothered.

I had done my research. Donnelly Marketing is a machine, efficient and relentless, driven by people who thrive on pressure.

Getting a foot in the door here is a privilege, even if that foot ends up fetching coffee for half the building. I would have settled for anything, a tiny opening, a sliver of daylight.

But the anxiety rose again, sharp as claws at the back of my throat. My mouth tasted metallic, the way it does seconds before you think you will be sick. What if I had misread everything? What if Mr Donnelly thought the light flirting was something more? What if he assumed I was offering myself rather than simply trying to be noticed in a world that overlooks women like me? The idea made my entire body twist with shame. God, Clara, what were you thinking?

Still, I could not ignore something else. The way he looked at me sometimes, as if he was studying the shape of my thoughts rather than my face. As though he was already aware of the pieces of myself I prefer to keep hidden. The thought hit me so hard it felt like my ribs tightened around it. Is this how it starts, that slow blurring of lines until you no longer recognise your own boundaries?

There are rumours about him. Some flattering, many not. A seducer. A man who speaks with charm that borders on dangerous. Yet not cruel, never that, according to those who had worked with him. There was admiration mixed into their warnings, and perhaps that tiny glimmer of respect was the thing that gave me foolish hope.

Under the warm sunlight filtering through the high windows, I felt trapped between expectation and fear. My stomach knotted so tightly that I wondered whether anyone else could see it in my posture. Was I about to step into an opportunity, or into something far more complicated?

Then I heard it. A voice that rolled through the room with the certainty of thunder. Deep, smooth, carefully trained.

"Good afternoon, Miss Sullivan."

A tall man stood in the doorway, his broad shoulders blocking the light. His presence made me sit up before I consciously decided to move. Behind him, leaning casually against the door frame, was Mr Donnelly himself. He looked as if he had always belonged exactly where he stood.

"You were scheduled to meet with Elaine from recruitment," the tall man said, his tone carrying a playful edge.

"However, Mr Donnelly asked me to step in. He said he would like me to conduct this interview personally," he added, winking towards Donnelly.

Mr Donnelly did not smile. He simply watched me, his expression unreadable. A cool quiet focus. My spine tingled, and something inside me shifted. This interview was not protocol. It was personal. His choice.

I could feel my notebook trembling slightly in my grip. My heartbeat thudded loudly enough that I wondered whether the two men could hear it.

That is it, I thought. That is the click of the trap closing.

So now I am writing everything down before I lose control of the narrative. I wanted a single chance, a moment to prove myself, yet the room seemed to shrink around me the longer I stood there.

I am not naïve. Power rarely shows itself in the ways you expect. It is not only found in contracts or corner offices. Sometimes it comes in the shape of a simple smile. Sometimes it feels like a hand lightly guiding your back while you walk straight into decisions you do not yet understand.

I want this job. I still do. But tonight, when I finally close my eyes and try to sleep, one thought will remain: did I attend a job interview, or did I barter away something far more precious than I intended?

4

Sept 5th, 2008. Charlotte

The coffee before the storm.

"Third time lucky," I said out loud to the table. Or to myself. Or perhaps to the universe, since Clara had called to say she was on her way again. I ended the call and stared at my hands, trying not to read into the tremble that refused to settle.

Getting the six of us together used to be effortless. We would pile into cafes and pubs without thinking about childcare rotas or work deadlines. Now it felt like orchestrating a military operation, complete with tactical planning and fragile alliances. Jessie, Kim, Ciara, Lauren and I still made the effort. We squeezed each meet-up between jobs, responsibilities and the occasional emotional collapse. Clara, though, had become slippery. One unread message at a time. One rain check after another. She always had a reason, always something else pulling her away.

When I was starting to believe she might let us down yet again, a singsong, drawn out Hey floated across the coffee house. It drifted towards us like a ribbon unfurling through warm air. And just like that, Clara appeared. She strode in as if she had never disappeared at all. Her cheeks were flushed, her eyes bright. Her breathless energy had that intoxicating quality that made people forget they were annoyed with her in the first place. My heart squeezed in the way it used to when she would show up at my doorstep without warning. Back when it was still normal to knock on someone's door unannounced instead of sending three confirmation texts first.

"I am so sorry I am late, she said, her grin entirely unapologetic.

"But I brought presents.

We all turned as she rummaged through her bag with theatrical flair. She produced six snow globes, each a delicate glass world with a tiny silver Eiffel Tower suspended in swirling glitter. She handed them out as if we were guests at some whimsical party. When I tipped mine upside down, a neat inscription on the base caught my eye: Best Friends. The simplicity of it made something sting behind my ribs. I nearly cried.

"Wait" I said, frowning.

"When the hell were you in Paris?"

Ciara jumped in before I could tease her properly.

"They gave you a passport?!" she laughed.

Lauren placed a hand on her chest with dramatic sorrow.

"Where was my invite, bitch?"

Clara laughed along. The sound rang clear, although it had an oddly polished quality. Too bright, as if she were performing a version of herself she wanted us to believe in.

"Work trip. I swear. Not a holiday!"

She brushed away the questions with fluttering hands, shifting the conversation with the ease of someone who had perfected the art of diversion. She turned immediately to Kim, who sat nearest.

"So, how is the new job?" Kim smiled kindly.

"Better than college?"

College was the thing Clara shed like a skin that no longer fitted. She had promised to go back. She had said it with conviction, although the shine in her eyes always suggested she would chase something else before she ever returned. Life had offered her glittering distractions: snow globes from Paris, jobs with titles so vague they sounded made up, and the freedom to drift without consequence. She gathered those things joyfully, like a child selecting the biggest sweets from a jar.

I had admired her for that once. Now I felt something closer to unease. Her parents had waited decades to have a child. They had given her love, stability and room to grow. Yet Clara carried a restless fire, a need to prove she was not the miracle baby wrapped in bubble wrap. She wanted to be untouchable, unrestrained, entirely self-made.

We chatted, letting ourselves slip into the familiar rhythm. Mugs clinked softly. The hum of conversation settled around us with the comfort of an old blanket. Even Jessie and Lauren, who had sworn they would finally confront Clara about her excuses and her distance, forgot their plan. That was the effect she had. She could disarm you without speaking. She could make you forget why you were angry in the first place.

But I watched her closely. Each time her eyes flicked to her phone, something inside me twisted. First once. Then again. And again. By the seventh time, the irritation had become a solid lump in my throat.

"Do you have somewhere else to be? I asked, sharp and low.

Her eyes widened. Colour drained from her cheeks just a fraction.

"What? No. Why would you think that?

"You have checked your phone seven times," I said. "And do not tell me it is for the time. I can see the shiny Omega on your wrist.

The tension between us settled heavily at the table. I could almost feel the others sink away from it, not wanting to acknowledge the shift.

"Do you fancy a smoke?" I said quite loudly. The others groaned.

"Boo, smokers are jokers!" Ciara called out.

"Smell ya later," someone muttered.

Clara was already standing. She did not really have a choice. If she refused, the others would sense something was off, and Clara never liked to look weak or cornered.

Outside, late summer clung to the air with a stubborn warmth. I lit my cigarette, although my hand trembled enough to make the flame waver. Before I could gather my thoughts, Clara turned on me.

"You cannot call me out like that,", she hissed. "Alone and in front of them. What is this, an interrogation?"

"No, I said, trying to hold steady, although my chest tightened painfully.

"This is me being worried."

"I do not owe you an explanation," she snapped. "I do not owe anyone one. And no, I am not going back to college. I am done with that. I have a life now. A real life. A job. Opportunities. Paris!"

Her voice climbed with each word. The glass door behind us trembled with the force of her anger. Then her tone dropped.

"You are jealous. I got out. And you are still stuck in that same coffee house you have worked in since school. Same life. Same you."

The words struck harder than she could ever understand. Or perhaps she did understand, which made it ache more. I blinked. My throat felt too tight to answer.

"Well?" she challenged.

"What was so urgent? What did you need to ask me?"

I opened my mouth. Closed it. Tried again before a useless sound escaped. My mother's voice rose in my memory, the one she used when she barked opinions at footballers on the telly. Your words are your sharpest weapons, Little One. Wield them wisely. She swore constantly at the players, yet somehow still managed to sound wise when she said things like that.

I steadied myself.

"I've seen this before," I said quietly. There was steel under the softness.

"You checking your phone like it is a lifeline. You setting alarms. You losing weight so quickly you barely show up in photos. I remember the last time, Clara. The eating disorder. The routines. The secrecy."

My throat burned as I swallowed.

"You are fading. And I do not only mean physically."

"You trusted me with this before, and I kept it to myself. I am doing the same now. I only wanted to check on you. Not to interfere. Not to push. Just to make sure you are alright."

The tears arrived before I could stop them. I hated crying in front of her, the girl who hid her feelings behind charm and glitter. Yet I could not contain it. The pressure inside me needed to escape.

Her face softened instantly.

"Oh God, Lottie, I am sorry." She reached for my hand, but my instinct recoiled. I pulled back It was not spite. It was survival. I felt like a machine overheating, desperate for a reset or a quiet room.

I could hear my mother again in my mind. Do not swear. Trust your words. Let them carry the weight.

But the truth was simple. Words hurt. They hurt more than bones, and Clara had proved that in seconds. One sentence could crack something inside a person that might never fully mend.

Back inside, the atmosphere had shifted. No one else noticed. They chatted and laughed as if nothing had happened. But the fragile thread between Clara and me had snapped. When she offered a mild apology, it felt thin as tissue paper. And when I replied with It is okay, I felt the hollow echo of a lie.

That was the role I always played. The good girl, the mediator, the one who made herself smaller so others would feel bigger.

It would be more than ten years before I saw Clara again. If I had known this would be our last afternoon together, just the six of us, I might have held tighter. Or perhaps I would have let go sooner, before everything became so tangled and sharp.

5

22 August 2025: Charlotte

Is this even my life anymore?

I know what you are probably thinking. No one should pry into someone else's diary. It is meant to be sacred, private, a sealed corner of a person's soul. Reading it feels like trespassing. Normally I would agree. Ninety-nine times out of a hundred, I would shut the cover, set it back where I found it and pretend I had never laid eyes on it.

But this is the rare one per cent moment where everything is different.

What I did was still a violation. I accept that without question. Reading Clara's journal felt like betraying a friendship that had already been strained to breaking point. Yet what I found within those pages was not only grief and memory. It was revelation. It was a quiet voice speaking from the past, reaching through ink and paper to tap at my conscience.

Because I have questions. So many questions. The kind that claw at you in the quiet hours. The kind that never let you rest. And the only person who could have answered them has been gone for years.

Except now, somehow, she is here again. In her own handwriting. In the margins she doodled on. In the confessions she never had the courage to speak aloud.

She had not taken that job at Donnelly Marketing because she was drifting through life or avoiding university, as I once assumed. She had a plan. She had goals. She was saving her wages for her tuition, determined to shape her future. Clara was driven in ways I had clearly misunderstood. Then something changed. Something dark enough to shift her course completely, something powerful enough to make her question the very foundation of her life.

The journal did not spell out what happened. It only hinted at why. Now I can hardly stop myself from asking: what happened to you, Clara, and why did you hide it from me?

My fingertips tremble as I run them along the journal's spine. The leather feels soft and worn, familiar in a way that makes my chest tighten. I know I should stop reading. I know the right choice would be to place the diary back in the box and walk away. Yet the temptation pulls at me. The answers I need are buried in these pages and I cannot look away now. Not when each entry feels like a breadcrumb trailing toward a truth I have somehow missed all these years.

And then there is the question pushing at the edge of my mind. The one that refuses to be silenced no matter how hard I try to reason with myself. Could Clara's mysterious Mr Donnelly be my Mr Donnelly?

It sounds absurd at first. Completely ridiculous. Yet the more I think about it, the more the name, the timing and the tone of her entries align. My heart races as the possibilities flicker through my thoughts. My instincts plead with me to remain rational, to stay calm. My gut whispers something different: you cannot trust what you think you know.

According to Clara's notes, he was unmarried when she met him. That much is clear. She described him as charming, even magnetically so. A playboy. A clever man in business with a streak of control he hid behind easy smiles. That portrait does not resemble my Niall. Or at least not the version of him I believed I knew.

When Niall and I met, he was quiet, almost cautious. Soft around the edges in a way that disarmed me. It took us months to open up to each other properly. We approached our relationship gently, as though afraid of damaging something fragile. He did not chase or boast. He listened. He folded laundry without being asked.

He brewed two cups of tea, one sweet and one plain, depending on the tilt of my mood. He felt safe.

And the businessperson Clara described, the sharp and calculating strategist, does not line up with the man I see at work events. Niall is generous in business, sometimes too generous. He gives people chances they have not earned, makes deals that prioritise humanity over profit. His kindness was what drew me to him. That softness in a world shaped by ambition felt like a relief.

So who is he really? Is it possible that both versions are true? And if so, which version did I marry? The thought makes my stomach twist. I pause, listening as footsteps thud across the floor upstairs. The twins are awake at last.

Their voices drift down the staircase along with the familiar groan of protesting floorboards. The sound stirs a strange mix of affection and tension in my chest. When they appear at the bottom of the stairs, I feel my heart pull in two directions at once.

"Morning, Rory. Morning, Emily. Did you sleep alright?" I ask, forcing my tone to stay light.

They look exhausted. Dark circles cling beneath their eyes. Their movements are slow, dragging, the kind that speak of restless dreams.

Yeah, it was alright," Rory says, his voice deeper than I ever expect. He has grown so tall. He must be six feet by now. Fifteen going on twenty-five. When did that happen?

"I would need to have got some sleep to answer that," Emily mutters with a narrow-eyed scowl as she rubs at her face.

Her sharpness is so familiar that it knocks the breath from me. She has her mum's spark. Even the red curls are unmistakable. They catch the morning light like a burning flame, just as Clara's always did. The sight makes my throat tighten.

They are her children. Yet they are mine as well. Are they not?

A rush of guilt surges up inside me. I was supposed to be the fun, eccentric godmother. I was never meant to stand in this space, trying to fill a void that should never have existed. This is not the life I dreamed of. Not the imagined family with lazy Sundays and laughter. This life is heavy with shadows and questions and layers of silence.

Somewhere in the midst of that silence, a monstrous truth has begun to take shape. Clara was Niall's first wife. And I, her closest friend, knew nothing of it. How does someone hide something so monumental from the one person who should have known? Marriage. Children. A life. Then her death.

Not a single old friend mentioned it. Not even a whisper. As though her existence had been carefully wiped away. Like a mark someone had been desperate to remove.

Did Niall orchestrate that silence? Or did I step into it willingly, frightened of what might surface if I pushed? I replay the last conversation I had with Clara in the coffee shop. Her face was tight with fear. Her hands trembled around her mug. She blinked back tears she refused to let fall. I let her walk away thinking we would talk again, thinking time would soften the edges. But time never came. She was gone within weeks.

And now I am raising her children, married to the man she once loved, and I do not even know if she left him or if she never got the chance. Could he have had a hand in what happened to her? The very idea horrifies me. Yet the thought persists, circling back like a dark tide.

I look at Emily, her features so like Clara's, and manage to smile.

"Do you want a lift into town, love? I was going to pick up some new bedding, something soft. Fresh start, fresh sheets."

She hesitates before answering.

"Could you come with me instead?"

The vulnerability in her voice takes me by surprise.

"Of course," I reply.

"I can come with you, no problem."

I try to sound relaxed, but something warm and strong unfurls inside my chest. Perhaps I am not failing them as badly as I fear.

"Maybe we could get lunch while we are out?" I add lightly, thinking of the argument the twins had about Emily barely eating last night.

"Or we could just grab a smoothie if that feels easier."

She gives an exaggerated eye roll.

"Lunch is fine. You did burn the bacon again."

I laugh, relief rising through me like a bubble.

"Listen, young lady, I have many talents, but bacon is not one of them."

It is a silly moment, almost trivial, but I cling to it. It feels like a lifeline in a sea of uncertainty. Even so, while we banter, my thoughts drift back to Niall. To the way he always insists on cooking the bacon. To the way he takes over small tasks. Is it affection or control? I never questioned it before, but now even his gentleness seems like something I need to examine more closely. Could I truly have missed the truth?

I push the thought aside as Emily heads upstairs to get ready. When she disappears, I walk into the room we half-use as an office. The morning light spills through the windows and paints soft gold across the floor. For a moment, the room feels calm. Almost ordinary. Yet my heart tells me that nothing is ordinary any more.

I sink on to a cushion and pull the box closer. Clara's journal rests inside. The weight feels different now, almost sacred, as though I am holding a heartbeat that once existed and still echoes faintly.

When I turn the page, the date leaps out at me. Our last big get-together. My pulse quickens. I skim the opening lines. The entry starts with laughter, warmth and the sweetness of routine. Then it shifts. The tone darkens. The words twist. The page ends in anger, raised voices and tears.

I draw a steady breath. I know that whatever comes next may break open everything I thought I knew. And I am no longer sure whether I want the truth or fear it. But either way, I brace myself. Because what I am about to read could change everything.

6

5 September 2008: Clara

(~~Have I~~) I have made a terrible mistake.

Six months. Just six. And somehow, I have become known as the one who gets things done. It still surprises me how quickly that reputation formed, particularly in an office filled with hidden agendas, clever smiles, and ambition dressed up as cooperation. I have learned that solving problems is not about finding the correct answers. It is about reading people, anticipating what they will need, and stepping in before they even realise the gap. Offering value before asking for support.

Others call it strategy. I call it survival. What I did not expect was how much I would grow to enjoy it here, especially the quiet thrill of negotiation. I live for the tense pauses in meetings, the measured glances across the table, and the delicate tug of influence during strategy calls. Yet when I first arrived, no one cared about my potential. To some, I was simply another pretty face, specifically a pretty face assigned to Mr Donnelly. A placeholder. Decoration. They made their assumptions clear, and they were hardly subtle. Even so, I was determined to prove them wrong. I still am.

In the beginning, the whispers hurt. The cold shoulders from the women stung more than I cared to admit. I tried to brush it off, yet it gnawed at me until I found myself questioning whether I belonged here at all. But something shifted at the summer party. That night, I caught a glimpse behind their smirks. It was not hatred. It was envy, or perhaps respect wrapped so tightly in intimidation that even they could not recognise it. The things we women say to one another in the restroom, offering kind truths and sharing sanitary products, are far more revealing than anything said in the boardroom.

It felt like secondary school again: power dynamics, unspoken alliances, and the constant pressure to fit into the right spaces. Only this time, I refused to fade into the background. I had grown past that. Except there was one person whose opinion I could not escape, no matter how hard I tried: Mr Donnelly.

His condescension is like a poison that drips into my day. He interrupts, undermines, and rolls his eyes whenever I speak, as if every contribution I make is an inconvenience. It becomes even worse when other partners are present. Their interest in my work should reassure me, and in a way it does, yet it also seems to provoke him. The more they listen, the harder he works to diminish me. And when it is just the two of us, the shift in him is unsettling.

Today, after another draining meeting, he cornered me by the printer. He lowered his voice as though we were co-conspirators sharing some ridiculous secret.

"Oh, Clara," he chuckled, leaning in. Whispering.

"You know I am only teasing you because I cannot let anyone catch wind of our little secret."

His breath carried the faint scent of espresso mixed with something sharper. His smirk looked familiar, yet the glint in his eyes had changed. It was no longer playful. It was possessive.

Before you get ahead of yourself and imagine my next line is something like: then he lifted me and threw me onto the printer to make passionate... well, no. Just stop. This is not that kind of journal entry. Not even close. I loathed the man. I hated the way he wormed his way under my skin, the way his presence twisted something deep in my stomach. Still, I had to stay composed. I could not let him see how much he unsettled me. Not the full weight of it. That kind of power is something I cannot afford to hand over.

I steadied myself.

"Mr Donnelly, we have been over this. There is no secret. We had one so-called date. It did not work. I thought I had made that perfectly clear."

His face tightened, although he pressed on. He looked too proud, or perhaps too entitled, to accept rejection.

"What are you talking about? We had a fantastic night. The restaurant. The champagne. That watch I got you. How could you forget?"

He spoke as though he expected gratitude, as if his gestures were meant to dazzle me. He remembered generosity. I remembered manipulation.

I kept my voice level, folding my hands to hide the slight tremble.

"We agreed to a drink. You changed it at the last moment to dinner in a restaurant where I felt completely underdressed. You made a scene about the food, belittled a couple because they sat in what you believed was your table, and you asked me about my dreams only to turn them into a checklist of things you could buy me."

The memory burned through me, sharp and humiliating.

"The Omega watch was never about the brand. It was about the idea of earning it myself. You missed the point entirely."

For a brief moment, I felt powerful. Clear. Unafraid. Then his expression hardened. The easy grin vanished, replaced by something colder. He looked at me as if I had shifted from amusement to obstacle.

The air tightened around us, as if the corridor had shrunk. I turned to leave, adrenaline rushing through my veins.

"And the way you treated the waiter that night was disgusting."

Then, God help me, I whispered as I walked away:

"You entitled prick."

Regret prickled across my skin the instant the words escaped. Why did I swear? Lottie always tells me never to lower myself like that. Yet in that moment, I needed something raw. Something honest. Besides, he is an entitled prick.

I threw myself into answering emails, fingers flying across the keys as if I could outrun the knot twisting in my chest. I wanted to believe I had stood up for myself. Nevertheless, beneath the surface, a sour thought festered: have I made a terrible mistake?

What frightens me most is the quiet truth I have been avoiding. Deep down, I already knew what he was. I simply refused to see it.

Mr Donnelly is not just powerful. He is dangerous. He does not understand the word no. He is the kind of man who trades favours behind closed doors, who makes threats sound like harmless advice, who pulls strings without breaking a sweat.

And what terrifies me is how easily he could erase me. Not only my job or my reputation, but me as a whole. Completely. As though I never existed.

Yet I am stuck. I missed the deadline to resume my course, and I will need to start over next year. That means saving more money. That means staying here, under his gaze, far longer than I ever wanted.

Mum and Dad offered to help. Bless them. But they have earned their peace. After decades of sacrifice, they finally have time for themselves. I cannot drag this burden back home.

After dodging endless tasks and back to back interruptions, I finally carved out a moment to see the girls. We have been trying to arrange a simple coffee for weeks, and every cancellation left me drowning in guilt. They are more than friends. They are my grounding point. My people. I need them more than I have been willing to admit.

I tried to slip away from the office twice, each attempt more desperate than the last. Both times, Mr Donnelly conjured some invented nonsense, an urgent matter that miraculously demanded my immediate attention the moment I stood up. The man had a talent for trapping me in place. I was about to give up entirely when Mrs Kenny swept into the room with the force of a kind-hearted storm.

"Clara, dear, you have not had your lunch yet," she said, her eyebrows lifting in exaggerated horror that made me want to laugh and cry at the same time.

Before I could offer even the weakest excuse, she turned to Donnelly with a glare sharp enough to shave metal.

"She deserves a break, do you not agree?"

It should have been a small moment, something barely worth noticing. Yet it meant the absolute world to me. A tiny rebellion on my behalf. A reminder that not everyone in this place was a wolf in a suit, waiting for the next opportunity to bite.

She pressed a few notes into my hand for her favourite croissant and insisted that I go enjoy the coffee house she knew I adored. The gentleness of the gesture cracked something in me and I nearly cried with relief. I gathered my jacket, handbag, gifts, phone, all of it, and bolted before anything else could rise up and swallow me again.

There was a surprising lightness in my step as I left the office, although my heart still hammered from the earlier tension. There is real power in walking away, even if the escape lasts only a short while.

"I am almost there, I promise," I panted into the phone, weaving through strangers on the packed street as if the pavement were shifting beneath my feet. The warm September air filled my lungs in greedy gulps, although it did nothing to cool the fire blazing in my cheeks. My bag bumped against my hip with every stride like a ticking clock, marking each unforgiving second that confirmed I was late. I hated being late with a passion that bordered on panic.

"Cannot wait to see you all," I forced out, shaping my voice into something cheerful, although the smile behind it strained.

The bell above the coffee house door jangled violently as I burst inside, a chaotic mixture of limbs, breathlessness, and jittery nerves. I must have looked completely unhinged, my hair wild from the wind, my eyes darting everywhere, and my bag swinging at my side like a blunt weapon. Reya, the new barista with eyes that glowed like candle flames and a laugh that always seemed to brighten the room, flashed me a knowing grin.

"Hi," she chimed, her voice warm and bright enough to steady me a little.

The comforting scent of roasted beans and cinnamon wrapped around me, softening the edges of my frantic energy. Even so, my nerves hummed beneath my skin as I scanned the shop. Then I saw them. My girls. My constants. All gathered around our old corner table as if time had not shifted beneath us. Yet it had. Six months had vanished, swallowed whole by silence, work, and him.

They looked just the same, beautifully and comfortingly the same. Jessie, our radiant leader, lit up the entire place the instant I spotted her. Her laughter rose above the chatter like a familiar melody, bright and contagious, drawing the room into its warmth. She had gone blonde again, of course, her hair a living canvas for whatever colour her soul felt like displaying that season. Every shade looked as though it had been designed solely for her.

Next to her was Kim, tiny and luminous, vibrating with her usual boundless energy even while perched carefully on the edge of her seat. She was mid-story, naturally, her soft and melodic voice carrying across the table with that soothing charm I had missed more than I could admit. She radiated sweetness and quiet strength, as though she possessed a secret reservoir of kindness that she drew from without ever running dry. All five feet of her seemed to glow with a fierce tenderness that made you feel instantly welcome.

Beside Kim sat Ciara, her arms crossed in the same familiar pose, her expression guarded, although her eyes remained gentle and impossibly perceptive. She wore her strength like armour, yet those of us who knew her recognised the deep empathy beneath the surface. No one understood anxiety quite like she did. She could sense it in you before you spoke a single word. She was our quiet rescuer during chaos, offering either the right words or the right silence with perfect instinct.

And then there was Lauren. Steady, calm, impossibly observant Lauren. Her gaze held a depth that could steady even the worst storm inside you. Beneath that calm sat a spark, the precise amount of fire needed to nudge you forward when fear tried to root you in place. She had a gift for supporting you exactly as you needed. Never too much, never too little, always just enough. Her belief in you was the sort that made you believe in yourself.

They were all there, just as they had always been, each one a cherished part of something sacred. My heart felt tight in my chest with how much I loved them.

Lottie sat directly across from the door. Her eyes met mine the moment I stepped inside, and something unspoken passed between us. It felt like a pull, strong and heavy, carrying warmth and warning in equal measure.

"I am so sorry I am late," I said, grinning in a way that made it impossible to pretend I truly regretted it.

"But I brought presents."

I had not taken even three steps towards them before my phone buzzed violently in my pocket. I flinched. Of course. Mr Donnelly.

The familiar dread curled through me as the screen lit up. "Where the hell are you?"

My stomach plummeted. Eight minutes. I had only been away eight minutes. Yet to Mr Donnelly, it might as well have been a week.

I did not open the other messages. I could not. Not with all their eyes on me. Instead, I gave a bright little wave and offered a soft "Hey" before slipping into the safety of our circle.

I pulled out the small trinkets I had picked up in Paris, souvenirs from a trip that had felt like a beautifully wrapped nightmare. The snow globes clinked against one another in my bag like restless spirits. The girls adored them, of course, although my smile wavered as the memory rose sharply behind my ribs.

Paris had been beautiful, almost painfully so. The trip itself had been a complete disaster. Suffocating in every possible way. Mr Donnelly had booked a lavish three bedroom apartment for himself, his valet, and me. He insisted he needed me close, claimed he could not manage without my help. The truth was far uglier. He wanted me cornered. Called me his assistant. But the moment I pushed back against his unwelcome touch, he snapped, revealing exactly what he had intended all along.

"What do you think I brought you for?" His voice cracked like a whip as he grabbed my arm to pull me close. I remember freezing, the air sucked clean from the room as if someone had opened a vacuum behind me. For a heartbeat I felt suspended, unable to move or think.

"You could not have booked the flights without me, sir," I said, forcing calm into my tone, although my insides screamed and twisted. I tried to steady my breathing. I tried to keep my voice level. I failed at both.

"So I assumed I was here to assist you, not fucking service you."

His eyes darkened, the light in them swallowed by something cold and dangerous. His grip tightened with a painful precision that made my skin prickle. In that moment, the one where my fear belittled my fury, I knew I needed to escape before the situation became something I would not recover from. My temper often made me say things my brain had not yet vetted, and the consequences usually followed like shadows.

I ran, not with my feet, but with everything inside me. Emotionally and spiritually I fled. I drifted along the quiet, cobblestone streets of Paris, letting the city swallow me as dawn crept over the rooftops. Rue Crémieux, usually crowded with tourists, lay beautifully still in the early morning light. The pastel façades glowed softly, and for a moment the world felt like it had stopped spinning.

The snow globes were never part of any plan. They were nothing more than a small, desperate gesture, an attempt to salvage something gentle from a night I wished I could erase. I stumbled upon a tiny stall just as it opened, the vendor half asleep, and the simplicity of choosing something delicate made me feel anchored. It felt like a thread to hold onto as I made my way back to the apartment.

Back at the table, laughter bubbled around me, warm and careless. My phone buzzed again. Another message. Then another. His name lit up the screen like a warning flare.

"You would be nothing without me. I could end you in one call."

The words hit like a punch to the gut. My fingers trembled under the table, wrapped tightly around the stem of my coffee cup as if it might steady me. The worst part was the tiny whisper in my mind agreeing with him. I had no qualifications. No backup plan. Only him, this job, and the bloody Omega watch I wore like a collar that gleamed every time I lifted my hand.

Lottie noticed. Of course she did.

"Do you have somewhere else to be?" she asked quietly. Her words cut sharper than I expected.

"What? No! Why would you think that?" I laughed too quickly, too defensively. My fingers twitched, betraying me before I could hide them.

"Because that is the seventh time you have checked your phone," she said evenly and nodded toward my wrist.

"And do not tell me it is to check the time. I can see that shiny Omega on your wrist."

Something cracked inside me. Lottie had seen the watch, the lie, the cost of everything I had traded. And there was no judgment in her voice, only concern. Somehow that was worse, because concern required closeness, and I had pushed everyone away.

"Do you fancy a smoke?" she offered casually, loud enough that the others heard.

The girls groaned in a chorus of playful disapproval. "Smokers are jokers."

I managed a grin, though my stomach churned. I was not ready to talk. I had not even figured out how to think. We stepped outside. The heat slammed into me, thick and heavy. It clung to my skin. But the weight of what I carried pressed much harder. When she turned to me, I felt the pressure reach its limit. I broke.

"You cannot just call me out like that," I said. My voice cracked, betraying everything I wanted to hide.

"Alone. In front of them. What is this, an interrogation, Lottie?"

"No." Her eyes widened, pain flashing through her like lightning streaking across a dark sky.

"This is me being worried."

"I do not owe you an explanation," I snapped. My eyes stung, and my temper flared.

"I do not owe anyone anything. And no, I am not going back to college. I am done with all that. I have a life now, a real life. A job. Opportunities. Paris."

A lie. Every word tasted wrong. It was as if something darker had taken over, my fear pulling the strings and using my tongue as its puppet. And then I went too far.

"You are just jealous. I got out. And you are still stuck in that same coffee house you have worked in since school, same life, same you."

Silence. I felt the moment she cracked. Something inside her buckled, and I swear I heard something breaking. Fragile. Final. God. I did not mean it. I did not mean any of it. She looked at me as though I had slapped her, and maybe, in a way, I had. Still, I pushed forward, desperate to recover what I had shattered.

"Well?" I asked, more softly this time.

"What was so urgent? What did you need to ask me?"

She hesitated. Swallowed. When she finally spoke, her words landed with the force of a hurricane.

"I have seen this before," she said, her voice soft, but with steel underneath.

"You, checking your phone like it is a lifeline. You, setting alarms. You, losing weight so fast you vanish in photos. I remember the last time, Clara. The eating disorder. The routines. The secrecy."

I froze.

"You are losing weight. You are disappearing. And I do not mean just physically."

She had seen me, not the polished, put together assistant I pretended to be, but the girl who once stared down at a slice of bread and saw failure. The girl who measured her worth in skipped meals and numbers on a scale. The girl I had sworn I would never become again.

I could not breathe.

"You asked me to keep it quiet. I did. But this feels the same. I just wanted to talk. To ask if you are okay. No judgement. Not a fix. Just a question."

A lump formed in my throat, heavy and hot. My vision blurred. I reached for Lottie's hand instinctively, searching for comfort, but she flinched. That small motion, her pulling away, gutted me more than any insult could. I had broken something sacred.

Lottie was the type of person who picked every word with care, as though laying stones across a river. And now I had stomped through the water and scattered everything. Her silence was not punishment. It was grief.

I want to fix this. I want to claw my way back to her trust. But right now, the silence between us screams louder than anything I said. I made this mess. I made this bed. And tonight, I will lie in it. Alone.

7

Mar 16th, 2009: Clara

What Was Hidden Is Now Proof

I have not written in a while. Even though I refuse to apologise to an inanimate object, you are my journal, which means you are meant to witness my mess, my progress, and every stumble between the two. So maybe I should say it. Sorry for the silence. The past few weeks have been a storm, wild and relentless, and I am still clawing my way through it. I need to pick up where I left off because the weight of everything feels like it is pressing the breath out of me.

It began with Mr Donnelly's voice, sharp and cold, slicing through the glass walls of his office and spilling into the hallway like acid that burned its way into my skin.

"If you don't come to London with me, don't bother being here when I get back, Clara. What good are you if you can't do your bloody job?"

His finger jabbed the air and landed on me as if I were a broken object he wished someone would toss into a skip. People walking past slowed, eyes darting between us, but none of them intervened. I stood frozen, exposed under an invisible spotlight that seared me with shame, confusion and a sudden sense of worthlessness. His words crashed into me, yet beneath his fury I noticed the cracks in the performance. Only yesterday, when it was just the two of us, he had practically begged me to come on the trip, dressed it up as some sort of celebration of my first year. As if that were something I would ever want to celebrate with him.

His enthusiasm had curdled overnight into a weapon. That shift was when I realised something important. Mr Donnelly manipulated everyone around him, not just me. A predator wrapped in charm and seniority, a man who thrived on control. His yelling had not been a fit of temper. It had been calculated, precise, a game designed to break me down and make me flinch like a child who had done something terribly wrong.

I thought of Lottie then, and of how strangely similar our childhoods had been despite the gap in our parents' ages and quirks. We grew up quite differently from most Irish kids. Neither of us lived under the shadow of the Irish mammy's wooden spoon. For many children it was a symbol of fear and punishment. For us it meant laughter, dreadful baking experiments, and faces streaked with flour. The count to three was not a threat; it was the signal for a chase around the kitchen, a gleeful challenge that usually ended in squeals and sticky hugs. It took us years to understand that not everyone had that.

Which made what I was facing now feel all the more alien. This was not simply unfair or exhausting. This was abuse. It took me far too long to admit that, to understand that Mr Donnelly's tantrums and invasive remarks were neither normal nor deserved.

The other partners dismissed everything at first, turning it on me, suggesting I had provoked him or that I was not up to the job. Yet when I took on more of their work and kept everything afloat, they could no longer deny the truth. I was capable, reliable and valuable, no matter how hard he tried to paint me otherwise. But even then, despite recognising what was happening, not one of them said a word in my defence.

Then came the day that changed everything. Thursday, March fifth, etched into my memory like a scar that refuses to fade.

The canteen buzzed with lunchtime chatter. Trays clattered and the smell of lasagne and burnt coffee drifted through the air. I queued for food with my hands wrapped around an empty plate, palms damp with nerves, when I felt Mr Donnelly move in behind me. Far too close. His presence pressed down on me like a storm about to break.

Then his breath brushed my ear, hot and intimate in a way that made my stomach twist.

"We are going to have so much fun in London."

My fingers slipped and the tray crashed onto the metal rail, sending lasagne sliding across it. Panic roared through me and my body moved before my mind caught up. I bolted for the coffee room, the only place with proper walls and a door apart from the toilets, desperate for air and distance. But he followed, footsteps quick and determined. I should have eaten in the loo, honestly.

The door clicked shut behind him, final and unmistakable, and suddenly I was trapped. He cornered me against the counter, his grip locking around my wrist, the other hand stroking the braid that lay over my shoulder and brushed against my chest. The sensation made my skin crawl. His hands had hovered too close before, but now they were on me and I could not escape.

His voice dropped to something low and poisonous.

"You can play the innocent little girl in front of everyone else, but I see you for the tart you are."

If anyone has ever wondered why a woman does not always scream or fight when cornered, let me say it clearly. It is not weakness. It is not submission. It is paralysis. Your mind begs you to run, to shout, to shove him away, but your limbs shut down as if someone has pulled out the plug. Inside I was fighting, clawing, screaming. But my body stayed still, frozen by terror. I felt small, filthy, and violated. Paris had already left its mark on me, but this was different. This was my workplace, broad daylight, people only metres away. Something inside me cracked open.

What I did not know was that Mr Skelly, one of the oldest and kindest managers in the company, had walked by and seen everything. He stood in the doorway for a moment that seemed impossibly long although it could only have been seconds.

He came in with his assistant, Mrs Kenny. His laughter filled the room at first, a carryover from whatever joke they had shared, but it died instantly when he registered what he was looking at. His face shifted from cheerful to horrified disbelief. Relief flooded me so suddenly that my knees nearly gave way.

"Why don't you take Clara over to the coffee dock for a break?" he said gently to Mrs Kenny. His meaning was unmistakable. Get her out, now.

Mrs Kenny placed a guiding hand on my arm, steady and warm, and I clung to that small kindness. I could barely hold myself upright. My body trembled and my mind felt detached, as if watching from a distance.

I glanced back as she led me out and saw Mr Skelly blocking the doorway, preventing Mr Donnelly from slipping away. He closed the door with careful, deliberate control. Then I heard his voice, stripped of any softness.

"What the actual fuck are you playing at? She is a child, and that did not look consensual."

For the first time in months, I braced for something other than fear. HR meetings, questions, gossip, yes, but behind all of that, something else stirred. Hope. Someone else had seen the truth. My secret was no longer buried beneath shame. The walls I had built around it were beginning to crumble and I was no longer carrying this alone.

When I returned to my desk, a letter awaited: not the termination notice I had braced myself for, but an approval for twelve days of annual leave that took effect immediately, despite the fact I had never submitted a request. In almost a year, I had not taken a single day off. My pulse slowed, not quite relief, but something close.

It was not celebration, but it was space. A breath. The first one I had taken in far too long.

Those days passed in a haze of indulgence: good meals that reminded me I still had taste buds, too much gin, long sleeps that felt almost medicinal. I let myself unravel a little, loosen the knots I had carried for months. Yet I saved a sliver of strength to write this, because what followed next still leaves a taste of disbelief at the back of my throat, as if I lived it in a dream I have not fully woken from.

My first day back. I told myself the nightmare would end, that maybe time had softened the edges, that silence had finally been respected. I had almost convinced myself of that lie. But walking into the office made the world shift beneath my shoes, as if some quiet betrayal had taken place in my absence.

A stranger sat in my chair. She looked young, perhaps younger than me, and I was only just shy of twenty-one. Blonde hair, bright eyes, a smile that suggested she knew things I did not.

'Oh, it's you,' she said, her voice thick with sarcasm.

'Yes,' I replied, my voice trembling despite my best efforts. 'And who are you?'

She straightened in the chair as if claiming territory.

'I'm Megan. Mr Donnelly's new personal assistant. Been here since you walked out.'

My chest tightened as though something inside me had snapped. Walked out? I had not walked anywhere. I had been told to take leave, but no one had whispered a word about being replaced. No warning, no explanation, nothing.

Then Mr Skelly appeared, stepping into the tension like sunlight cutting through fog. His warmth was an unexpected balm. He greeted me with the easy familiarity of an old friend.

'Well, don't you look refreshed and replenished and raring to go,' he said, quoting one of my favourite films with a grin that reached his eyes. 'Did you enjoy your time off?'

Megan's expression faltered at once. Confusion flickered across her face as she stumbled into the truth she had not been given.

'Oh god, I'm so sorry,' she whispered. 'I thought you just walked out, I didn't know it was...' Her words tangled together as if she feared they might break apart if she spoke too slowly.

'No, don't be sorry,' I said gently, my voice softening without effort. 'It's fine. Truly.'

Because what else could I do? I would not fight a young woman caught in the web Donnelly spun around anyone who dared to exist near him.

Mr Skelly guided me into his office. The moment I stepped inside, it felt like entering another world entirely, one built from kindness rather than control. There were family photos that showed decades of laughter, trophies from egg and spoon races his grandchildren had long since outgrown, shelves packed with well-loved murder mysteries and comedian biographies. It smelled like old paper, lemon polish, and humanity.

He gave me a hopeful smile.

He explained that he wanted me on his team, that Mrs Kenny had been forced to take indefinite leave after dislocating her hip during an overambitious attempt to keep up with her grandson's skateboard tricks. His words lit something in me that had been dormant for months: purpose, validation, even a fragile sense of excitement. I worried for poor Mrs Kenny, of course, yet at the same time I felt the universe tilt ever so slightly in my favour, as if someone had finally seen the potential I had been trying to show for so long.

'You are an invaluable asset, Clara. Never let anyone make you feel less than you are, because you are worth far more. So, what do you say to my offer?' His words wrapped around me like a soft scarf after a bitter storm.

I paused to savour the moment: the silence, his sincerity, the way my lungs filled without ache.

'I say,' I began, letting the air thicken with drama the way I always did, 'two steaming cups of coffee with just a splash of milk and two sweeteners coming up, sir.' I beamed, letting a grin burst free, bright enough to power the floor's constantly flickering lights.

Inside, my pulse fluttered like a small bird finally coaxed out of its cage. After almost a year suffocating under Donnelly's iron hand and his lingering stares that crawled over my skin, it was ending. Finally.

I headed for the break room, nerves fizzing beneath my skin. Even with the shift in personnel, my body had not caught up to the change. Shadows still made me flinch. Sudden noises still rattled my ribs.

I nudged the door open and left it ajar behind me. Just a sliver, but enough. A tiny escape hatch I could bolt through if needed.

Someone was already inside, headphones clamped over their ears like armour against the world. They barely glanced up, which was a blessing. I gave a small wave anyway, a polite offering to keep the peace. We all had our own methods of survival here.

I turned to the coffee machine, letting the hum of heating water and the clink of mugs ground me. The scent was soothing, warm, like a memory of mornings where no one barked your name with malice. I reached for two cups, humming under my breath.

Then a voice burst through the air.

'Where the hell have you been?'

The words hit me like a slap. His voice. My stomach plunged. My hand froze in mid-air. For a heartbeat I could not breathe.

Mr Donnelly?

I spun so fast my spine protested, but it was not him. It was Niall.

And the relief that washed through me made my legs go weak. It felt foolish, almost childish, yet there it was: a tidal wave crashing through the fear.

'Hi Niall,' I said, though my voice still trembled. 'You frightened the holy bejesus out of me.' I tried to laugh, but it came out thin. 'I didn't vanish off the planet. I just took annual leave.'

His grin was easy and boyish, softening the space between us.

'Nice for some,' he snickered, then raised his hands in surrender. 'No, I'm teasing. Did you do anything good?'

Niall always looked as if he had stepped out of a heartwarming film, not as the lead, but as the best friend you only realised you adored once it was far too late. He had the solid build of a rugby player and a smile that could coax warmth out of winter. God help me, I could not look at him too long without my mind drifting toward places that had very little to do with office etiquette.

He was not perfect, thank goodness. Perfection would have made him untouchable. No, Niall was the kind of handsome that felt lived in, believable, the sort you could imagine teasing you in the supermarket aisle, then pinning you against the fridge once the children had finally gone to sleep. It was ridiculous and human and far too tempting for someone who had spent nearly a year feeling invisible or, worse, watched.

Oh my god. I needed to stop. Now.

"Hello?" he laughed, waving a hand in front of my face as if checking whether I was still breathing.

"Earth to Clara. You sure you didn't drift off to another planet? I asked if you did anything nice on your time off."

I snapped back to the moment, far more awkwardly than I wanted to.

"Oh, right. Honestly, I just caught up on sleep," I said, clinging to the lifeline he offered.

"I hadn't realised how exhausted I was until I finally stopped moving."

Niall nodded in that knowing way of his, like he understood something deeper without needing to say it aloud.

"Completely fair. I mean, look where you work," he paused, then rushed on.

"I, oh no, I didn't mean that as a complaint. I love my job. Love it. So much love," he added with theatrical solemnity, hand over his heart as if swearing an oath.

"But I am allowed to say it, since I'm related to half the people in here."

Shit.

Shit.

His name. Donnelly. How had I missed it? My stomach flipped, a cold wave rolling through me. I had assumed it was a common enough surname, something like Smith or Murphy. There were hundreds of people here, surely it was possible. Surely.

Still, I didn't ask. I wouldn't ask. I couldn't afford to dig deeper. My new chapter had only just begun, and I was not about to rip out the first page. Besides, I reassured myself, there is no way they are related. They do not share any of the same features. Maybe he has a distant uncle in the building, someone on a completely different floor. Anything but the truth I feared.

"Right," I said, my voice far brighter than I felt as I lifted the two hot coffees.

"Well, that's me." I turned to go, hoping my legs would not betray me.

"Wait, Clara."

His voice stopped me. Lower now, more serious, as if the air between us had shifted.

I turned, half expecting him to announce that I had taken the wrong mug or dropped someone's order.

"If I ask you something, and it's not your cup of tea, feel free to tell me to feck off," he said, the words tumbling out too quickly. He looked at me with an intensity that made my breath falter, waiting for an answer to a question he had not yet asked.

I blinked. "You haven't asked anything yet."

He ran a hand through his hair, nerves flickering across his face. Niall never looked nervous. It unsettled me more than it should have.

"Right. Alright. I'm just going to say it. Although please note that I don't usually do this. I missed you while you were away. And I figured if I didn't say something now, I might regret it. I know we barely know each other, but that can be fixed easily. Ya know?"

My mouth dried. Words scrambled for the nearest exit, abandoning me with ruthless efficiency.

Was he? Was he actually asking me out? Surely not. He still had not quite formed an actual question. For a heartbeat, I found it almost adorable how bad he was at this, if this was in fact him asking me out.

Then my brain flooded with static. A thousand thoughts crashed over me at once.

Shit. He is asking me out.

Do not blush. Do not faint. Do not scream. Be cool, Clara. Be normal. Act like someone who has been asked out before without combusting.

But my pulse was a war drum, beating loud enough to echo inside my skull.

"I've offended you," he said quickly, eyes widening.

"God, I knew this would get awkward. We can forget I said anything, and if you ever want to talk to me again after they surgically remove my foot from my mouth, I'll be in the breakroom. Forever. Alone."

I needed to respond. Say something, Clara. Anything. Even a sneeze.

"You said tea," I managed at last.

"What?" He looked completely at sea.

"You said tea, and it threw me. I'm more of a coffee girl. How about we grab one together sometime? Outside the office, I mean?"

His grin erupted across his face, bright as sunlight breaking through cloud.

"Yeah. Yeah, I'd love that."

The tension between us cracked, replaced with something lighter, warm and sparking in the air.

"Wait," he said, pretending to ponder with exaggerated seriousness.

"Did I ask you out, or did you ask me out?"

I winked. "Team effort."

I walked away with a spring in my step, and maybe a slightly intentional sway, praying I did not trip and destroy my moment before it had even begun.

"After work?" he called.

"Absolutely," I replied without looking back. Inside, I was nothing but fireworks and glitter, an entire carnival set loose in my chest.

Back at my new desk, I sat in a haze of post-adrenaline happiness. For a brief, gentle moment, I let myself enjoy it: the warmth, the flutter, the possibility of something new and bright taking shape.

I reached for my phone. I wanted to call Lottie. She would have screamed. She would have demanded every detail. But it had been six months since we last spoke. Six months since that fight: the awful, bitter words I spat at her that still haunted me on quiet nights. How can I call her now and blurt out my joy? My racing pulse? My ridiculous grin?

I had not messaged the girls in months. Not properly. They tried at first, God, they tried. But I never replied. The days blurred together, work swallowed everything, and when you live in survival mode, even responding to a meme feels like climbing Everest with bare hands.

Eventually, their attempts fizzled out. Silence settled in the space where our friendship used to sit. Now I was sitting here, full of light and excitement, with no one to share it with. No one to ring and say, guess what just happened.

The realisation hit me like a gut punch. I did this. I pushed them away. I chose silence. And silence rarely waits around to be filled again.

Friend groups are like lifts. The last ones in are usually the first ones out. So here I am, holding two coffees, a heart full of possibility, and no one to call.

God, I feel so stupidly and achingly alone.

Shit.

8

June 20th, 2009: Niall

The weight of small things.

I should probably let Clara drive more often. That thought hit me about twenty minutes into our trip, somewhere between a glance at the road and one at her. There is something peaceful about watching her from the passenger seat, not in a creepy way, more in a way that feels like awe. It is the strange disbelief that someone like her exists at all and that she is right here beside me, breathing the same air and trusting me with a day that was supposed to be simple.

It has only been three months, yet I can read her face like the morning paper. Happy Clara has bright eyes and a soft laugh that curls at the edges. Sad Clara has a quiet mouth and a gaze that drifts far beyond whatever is in front of her. Angry Clara is even easier: tiny frown, sharp sighs, a jaw that tightens before she realises it. And hungry Clara, oddly enough, is a hybrid of the last two, which is both amusing and slightly terrifying.

But today she wore a new expression. Worry. Not the dramatic kind people put on when they want saving. This was the quiet type, neatly folded behind her eyes like a note she hoped I would never read. I hated it and hated that I could not immediately fix it.

"Hey, gorgeous, you hungry?" I asked, keeping my voice light enough that she would not hear the tension threading through it.

"We could grab something before we hit Howth?"

She smiled, but the real one, the one that reached her eyes, was nowhere to be found.

"I'm sorry," she said softly, looking out the window as if the sky might offer her an escape route.

"I've been feeling ill all day. I don't think I'll be much company."

That quiet worry deepened. Her skin looked paler, her voice softer, and in that moment I wanted to wrap her in warmth and reassure her that everything would be all right, though I had no idea what all right would even look like.

"Don't be sorry," I said quickly, studying her face as though it might reveal a puzzle piece I had missed.

"Want me to take you home?"

She hesitated. She always hesitates when it comes to her own needs. I have learnt that about her, the way she lives as if she owes the world something she can never repay. I still do not know the whole story, only fragments. A falling out with friends last year. Nights when she talks in her sleep and her voice cracks around a pain she pretends I have never heard. I let her believe that. One day she will tell me when she is ready, although I sometimes wonder if she will ever feel ready.

We arrived at Howth Head Summit soon after, one of our favourite places. Sometimes we walk the trails until our shoes are soaked or our limbs ache in that pleasant, satisfied way. Other times we sit in the car and watch the tide come in, then slip back out again, pretending for a blissful moment that time is something we can ignore. Today, though, the air inside the car felt heavier than the clouds pressing down on the sea.

I parked and turned toward her, the afternoon sun casting a soft gold halo across her profile. She looked fragile, caught somewhere between here and a place she could not name.

"What's going on?" I asked gently. My hand found hers without much thought. Her fingers were cold, colder than they should have been.

She looked at me, really looked, and I saw it. Fear. Not the quick jolt of it, but the kind that settles deep inside a person and refuses to move. It lodged in her throat and shimmered behind her lashes.

Then she said it.

"I think I might be pregnant."

Time stopped. Truly. For one floating second the world seemed to tilt and leave me scrambling for balance. My heart sprinted and my mind turned into a cartoon bunker, alarms everywhere. Outwardly, though, I forced myself to nod, calm and adult, as if panic were something only other people felt.

"You think?" I repeated softly.

"What makes you think that?"

She fidgeted, twisting her fingers together in that way she does when fear grips her.

"I'm late. I'm never late," Clara said, her eyes wide with disbelief.

"I could plan a trip, to the day, around my cycle, but this time nothing. So I took a test." Her voice cracked slightly.

"It came back positive."

There it was. Truth, fragile and loud in the small space between us. Her face crumpled as panic threaded itself into every line. I wanted to scoop that panic out of her and hold it away, to tell her not to worry, that we would figure this out. Yet I did not know what figuring it out even meant. I felt the ground shift under us, subtle but unmistakable.

"You took more than one test, did you not?" I asked. I tried to keep it light, though I knew exactly what she would have done. Clara does not accept a single answer when fear is involved.

She laughed, shaky yet real enough to reach me.

"Four. I took four tests."

I nodded slowly and held her gaze.

"And all of them were?"

"Positive," she whispered, and as she said it the truth seemed to strike her again.

"I suppose I do not think I'm pregnant. I am pregnant."

Her voice cracked like thin glass underfoot, and then she broke. Quiet sobs, her shoulders trembling as though the weight had finally become too much. I froze for a heartbeat, then moved closer and wrapped my arms around her, holding her as if I could shield both of us from everything rushing in.

Inside, I was still panicking. Not simply about the baby, although that worry hummed somewhere in the background. I was panicking because I did not yet know which part I should be most afraid of; which unknown was the one that might undo us. I cared more about Clara in that moment, about the way her world had tilted. About us. I have always been the planner: the one who sorts the lads' trips, who organises holidays, who builds detailed itineraries because planning makes the world feel manageable. And this situation, this life changing twist, was the complete opposite of manageable.

Yet through all the chaos something settled with a clarity that surprised me. I wanted to be her anchor. I wanted her to feel the certainty that she would not face any of this alone. My nerves kicked into gear, and I began talking without much thought. Talking and planning out loud, the words tumbling as easily as breath.

It was the only way I knew to keep us both from falling.

"Right, so first things first, we will find a doctor. Yours, mine, a new one, whatever you want. We can talk about vitamins and supplements after that. You mentioned your iron was low recently, so we will ask about that as well. Then we can prepare your flat. Mine too. Or, well, maybe we could even talk about moving in together? Only if you want it. No pressure."

She blinked at me as if I had announced that the sky had fallen.

"And coffee," I added quickly, the words tumbling out of me before I could stop them.

"I read you can have one cup a day. Although, if you want to cut it out completely, we can make fruity teas instead. A whole tasting menu of them. And hot chocolate, of course. You adore hot chocolate."

I was rambling. I knew it, and I could not make myself stop. My brain had turned into a runaway train, picking up speed with every heartbeat.

"And I am not convinced I can survive your caffeine withdrawal for nine months, so we might need to start slow."

"Oh my god," Clara said at last. Her eyes widened, filling the car with a stunned sort of quiet.

"You have already got everything planned."

Panic surged again, sharp and bright. Shit.

"No, honestly, no," I said, lifting my hands in surrender.

"I only did not want to be the sort of bloke who freezes. I wanted to be the one who showed up. But I should have asked you first." My voice dropped to something small.

"Do you want to have this baby?"

Her silence felt like a crack in my chest, thin at first, then widening.

Then, softly, she said, "This is wonderful." She drew in a breath.

"I mean, I am shocked. For someone who claimed he had no idea what to say, you said all the right things."

The breath I had been holding since we pulled into the car park finally slipped out of me.

She looked at me again, more steady this time.

"But we have only been together a few months. I did not want you to feel trapped."

Trapped? I nearly laughed. If anything, the idea that someone like her wanted to be with me at all still felt surreal.

"Clara," I said carefully, searching for the right words.

"I am all in. I have been in love with you since we shared that awful curry in Tallaght. You laughed with your whole body when I thought I was going to spit fire, and I knew I was done for. Completely gone. I have not stopped falling since."

Her lips parted in shock, which was strangely lovely in its own right.

"You are in love with me?"

"Madly," I whispered.

"I even wrote it down weeks ago, if you need proof. I keep a journal."

Her smile emerged slowly, the first true one I had seen all day.

"I journal too. I have kept journals most of my life."

Of course she had. It suited her, thoughtful and curious as she was.

"You are kind," I said, my tone becoming more serious.

"You are loyal, brave, beautiful, and you somehow manage to find good in everyone, even when they have done nothing to earn it. I love you, Clara. Every part of you. And I want to do this with you."

She cried then, but these tears felt lighter. Joy mixed with disbelief, like a small burst of sunlight breaking through rain.

"So we are doing this?" she asked. Her voice trembled in a way that made my throat tighten.

"We are doing this," I said, and I felt every word settle firmly inside me.

"Brilliant," she whispered. She gave me a look that made my chest feel too small for my heart.

"Please do not be mad."

"Mad?" I laughed, almost breathless.

"After all this? Go on. Try me."

She gave me that look again, wary but now clearly amused.

"Now that I am no longer in full crisis mode, I am absolutely starving."

I laughed properly this time, all the tension of the afternoon unravelling at last.

"I knew something was wrong when you turned down food," I teased as I turned the key in the ignition.

The car rumbled to life, a familiar comfort. I gave her a cheeky wink.

"Donnelly, party of three, cleared for take off."

I caught her grin at the edge of my vision. For the first time all day, a fragile but steady feeling took root inside me. It felt like the beginning of something we might be brave enough to build.

I might wait until after we eat to tell her I would love two children. A boy and a girl. Yes, best saved for after food.

9

Aug 22nd, 2025: Charlotte

Two can keep a secret.

I think I have officially lost the plot. Reading Clara's journals felt justifiable. She is gone, and her silence presses on every part of my life. How else am I supposed to uncover the truth she left behind? But Niall's journals are different. He is alive, breathing, sharing a bed with me, warm beside me every morning. And I still went there. I crossed that line with full awareness, as if something inside me insisted it had the right to look. What is my excuse now? Curiosity, fear, the desperate need to understand the man I am slowly building a life with. He has never even said his late wife's name aloud. Not once. How am I supposed to ask him about any of this when he has sealed those memories away as if they belong to another lifetime. I need to talk to someone. I feel like I am drowning in secrets that do not belong to me, yet cling to me all the same.

Clara was not angry with me. Not properly. Not in the sharp way I feared she might have been. She was stuck. Torn between loyalty to me and the nightmare she had been pulled into. That man she worked for, that monster masquerading as opportunity, twisted her dreams into a cage. She had been drowning while I stayed blissfully unaware, and now that truth sits heavy in my lungs.

This ache inside me is maddening. It is like a scream I cannot release. I want to call her, just dial her number and say, I understand now, I finally see what you were going through. But I cannot. She is gone, and all I have are inked fragments of her life, scattered in boxes like bones. It feels unbearable to hold so much truth with no one left to share it with.

And then there is Clara and Niall. God, they were so young. I always knew they were young when they met, but reading his words, his raw and trembling affection for her, altered something in me. They were not simply a young couple. They were practically children, learning who they were while trying to build a family. A life with two babies before most people have worked out how to pay their own council tax.

The way Niall wrote about her caught me completely off guard. His tone carries a tenderness that stirs something I cannot name. It is not jealousy. It is a strange unfamiliarity. I do not recognise this version of him. His early twenties self, poetic and unguarded, adored Clara with a force that feels almost mythic. Sunrise and storm. Light and threat. That version of him belongs entirely to her.

And yet I remember her so clearly. Clara in her twenties burst with fire and colour. Her laugh was sharp, quick, infectious, bouncing from walls and people alike. Her dreams tumbled out of her faster than she could keep up with them. Reading how he saw her did not wound me. It warmed me and made her feel close again, as if I was getting a glimpse of a home video I never knew existed.

Then warmth turns to grief. It always does. Every line of love he wrote for her is now a relic of a life that ended far too soon. Their story is closed, sealed by something too cruel to accept, and now I am the one living beside the man who once poured poetry into pages for my best friend.

He is mine now. Yet a tiny part of me whispers a question I hate. Would he ever write like that for me? Does he feel that same wild pull toward me, that helpless urge to immortalise me in metaphor, or does that kind of love only strike once in a lifetime?

My thoughts are spiralling again when I hear her.

"Chaaaarlotte?" Emily's voice sings through the hallway. Light, high pitched, sweet like spun sugar, and far too cheerful for the emotional crime scene I have made on the office floor.

I nearly jump. Pins and needles flood my legs. I have been sitting cross legged for who knows how long, lost in a world that is not mine. I scramble to shove the journals back into their box. The lid snaps shut just as Emily steps into the room. Her eyes land on the framed photo still in my hand. I freeze.

"What are you doing?" she asks. Her head tilts with that confident little smirk. That tone with its mix of innocence and interrogation. She demands answers with all the authority of a child who believes she has a badge hidden somewhere.

I smile and try to look relaxed.

"Just going through some old boxes. Found some pictures I had not seen before."

She steps closer. Her eyes narrow at the portrait, then soften in a way that squeezes my heart.

"That is my mum," she whispers.

"I know," I reply, forcing a gentle smile even as guilt drums inside my chest.

Her gaze flicks to mine.

"What? Wait. How did you know that was my mum?"

Shit. I fumble for a lifeline.

"Well, your dad is there. And that is you, obviously. I would know that smile anywhere. And Rory is right beside you with those enormous eyes. So I figured the woman had to be your mum. You have her dimples and Rory has her eyes."

Emily squints at me for a beat too long.

"Really? That is how you know?"

Shit. Shit. Shit.

Before I can trip over another lie, she grins.

"Not because we are all curly, roaring redheads?"

I laugh far too quickly.

"Well, the curls are a bit of a giveaway."

Crisis averted. Barely, but I will take the win.

"Shall we get going?" I ask. I need to get out of this room before its ghosts start whispering again.

"Absolutely. Can I sit in the front?" she chirps as she bounces toward the door.

"Of course. Where else would you sit? In the back like some stranger? I am not your chauffeur."

She giggles and calls back, "What if I get you a chauffeur hat? You could totally pull one off."

I laugh as the tension drains from my shoulders. "Yes, I will have a look on Amazon. See if I can get one."

"Oh my god, really?" she says as she disappears down the hall.

I pause for a moment with my hand on the box. I already know what I will do the second we get home. I will open it again. Somewhere within those pages, beneath the love and the tragedy and the secrets, is a truth I have not yet uncovered. I am not ready to leave it buried.

Then her question catches up with me.

"No. Not really," I call back with a laugh.

"Get in the bloody car, Em."

Dublin is drenched in sunshine this morning. The kind that tricks you into believing summer will linger a little longer. The streets pulse with life. Buskers pour their souls into every note, coffee carts hiss and clatter, toddlers shriek with delight as they chase pigeons down the pavement. The sunlight glints off shop windows like gold leaf, and a soft breeze brushes my skin, a quiet reminder that autumn is already creeping towards us.

As Emily and I weave through the bustling crowd, a wave of nostalgia hits me so sharply that it almost stops me in my tracks. Dublin City used to be our playground, a maze of streets where Clara, the girls and I carved out our own tiny universe. Skinned knees, failed skateboard tricks outside the Central Bank, the three of us pretending we were far cooler and far braver than we actually were. Back then, the world felt soft and malleable, something we believed we could shape with our bare hands if we only pushed hard enough.

Now I watch Emily walking beside me, calm and self-possessed in that quiet way she has, and my heart tightens. She is growing into someone fierce and thoughtful, a girl with a spine of steel and a mind that sees far too much for her age. We slip into Penneys, letting the familiar chaos swallow us. Fluorescent lights hum above, hangers slide along metal racks with a soft crinkle, and the earthy scent of fresh cotton settles around us. For a moment, it feels like stepping into a place that hasn't changed, even though everything else has.

"I just need socks," I mutter, although we both know I am lying to myself.

She laughs lightly. "Sure, me too."

Emily loves Penneys for the small treasures she can pick up for a few euro: glittery hair clips, novelty socks, earrings shaped like gummy bears. The rest of her wardrobe comes from thrift shops, where she hunts for pieces with hidden histories and frayed seams that speak of other lives. She is not like most girls her age. She carries a quiet gravity, a stubborn streak of individuality. She is like Clara.

Clara. Her name floats through my thoughts again, soft as a whisper and sharp as broken glass. It rises inside me like a bruise I keep pressing, even though I know it hurts every time.

How do I tell Emily that I knew her mum, that I loved her fiercely once, in a way that shaped every part of who I became? That a foolish, bitter argument pushed us apart, and I never had the chance to mend what we broke before she died. I did not know how much she struggled. I did not know she had children. I certainly did not know that the man I fell in love with, the man I married, had once been hers.

What would I say? Something absurd like: "Oh hi, by the way, your mum and I used to be inseparable. I did not steal your dad, I swear. I simply stumbled blindly into the wreckage of a life I never realised was connected to yours." Yes. That would go down beautifully.

I try to shake off the guilt but it clings to me stubbornly. I respected Niall's desire for privacy and boundaries, but now the silence feels like a betrayal. Why did he never tell me about Clara? I am raising her children. It feels unnatural that she rarely surfaces in conversation after three years, and not for lack of trying on my part. He would offer crumbs of information before gently steering the subject elsewhere. It makes me wonder. Was Clara afraid of him? Was he the Mr Donnelly she wrote about?

No. I stop that thought before it gathers momentum. She made a distinction between them, I remember that clearly: Mr Donnelly and Niall. Still, the question gnaws at me. Was he involved in her suffering in some other way? Did he know more than he admitted? Did he stand by while someone else hurt her, or worse?

My stomach twists. I do not want to believe such a thing. Niall is gentle. He is attentive. He is the man who reads beside me in silence because he knows the presence of another heartbeat can be comforting. He is the warm hand I reach for when the dark feels too close. He steadies me.

Yet history is crowded with women who built families with men who hid monstrous truths behind soft smiles. That thought alone is enough to make my breath falter. I cannot keep picking at this alone. I need to talk to Reya. I need a tether before I unravel completely.

A small voice cuts through the din around us.

"Aunty Lottie!"

I turn, my heart flipping, and spot Sammy bounding toward us. Niall's niece, Conor and Samantha's little firecracker, her curls bouncing and her grin bright enough to light half the shop.

"Well, if it is not Miss Sunshine herself!" I crouch a little to meet her eyes. "What are you up to, madam?"

"Nicky and I came into town." She beams. "He is at that comic book shop on the quays. I wanted to look around."

"Alone?" My brow arches before I can stop it. A surge of old panic rushes through me: all those teenage nights wandering home after random house parties, the narrow escapes I never realised were narrow until years later.

She shrugs with an impressive confidence. "I am fifteen now, Aunty Lottie."

Emily snorts. "Already braver than me walking around town on your own."

"Right," I say, forcing a smile that hides more than it reveals. "Well, you are both coming home with me. No buses today. Tell Nicky to meet us at the coffee house for lunch when he finishes. My treat."

"Yes." Sammy practically vibrates with excitement. "Nicky will be delighted. He has the biggest crush on Reya."

Emily bursts into laughter. "Please, as if he stands a chance. Have you seen John? That man is actual perfection."

I groan dramatically. "Girls, I do not want to hear this."

Their laughter spills out across the shop, bright and unguarded. I cling to it, grateful for the brief escape from the heaviness in my mind.

"What brought you into town today?" Sammy asks as we pause by the shopping centre railing.

"School shoes," Emily mutters.

"This close to school starting? That is not like you at all," Sammy says, feigning shock.

Emily tries to shrug it off, but I catch the flicker of something beneath her expression, something tender and raw.

"Mum used to sort all that weeks in advance," she murmurs.

Silence settles over us for a moment. Then she smirks gently.

"She always picked the sensible ones. Which, let us be honest, was code for ugly."

The girls erupt into laughter, and I smile along with them, even as a familiar ache blooms in my chest. Should I have stepped in sooner to take over the simple rituals Clara once handled without thought? Or am I reaching for a role I can never fully fill, no matter how hard I try?

The question lingers as we move through the crowd, buzzing around me like a wasp I cannot swat away.

Sammy was saying there is this cool shop in Stephen's Green, Emily adds, breaking the quiet with a little spark in her voice.

Oh? I ask, raising a brow as if I have never heard any of this before.

Yeah, vintage stuff. Handmade jewellery. Band T-shirts. You would love it, Sammy chirps, practically bouncing in her seat.

Nicky told me about it.

I fake surprise, although the truth sits heavy beneath my ribs. I know the place far too well. Clara and I used to get lost in there for hours, slipping between rails of forgotten treasures, buying things our parents swore we would never wear. The joke is on them. I still have that old Metallica hoodie tucked in the back of my wardrobe. It smells faintly of dust and adolescent rebellion, and I am not sure I would ever throw it away.

I want to freeze this moment, to pin it like an insect beneath glass. Emily's wide and eager eyes. Sammy's soft laughter. The dizzy scent of warm pretzels drifting from the food court and the gentle murmur of passing shoppers. It should feel simple and sweet, but it does not. All I can think about is her. Clara. And him. Niall.

Why did he not tell me? Did he think it would not matter? Or worse, did he already know everything and choose silence anyway? A strange plan begins to form as the questions swirl. It rises from a place I have not touched in years, something sharp, instinctive and cunning.

In the attic of our last home, Cherrywood House, I found my school yearbook buried in an old box beneath broken Christmas lights. Pressed between the pages were faded photographs, curled at the edges and soft from too many hands. One caught my eye. Clara and I were practically on top of each other, grinning like fools as we tried to fit thirteen of us into a single frame. The flash had caught the shimmer in her eyes. Innocence. Trust. Youth that felt indestructible at the time.

I will fish that photo out and leave it somewhere obvious, perhaps right on the kitchen table. If Niall sees it and flinches, I will know. If he acts like nothing is wrong, I will know as well. Either way, the truth is coming, slow and unstoppable. And God help us all when it finally arrives.

You would think that by now I would be used to the way my heart hitches every time someone calls me Boss. Yet the moment John's voice rings out from the corner table, it still hits the same way.

"Hey there, Boss."

A thousand tiny butterflies erupt in my stomach, ridiculous and persistent. There is always something theatrical about the way he says it, as if he is performing for an invisible audience or hinting at some inside joke that only he finds amusing. Or maybe it is just me overthinking everything again.

The smell of roasted beans and cinnamon buns reaches me before I even turn toward him. It is comforting and grounding, although shaded with a nostalgia I am never sure how to handle. I smile anyway and roll my eyes.

"Seriously, John? I have asked you a million times not to call me that. It makes me sound ancient or like I secretly run a criminal organisation."

John laughs and flashes that lopsided grin of his, the one that seems to soften the whole room.

"Oof, someone is cranky. Emily, how long has she been caffeine deprived?" He rests his arm on little Emily's shoulder.

Emily leans into the moment with a smirk.

"At least three hours. You are brave to provoke her."

"Three hours?" Reya gasps with exaggerated horror as she approaches from the back room.

"I thought we had an agreement. Two hours max."

"Oh, so this is a mutiny now?" I tease, throwing my arms up in dramatic surrender.

"I see how it is."

Warm laughter fills the air and mine joins in, although something fragile hums beneath the humour, a thin thread tugging tighter and tighter.

"John, round of ham and cheese toasties and strawberry frappes, please," I say, mostly to feel in control again, even if the moment is a small one.

That is when Nicky strolls in, smooth as ever, a wink tossed toward Reya as if he is dealing cards in a game only he understands.

"No frappe for me. Just coffee," he says, letting his smile linger on Reya a little too long.

John narrows his eyes.

"Dude. I am standing right here."

Nicky grins, completely unfazed.

"Relax, old man. Reya only has eyes for you. I am just here for the toasties."

"Careful, kid," John says, raising an eyebrow. "Respect your elders. You might be young, but I can still…"

"Take a nap mid sentence?" Nicky offers, all innocence and cheek.

"Now, now, boys," I cut in, hands raised like a referee stepping between two overeager players.

"Let us keep the testosterone at decaf levels, shall we?"

I glance around and something loosens in my chest. Despite everything, these people, my people, have made space for Niall's family as if they have always belonged. It should bring comfort. Instead, it sharpens the contrast between the life I am building and the truth that lurks beneath it.

I catch Reya's eye.

"Can I have a quick word? Alone?"

She nods without hesitation.

"Yeah, sure thing, love. Lead the way."

We slip into the back office, the door closing behind us as the clinking of cups and lazy chatter fade. Before it fully clicks shut, John's voice sails after us with exaggerated despair.

"I suppose I will just make all the toasties and frappes myself then, yeah?"

Nicky's voice follows, too loud and far too pleased.

"Coffee for me, old man."

John chuckles.

"Yes, yes, you are grown. Drink your bitter bean juice in peace."

Once the door seals, the noise dims to a muffled hum.

"Jesus, Charlotte," Reya whispers the moment we are alone. The colour drains from her face as I tell her what I have held in far too long.

"Are you serious?"

I nod, pulse racing hard enough to feel in my throat. "Yeah. Dead serious. Christ, sorry, that came out wildly inappropriate."

"Did you know?" she asks quietly, the words sounding as if they taste wrong on her tongue.

I swallow, uncertain if my answer will steady the room or knock the world off its hinges.

I blinked.

"No, God, Reya, of course not. But I still can't stop asking myself how this never came up in the three years I've known Niall. Not once. Not even in passing."

She reached for my arm, her touch steady and warm, almost enough to anchor the ground beneath me.

"Yeah, sorry. That was unfair. I know you and Clara had a messy end back in '08. I wasn't implying you swooped in."

I hesitated, a small pause that felt heavy.

"But 2008 wasn't the last time I saw Clara."

Reya froze. Her fingers tightened around my wrist as if she needed to hold on to something solid.

"What?" Reya said, much louder than I am sure she intended.

"Hush," I whispered, glancing at the thin office door. Even the hum of the espresso machine sounded sharper.

"I ran into her here. In this coffee house. Just before she died."

Reya's gasp cut through the stillness.

"How was it?"

My mouth dried as the memory surfaced.

"We laughed at first. It felt warm. Familiar, even, like stepping back into a version of ourselves we thought still existed. But it faded fast. She was distracted. Kept checking her phone as if she was waiting for something. Or someone. And then she changed. It was like watching someone flick a switch and turn the room cold."

Reya leaned in, unease growing in her eyes.

"Do you think she was afraid of Niall?"

The question lodged in my chest like broken glass.

"I don't know," I said eventually.

"But I can't stop replaying it. The tension. The fear. The way she rushed off. It felt like she wanted to tell me something but couldn't make herself say it."

Reya's expression flickered. She adored Niall. Even considering this possibility made her stomach twist, yet she stayed with it instead of shutting down.

I drew a shaky breath.

"Unless Clara wrote it down in her journals."

Reya's eyes sharpened with disbelief.

"Wait, what journals? Her journals? You found Clara's journals?"

"I did. And I've been reading them." The confession hung between us, thick and unforgivable, although the truth itself felt strangely inevitable.

Reya stayed silent for a moment that stretched long enough to sting. I saw the judgment rise in her eyes before she blinked it away, replaced by something softer.

"Look," she said quietly.

"I won't ask what they say. I don't want to know. But I understand why you're reading them. Just be careful with this, Charlotte. It's a powerful thing, other people's secrets."

I nodded, my throat tightening.

"What's your next move?" she asked.

"I have a plan, kind of," I muttered, aware of how flimsy it sounded.

"I just need to act before I talk myself out of it."

She hugged me without hesitation.

"Whatever it is, I've got you. I love Niall, but I love you more. And if it comes to it, I'll be right beside you."

Her loyalty almost broke me open. I clung to her, grateful, then suddenly remembered.

"Shit. Your appointment. How did it go?"

I saw it straight away, the dimming of her smile and the way her shoulders dipped.

"We've decided to take a break."

A cold knot tightened in my stomach.

"You and John?"

"No, no, we're solid," she said quickly, her eyes bright again, though the shine looked fragile.

"We had to have the conversation. The one where you admit this might never happen for you. And we promised each other we'd survive it. Because what we have, that's enough. A baby would be a blessing, not a requirement."

I wanted to be steady for her, but instead a laugh bubbled out of me. It was ridiculous and inappropriate and exactly what my frayed nerves produced.

"What?" she asked, squinting.

"I just... we are so different; you know? You and John are facing this monumental life crisis and somehow it's making you stronger. Meanwhile, I think my husband might be the villain in a psychological thriller."

Reya snorted, laughing so hard she had to wipe away a tear.

"Jesus, Charlotte. That's dark."

"But true," I said, laughing with her.

"You've got love. I've got suspense."

We were still laughing when we walked back out, breathless and red-faced, trying and failing to compose ourselves.

"You ever notice how they sound like witches when they laugh like that?" Nicky said to John as we approached.

John did not miss a beat.

"Why would you say that out loud? That's how you get cursed. Don't look them in the eye."

We said our goodbyes and headed for the car park. My car sat gleaming in the sun like a cherry red promise. Totally impractical. Entirely mine. I'd fantasised about a red SUV ever since watching Ghost Whisperer as a teenager. Other girls dreamt about the perfect wedding. I wanted cruise control and leather seats. Something that felt like freedom.

After surviving the obstacle course of the multi storey car park and slipping out of the city, I finally reached the N7. I flicked on cruise control, and silence wrapped itself around me like a cloak. The road stretched ahead in a long shimmering blur.

My thoughts drifted inevitably to Clara, her journals, and the scan she mentioned in those months that followed. And to everything she never said but might have been desperate to.

10

July 25th, 2009: Clara

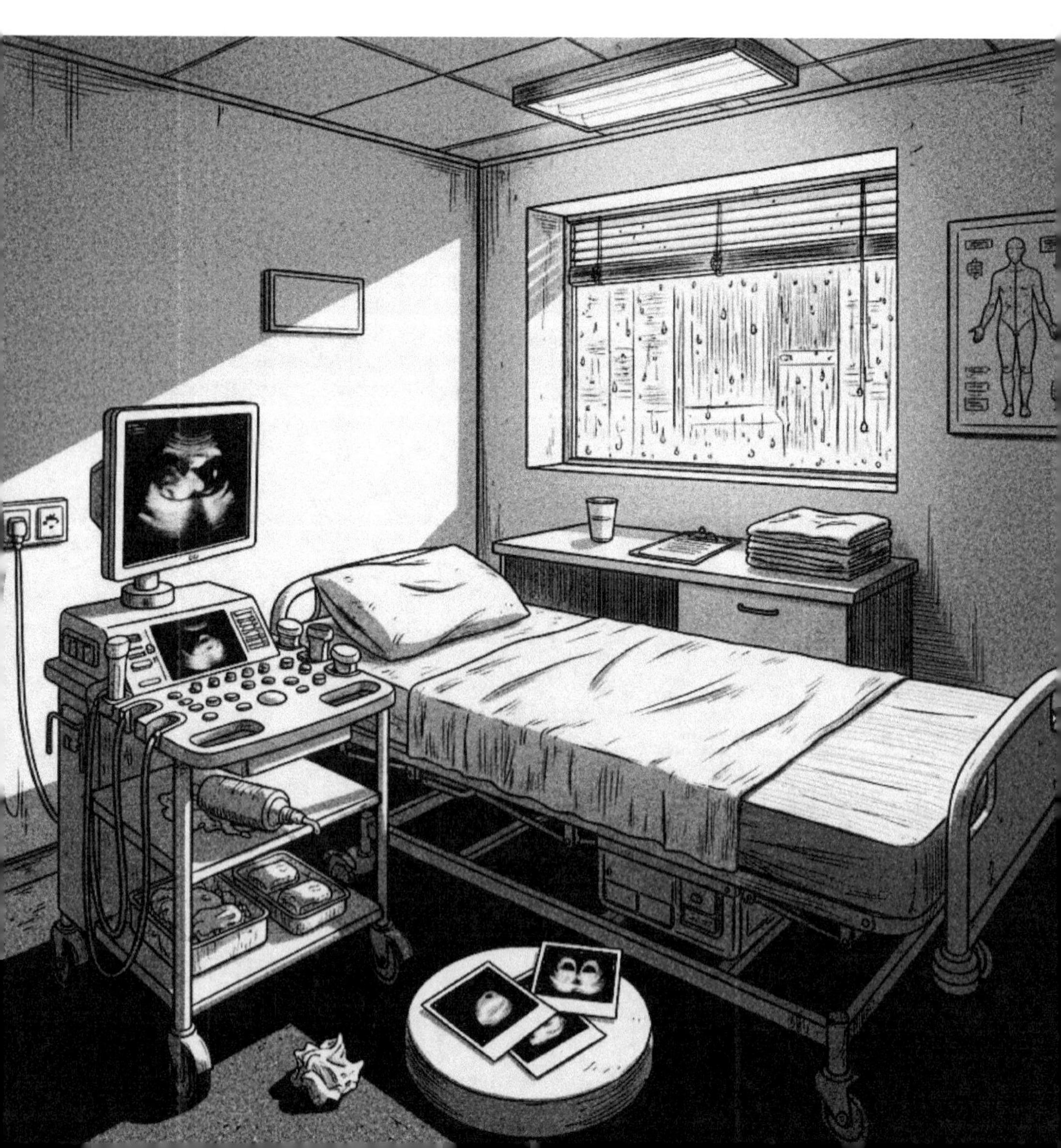

I held my breath and prayed.

I can barely hold the pen. My hands will not stop shaking. Even now, long hours later, my heart is still galloping in my chest, as if it is trying to outrun what almost happened. The memory is so fresh that it clings to me like steam after a hot bath.

This morning, I thought I was losing the baby.

The rain was hammering the car windows, steady and relentless, almost as if it sensed that I wanted to scream yet had decided to offer its own kind of comfort. Streetlights blurred in long streaks through my tears. Every colour looked washed out, as though the whole world had been drained to greys and silvers. I clutched my belly with one hand and Niall's knuckles with the other, gripping hard enough to hurt. The pain came in waves: sharp, twisting, hot, each one stealing my breath a little more.

"Oh, Niall, I'm so scared," I sobbed. My voice cracked and splintered. The words tasted metallic, as though fear itself had coated my tongue.

We had been so careful. I had followed every rule with almost religious devotion. All the supplements, the folic acid, the endless green smoothies that made me gag but I drank anyway. Had we jinxed everything by buying the crib too early? Did the stupid fall the other day count for more than it seemed, that tiny stumble in the hallway when I brushed it off as nothing? Was this my fault?

My face pressed against the cold window, and the city flew past in streaks of grey and gold. I wished I could wipe dread away as easily as I wiped my tears, but it clung to me like a second skin, impossible to peel off.

Last night, we had been in A and E. I was nine weeks pregnant. I will never forget the way the nurses looked at each other, those small, tight glances that were meant to seem routine yet carried too much meaning. Ectopic pregnancy, they said, only a possibility, but the word lodged itself inside me like a shard of glass.

I barely slept. I kept pressing my hand to my abdomen, waiting, hoping, praying to feel something that might reassure me, anything besides the hollow throb of fear.

This morning, they told me to return for a scan. Just to be sure. That phrase. It always sounds gentle, almost soothing, yet I have learned it is often code for prepare yourself for the worst.

Niall dropped me at the hospital entrance. His hand slipped from mine too quickly, as if the world itself was tugging us apart.

"I'll be right there," he said. His eyes were already darting across the car park, hunting for a space.

His words followed me down the hallway like a thin echo. I did not want to walk into that place without him. I begged the nurse at the desk to let me wait.

She gave me an apologetic smile.

"We're on a tight schedule, pet. Best we get it over with."

Over with. As if this was not my entire world balanced on the thinnest edge.

There were eight of us in the waiting area. Only two were there for planned scans, but it made no difference. We all sat in heavy silence, staring at our laps, our thoughts writing tragedies none of us dared to voice. No soft laughter. No glowing parents to be. Only the eerie quiet of hope holding itself perfectly still.

I called Niall. He was still stuck in the queue.

"I'll abandon the car if I have to," he said, trying to sound calm. I heard the fracture in his voice. It made something in me splinter all over again.

The scanning room was cold. So bright it felt surgical. The air smelled of disinfectant and latex gloves. A thin curtain hung from a ceiling track, pretending to offer privacy. I climbed onto the bed, and the paper beneath me crackled like brittle bones.

The nurse who entered was older, with gentle eyes that reminded me of soft rain. Her voice was warm, almost musical. She even made me laugh, warning me about the cold gel as though it were a scandal she was too delighted to reveal. I was still laughing when everything changed. Her smile faded. Her brow folded. She glanced at the second nurse in the room, then at the student. A whisper. A nod. A sudden stillness that made every hair on my arms rise.

Then she said it.

"Lovey, I'm going to need to do a transvaginal scan."

I nodded. My mouth had gone dry. I did not dare ask why. The nurse lifted the probe. It looked strange, intrusive, so far removed from anything I ever associated with motherhood that I wanted to vanish. I inched down the bed until I felt as if I might fall straight off the world.

The probe entered. I winced, not from the discomfort but from dread, from the unbearable anticipation. The nurse spoke softly.

"This will let us confirm a heartbeat and check for signs of an ectopic pregnancy."

She paused.

My eyes filled with tears. I stared at the ceiling and counted the tiny holes in the tiles, trying to prepare myself for a verdict that would shatter me. I was bracing for emptiness. For silence. For the confirmation that the spark inside me had gone out.

Then her voice changed completely.

"Is there a history of twins in your family, lovey?"

I blinked. The question did not make sense.

"Yes, my mum is a twin. Two sets on her side." I answered without thinking. My mind was still fixed on grief, not possibility.

She smiled. A slow, delighted, utterly genuine smile.

"You're having twins, my love."

The room tilted. Twins. Not empty. Not lost. Two. Two heartbeats flickering in the dark, like tiny lanterns. I sobbed, loud and unrestrained, tears spilling everywhere. The student nurse turned away and sniffled. I learned later that she was new. Every scan she had done until that morning had ended in silence.

But mine was life.

I could not stop crying.

"Oh my god, oh my god." The words kept tumbling out, as if my mouth could not keep up with my heart.

The nurse asked if she should fetch someone.

"No, these are happy tears." I could barely speak.

I did not know joy could feel sharp. I did not know joy could ache the way fear does. She handed me three photos: Twin A, Twin B, and one of them together. I held them as if they could break under the slightest pressure. My hands shook.

I tried to call Niall, but the signal was patchy. Perhaps it was meant to be. Saying it over the phone felt wrong. It did not belong in a text either, yet I sent one anyway because I needed him with me.

"I'm out. Will you pick me up at the door?"

When his car pulled around, I ran towards it. He looked so guilty, as if every moment I had spent alone had been a burden he could never repay.

"I'm so sorry, Clara. You had to do that alone. That was my first big test as a baby daddy, and I failed it."

He looked as if the words weighed on him. I passed him the first photo, and the worry in his eyes sharpened.

"Is the baby okay?"

"Perfect," I said, then placed the second picture into his hand, letting him take a moment with it.

He stared at the scan, tracing the faint outline with his thumb, as if touching it might make the moment more real.

"So tiny," he whispered.

"So perfect."

Then came the question I knew was coming, the one that had been hovering between us since I first sat down.

"Why the pain though?"

I drew a steadying breath and handed Niall the third image. The shift in his expression was instant.

"Holy shit," he said as he squinted closer at the grainy shapes.

"Wait, are there two?" His jaw dropped, and he looked at me as though the world had tilted.

"Are you serious?"

"Yeah," I said, a laugh breaking through even as my eyes stung.

"Baby's bringing a friend."

I was honestly impressed that he spotted the twins so quickly. Most men would have assumed it was a glitch or a smudge on the screen. For a heartbeat, pride warmed my chest.

Niall's whole body loosened with relief, then tightened again as understanding settled.

"Okay. Okay. I've read about this. The hormone, what is it called, Relaxin, right? Your joints are expanding. That explains the pain. They are already fighting for space. Sibling rivalry before birth."

I blinked at him, stunned that something from those parenting books had actually stuck in his mind.

"You're alright with this?" I asked. My voice wavered before I could stop it.

"I mean, I'm fricken terrified," he said, rubbing the back of his neck.

"But I think that is what being a parent is. You would be mad not to be scared. Still, I am here. I am all in. I am going to be a twin dad."

The breath I had been holding for days finally left me, slow and shaky. We sat together and talked about how we would tell Niall's family and what the twelve week reveal might look like. He joked that my parents were wonderful, although his would need a little advance warning.

"I need to feed my lady and her two little passengers," he said, and there was this soft awe in his voice that made my chest ache in the best way.

I laughed, although the moment faltered when he added, "Maybe that explains the moodiness, you're hungry. You are eating for three after all."

I shot him the glare of death.

"Sometimes it feels as though you have never held a conversation with a woman."

"Please do not leave me," he said with a laugh, both hands raised in surrender.

Today had begun as the worst day of my life. It was ending as one of the best, although a small knot of unease lingered under the surface. I could not quite name it, yet it refused to let go. Something told me this journey, our journey, would not be simple.

Even so, tonight I would let the joy in. I would hold it close before the fear crept back.

Because right now, in this moment, I have two tiny heartbeats living inside me.

And that is enough to believe in.

11

Aug 22nd, 2009: Niall

Secrets at the doorstep.

I nearly wrote them a letter. I imagined folding my nerves into tidy lines on a page, as if written words might steady the storm I knew was coming. If I could just set it all down: Clara, the move, the babies. Somehow I convinced myself that a letter might soften the explosion. As if ink on paper could shield me from my parents. It never could.

They are not calm parents. They never have been. Rita and Conrad specialise in turning minor tremors into full quakes. I love them, but they treat panic like a family tradition. A drama played out over tea. You would think I was confessing to a violent crime rather than, well, growing up and making choices of my own.

To them, everything is exaggerated. Every decision that wanders even a fraction from their version of the proper path becomes a spectacle. Sometimes I wonder who exactly they think we are. Royalty in exile. Curators of a perfect family image. I do not know what reaction I hoped for. Support. Calm. Some small kindness. I was not being realistic.

This morning my mind kept drifting back to one particular evening in 2004. I was young, more boy than man, but I remember it clearly. Conor was twenty then. He had just ended things with his long term girlfriend. Their relationship had been a slow collapse for years, both of them keeping one foot pressed against the door as if ready to bolt. When she told him she might be pregnant, he had come to our house with a tremor in his voice and his hope clinging to him like a thread. He wanted help. Advice. Reassurance from the people who were meant to guide him.

What he received was nothing close to that. My father accused the girl of trapping him. My mother blamed Conor for choosing someone, as she put it, with no morals and even less sense. They spoke about her as if she were some parasite feeding on his future. As if Conor had not left school at sixteen, worked like mad and earned his degree the same year, determined to build something better for himself. He wanted to travel. Breathe. See life before letting it pin him down. He was not abandoning anyone; he was protecting the little freedom he had carved out.

I was eavesdropping from the hallway, frozen in place, listening to them dismantle him piece by piece. Something inside me hardened that night. A quiet truth: these are not the kind of parents you turn to when life goes sideways. They made him feel as if he had committed some unforgivable sin. The girl was not pregnant. It had been a false alarm. Yet the damage lingered.

Now it is my turn. Only this time the fear is not imaginary. It is real, breathing down my neck.

I am twenty two. I have an associate degree. I have travelled. I have lived more than they realise. Yes, my bachelor's degree will be delayed and yes, my path has twisted in ways they dislike. But it is my life, shaped by choices Clara and I make together. We are not spiralling. We are building something. And still I can hear their voices as if already shouting in my mind, trying to plant shame in me the same way they tried with Conor.

But I will not let them. I refuse to let that seed take root.

Even so, the thought of telling them makes my stomach knot. Maybe tomorrow. Maybe next week. I keep shifting the reveal like it is a calendar appointment I can rearrange. Yet this is supposed to be joy. Two babies. The woman I love. A future starting to form. I wish I could share that joy with them without fear.

I drafted a letter in my mind anyway, a kind of last resort.

Dear Mother and Father, I hope you are sitting down because what I am about to tell you will probably dislodge the foundations of your perfectly ordered lives. Clara, my girlfriend, is moving in with me because she is pregnant. Also, it is twins. Love from your ever disappointing son.

My mother would faint or pretend to. My father would glance at her, waiting for permission to type his reaction along the usual lines. And I would be left standing somewhere between their horror and my disbelief that this is my actual life.

None of that prepared me for what happened next.

We drove out to the family place in Kildare. My mother calls it the lodge, although it feels more like a countryside manor that has collected stories the way trees collect rings. Some joyful, others darker. It used to be a sanctuary when I was small. Now the gravel path feels like a corridor back into a summer I try not to think about, the one that divided my childhood from everything that followed. The memory clings to me like burrs on a jumper.

Still, I tried to keep the mood light as I parked and unbuckled my seatbelt. The air out there always catches me off guard. It is sweeter than the city, threaded with wildflowers and the faint scent of rain soaked earth that you can almost taste. I hurried round to Clara's side and opened her door. She gave me that amused look again, the one that says she appreciates the gesture even if she does not quite need it.

She winced as she swung her legs out. One hand drifted to her hip. That persistent pelvic pain has become her shadow. She carries so much in silence, not only the weight of two lives growing inside her but all the aches and worries she hides so I will not fuss.

"Such a gentleman," she teased, although her fingers tightened on mine as she stood.

My mother was already outside before we had taken ten steps. Her arms were open, her smile wide, yet something sharp flickered behind her eyes. Intuition. Suspicion. That uncanny ability she has to sense a shift in the air long before anyone speaks.

"Well, this finally makes sense," she said at once. My stomach lurched so hard I lost my breath.

She knows. Or thinks she does.

I looked at Clara. Clara looked at me.

I should have realised this visit was about more than introducing a new girlfriend, my mother said, her voice simmering with smug certainty. My heart thudded like a fist on a locked door.

Niall has never brought a girl home before. She turned to Clara with the assessing look of someone reviewing a guest list rather than meeting a real human being.

But you are not just a girlfriend, are you. You look like the whole package.

Clara offered her best smile, polished and cautious. The kind you rehearse before meeting in laws who can make or break a welcome with a single raised eyebrow.

And I felt the first tremor of the quake I had feared for weeks.

"I'm Clara. It's a pleasure to meet you finally. Niall's told me wonderful things."

"Oh, really?" His mother narrowed her eyes at me, playful yet sharp, as if weighing truth on an invisible scale.

"I never taught him to lie." She smirked, a quick twist of amusement that made Clara stiffen before she let out a bright, nervous laugh.

"Anyone who can make an Irish stew like I hear you do has to be good people."

My mother beamed at that, delighted.

"Oh, you're quick. I like that. We'll keep you." And just like that, she wrapped an arm around Clara's waist. Clara flinched. Only a flicker, barely a shiver under the surface, but I caught it. So did my mother.

"Oh, sorry, love." She stepped back at once, her gaze flicking over Clara's middle with something between concern and curiosity. "I wasn't getting fresh with you. That's Rachel's job."

"Jesus, Mother." Heat climbed up my neck.

"What? It's nothing Rachel wouldn't say herself." Mum laughed. A full, booming laugh that filled the porch before spilling into the house behind her.

Inside, the house swallowed us with its familiar cluttered warmth. It always felt loud, even in silence, as if every creak and cushion carried its own memory. Antique armchairs sat beside strange nautical trinkets that my father collected from car boot sales. Nothing matched, yet nothing felt out of place. My parents never agreed on style in their lives, although they somehow created a home that held together like two stubborn puzzle pieces forced to fit.

Clara's eyes widened as we walked through the hall.

"This place is wow."

Yeah. Wow was right. She said it like she meant it, but a faint unease still hovered around her, subtle enough that no one else would notice.

Introductions came next: Rachel, with her wild grin and mischievous spark that lit every room; Conor, calm and steady, the anchor to Rachel's whirlwind; and Samantha, who assessed Clara with the cool focus of someone who enjoys solving people more than greeting them. I barely looked at Sam. We had never exactly got on, and though we kept things civil for Conor's sake, our conversations rarely stretched beyond polite nods.

Then little Nicky toddled over, his clubfoot brace clinking rhythmically as he collided into my knees, arms lifted like a toy winding itself up for affection. My chest tightened with pride and a softer ache that still surprised me. Two years, and he had fought more battles than most people face in decades. Watching him grow had been one of the few things that made the world feel steady.

Lunch came together beautifully. Sunlight poured through the kitchen windows like golden syrup, warm and thick. Lemonade spritzers fizzed in tall glasses, and a slow roast simmered in the oven, filling the room with an aroma that tugged at every old childhood memory at once. For a moment, the scene felt almost peaceful. Almost perfect.

But Clara looked pale, too pale, and she pushed her food around more than she ate it. She murmured something about nausea, far too polite to admit she felt awful. Then the chef swept in with a tray of sushi.

Sushi. I should have warned them. I should have said anything at all to avoid this moment. Instead, the room tightened around me until Rachel casually raised her voice.

"Veggie sushi for Clara, please, chef, remember?"

Clara blinked in surprise.

"Oh, thank you. Yes, that's great." She looked at me, puzzled, as if trying to place what she had missed.

I turned to Rachel.

"I never told you Clara was a vegetarian."

She grinned, wicked and knowing.

"I know she's not, but you also never told me she was pregnant, so aren't you glad I had a quiet word with the chef?"

The whole room seemed to tilt. Clara stared at her plate. My pulse stumbled.

"I'm sorry." The words felt slow, clumsy. "We weren't sure how to say it. It all feels so fast."

Rachel leaned in, lowering her voice.

"Fast doesn't mean wrong. You two are happy. That's more than most people get. Trust it."

Then came that moment. The one where time pauses, waiting for you to breathe first. I stood with my glass half raised, ready to share the news, but when I looked up, every face was already turned towards us. Expectant. Soft. Knowing.

They knew. Somehow, they had all known.

"You already know, don't you?" My voice dropped into a whisper.

Laughter burst around the table, warm and unguarded.

"Yes, my love," my mother said, eyes gleaming. "You've never been able to hide anything. Your face gives you away every time."

"Clara and I, we're expecting." The words finally came out, although a strange hollowness settled beneath my ribs.

Polite applause. Cheers. Smiles all around.

"Tell them the rest." Clara nudged me, small and firm.

"Oh, right." I straightened a little. "We're having twins."

Gasps, real ones this time. The delighted kind. The kind that said everything was about to shift, and everyone was ready to shift with it.

"To the Donnelly party of four!" Conor roared.

Glasses lifted. Voices chimed together. Joy wrapped loosely around the room, easy and bright.

For a moment, I let myself believe that nothing could spoil it.

Later, as we gathered our things to leave, something shattered that illusion. Clara stood in the hallway with my father. Their backs were turned, voices lowered. His expression was rigid, unreadable. Hers was tense, strained around the edges.

When I asked what they had been talking about, she waved it off.

"He just said to speak to Mr Skelly if work gets overwhelming. That's all."

My father never commented on emotions, barely acknowledged his own. A warning tugged at me. What could he have said to Clara that she felt she could not share?

The drive home drifted into quiet. Clara rested her head against the window, half-asleep, while the countryside blurred into muted greens. I kept my eyes fixed on the road, although my thoughts twisted endlessly.

Not about the twins. Not about the lodge. Not even about my family's reaction. All I could think about was Clara. And my father. And a flicker of unease that refused to die.

12

Aug 22nd, 2009: Clara

The face behind the mask.

There is a strange kind of silence in me tonight, almost like the eerie stillness that follows an explosion when everything has settled into dust and a faint ringing fills the air. It sits beneath my skin, waiting for a moment to break.

Today should have been simple. It should have been about joy and nothing else. And in a way, it was. On the surface at least. Smiles passed around the room, laughter bouncing off warm kitchen tiles, hugs that felt genuine. A family welcoming me, welcoming us, into their space. A home full of heat from the oven, Sunday roast, wine poured generously, siblings teasing each other across the table with the kind of ease that comes from years of being stitched together by shared stories.

Yet I felt separate from it all, as though I were standing behind glass. Close enough to see everything with painful clarity, but far enough that I could not quite touch the moment. It began the instant I stepped through their front door and saw him.

My mind lagged behind my body. My lungs stopped first, then my hands began to tremble. A face I had not seen for months, a voice I had buried beneath therapy sessions, late night journalling, and the slow passage of time.

Mr Conrad Donnelly.

The man who held eye contact for a bit too long in meetings. The man who always closed his office door when I stepped inside. The man who told me I was too ambitious to be that naive, and then proved exactly what he meant when he cornered me and crossed a line I could never uncross. His hands. His body. His entitlement.

And now I learn he is Niall's father. Of course he is. Life seems to enjoy cruel symmetry.

I did not say a word. I could not. I smiled as if I had not just swallowed a scream. I shook his hand with a steadiness I did not feel, let him kiss my cheek while every muscle in me recoiled. The house felt as if it were shrinking around me, every hallway narrowing until my only option was to move deeper inside it.

The rest of them were lovely. That was the hardest part. Rita, Niall's mother, embraced me with a warmth that felt almost maternal. She fussed gently, offering tea before I even reached the sofa and asking a dozen questions about the drive and the weather and whether I liked the roast lamb.

Rachel and Conor were loud and charming, full of sibling chaos. They had that easy rhythm, the shorthand of family, but they made room for me without hesitation. Rachel spoke to me as if we had known each other for years. Conor cracked jokes that cut through my tension even though he clearly thought of himself as the responsible older brother.

They were good people. Kind people. Their kindness made the contrast sharper, the lie heavier.

When Niall stood to speak during lunch, napkin still on his lap and a grin creeping up his face, my stomach tightened. He glanced around the table at the people who had shaped him, and for a moment I wondered if I was corrupting something pure simply by being there.

He cleared his throat and said, "Clara and I have some news."

The room shifted at once. Rita had already hinted she suspected something since Niall never brought anyone home. Still, even with their guesses, the truth dropped like a spark into dry grass.

"We're expecting," Niall said. Rita's eyes glistened immediately.

"Twins," he added, and that was when the shrieking began.

Laughter. Tears. Toasts being raised. Conor demanded naming rights as a joke, Rachel pleaded to plan the baby shower, Rita held my hands so tightly I could feel her pulse. I played the part effortlessly because I had practised for years: smiling, nodding, laughing at the exact right moments. Inside, though, my mind drifted somewhere dark and familiar.

I was back in that office break room, hearing the way Mr Donnelly said my name as though he owned it. Back in that moment when he closed the door and I understood too late that I was trapped.

I had not let myself revisit those memories for a long time. Today gave me no choice. He sat across from me at the table, chatting, joking, appearing every bit the devoted father. And I sat there pretending not to notice the truth under his polite exterior.

After dessert, I excused myself quietly. I felt as though the house was suffocating me, pressing warmth into my skin until it burned. I said I needed the bathroom and slipped away, grateful for a few seconds of solitude.

I had not even reached the stairs when I realised he was behind me.

"Clara," he said, voice low, so familiar it made my stomach clench.

I stopped, cold from the inside out.

"I have been trying to place you all day," he said, eyes sharpening.

"It took me a moment, but I have worked it out. You are a shark."

I stared at him, words stuck in my throat.

"Unbelievable," he continued, as if he were the injured party.

"I knew you wanted to get ahead, to make a name for yourself, but I never thought you were this ambitious."

I could hardly breathe.

"You trapped him, did you not?" he sneered.

"You saw the last name. Saw the opportunity. A pregnancy. Twins at that. Quite a strategy."

"Do not speak to me," I managed, though my voice was smaller than I hoped.

I moved to pass him, but he grabbed my wrist with far too much force.

"You may have fooled them. But I know exactly what kind of girl you are."

And then:

"Niall?"

Mr Donnelly froze. I did too. We turned, and there he was at the bottom of the stairs, arms folded, expression tight.

"What is going on?" he asked.

I swallowed and smiled out of habit.

"Nothing. Just about work. Your father was checking if I was alright."

Niall looked between us. His jaw shifted. He said nothing, but something in him changed. A faint shadow flickered behind his eyes. Doubt. The first I had ever seen.

Now we are home, and the silence between us feels heavier than before. I keep pretending it was a lovely day spent with a wonderful family. My body disagrees. My skin feels raw. My heartbeat is too loud, thudding as if it wants to escape.

I do not know how long I can keep this façade. I do not know how long I can carry a truth that gnaws at me every time I close my eyes. The past never disappears.

Sometimes it sits across from you at the dinner table, smiling politely, pretending nothing ever happened. And all you can do is smile back and try not to break.

13

Jan 27th, 2010: Clara

My last day, my first step.

The office hummed with that familiar, low fluorescent buzz, the sort of sound that settles into your bones until you stop noticing it. The lights above cast everything in a cold, washed-out glow, the kind that makes the walls look grey instead of white and leaves even healthy skin a little sallow. I leaned back in my chair and cupped my hand beneath the weight of my aching back. The twins were restless again, pressing and shifting as though they were trying to stretch into corners that did not exist. They crowded me from the inside and stole what little ease I had left. I let out a deep, frustrated sigh before realising that the words tumbling from my mouth were not meant to be spoken aloud.

"Oh my God, why am I still working?" The complaint drifted across the glass walls like steam escaping a kettle, soft yet impossible to take back.

Mr Skelly sat comfortably at his desk, perched with the quiet contentment of an old owl in his favourite tree. He looked up, eyes bright with amusement.

"Well, I assumed you liked my company," he said, pulling a face as if wounded by the thought.

I managed a tired smile. The attempt at humour felt thin, yet it steadied me for a moment. Another sharp bolt of pain shot across my lower back and I winced.

"Of course I do. I am only having a bit of a whinge. My back is killing me today, sorry if I sound like a cranky cow."

He leaned back, fingers interlaced over his rounded belly, and for a moment he looked like a grandfather about to embark on a bedtime tale he had told a dozen times yet still enjoyed.

"Since today is your last day, I feel bold enough to say this. I told you weeks ago to take your sick leave. You are carrying two people inside you, Clara. That is not a part-time job. You should not be here making me coffee or sorting through accounts."

This time my laugh was genuine, though still edged with discomfort. He always had a way of cutting through my fatigue and finding some scrap of warmth beneath it. Even so, he seemed to realise how his words might sound and softened his tone.

"I would never make light of what you do here. You have become essential to me. You run this place as much as I do, and if we are being honest, you do it with far more efficiency." His grin turned sheepish.

"My wife is dreading my retirement. Not because she fears I will be under her feet. It is you she will miss. She keeps saying she is not ready to share your full-time motherhood yet."

His words settled gently, yet with a weight I could feel across my chest. He should have retired months ago. Everyone knew that, including him. His eyes darkened slightly, touched by memory, and the room grew still enough that I could hear the soft whir of the printer down the hall.

"I think we both know why I have not retired," he said quietly.

The past curled inside me like a tightening spring. That day. The day he walked in on Mr Donnelly. The image rose without permission, stark and intrusive. It still lived beneath my skin like a half healed burn. I had felt trapped, cornered, frightened that if I allowed myself to think too deeply about it, the entire tapestry of my life with Niall might begin to fray. I had been clinging to the threads, desperate to keep everything intact.

He had saved far more than my job that day. He had given me dignity when I felt stripped of it, and space to breathe when the world felt too close.

"Yes," I said softly. The word caught on something tender inside me.

"We do."

He nodded once, slow and thoughtful. Then he reached for his bag as if keen to draw us both back toward lighter air.

"Oh, I nearly forgot."

He pulled out a small parcel wrapped in cheerful lemon-yellow paper, tied with a delicate ribbon that looked as though it had been chosen with care.

"My wife made this for you. A sort of end of your pregnancy survival kit."

The gesture startled me with its sweetness.

"Oh, she did not have to—"

"She wanted to. She said these are the little comforts that helped her through her pregnancy with Shane. He is thirty-eight now and still her baby. God help whoever marries him."

I laughed, and the sound surprised both of us. It felt like a tiny release, a brief return to myself.

"She tried to recreate it with more modern things, of course. Products have changed, but she stands by some of the old favourites."

I traced the smooth edge of the paper, moved by the thought behind it. A lump rose in my throat that I tried to ignore.

"I was not expecting this. Lately everything people give is for the babies. But this is for me, is it not?"

"Exactly." He smiled with quiet pride.

"She said people always forget the woman. Everyone is so focused on the bump and the babies. This one is for the mother bear."

The words struck something tender inside me. I blinked quickly, trying to steady myself as the heat behind my eyes grew warmer and far more insistent than I expected.

"Please tell her thank you. Really."

It was harder than I expected to say goodbye, even though my body felt long past ready to clock out for the day. Today marked my last shift at work. The official end of one chapter. The hesitant beginning of something I still do not know how to name. Marriage. Twins. A life reshaped in ways I am only starting to understand.

Niall and I are getting married this weekend. A small ceremony, intimate and ours, something quiet before the storm of parenthood rolls in and swallows us whole. I never believed the timing of a wedding could matter so much, yet now it feels sacred: our final adventure together before the world at large meets the twins and everything changes again.

Living with Niall is both wonderful and maddening, although I suspect that is part of our charm. Our tastes clash like mismatched wallpaper, colours and patterns that should fight with each other, yet somehow we keep discovering a way to blend them into something new and strangely beautiful. We are learning to bend, to compromise, to create a rhythm that belongs only to us.

And the emotions, good Lord. I am swollen, hormonal, and apparently capable of crying over adverts for instant coffee. Rachel has taken to hovering at my shoulder, protective and alert, ready to swoop in the moment she senses me begin to unravel.

Over Christmas, she, Niall, and I curled up on the couch and I dissolved into tears during a Nescafe house commercial. Niall blinked at me in open horror, utterly unequipped for the meltdown. Rachel simply pulled a blanket over us, offered me chocolate, and pretended it was all perfectly normal. In that moment, I felt held in a way I had not realised I needed.

Sometimes I swear Rachel and I must have been sisters in a past life. Her strength is quiet and hard earned; life has dealt her more than her fair share of cruelty, yet she still gives out kindness as if she has an endless supply of it tucked behind her ribs. Her relationship with Kathy remains another delicate tightrope, one complicated by Kathy's family, although Rachel walks it with remarkable grace. Even when her heart falters, she never quite loses her balance.

She is teaching me about resilience, about the shape of grace under pressure, and slowly we are bonding in ways that feel both effortless and profound. And yet, there is something I have not told her. Something I have not told anyone.

Conor. Niall's brother will not be at the wedding. Not because he is too busy or uninterested. He will be absent because of what we know, because of what we share, because of a truth he begged me to keep buried. It was not guilt that drove his plea, not exactly. It was fear. Fear of what might unravel if the truth ever clawed its way into the open. He made me promise not to tell Niall, and I have kept that promise. I intend to keep it still.

Even so, the silence clings to me like damp clothes that refuse to dry. I feel its weight every time Niall mentions Conor's absence, confusion clouding his eyes with each unanswered question. He can sense the wrongness of it now. He has begun watching me too closely, with a suspicion he tries to hide, and I do not know how much longer I can keep smiling without splintering.

There are days when I feel the words rising, sharp and insistent, pressing against my throat and begging to be spoken. Other days, I remind myself that secrets, once released, never sit quietly. They grow. They shift the ground beneath your feet. They change everything, sometimes beyond repair.

And still, I know this much: if that secret ever comes out, if even the smallest piece of it slips into the light, everything could collapse. The wedding, the family we are trying to build, perhaps even the fragile thread Niall and I are balancing upon.

At times like these, I almost feel grateful that Lottie is no longer part of my life. If she were, she would already be running in frantic circles, waving a bright red flag and filling the room with her siren cries, shouting, "Get out. Leave. Danger. Danger." And for once, I am not entirely sure she would be wrong.

14

Aug 22nd, 2025: Charlotte

The more I ask, the less I know.

I pulled the SUV into the driveway and shifted into park, although my mind was still miles away. The whole drive home had slipped past in a fog, one long loop of thoughts circling in my head like a skipping record I could not steady. When I opened the door, the stale heat of the day rushed in, brushing against my face with a dull heaviness. It was not enough to pull me fully back into the present.

"Attention, all passengers," I called out in mock formality, my voice attempting a brightness it did not quite possess.

"Please ensure you have removed all personal belongings upon exiting the vehicle. I shall be visiting my dad early tomorrow, and I do not want any last-minute calls about forgotten jackets or earbuds or God knows what else." I paused, lifting one eyebrow before adding with a crooked smile, "Although if you do call, I shall probably still come back. I will simply be very, very cross."

They laughed, the gentle obliging kind you give someone who is clearly trying to pretend everything is perfectly fine.

It had nothing to do with clutter. I am not obsessive, not exactly. It is just that when the kids leave things behind, they do not call. And when they do not call, I worry they are afraid to ask. I am always there when they need something, always ready to swoop in and fix whatever needs fixing, yet they rarely reach for me. Not really. I would give anything to be needed, even for something as trivial as a jacket. Perhaps especially for that, because it would mean they still saw me as someone they could turn to without hesitation.

I was heading to Clondalkin tomorrow, not Timbuktu. Even so, the distance felt larger than it was. I would come for them at any time, no matter the reason: sick days, forgotten sports kits, broken hearts. I would always come. I am not sure they believe that yet.

"Dad texted," Emily announced. Her voice was muffled as she leaned back into the car to pull out the last shopping bag.

"He said he is going to be late and that we are supposed to order pizza."

"Oh, did he now?" I said, folding my arms and leaning against the car. A thin trace of sarcasm slipped into my voice. I did not bother to hide it. I was not angry, only tired. Weary in that way you become when something feels familiar but should not be. This was not usual for Niall, which only made the moment more unsettling.

"Yes." Emily replied too quickly. She flushed pink, her expression stretching into a forced nonchalance as she checked whether her lie might pass unnoticed.

"Fine by me," I said with a sigh.

"I am absolutely shattered. Shopping is brutal."

"Shopping is an extreme sport," she joked, rolling her eyes in theatrical exhaustion.

"You girls worked up a sweat, I see," Rory chimed in, leaning on the car door with a teasing grin.

"Did you hear that, Em? Sounds suspiciously like someone does not want pizza," I said sweetly, slipping an arm over Emily's shoulder in mock offence.

"Ladies, allow me," Rory said, reaching for the bags with exaggerated chivalry.

"Why is it always me?" Emily grumbled under my arm, although her smile betrayed her.

"Because you are tiny and cute," I said, kissing the top of her head.

"Embrace your destiny, girly."

"One day I will be an adult and I will not have to carry shopping bags," Emily announced as she tried to stand taller.

"One day you will be an adult," I echoed. "And then you will have bills, stress and back pain."

"The horror!" she gasped, and we both burst into laughter.

We stepped into the house and the feeling struck me again. That odd mix of excitement and disappointment. The place echoed softly, its emptiness strangely loud, as though the walls were waiting for us to justify their existence.

About half our furniture had not arrived yet. My coat had no hook. My bag had no resting place. Every room felt like a paused moment, suspended somewhere between arrival and departure. I wanted to love this place and wanted even more for it to feel like home, although it clung stubbornly to a sense of being temporary, like a waiting room we were only passing through.

I wanted to involve the kids in making this house our own. I wanted the small rituals of settling in, the choosing of colours, the placing of cushions, the debate over lampshades. Yet the thought made my stomach twist. What if they brushed me off. What if they said what they had said before: what is the point. We have been here already, Charlotte. We know how this ends.

And beneath everything sat the shadow of Niall. God, Niall.

I have never doubted him. I never questioned the late nights or the quiet spells, the occasional distance that he said came from work. I accepted it all without blinking. Until now. Something feels wrong and the certainty is heavy in my bones. I hate how easily suspicion creeps in now and how quickly my mind unravels. It has only been a day since I found Clara's journal, yet it feels as though the ground beneath me has already shifted.

Why is he working late this weekend, of all weekends, the weekend we finally moved in. And why does it feel as if this move was never really about us. Not in the way I believed.

I remember when I first walked into Cherrywood House after our wedding. The air felt crowded with ghosts of a life I had not been part of. The place seemed to beg for warmth, for noise, for someone to breathe a bit of life into its quiet corners. I tried to give it that. I tried so hard.

Emily and I spent evenings scrolling through Pinterest boards, matching colours with fairy lights and soft throws. Rory designed a games room with such fierce enthusiasm that my heart ached with pride. For a brief stretch of time, it felt like we were building something real, something that belonged to all of us.

Then one day, Niall told me to stop. Just like that. No more upgrades and no more plans. Because maybe we would be moving. No explanation. Only silence.

And now that silence feels like a warning I ignored.

And now we are in a new house that does not feel like ours at all. It feels like a new chapter that has been drafted by someone else, as if I have been written out of my own life and stitched back in without warning. I no longer know where I stand in this story. Some days I barely know who I am.

Where are you right now? Emily's voice snapped me back to the present. I blinked, startled, as if surfacing from a dream I had not realised I was sinking into.

Sorry, love. I was away with the fairies.

Faeries or fairies? she asked, a sly smile forming. She knew me far too well, my fondness for folklore, myths and legends that had filled so many quiet evenings.

The nice fairies, I reassured her with a soft laugh, grateful for the momentary lift of her teasing.

No need to worry.

Oh, I was not worried, she said, her eyes gleaming with mischief.

The faeries said you are terrifying. They would never dare cross someone who eats ham and pineapple on their pizza.

I gasped, clutching my chest in mock outrage. Traitors. I shared my pineapple with them and this is how they repay me.

We were still giggling when a sudden jolt of panic surged through me, sharp enough to steal my breath.

Oh no, the pizza. I completely forgot. I am so sorry, Emily. I will order it right now.

Relax, chill, she called back from the hallway.

I already ordered.

I exhaled, both grateful and faintly ashamed of how easily I had spun into worry.

Thank you, I called back, though she was already gone from sight.

Oh, Emily, I shouted after her one last time.

Her voice drifted back, full of glee.

Yes, I ordered yours with sweet corn. But honestly, adding fruit and vegetables to a pizza does not make it healthy.

I shook my head, smiling despite myself.

Corn is another fruit, you little smart arse. But you have already gone, so now I am simply talking to myself.

And just like that, I was alone again.

I wandered slowly through the house, each room feeling like a half finished sentence waiting for its ending. The musty scent of cardboard and unsettled dust clung to the air, mingling with the faint metallic chill of a place not yet lived in. Afternoon light bled weakly through the grimy windows, casting long streaks across the bare floors.

My footsteps echoed faintly across the wooden boards. Six boxes. That is all. Six boxes and a toiletry bag to contain an entire life that once felt fuller than this. How had everything collapsed into so little. How had it all come down to this.

I was sure I had left the box marked kitchen in the office, or what might eventually become one of our offices. But now it was gone. Not misplaced, not casually shifted, but moved with intention. I felt it deep in my gut, a subtle wrongness that prickled along my spine.

Someone touched it. Someone went through it. I need to find it. I need to see that photo again, the one where Clara's smile is warm and real, where her eyes sparkle as if she holds a secret she wants me to guess. I need her again. Not the ghost of a woman I barely recognised in that coffee house. Not the distant stranger wrapped in grief and guilt. I need my Clara, the version of her that felt alive in my hands when I turned those pages last night.

I needed to read those pages again. I needed to know what secret she meant.

I was standing by the doorframe, caught in that familiar ache that had settled like a bruise beneath my ribs, when Rory startled me back to the present. He glided into the room like a ghost, all six feet of him moving without making the slightest sound. I gasped and pressed a hand to my chest.

"How is it that there is six feet of you, yet you float like a butterfly," I asked, my voice a mix of laughter and accusation.

"Practice," he said, eyes bright with mischief.

I raised an eyebrow.

"Oh, I know. I had a front row seat to you practising sneaking in through the mudroom after curfew three weeks ago."

"Oh, you knew about that." He froze mid step and looked genuinely alarmed.

"Wait, Dad did not say anything. You did not tell him?"

"No," I said with a small grin.

"I saw someone drop you off, so I knew you were safe. The car was impressive. But just a heads up, your dad might have something to say about you dating someone old enough to drive."

I meant it lightly, although a flicker of unease twisted through me. A seventeen year old. My stomach tightened instinctively.

Then I caught myself. Rory is not twelve anymore. He is fifteen, though sometimes I still see him as twelve because that was the last version of him I felt certain of, before my world twisted into the shape it holds now. No one prepares you for how quickly teenagers slip out of your hands.

He laughed, clearly entertained by my discomfort.

"Ah, Charlotte, I should have just told you. I am sorry I kept you up."

He hesitated, then added quietly, "Her name is Anna. She is fifteen as well. Her older sister drove me. She would not let me walk home."

Relief washed through me.

"Anna's sister. A responsible teen stranger was the hero of the night. She deserved a thank you. But you are still a kid, Rory, even if you are taller than most grown men," I said with a grin softening the reprimand.

He leaned against the doorframe again, watching me carefully.

"You look like you lost something."

"Just a box I was going through yesterday." I nodded, although my voice came out a little too light.

"What kind," he asked, tilting his head.

My fingers twitched at my side.

"Photos. Old stuff. Nothing important," I lied, the words catching slightly in my throat.

"Oh. That may have been moved. Dad and I rearranged a couple of boxes while you and Em were out. They went straight up to the attic."

I looked at him sharply.

"Why did you take things straight to the attic. Your dad said not to bring anything unless you planned to use it and not leave it in boxes."

He laughed, unbothered by my sudden edge.

"You would be surprised how many boxes we have dragged from house to house just to stick them in the attic again."

"Your dad does that."

"All the time," he said with a nod.

"He said those boxes were never meant to be unpacked."

Something twisted in my gut, tightening with a cold certainty.

"Wait, what do you mean. I thought we only brought the things we packed ourselves."

Rory's expression changed, something shifting beneath the surface.

"Oh no. Some boxes came from before."

"Before. Like from the Cherrywood house," I asked, the name heavy on my tongue and thick with memory.

He shook his head slowly, a shadow passing over his face.

"No. Before that. From when my mum was alive."

The room grew colder, as if the air itself had held its breath.

"My parents bought a house long before we were born. It was the place we grew up in, the place we knew by heart, and we were happy there until the day my mum passed away. After that everything seemed to tilt. One evening Dad simply snapped. No warning, no slow build. We packed up and moved overnight to Cherrywood House. Just like that. No explanations, only a silence that felt too big to question."

I did not breathe. My pulse thudded in my ears with a strange insistence. Rory was talking about Clara. My Clara. His mum. He stared down at the desk as if the words had slipped out of him without permission, as if speaking aloud had broken an unspoken rule we were both pretending did not exist. I placed a hand on the desk to steady myself.

"Rory," I said softly.

"You can talk about your mum. Her name isn't a secret here."

He gave the smallest nod, glanced towards the hallway and lowered his voice.

"We were okay for a while after she died. Not great, just... surviving. But then Dad found one of her journals and whatever was in it, he just lost his shit."

I flinched at the word journal. Hearing it from Rory made everything feel too close, too sharp. The past was no longer buried; it was shifting under the floorboards, making its way back toward us.

"Language, Rory!" The words came out on reflex. I winced at myself a moment later.

"Sorry, mum," he said, then froze as if the word had burned him. His eyes widened in horror.

"Oh God, I didn't mean... Charlotte, I didn't mean to call you..."

"Rory," I cut in quickly.

"It's okay. Honestly. We're talking about your mum. It was just a slip of the tongue."

"Well, not exactly," he murmured. His voice had gone tender, almost fragile.

"I've thought of you as a mum for a long time. I just didn't know if saying it out loud would make things weird, or if you'd even want me to think of you that way."

I blinked against the sudden sting behind my eyes. For a moment the ghost of Clara stepped back. What stood in front of me was only Rory, my brave, brilliant boy, waiting for permission that should never have needed asking.

"Oh, Rory," I whispered.

"It's an honour even to be nominated."

His grin spread, eyes bright as he caught the reference to our shared love of award shows and their red carpet disasters.

"So, it's okay?"

"Yeah, son," I said, my voice thick with feeling.

"It's more than okay."

"Cool." His voice cracked in a way he tried to disguise with a half shrug. He straightened himself and the smirk returned, though emotion still shimmered underneath.

"Right, the box of photos. I reckon it's in Dad's upstairs office. Not this office, the other office. We've got too many rooms."

"Too many?" I echoed, distracted by the shift in tone.

"And none of them feel like home yet," he said with a laugh.

"Oh, so you don't want to help me design a games room?"

"Don't even mess, Ma," he teased.

I stared at him in mock shock at the sound of Ma slipping out.

"Have I ruined it already?" he asked, laughing at my expression.

"Immediately," I said, though I was smiling by then.

"Oh, also... I was thinking of inviting Anna over for pizza. Is that all right?" he asked, changing the subject with ease.

"Of course," I said.

"Do you want me to say hello, or keep a low profile?"

"You are the least embarrassing person in this house," he said with complete sincerity.

"But maybe let her settle in a bit first. Then I'll come get you."

"Perfect. Those are your boundaries."

He nodded, looking oddly proud of himself.

"Now here are mine," I said.

"If you go to your room, the door stays open. Or better yet, keep her out of there completely. It looks like a small hurricane passed through."

"Fair," he said with a guilty laugh.

"She'd never come back."

We both laughed, a warm sound that loosened something in the walls of Cherrywood House, as if the place finally exhaled with us.

"When we settle in a bit more, would you help me do something cool with my room?" he asked.

"No chance we're waiting that long. We'll blink and it'll be Christmas. Let's do it next week. Paint, furniture, the works."

"Okay. Thanks, mum." The word clung to him like a new hoodie he had not quite broken in, tentative yet loved.

"You're welcome, son," I said. My chest ached with something dangerously close to joy.

I kept smiling until the muscles in my face protested. Then the door behind him creaked as he walked off. The smile dropped.

Niall stood in the alcove of the front door. The dusky evening light framed him through the tall panes of glass that should have made him look gentle. Instead, he appeared as a silhouette:

unreadable, still, too quiet. He had not made a sound on his way in. No footsteps. No click of the latch. It felt as if the house itself had opened for him.

The air seemed to drain from the room. A heavy silence settled in its place.

"Hey, love, you're home late. Everything okay?" I asked too quickly.

My voice cracked in the middle, though I forced the rest out with a smile that did not touch my eyes.

Niall watched me without blinking. His gaze was sharp, calculating.

"Did Rory just call you mum?"

The way he said it chilled me. Cold, flat, almost delicate, like a knife wrapped in velvet. I could not read him. That frightened me far more than if he had shouted. Niall was usually easy to read, almost clumsily transparent. But this was something else entirely: a mask settling over his features, smooth and impenetrable.

I fumbled.

"Uh, yeah. I thought it just slipped out."

"Just then? That did not sound accidental."

I could feel my heartbeat in my teeth, a strange flutter that seemed to echo in my jaw.

"No, no, okay!" My voice came out shrill and too fast, the sort of tone that made even me wince. I was spiralling and I knew it.

"He swore, and I said, 'Watch your language,' messing, and he said, 'Sorry, mum', as in cheeky, you know. Then he apologised and said he did not mean to call me that, and I told him it was fine, probably a slip of the tongue. And then he said that he had been thinking of me as a mum for a while but did not want to make me uncomfortable. I told him I was honoured."

I stopped. My breath sounded too loud. I had talked myself into a corner and it felt like a confession. Why did it feel like I had admitted to something shameful?

He looked at me. Not at my face but through it, as if he were studying the edges of my thoughts. As if he were searching for deceit or waiting for the thing I did not say. Did he suspect me of trying to replace Clara? Of twisting Rory's grief into something that served me? Did he think I was the impostor in this house, the one pretending to fit into a life that was never meant to be mine?

The silence between us thickened, gaining weight. Then Niall's expression cracked.

"That is amazing, Charlotte," he said warmly. His tone shifted from wary to bright with an ease that made my stomach flip.

"That is really, really amazing. Just be patient with Emily, you know? She is a bit more sensitive. Let her come to you in her own time."

The sudden shift in his mood took me aback and left me blinking.

"I know," I murmured, forcing a small laugh.

"She is tremendously independent, but I am incredibly patient. I am feeling pretty chuffed though."

The smile I offered felt stitched onto my face, the kind of smile that hurt to hold. I could not look at him. The headache I had planned to fake so I could slip away and hunt for those journals had turned into a real one, a tight pulse behind my eyes. I needed a cigarette. I did not even smoke anymore, yet the craving rose sharp and sudden, as if something inside me wanted an escape hatch.

And then, mercifully, the doorbell rang.

"That must be the pizza," Niall said casually.

"You coming in?"

No. No, I was not.

"I have just developed a massive headache," I said, pressing a hand to my temple.

"Could you save me a slice? I think I will go lie down for a bit."

Niall frowned with soft concern.

"Oh no, you poor thing. Can I make you tea? Is it from being in town?"

His worry sounded genuine, and I hated that it soothed me. I needed to stay focused and not melt every time he offered kindness.

"Yeah, probably. It was packed. If Emily had not been with me, I might have turned around and come straight home. Oh, and we saw Sammy and Nicky in town."

"Great," he said, then paused.

"Were they alone?"

Ah. There it was. A question disguised as small talk. Not curiosity. Surveillance. I knew what he meant. Was Conor with her?

I offered a casual shake of my head, hoping he could not see the frantic thoughts flashing behind my eyes. He and Conor had always been complicated. Not quite enemies. Not quite friends. Something jagged between them that had never been smoothed over, no matter how many years passed.

I wandered into the kitchen before slipping away properly, intending to excuse myself. Rory was sitting at the table with a girl I had not seen before. She rose smoothly, offering a smile that was both shy and assured.

"Hi! I am Anna." Her voice was soft but steady. Something about her radiated a quiet bravery, the sort that comes from saying what you mean even when you are terrified you have got it wrong.

"I get awful migraines," she added.

"If you ever need anything, I always have supplies."

Then came the overshare.

"I also get tough periods. The cramps and migraines together are the worst." She stopped abruptly, cheeks flushing.

"Oh god, Mrs Donnelly, I do not know why I said that. I ramble when I am nervous!"

I touched her arm gently.

"Hey, you could have fooled me. You walked in here like a pro and even offered me your stash. That is a win in my book."

She smiled, her shoulders loosening. Then, almost whispering, she asked, "Do you take Cerazette?"

Caught off guard, I nodded vaguely.

"I do, yeah, why?"

Anna blushed again, though there was a spark of determination beneath it.

"My mum says I might go on it soon. To help with my period. And because I have a boyfriend. Not that we are that kind of serious or anything."

"Whoa, Anna!" I said with a laugh.

"You do not have to share unless you want advice. But I love that you talk to your mum about everything. That is a real gift."

Just then, Rory cut in, his voice proud and untroubled.

"Anna, this is my stepmum, Charlotte, but I have started calling her mum."

My heart thudded hard enough that I felt it in my ribs. There it was again. That new name. That tiny surge of hope that scared me more than anything else in this house. I tried to laugh it off, though something inside me shifted.

"It's new. We're just trying it on for size." Rory said with a casual shrug.

"Eh, no!!" Anna teased, slicing across Rory's words with theatrical outrage.

"You gave her the title. No takebacksies."

"I've tasted the power," I said with mock menace, deepening my voice for effect.

"And I'm not giving up the crown."

"Oh, you're terrifying. I love you." Anna flashed me a wide grin that made the moment feel light and familiar.

Rory leaned close, lowering his voice.

"Let me know if you need anything, or, you know, help finding boxes."

I blinked at him. Did he know? Of course he knew. Rory had a way of seeing beneath whatever surface you tried to hold. Yet there was something else in his expression, something that made me think he wanted me to keep digging, to uncover whatever secrets he suspected were hiding in the spaces we all pretended not to notice. I gave a small nod, then slipped away before either of them could ask more.

Upstairs, the house stretched out before me like a stage set waiting for its actors. The front door glowed faintly with its stained-glass arch, scattering small jewels of colour that drifted across the floor as the afternoon shifted.

Niall insists we use the front entrance, yet I always prefer the back door since I park my car there. It feels more private. More practical. Besides, it is easier to stumble straight into the kitchen while attempting my weekly ritual of carrying all eight grocery bags in one heroic trip.

I walked past the family room. Up the main staircase. Past bedrooms full of shadows and half-remembered echoes. Past the laughter that still lingered in the air from downstairs. Then I climbed higher. To the attic. Three floors up. Past Niall's tucked away office. The attic staircase was narrow and strange, hemmed in by walls that made the air feel tight, almost as if the house itself was paying attention. As I reached the top, the door surprised me. It did not creak or resist. It simply drifted open with an unnervingly smooth movement, almost hydraulic, as if it had grown too familiar with being opened in secret.

Inside was another world entirely. A little eerie, naturally, because what attic isn't. Rocking horses with cracked paint and old dollhouses slumped in faded corners. Trinkets from some forgotten dreamscape of childhood. The whole space felt like Clara's memory turned into décor, tender and ghostly. Then my gaze caught on something tucked in the corner. A box labelled Kitchen drawers on one side and Niall's office on the other. Misleading. Or deliberate. The kind of detail you notice only when your heart is already uneasy.

My hands were shaking as I lifted the lid. I could still hear faint traces of laughter drifting up from downstairs, Rory begging Anna not to finish a scandalous story, Emily giggling, Niall's deep laugh echoing through the floorboards. Yet the sound felt impossibly distant, as if I had stepped too far into another layer of the house.

I had not looked closely enough into the box last night, and I had certainly not expected what I found now. This was not Clara's handwriting. These were Conor's journals. Pages filled with his voice, his thoughts, his restless scrawl. Each entry marked with coloured tabs that mapped out time in a way that made my breath hitch. Why were the dates tagged. Who tagged them. Niall.

A cold ripple went through me.

I scrambled for Clara's journal, the one I had read before bed. That one had the same coloured tabs. Had Niall been comparing them. Tracking when Clara and Conor wrote entries near the same dates. Did he suspect something. Was there something to suspect.

Clara. My closest friend. She was not a cheater. Not then. Not ever, I had always believed. But time has a strange way of bending loyalties, of reshaping memories until you are no longer sure what the truth looked like when it was still fresh.

I stood there, suspended on the edge of a discovery that felt almost illegal in an emotional sense. That is the only way I can describe it. What am I doing. I am about to read my brother in law's private journal. What is wrong with me.

And yet I did not close the box.

15

Feb 3rd, 2010. Conor

I only went to get breakfast.

I turned into the sweeping curve of the garden drive, the car gliding beneath a canopy of green that always looked too serene to belong to the real world. For a fleeting second, I allowed myself to drift into that quiet. Then something buzzed against my chest, a small vibration that pulled me back. My phone.

I pulled it from my suit pocket, expecting some mundane update, perhaps a reminder from the office, but instead a message glowed across the screen.

"Twins born at 2:22 am. Mum and babies are doing well."

The words struck me like a warm breeze seeping through a closed window. Inviting, yet oddly distant. A broadcast, not an intimate whisper. Still, something in my chest shifted. A faint comfort, unexpected but unmistakable. Niall had included me. He had chosen to. He did not need to, not after everything that had happened. If anything, he had every reason to leave me out entirely.

I could still feel the echo of his fist against my jaw, a sharp, honest punctuation to the cruellest thing I have ever said. And I deserved every bit of it.

Four months earlier, we had gathered around the fire at our parents' estate. It was meant to be a celebration. Niall had announced, with a voice filled with hope and a joy I had not heard from him in years, that he and Clara were getting married before the babies arrived.

Clara. God, Clara. She was the very definition of radiance that night. She glowed in a way that made the room feel warmer. And I ruined it, because the darkness I carried would not keep quiet. Because bitterness has a way of growing heavy if you do not acknowledge it.

I heard myself say it before I could stop it.

"Oh, she has you trapped now, brother, your life is over."

The silence that followed felt like the world itself drew back, horrified by my cruelty. The punch came fast. Direct. Fair. More than fair.

But the story did not begin with that punch.

It began earlier that evening, when my wife leaned in close to Clara and whispered something so monstrous that it froze the blood in my veins. Samantha, drunk and careless, confessed with a soft laugh that she had stopped taking her pill months before our son was conceived. Then she added that she had poked holes in my condoms as if it were some mischievous prank, a clever trick between friends.

I knew it was bad before Clara reacted. She was steady, dependable, measured. Her face fell only when something truly cut her. And there it was. Alarm. Disgust. Pity.

And I did nothing. I stood there, rooted to the floor, watching the life I thought I had built collapse in on itself.

So yes, I was already breaking apart that night. Jealous, exhausted, trapped inside a marriage that felt like it had begun to drain the air from my lungs. Seeing Niall and Clara so full of joy, so unburdened, cracked something in me that had been straining for years.

I am ashamed of what I said. I carry it like a smouldering ember beneath my skin. Yet shame is only part of it. What haunts me more is the knowledge that this feeling is not new. It is ancient, woven into my bones. It belongs to my childhood.

My marriage is not the root of the problem. Not entirely. The deeper issue is the legacy I inherited. The silent vow to endure what should have been abandoned long ago. I once swore I would never stay with someone purely for the sake of the children. My parents did. And it nearly destroyed us.

People tend to believe that a broken home appears only when divorce enters the picture. They are wrong. A home shatters long before that, when two people remain together out of fear, dragging their children through the ruins of their disappointment.

My parents, Conrad and Rita, should have separated years before we were old enough to understand the meaning of their words. Instead, they clung to each other like survivors of a wrecked ship, pretending the rising water was not creeping up around their throats.

We grew up submerged.

Their fights cracked walls and shattered glass. They never stopped shouting simply because we were in the room. Our small bodies might as well have been invisible. Someone had to take charge, so I did.

At ten years old, I became the shepherd for three lost souls. Niall, only seven. Rachel, five. And baby Greg, barely toddling, always searching for a leg to cling to.

I called them my soldiers. I marched them out of rooms when voices turned into knives. I set them in front of cartoons and tried to keep the shadows from slipping in.

But the shadows always returned.

I remember one summer morning. It should have smelled of sunshine and breakfast, but instead the first sound that pierced the air was a mug smashing on the kitchen tiles, followed by a scream and another wave of rage from behind closed doors.

I gathered my soldiers and led them to The Den. Our secret sanctuary at the edge of the property, wedged between hawthorn trees and ivy dressed walls. It had once been a bright little playhouse. Now it was weathered, chipped and moss covered, but it remained ours. A tiny kingdom free from the war inside the house.

I left them there for only a moment. Just long enough to fetch food. Toast, fruit, something warm that felt like comfort. But by the time I returned, tray balanced in my hands, I saw Niall sprinting towards me.

Running. Really running.

His face was pale as chalk. Panic twisted every line of him.

"Something is wrong with Greg."

The tray slipped. Toast scattered like dead leaves across the grass.

I ran. My heart thumped violently as I reached The Den and found Greg lying still on the ground. Too quiet. Too pale. Something inside me tore.

I did not think. I scooped him up and bolted toward the house. Niall ran ahead, shouting for help. Begging. But our parents were locked in another of their battles, too consumed by their own venom to hear him. Even with Greg growing limp in my arms, they did not listen.

I burst into the kitchen, breath ragged, and shouted with everything I had left.

"Would you two ever shut the fuck up and listen?"

That stopped them.

My mother turned. Her face drained of colour when she saw Greg.

"Oh my God, Greg. What happened, Conor?"

"I do not know, Mother. Niall came looking for you, but you would not listen."

Niall collapsed to the floor, shaking and crying. I wrapped an arm around him. He needed to know that none of this, not a single piece of it, was his fault.

"You did great," I told him, voice thick with a pride that already felt fragile.

Rachel burst in a moment later, panting hard, her eyes wide with something close to terror.

"Greg got a bee sting!"

Time froze. My father's face drained of colour.

"Get the EpiPen. Call an ambulance," he barked. Mr Clark, my father's assistant, dashed from the room with a speed I had never seen in him.

And then my mother whispered to my father, barely audible, yet somehow slicing through the air.

"Oh Jesus, Conrad."

At first, I did not understand.

"What? It's just a bee sting. Right, Rachel? Just one?"

"Yeah," she managed, her voice shaking.

"Just one."

My father placed a steady hand on my shoulder, although the tremble in his fingers betrayed him. His eyes locked onto mine.

"Greg is like me, buddy. He's allergic."

The room tilted, spun, warped. I knew that. I had always known that. He had told us countless times, drilling it into our heads as if repetition alone could save us. The signs, the symptoms, the danger, all of it had been laid out for us. But in that moment, the only thing that looped in my mind was:

"But I only went to get breakfast."

The words collapsed inside me. I dropped to the floor, cold and hollow, watching through a haze as Father lifted Greg's limp body, shouting for help that already felt too late. Niall's cries tore through the room and through me.

Rachel was sobbing now, shaking so violently it looked as if she might come apart entirely.

"I couldn't keep up with you, Conor. I should've told Mammy sooner. I tried"

I wanted to scream until something broke. I wanted to claw at the walls, to turn back time, to do anything other than witness the world folding in on itself. But all I could do was sit there, frozen, watching everything crumble while wondering how I ever convinced myself I could protect them. Any of them.

God help me; I was just a child. And even now, as a grown man, I still have no idea how to mend what shattered that day.

I cannot pinpoint the exact moment my parents stopped fighting in front of us. One day, the screaming simply ceased. Not because they had healed, not because the love had rekindled, but because they had decided they were done performing their misery for an audience.

The silence that followed was not peace. It was absence, a ghostly echo of something far worse. Smiles turned stiff, conversations became clipped and cautious, and whatever warmth had once existed between them had long since flickered out.

Eventually, I stopped caring whether they were happy, which perhaps makes me sound heartless. But when you grow up tiptoeing around emotional landmines, your survival instinct becomes focusing on someone else, someone smaller, someone who needs you.

For me, that was my siblings, my sister and now the only brother I have left. Protecting them became my purpose, the one thing that felt solid in a house made of shadows. I could not save Greg, but I could try my damned hardest to keep the rest of my family from disintegrating.

That instinct, that compulsion to protect, has seeped into every part of my life. Even now, even in a marriage that feels more like a held breath than a shared future, I protect what is mine. I play my part. I wear the face. Samantha has no idea that I know. She has no clue that I heard the words that scorched everything to ash.

She did not hear me approaching the drawing room, but Clara did. I stopped just outside the door, frozen, listening. Samantha's voice was low and raw, each word spilling out like venom she had kept bottled for far too long.

And Clara, God bless her, sat there absorbing it all, her expression soft with concern. When she noticed me, our eyes met. Panic flared in hers, quickly chased by something deeper: sadness, loyalty. She placed a gentle hand on Samantha's arm, halting her, as if trying to protect me from the last of the poison.

I should have walked away. Instead, I drank. Too much and too fast. Four whiskeys in, my mouth began outrunning my better judgement. I said something reckless enough to summon my brother's fury. His fist connected with my jaw in a flash of righteous anger.

"That was for Clara," he spat, as if I had morphed into the villain of our family story. But Clara knew the truth. She stepped between us before things spiralled further, her voice the only thread pulling me back to myself.

I was never angry at her. Not once. I was drowning in a quiet hell of my own making, trapped inside a life that had stopped feeling like mine.

Niall left first, brushing past with barely a glance, heading out to get the car. Clara lingered near the doorway, my mother beside her with a hand on her back like a guard standing at attention.

I approached them, heart thudding, my jaw aching. Before I could speak, my mother's voice cut through the space, sharp enough to wound.

"Go sleep it off, Conor. I cannot begin to tell you how disappointed I am."

Disappointment. From her. The same woman who once shouted that love was a lie while throwing a vase at my father's head. Somehow, that single word hurt more than Niall's punch.

"I need to apologise, Mother, please," I said, desperate to undo at least one mistake from the night. But she recoiled, disappointment etched across her features like a long-standing fracture.

I turned to Clara instead.

"I cannot apologise enough for what I said. There was no weight behind it. You and Niall, what you have is real. Marriage, children, all of it belongs to you, and rightly so. I do not expect forgiveness. Truth be told, I might respect you more if you never spoke to me again."

I began to walk away, but Clara reached out and caught my arm, her hand trembling.

"I can explain it to him," she whispered.

"He will understand if I just tell him."

My stomach plummeted. I prayed to God she was not speaking about Samantha's confession. My heart hammered so violently it felt as if it might break free of my ribs.

"Explain what?" I asked, too quickly, far too revealing.

"You heard what she said, Samantha," Clara said gently.

"That is why you snapped. He will understand. They all will. I am on your side, Conor."

A part of me wanted to collapse into her kindness and let the tears come. But no. Not this time.

"No, please. Do not. Especially not my parents."

The words caught in my throat and barely made it out.

"Just thank you for understanding. And God forgive me, welcome to the family, sis."

She smiled, soft and sad, the sort of smile that carries a truth no one dares to voice. I pressed an ice pack to my cheek, the cold stinging sharply, and turned away as Niall's voice rang out from the hall.

"Clara, love, come on!"

He sounded irritated, clipped, worn. I suppose I would have sounded the same once upon a time, back before I learned what it is to share a house with someone who wears a stranger's face every morning.

Four months. That is how long Niall has ignored my messages and my calls. Four months of silence that grew heavier every time I reached for my phone. When I heard about the twins, I hesitated. I did not know whether I had earned the right to send anything at all, yet something inside me refused to stay quiet. I wanted to be part of their lives, not merely as an uncle, but as a shield. As someone determined to grow into the person our own family never gave us.

My thumbs hovered over the screen for what felt like ages before I finally wrote:

"Wow, that is amazing news, little bro! I cannot think of a better couple than you and Clara to support them. I will do my best to hold down third place. I am always here, day or night. Looking forward to chatting soon!"

I hit send at the exact moment the front door burst open. Nicky's laughter spilled into the air, bright and warm, like sunlight breaking through a sky that had been grey for too long.

"Daddy, Daddy!" he shouted, racing into my arms with boundless excitement. Samantha followed close behind, beaming. Radiant. Perfectly timed, as if the moment were part of a script only she had read.

"Show Daddy, Nicky," she encouraged.

Nicky tugged open his cardigan with theatrical flair only a four year old could believe in. My breath caught. His T shirt read: Big Brother in the Making. My legs turned to stone.

I stared at the words, blinking, half expecting them to rearrange themselves into something harmless. Anything harmless. Big Brother. She made him wear this?

"You are going to be a big brother?" I forced out, my voice chipper, almost cheerful, although I could feel it cracking beneath the surface.

"That is amazing, buddy."

I kissed the top of his head and nudged him gently inside, my mind already spiralling.

"Did I do okay, Mummy?" he asked, wide eyed and hopeful.

"You did great, baby," she said. Then she turned towards me with that same smile, fixed and glossy, as if glued to her face.

"Well? What do you think?"

My voice came out ragged.

"Would you care to explain how we have barely spoken in months, have not shared a bed, and yet you are pregnant?"

Her expression did not shift. Not even a flicker.

"I do not know what you are trying to imply, Conor, but I am pregnant. It is your child. No questions." She placed a slow, deliberate hand on her belly, a gesture that felt more like a warning than reassurance.

"Eighteen weeks," she added, as if that detail might soothe me or somehow stitch us back together.

"I thought you would be excited, but if you are not, I can leave with Nicky."

It was a calculated strike and it landed with precision.

"No. I am happy," I lied, scrambling to sound steady. The word scraped at my throat. I had to pivot quickly, to throw any gentle distraction between us.

"Maybe it is a girl?" I said lightly. That surprised her.

She raised an eyebrow.

"You know carrying high or low is a myth, right?"

"Yeah, I know. Just this pregnancy feels different. You had awful heartburn with Nicky, remember? Maybe that is how we did not realise," I said with a thin laugh that did nothing to hide my unease.

She paused before shrugging.

"Now that you mention it, I have not had heartburn this time. Maybe you are right."

I smiled, although it hurt more than my bruised cheek.

"Let us spread the news," she exclaimed, clapping her hands together.

"Let us wait a few days. Give Niall and Clara their moment to shine. Twins are big news."

Her face tightened for a second.

"I suppose. I do not want to wait too long. It has been all about them for months."

The bitterness in her voice made my stomach twist. I had spent years excusing it, pretending not to notice the way she carved people up with her tone.

"Our pregnancy is not more or less important," I said carefully, choosing each word like it might explode.

"Let us wait for the anomaly scan. It will give us something solid to share."

Her face softened slightly, barely a shade of change, but enough for me to pretend everything was normal. I stood there holding a woman I no longer recognised while pretending this was still the life I wanted.

I had been minutes away from leaving this marriage. Minutes. Now I am tethered to her again, not by love but by guilt, by children, by a fear I cannot quite name.

How did I end up here, repeating the very cycle I once swore I would escape?

I thought walking away would be simple, that I would know when the moment arrived. Instead, every path ahead feels like a trap, built from lies or paved with obligation, and I am caught in the centre, struggling to breathe.

And here I am again, pretending not to drown.

16

Aug 22nd, 2025: Charlotte

It burns, but I cannot look away.

The house could have gone up in flames and I swear I would not have noticed. Conor's journal held me completely captive. Every line pulled me further in, as if I were sitting beside him in the dark, watching the scenes unfold with no power to intervene. It amazes me how the people around me seem able to write like seasoned memoirists, yet I struggle to capture a single week of my own thoughts without abandoning the page in frustration.

My chest aches, no, it blazes, for Greg. Sweet, fragile Greg. I always knew that Niall had a younger brother who died young, but the details had lived in my mind like fog on glass, blurred and convenient to ignore. Conor's words scraped away that mist with brutal honesty. The way he wrote, raw and terrified yet fiercely protective, made me feel as if I could hear his sobs vibrate through the paper. I could feel the heat of tears on his cheeks, taste the metallic panic in his mouth. Loss like that reshapes a person. It rewires the soul. And now, reading him like this, I understand why Conor carries so many silences. I am beginning to see the cracks beneath the Donnelly family's immaculate surface.

I used to chalk up their distance to old-fashioned manners and that particular brand of repressed Irish Catholic stiffness, the sort that insists on leaving room for the Holy Ghost. Conor's entries show something different. It was not decorum. It was misery, and a house that never truly healed.

I still think Rita is the warmest of them. When I first met her, she pulled me into her orbit and made me feel like part of something, as if I were not stepping into a role someone else had abandoned. But Conrad, God, Conrad. Cold, formal, always holding himself just out of reach. I had once mistaken it for awkwardness. Now I see the truth.

A predator.

It is hard to even type that word. Harder still to let my mind linger on it. Yet nothing else fits. If Mr Skelly had not walked into that break room at that exact moment, I cannot imagine what might have happened to Clara. The memory loops through me like a warning bell that never loses its urgency. If that was one moment that got interrupted, then how many did not. And then to learn that Conrad accused Clara, that he dared claim she tried to trap Niall for the prestige of the Donnelly name, it makes my skin crawl so sharply that I feel it under my nails.

How can one person act with such revolting entitlement?

The logic never lined up. There are a dozen Donnellys at Donnelly Marketing. Nine still work there today. Clara could not have known which one Niall was related to, if any at all. And Conrad played the part of a single, possibly divorced, middle-aged bachelor. No ring, no casual mention of a wife, nothing that suggested family. Niall had been full-time for only four weeks when he asked Clara out. He had been travelling, barely settled in the department. There was no way he knew his father's assistant was the same woman he was beginning to fall in love with. Their paths had only crossed in the break room or the busy canteen, fleeting meetings that meant nothing at the time.

But now my thoughts spin. They twist and snarl like thread caught on thorns. Because I always run to Niall. When my world tilts. When the anxiety claws. When everything feels too heavy to hold alone. He steadies me. Yet this, this storm, is mine to face without him. I cannot burden him with what I am thinking. Not yet.

What did he believe happened between Clara and his father?

Is that why he marked the journals with dates? Was he trying to catch Clara or Conor in a lie, attempting to piece together a timeline that would either confirm or disprove something terrible? The thought sits in my stomach with the weight of lead.

Rory's voice returns to me as if summoned. He had said that Niall read his mum's journals and lost his mind. That he uprooted the children from the only home they had ever known. But why. What had he discovered in those pages that shattered him so deeply he felt he had to tear down the past itself. What could have driven him to erase every trace of Clara and move them all to Cherrywood House?

The truth is that Cherrywood House never felt like a place where a wife and mother had once lived. There was not a single imprint of her in any room. No photos. No keepsakes. Nothing tucked away in drawers. It was not even that they had been stored. They were simply gone. As if removing her from sight could soften the ache of losing her.

Now the pieces fit. Painfully well.

I used to think the house lacked a woman's touch. I told myself it needed warmth, colour, softness. What it needed, and never had, was Clara. Her careful eye for detail. Her favourite prints and textures. Her framed memories. She was the sort of woman who would have filled the walls with photographs instead of leaving them locked away on a camera roll. She would have created a gallery of love, a home built from moments.

If I had known from the beginning, if we had pieced the truth together years ago, would it have changed anything? Would Niall and I have grieved together and found a way through the storm, or would we have drowned beneath the weight of it? Would I have become a reminder of her in his eyes, a ghost haunting the life he was trying to rebuild? I do not know. I really do not.

I shift my legs and lean back against the heavy trunk. The cool wood presses through my shirt and steadies me for a breath or two. My fingers tremble slightly as I reach for the next journal in the stack. My breath catches the moment I see the name written at the top.

Clara.

Oh God.

I close my eyes for a moment. Steeling myself. Whatever is contained in these pages, whatever secrets Clara left behind, I am not ready.

But I open it anyway.

17

Mar 1st, 2010: Clara

Coffee, Mum, Sleep, Repeat.

Nothing, absolutely nothing, prepares you for the exhaustion that crawls into your bones like slow rot in the weeks after giving birth. Every book, every chipper mummy blog, every lullaby-singing Baby and Me group presents sleep deprivation as something almost adorable, something you tackle with coffee, cuddles and the occasional nap. They never mention what it becomes when you have newborn twins, both blessed with colic. The tiredness stops being tiredness. It becomes something sharp and feral, something that makes the edges of the world feel distorted. I genuinely think the government could use it as a form of interrogation, and it would work frighteningly well.

And yet. God, and yet.

The love I feel for Rory and Emily is not soft or pastel coloured. It is not tender or serene, and it definitely is not anything I imagined. It is primal, unsettling, almost frightening in its intensity. I look at their faces, those tiny perfect features. Emily with her delicate lashes that flutter like moth wings each time she dreams. Rory with his little hand curling around my pinkie as if claiming me by right. When I watch them, something inside me feels like it might crack open under the sheer force of it. This is a love that does not feel safe. It is too big, too consuming, too ready to swallow every breath I take. If anything ever happened to them, I swear my body would forget how to breathe.

Thank God for Rita.

Niall's mum arrived like a warrior angel in those first days. I still do not know how I would have managed without her. My own parents were stuck in Australia when I went into labour. They missed everything, and I think my mum cried for twenty minutes straight once she heard the news. Her guilt came through the phone in waves and made my already fragile nerves tremble.

At one point, Rita gently took the phone from my shaking hand and stepped out of the room. I fully expected her to tear my mum apart for letting her emotions spill, but she understood perfectly. I remember hearing her say, in that low warm voice of hers, that she knew a guy who knew a guy who could help my mum rob a private plane if that was what it took to get her here. Then came that laugh of hers, the one that makes you think she might actually follow through.

Now my mum and Rita are good friends, real friends, not the polite in-law type. They have coffee together every Thursday, chatting like women who have survived something together. There was never any hope of keeping church and state separate after that.

But Conrad. God, Conrad.

Niall's father claims he is not a baby person. Thank Christ for small mercies. His appearances have been blessedly rare, limited mostly to the obligatory hospital visit. That one visit was more than enough. Watching him hold my babies, my babies, twisted something deep in my stomach. He traced their faces with those soft hands of his, hands that had never seen real work, hands that had once slid beneath a boardroom table and pressed into my thigh. Hands that brushed across my lower back when I reached for a folder, that gripped my shoulders from behind while his apology ghosted against my ear: Oops, did not mean to crowd you.

I hate those hands. I hate the memory of them on my skin, the way they turned me into a silent, shaking mess in a break room. And now those same hands have touched my children.

The bile rises even now when I think of it. The sight of him cradling Rory, rocking with this gentle sway that made him look like the ideal grandfather. A lie. A mask. All while I stood there, frozen in place, wearing the smile expected of a good daughter-in-law. Pretending nothing had ever happened. Pretending I was fine.

Because Niall can never know. He cannot.

I do not know how he would react. Would he believe me, would he want to burn everything down to protect us, or would he laugh it off with that awkward little shrug of his and say his dad is simply a bit too friendly. The truth frightens me. Either answer frightens me.

I love Niall. I do. And I believe he loves me. But there are moments when I feel the walls closing in, like the door of some invisible cage clicked shut behind me and I did not realise until long after. I have a beautiful home and two perfect children. I have a sister-in-law who feels more like a soulmate than anyone else ever has. Rachel is the person who holds me steady when everything tilts sideways. She sees me clearly, even when I cannot see myself. I keep telling myself I can help mend the tension between Niall and Conor. Conor, who is nothing like their father. Conor, who is gentle, steady, kind.

But none of that matters when Conrad Donnelly is still breathing the same air as me.

I am still going to therapy. I sit on the sofa and fold my hands neatly, and I lie. I lie through my teeth. She thinks I am on parental leave from a safe job. She does not know I left because Mr Skelly is gone and the idea of returning makes my chest tighten. She thinks I am happily married, which I suppose I am, but she does not know that my husband is the son of the man who assaulted me. She does not know I must sit across the dinner table from that man. She does not know I stood in a hospital room and watched him lift my daughter and press her to his chest.

She does not know any of it. And I cannot bring myself to tell her.

I never pressed charges. And now it feels as if too much time has slipped away, carried off in silence. Too many unspoken moments, too many days when I pretended everything was fine because pretending felt easier than speaking. I know what people would say: Why did you stay quiet? Why would you marry into his family if any of it were true? Did you flirt with Mr Donnelly to secure a place at his marketing company? Perhaps he misunderstood you, or perhaps you misled him.

Perhaps. Perhaps. Perhaps I deserved it because I wore a short skirt to the interview. Because being a woman often feels like a cruel riddle, an exhausting puzzle with no right answer and no promise of fairness.

The twins will be four weeks old soon. I want to do something nice, something ordinary, something that might trick my mind into believing that life is simple again. I keep thinking about planning a picnic in the garden, just the five of us gathered under the apple tree. I wish I could take them to the park with the other parents who seem to know what they are doing, but my healing is slower than I ever imagined. Not the scar, that is closing well enough. It is the numbness that unsettles me. From my belly button downwards my body feels as if it has simply given up, as if someone has flicked off a switch and left my nerves in the dark. I poke at my skin sometimes, testing its loyalty, trying to decide whether it still belongs to me. It never feels quite right.

Sometimes I stand over the cot and watch them breathe, caught between awe and terror. I lose whole stretches of time like that. Midnight melts into dawn. My legs ache, my eyelids burn, yet I remain rooted there, hypnotised by the fragile rise and fall of two tiny chests. I tell myself this is normal, just new mother nerves, the usual storm of worry and instinct.

But it is not only worry that keeps me anchored to that cot. It is fear, quiet as dust and just as suffocating, fear that something will go wrong if I look away. If I blink for too long, one of the babies might stop breathing and the world might decide to take them back. The thought claws at me, steady and cold.

I think about that night a week after we brought them home. I was rocking Emily and pacing the nursery in the pitch dark. She would not stop crying, and I was so tired it felt like my bones were humming. Niall was snoring downstairs on the couch, worn out after another fractured day. I could barely remember my own name, let alone the hour. Then there was the noise. I still hear it, clear as glass. A single footstep on gravel. Not a shift of wind or a wandering fox. A deliberate sound.

I froze. Emily stopped crying as if she sensed something too. I went to the window and peeled back the curtain a fraction, hardly daring to breathe. Nothing. Only the hedge, the shadows, the night holding its breath. But I know what I heard. I held her so tightly that I left faint little half moons on her back with my nails.

Perhaps it was a neighbour coming home late. Perhaps it was nothing at all. Yet something inside me refuses to believe that simple explanation, as if my instincts are warning me to stay awake.

I do not want to spiral. I cannot let myself spiral. If I start naming every fear that lurks inside me I will never stop. I will become one of those women who live behind permanently drawn curtains with too many locks on the door and alarms that beep at every movement.

But there is something I know for certain. Conrad has keys to this house. He gave them to Niall after we married, calling it a gesture of trust and family unity. Niall accepted without a second thought. Why would he question it? He loves his father and trusts him completely. His phone is still set to ring with the name Da Bear, a silly remnant from childhood. We could not afford a family home at the time, so we accepted Conrad's offer without hesitation. Yet this house feels no different from that Omega watch he gave Niall. The watch was a shackle, tight and gleaming. This house is a dungeon with freshly painted walls.

I have thought about asking Niall to change the locks, but how could I explain why without unravelling everything? And if I did tell him the truth, I cannot imagine what that revelation would do to him, to our marriage, to the fragile life we are trying to build.

And now there are these children between us, our flesh, our blood, our proof that life continues even when the past still clings. Rory's eyes crinkle exactly like Niall's when he attempts a sleepy smile. Emily frowns in her dreams, just as I used to before all this began. They are stitched together from us, small and perfect. I feel I owe them a life that is not soaked in old ghosts and unspoken shame.

But Conrad's face still floats behind my eyelids whenever I try to sleep. I see him in the glow of that boardroom projector, smiling as though he were untouchable. I remember the twitch of his mouth when he leaned too close. I remember the final day, the day I walked out and returned to a new beginning with Mr Skelly. His breath touched my skin as he whispered, you know no one is going to believe you.

He was right. No one ever would. So I became someone else. I became Niall's girlfriend, then his fiancée, then his wife and finally the mother of his children. People said I was fortunate. They said, Clara, you landed a Donnelly, that family is money and stability, they are like something out of a Stepford dream. If only they knew what lay beneath the glossy surface.

I do not know what I am doing. I barely recognise myself. I should have burned it all down before it started. I should have screamed the truth the second it happened. Instead, I said nothing. I was barely twenty one, afraid and desperate for that job, desperate for any chance at independence. So I swallowed it, as countless women do, and carried the weight of it alone.

And now I live in a beautiful house with white curtains, a garden swing and a kitchen that always smells of breast milk and lavender. Yet I carry a rot inside me. It is small, but it spreads quietly. I feel it in the tremble of my hands when the doorbell rings unexpectedly, in the way I triple check the curtains before feeding the babies, in the way I repeat I am fine until the lie feels almost true.

They will cry again soon, one or both of them. The clock tells me I have ten minutes of peace, perhaps fifteen if I am lucky. These small pockets of time are all I have. They separate the versions of myself: the one who is warm and maternal, and the one who is terrified of shadows in her own home.

Tomorrow I will ask Rachel to come over. We will sit in the garden with tea and pretend for a short while that everything is exactly as it should be. But tonight I will sleep with the nursery door open.

And the hallway light is on, just in case.

18

Mar 1st, 2010: Niall

Be a good Father, there is no Option B.

No one tells you the crying will sound different at night. I do not mean louder, though God knows it is louder, I mean different. Almost haunted. There is a resonance to it that never appears during the day, a strange hollowness, a kind of echo that makes it feel as if the sound has more room to unfurl. As if it can coil through corners and cling to shadows that are not there when the sun is up. At night, the walls seem thinner and the cries seep through the floorboards, sliding under doors and digging straight into the marrow of your bones.

Emily has this sharp, hiccupping wail that slices through the quiet like a razor. The kind you feel before your brain has time to register it. Rory's cry is different. His is a low, broken whimper, guttural and strained, as if he is desperate to stay composed but simply cannot manage it. There is something weary in it. As if a small part of him already knows there is no use pretending things are fine when they are not.

They are both crying now. Not unusual. They take turns most nights, almost organised, little sentries passing the baton of misery back and forth. Tonight, though, they have synced. A duet of distress rising and falling in an uneven rhythm that refuses to settle.

Clara is already up. I heard her stir before I even opened my eyes. She moves like someone caught between sleep and duty, part woman, part machine. No hesitation, no sigh, just an immediate shift from bed to hallway. Her body reacts before her mind has a chance to form a thought. That used to impress me. I used to think it made her strong. Now it frightens me because it feels like watching someone slowly vanish inside themselves.

She never wakes me. Not on purpose. Maybe she does not trust herself to ask for help or maybe she does not trust me to step in. I keep wondering whether she thinks I will fail her or whether I already have.

I am trying. God, I am trying. Yet it does not always feel like I am making any difference.

Tonight I forced myself up. I changed Rory's nappy, rocked him until his breathing softened and the tension drained from his tiny limbs. He sleeps now, curled against my chest, warm as a small furnace of milk and innocence. When I walked out onto the landing I passed Clara, or perhaps she passed me, and it felt like brushing shoulders with a ghost. Her skin was pale under the dim light. Her eyes looked bruised, her hair twisted into a wild, matted crown of exhaustion. She did not speak, simply nodded and drifted past me as if we were strangers on a train platform, standing too close yet travelling to entirely different destinations.

There was a time when we laughed in the dark. When we whispered about the future under the duvet, our legs tangled, our fingers tracing lazy shapes across each other's skin. Now there is silence. Or sobbing. Or the rhythmic creak of the nursery floorboards as we pass each other in wordless shifts, ghosts haunting our own home.

I once believed love would be enough.

I remember standing in that hospital room with its harsh lights and scratchy blankets, the sterile bite of antiseptic lingering in the air. I remember holding them both for the first time, Rory in one arm, Emily in the other, two wrinkled, red-faced little strangers who somehow already owned every part of me. I was terrified I would drop them or breathe wrong and ruin something precious. Yet at the same time I was in awe. I would have died for them without hesitation. I still would.

But something is fraying at the edges. Something invisible but unmistakable, a seam pulling apart one quiet thread at a time. I do not know how to mend it.

Clara barely talks to me. Not in any meaningful way. She goes through the motions. She smiles when required, kisses me goodnight as if ticking her way down a list, bath, bottles, blankets, bedtime, husband. Her warmth feels rationed, measured out in small, careful portions, and I cannot shake the feeling that none of it is meant for me anymore.

She tells me she is tired and I believe her, but there is something heavier beneath the surface. A weight. A slow sinking. I see it in the way she stands at the window with an empty stare, as if she is somewhere far beyond the glass. I see it in how she grips the side of the cot for balance, fingers whitening, as if she might topple forward. I see it in how tightly she sometimes holds Emily, clutching her as though the moment she loosens her grip, everything in her life will simply drift away.

I asked her last week if she was alright. She laughed. Not a laugh that reassures, but one that feels like a sob forced into a different shape. It left me speechless. After that she mentioned planning a picnic in the garden, something gentle and light, strawberries, white wine, a blanket on the grass. She spoke of it with this soft wistfulness, as if imagining something she hoped might anchor her. She never planned it. She forgot. Or changed her mind. Or perhaps it was only ever a way to stop me asking questions she could not face.

The thing is, I do not know how to help. And that makes me feel useless in a way that settles under my ribs like a weight I cannot shift. I keep doing the practical things: sterilising bottles, folding onesies, bringing Clara mugs of tea she forgets to drink as soon as it cools.

I hold the babies so she can show er, although sometimes I suspect she locks the door and simply sits on the tiled floor, crying quietly while the running water hides the sound from the rest of the house.

Tonight, I found a tear-stained muslin cloth balled up beneath the changing table. The sight of it: this small, discarded piece of grief that no one was meant to see, hit me hard in the stomach. It frightened me in a way I struggle to explain, as if I had stumbled across a secret so fragile that touching it might cause everything around us to crack.

I miss her. I miss us. The before us. The soft, joking, intertwined version of us who whispered names in bed and argued playfully about whose turn it was to make tea. Now there seems to be a wall between us, not a wall made of brick, but something built from exhaustion and silence that grows a little taller every day. Sometimes I feel as if I am shouting across it, trying to reach her, yet hearing only the echo of my own voice fading.

I know things are meant to change. I wanted them to change. I wanted this family, this life. But I never imagined Clara would slip away from me while everything else shifted into place. And there is something else, something I have not dared to write down until now because even thinking it feels like stepping onto dangerous ground.

Sometimes, late at night, when Clara is asleep and the house feels suspended in a strange hush, I sit alone in the nursery. I stare at the shelves I built, the tiny shoes that still have stuffing in them, and the soft toys propped neatly in rows. And for reasons I cannot quite name, I think about my father.

I remember the way he looked at Emily in the hospital, his fingers brushing her cheek as if she were made of glass. There was a gentleness in his eyes I had never seen before. People say becoming a grandfather softens a man: perhaps that is true. I did not see it with Conor when Nicky was born, but then again, my father and Conor have always been like sandpaper and silk, two textures that never settle comfortably together.

But the truth is, I do not trust my father. Not entirely.

He says all the right things. He brings flowers for Clara and tells neighbours and strangers about the twins as if they are a personal triumph. Yet there is something rehearsed about it, something that feels more like performance than emotion, as though he is trying out lines for a character he has not fully grasped.

I used to worship him. He was everything I thought I wanted to be: sharp, intelligent, impossible to ignore. But since the twins arrived, I have begun noticing small shifts in the atmosphere. Clara stiffens when he comes too close. She makes excuses to leave the room when he enters. Once, I saw her flinch when he touched her arm, a simple, fleeting gesture that should have meant nothing, but the look in her eyes suggested otherwise. She covered it quickly, brushing his hand away with an awkward laugh, yet the moment has stayed with me, replaying in my mind more often than I care to admit.

It did not look like nothing. It looked like a memory pushing through the surface of her calm, something she refuses to speak aloud. I do not want to believe my father could ever... no. I will not finish that thought. Because if I allow the idea to form, if I give it shape and language, then I must face what it implies about him and about the past, and I am not ready for that reckoning.

Still, the thought is there, lodged deep inside me like a splinter I cannot remove.

I need to talk to Clara. I need to reach her. But every time I try, she turns away or folds into herself like a flower closing at dusk, shutting out the world. I do not want to push her. I am terrified that if I do, she might retreat even further, and I will lose the part of her that still remains within reach.

Tomorrow, I will cook breakfast, a proper one with eggs, toast, and coffee that does not come from a pod. I will let her sleep as long as she needs. Maybe she will wake to the smell and feel for a moment the old warmth between us. Maybe she will smile. Maybe she will look at me as she once did, as though I was still the man she chose without hesitation.

Maybe she will let me in again. Even a small step would feel like a lifeline.

For now, I stay in the nursery a little longer. Rory is asleep on my chest, his breath warm and steady against my skin. His tiny fist is curled into my shirt, holding on with surprising strength, as if he is anchoring me to something I am scared of losing. Emily is still fussing in the next room, her cries shifting into softer sounds as her energy fades.

And Clara... Clara is somewhere I cannot reach, somewhere shadowed and silent.

But I will wait. I will wait for as long as it takes. Because love may not be enough to fix everything, but it is what I have left, and I will keep offering it: quietly, stubbornly, endlessly. One day, I hope she will find her way back to me. One day, I hope she will choose to stay.

19

Aug 3rd, 2010: Conor

Built from broken things.

There is something cruel about silence in the early hours. It echoes. It lingers. It presses into the thin spaces between the words we never manage to say. It feels almost alive, like a presence sitting in the room with us and waiting for someone to break.

It is worse when you are sitting across from the person you built your entire life around, and all you can think, tight and hot behind your ribs like a fist refusing to unclench, is: Why did you not tell me?

The kitchen was dim. One overhead light buzzed in its tired way and cast a dull circle across the clutter we had not cleaned up. The remains of dinner. Bottles. Sammy's discarded toy truck lying on its side as if someone had abandoned a tiny accident scene. The baby monitor in the corner blinked a steady green and looked calm, almost serene, as if it knew something we did not or could not face.

She held a glass of wine she had barely touched. Her fingers curved so loosely around the stem that I half expected it to slip from her hand. Her shoulders were tense, pulled tight, a thread wound to its limit. Her mouth twitched now and then as she stared at the fridge and through it, seeing everything except me.

I do not know why I finally spoke tonight. Maybe it was Sammy settling at last after hours of fussing. Maybe it was the pinched look in her eyes that never eased, not even when she smiled. Maybe it was the unfinished wine, or the heavy shadows under her eyes, or the way she reached for my hand out of habit and I flinched before I knew why. As if some deeper part of me remembered the truth long before I admitted it.

But I said it.

"You told Clara," I murmured. My own voice startled me. It sounded too loud in the hush.

"At the engagement party."

She froze. Her back stiffened, her breath caught, and she did not need to ask what I meant. I watched the tiny flicker cross her face. Recognition. Guilt. Fear. Relief, perhaps, that the moment she had dreaded had finally arrived. The words came to me more easily than I imagined. They had been fermenting for over a year, turning bitter in the dark.

"I heard you in the drawing room. You were drunk. You told her you had stopped taking the pill. You said you got pregnant on purpose. That you could not risk me leaving."

Silence again. Deeper now. Sharper. She did not speak. She did not deny it. She did not even look surprised.

That party was over a year ago. Nicky was already two by then. The lie had settled into the foundation of our family and hardened there. I was never meant to hear it.

But I did. And I carried it. Buried it. Let it fester like a splinter too deep to reach with anything but pain.

Clara never told me. She kept Sam's secret, the way Sam begged her to. They both pretended that night had never happened, and I pretended not to know.

I have been holding it ever since, letting it rot quietly between my ribs. Smiling through it. Parenting through it. Sleeping beside her. Loving her, in the way you love someone while also trying not to look at the wound they left in you. What was I supposed to say?

"Hey, I know you manipulated me into fatherhood, but it is fine"?

No. I kept quiet until tonight.

She looked like she might cry. Her eyes glossed with it, but the tears did not fall. She blinked slowly as if her mind had stalled and needed to catch up with her body.

"You have known this whole time?" she asked.

I nodded. The air between us felt radioactive, as if one wrong movement would split the room.

She leaned against the counter and wrapped her arms around herself. She looked smaller than the woman who had cornered me years ago with wide, terrified eyes and whispered, "We are pregnant." I had smiled. God help me, I had smiled.

"I thought if I told you," she said, her voice rough, "you would see me the way you see your dad's mistresses. Weak. Scheming."

I swallowed and leaned against the counter beside her, careful not to touch her, steadying my breath.

"You thought I would leave?"

She nodded. Her lips trembled. Her eyes shone with tears she refused to release.

"You were not happy, Conor. Not back then. You were quiet and sharp. Distant. I thought if I did not do something, if I did not anchor you, you would vanish. Like your dad did. I was scared."

Her voice cracked. That one word, scared, sounded like an old bruise pressed too hard. And here is the worst part, the part that cuts through me like glass: I understand.

I hate that I understand. But I do.

I remember who I was then. Cold. Closed off. Running from the man I feared I would become and doing it by walking so close to his shadow that I hardly knew where he ended and I began. Keeping my emotions buried. Keeping my future undecided. One foot always near the door and the other planted in uncertainty.

She did not trap me because she was cruel. She trapped me because she believed love alone was not enough to hold me. Because I had made her feel that way.

But still, I said softly, "You took away my choice."

Her mouth parted. I could see the instinct to lie, to soften it, to repaint the truth in kinder colours. She did not do it, because she could not. The truth sat between us like a live current.

She turned away and covered her mouth with her hand. Her chest rose and fell in uneven pulls, her ribs trembling with breath she could not steady. I thought she might scream. Instead, she whispered, barely audible:

"I am sorry."

God, she looked wrecked. Like something fragile after a storm: standing, but barely holding together. Her shoulders curled inwards as if she were bracing against a wind that had already passed, yet somehow still tore at her. All I could think about was the years we had spent building this life, brick by careful brick, and how much of it had been standing on something rotten. Something we both pretended was solid until it finally cracked.

And yet, whenever I look at Nicky, everything tilts back into place. That boy is everything. His wild laughter, his sticky hands reaching for my face, the way he calls me Daddy as if it is a magic word that can fix anything. The way he runs to me when he is scared, trusting that I will be something steady even when I feel like I am collapsing inside. He is the reason I know who I am now. He is why I stayed, why I softened, why I finally stopped running from myself.

So, no, I do not hate her. I want to. God knows I have tried. But I do not.

I told her that, quietly and with a steadiness I did not feel. It came out as a truth I had not wanted to face, one that loosened something tight in my chest the moment I said it aloud.

"I don't hate you."

That was when she broke. Not with sobs or screaming, not in any way that would have been easier to turn away from. She broke in the quiet way that hurts more, the way that slides beneath your ribs and stays there. She kissed me like she thought it might be the last time. Like she could not bear one more word between us because words were too sharp, too heavy, too dangerous.

I kissed her back because I did not want words either. Not anymore.

It was not sweet.

It was not gentle.

It was a wildfire.

It was teeth and nails and bruises we would not explain in the morning. It was uncontrolled, vicious, and absolutely necessary. We tore at each other like two people who were no longer sure they would still be together tomorrow, yet needed this tonight with a hunger that bordered on fear. Her lips bruised under mine, our breaths tangled and hot, her hands yanking my shirt over my head as though she needed proof that I was still real. Every scar, every tense muscle, every inch of the man she lied to and loved left nowhere to hide.

Her legs wrapped around my hips as I lifted her, weightless for a moment, as if gravity had stepped aside to let us ruin each other properly. Bottles clattered off the table. Plastic skittered across the floor. Somewhere in the corner, the steriliser beeped again, steady as a metronome we refused to listen to, a reminder of the life we had made and the one we were close to losing.

She clawed at me like she hated me, like she loved me, like the two feelings lived in the same place in her chest. My mouth pressed against her throat, her collarbone, her breast, every touch a mix of biting, licking, gasping. Her nails raked down my back and the sting made something inside me snap free. I bit her name into her shoulder. She moaned into my skin like a prayer she no longer believed in but could not stop saying.

We did not make love. We devoured each other.

Every gasp was a confession, every claw and thrust and desperate, shaking kiss a reminder that we were still alive inside this beautiful, broken thing we had made. She swore under her breath, filthy and trembling, each word landing as both permission and punishment. Words I never thought I would hear from her again, words that unravelled me.

We did not care about the mess or the neighbours or whether we broke the table. We only needed to feel something real, something that belonged to us and no one else.

And when it was over: when our bodies finally gave out, messy and wild and utterly silent except for our gasping breaths, we collapsed onto the cold kitchen floor. Tangled. Spent. Changed. The tiles leeched the heat from our skin while our pulse stayed frantic, as if the world had not quite caught up to what we had done.

The fridge hummed like it always does. The baby monitor blinked steadily in the background. The world did not end. We were still here.

She looked at me with red-rimmed eyes and asked, in a small and terrified voice, "Do you still love me?"

For once, I did not hesitate.

"I never stopped."

She stared at me for a long moment, studying my face as if searching for cracks. As if waiting for the lie. And then, slowly, something in her eased.

This time: this crazy, broken, perfect time, she believed me.

20

Dec 25th, 2010: Clara

Consent is a gift.

Emily cried during the entire car ride, her little face blotchy and furious, and Rory projectile vomited down the front of his adorable Christmas jumper before we had even backed out of the driveway. I wanted to cancel the whole thing on the spot. It felt like a warning, as if the universe were whispering that today would not bring the peace we were hoping for. Still, Niall had been so hopeful that this day would be the moment things finally felt normal again. Joyful. Like we were a proper family finding our way back to each other. So I swallowed it. All of it.

I cleaned Rory up as gently as I could, sang through gritted teeth to settle Emily, then touched up my makeup with hands that would not stop trembling. By the time we pulled up to the Donnelly home, my nerves were fraying. I stepped inside with the stiff smile of someone walking into a minefield, fully aware that one wrong step could make everything explode.

The house smelled of cloves, roast ham, and the faint sourness of whiskey that clung to the furniture no matter how often Rachel aired the place out. She greeted me at the door with an armful of gifts and warmth, pressing a mince pie into my hand before I could even shrug off my coat. She was the only reason I did not turn around and run back to the car.

Conor was already inside, sitting cross-legged on the rug with baby Sammy in his lap. He was making ridiculous faces, pretending to lose a staring contest. Nicky was doing chaotic laps of the family room, shrieking with laughter as he zigzagged between chairs. Niall hovered nearby, grinning with pride as if this buzzing, lively chaos was exactly how he always imagined fatherhood would be. It almost looked like one of those glossy Christmas adverts, the ones that pretend everything can be perfect if you smile hard enough.

For a fleeting moment, I let myself believe it. Almost.

Then Conrad walked in.

He made a loud, attention-grabbing entrance, voice booming with forced grandfatherly cheer. He called Rory his little soldier and Emily a heartbreaker in the making. The words might have sounded harmless to anyone else but I felt the sharp sting hidden inside them, a private jab meant only for me. He wore that same calculating grin, the one that fooled most people into thinking he was a harmless old charmer. But when his eyes met mine, something behind them flickered. Recognition. Ownership. Like I was still his secret.

I kept my distance. I floated from group to group with excuses on my tongue, always keeping Rachel within arm's reach like a shield. But of course, he found me alone eventually. It always happens that way, as if he can smell vulnerability in the air.

It was just after dinner. Niall had taken Rory upstairs for a nappy change. Rachel and Conor were in the kitchen, cleaning up and bickering about whether vegans can eat gravy. I stayed behind in the living room to gather the shredded wrapping paper from under the tree. I was kneeling, my back turned, when I felt him behind me. His shadow reached me before his voice did, stretching across the floor like something alive.

You have always looked so beautiful on your knees, he said.

I froze. The sound of him knocked the breath from my lungs. I stood too quickly and the blood rushed to my head. My vision tilted for a moment before I steadied myself.

Do not, I said, my voice low and sharp.

He stepped closer. Close enough that I could smell the scotch on his breath and the heavy cologne he always drowned himself in. His voice dropped.

You think they would believe you, Clara? After all this time? After you married into the family?

He seized my wrist with one hand. The grip was bruising and deliberate. His other hand slid to my waist, pulling me towards him with possessive force. My breath caught, jagged and painful. I could feel bile clawing its way up my throat, acidic and urgent. He tightened his hold, twisting my wrist back just enough to remind me he was in control. It felt as suffocating as a hand around my throat. I could not breathe.

I did not want this. I tried to scream, to force sound past the terror lodged in my chest, but my voice collapsed in on itself. Only tears came, hot and relentless, spilling down my cheeks as I shook my head in silent panic. My body trembled, frozen in fear, while inside I screamed so loudly it felt like the room should have heard it.

I stared up at him. My pulse hammered against my skin. I thought of the babies upstairs, safe and unaware. I thought of the home I desperately wanted for them and how unsafe I felt in that very moment. I opened my mouth, unsure what I meant to say, only knowing that something had to break.

Get away from her.

Conor's voice cut through the room like a blade.

We both turned. He stood in the doorway, his expression unreadable for a heartbeat. Then the colour drained from his face, replaced by something darker, something fierce and controlled.

Conor, Conrad began, trying to recover himself, stepping back as if everything were perfectly innocent. We were just...

I saw what you were just, Conor said. His voice shook. Your hand on her waist, and I saw her face.

The silence that followed was so heavy it felt like the air itself cracked open.

Conrad let out a chuckle, brittle and desperate. She misunderstood...

No, Conor said. I misunderstood. I used to think you were just an arsehole. Now I think you are a predator.

Conrad opened his mouth to lie again, to twist the story back into something convenient, but Conor cut him off, stepping closer with every word, each one careful and weighted.

If you ever touch her again, if you ever come near her again, I will tell everyone. Rachel. Mum. The board at Donnelly Marketing. The press, if I must. I will make sure no one ever looks at you the same way again.

Conor...

No. You do not get to say my name. You do not get to be part of this family if this is who you choose to be. His voice cracked. I should have seen it sooner. I did not want to. But I do now.

I could not breathe. My back was pressed against the corner without my noticing. It felt as if my life had split cleanly in two: everything before this moment and everything after.

Conor turned to me and something in his expression broke me entirely.

I am so sorry, he said softly. You do not have to pretend anymore. Not with me.

I nodded, but the words stuck in my throat. My hands were shaking too hard to hide. I wanted to cry. I wanted to scream. I wanted to step into his arms and thank him for seeing me at last.

And I wanted, more than anything, to feel safe again.

Rachel came in a moment later, asking what on earth was going on. Conrad slipped away like smoke, muttering something about needing air, as if the walls themselves had begun to suffocate him. Niall came down moments after that, confused and half asleep, holding Emily out in front of him like a peace offering he did not fully understand. No one told him what had just happened. Not yet. No one seemed ready to let the truth settle in the open.

Conor began to speak, rage still boiling beneath his skin, until I squeezed his arm in a panic. I chose the spot carefully, the only place hidden from the room's gaze.

"Dad went to bed early. He is not able to keep up with the youth these days," Conor announced, raising his voice just enough for the room, now full again with family, to hear.

A lie for now. Yet the truth was finally present in the room. Someone else had seen. Someone believed me. Someone other than Mr Skelly, who I had always feared would be dismissed as an overprotective employer if I ever dared to come forward about Conrad. But now one of the inner circle had witnessed it. For the first time since that man touched me in the breakroom, I felt the smallest shift inside me, a sense that maybe, just maybe, I was not alone anymore.

The house settled into a strange stillness then. The kind that follows a storm, when the air cannot decide whether it is safe to breathe again. Niall was upstairs, asleep with the babies curled into their cribs at either side of him. Rachel hummed carols under her breath while she packed away the leftovers, still blissfully oblivious, then drifted off to bed just after midnight.

Conor asked me to stay behind. He said he wanted to talk. I followed him into the sitting room, our old familiar refuge. Tonight it felt different, unfamiliar, heavy, full of everything we had not said.

The Christmas tree lights blinked behind him, slow and steady, almost like a warning signal.

He did not sit. He paced the length of the room for a moment, running both hands through his hair before turning to me with that same fierce determination burning in his eyes.

"We have to tell them," Conor said, voice low but firm.

"My mother, Rachel and Niall. They need to know who he really is. What he has done."

I sank onto the very edge of the sofa, my heartbeat thudding painfully in my chest.

"Conor, no."

He stepped closer, frustrated.

"Clara, he cornered you. And if I had not walked in when I did…"

"But you did," I interrupted, the words rushing out.

"You did walk in. And that is enough."

"It is not," he snapped, not at me, but at all the weight pressing down on both of us.

"You are not safe if he thinks he still has a hold over you. And my mother deserves to know the man she married. Niall, Christ, Niall should know what his father is capable of."

"I know," I said, my voice cracking at the edges.

"I know. But it is not that simple."

"It is that simple," he insisted.

"You did nothing wrong. He did."

I stood as well, my legs barely steady. My hands trembled in the familiar way they always did when fear and shame tangled together.

"Conor, I am not just protecting myself. I am protecting the life I have built. My babies. Niall. I cannot predict what this would do to him or to our family."

Conor's expression twisted into something complicated, a mix of fury, hurt and helplessness.

"So what then? We pretend nothing happened? We let him keep coming around, smiling like the doting grandfather, while you have to shrink into yourself every time he walks into a room?"

"I am not asking for forever," I said softly.

"I am only asking for now."

He opened his mouth to argue, but I cut him off. I knew exactly how harsh the words would sound.

"I kept your secret," I whispered.

His whole body went still.

"When your marriage was falling apart. When you were sleeping on our couch for four long months, telling everyone you were renovating the spare room. I never told a soul what Samantha did. I never told anyone that you rang me at three in the morning because you were shaking so badly you could not speak, after Samantha told you she was pregnant with Sammy."

He froze completely.

"I kept your secret because you were not ready," I said, softer now.

"You asked me not to tell anyone and I did not. I waited until you could breathe again."

My throat tightened and tears threatened.

"All I am asking is for you to do the same for me."

Conor did not speak for a long while. He rubbed his face with both hands, then dropped heavily into the armchair across from me, the weight of everything settling onto his shoulders.

"You are not alone, Clara. You know that, do you not?" he said at last, his voice so much quieter.

"I cannot believe I did not see it before. I am so sorry I did not see it. Whatever you decide, I will back you. I will vouch for you. But it is tearing me apart, watching you shrink in your own skin because he is still allowed in the room."

I nodded and bit my lip so hard I flinched.

"It is tearing me apart as well. But this is something I need to handle in my own time."

He leaned forward, reaching for my shoulders with care. He stopped himself just before making contact, as if afraid the touch might shatter me, so he simply held my gaze.

"If he ever comes near you again, I will not wait. I am telling you now, that is not a threat, it is a promise."

"I know," I said, and stepped forward to embrace him firmly, lovingly, the way you would hold a brother you trust with your whole heart.

"And that is why I feel safe."

We sat together in silence. Not the comfortable kind and not peaceful either, but something more like mutual understanding that neither of us could quite name.

The tree lights blinked on.

Off.

On.

Off.

I do not know how long we stayed like that. Five minutes. Perhaps twenty. The fire had burned low, leaving the room lit only by the warm gold glow of the tree lights. They were gentle, far too gentle for the shadows they cast across the walls.

For the first time in weeks I felt safer than I had allowed myself to hope. Yet safety in this house always feels like borrowed time. A moment later the doorway filled with a familiar silhouette.

Samantha.

She stood there with her hand resting on the doorframe, wrapped in a silk robe that shimmered faintly in the fairy lights.

"Conor? Are you coming to bed?"

Her voice was soft, almost whisper-like, yet edged with suspicion. Concern arranged neatly over something sharper. Conor sat up straight, stiff as if caught doing something wrong. I shifted back instinctively, though we were already sitting on opposite sides of the room.

When she stepped further into the room and saw me, truly saw me, her eyebrows lifted in surprise. Not panic. Not alarm. Simply curiosity. There was also something lingering behind her eyes that I could not quite place. A flicker of doubt perhaps. Or was it fear?

"Oh, Clara. I did not realise you were here too."

She looked between us with a slow sweep of her gaze and the air shifted. It thickened as if the room had drawn a long breath and decided to hold it.

"Are you okay?"

The question was directed at me, yet it never felt like an expression of concern. It landed more like an assessment, a careful probe, the first note in a story someone else might later tell. I forced a smile and hoped it reached my eyes.

"I'm fine. Just needed a bit of quiet."

Conor rose then, standing in that unhurried way of his, rubbing the back of his neck as though he needed to ease some invisible weight.

"We were just talking."

Samantha's gaze flicked to him in a quick, sharp movement, then paused on me.

"Mmm. Were you?"

"It's been a long day."

I nodded. "It has."

But we all knew that was not what she meant, not really. Something unspoken hung between us, stretched tight like a thread that might snap if any of us pulled too hard. She said nothing more. She turned and slipped back into the hallway, a swish of silk trailing after her with a chill that felt colder than the air itself. Conor gave me a brief, apologetic glance before he followed her out.

I stayed where I was for a long while, alone in the fading glow of the fire. The embers pulsed weakly, collapsing in on themselves as I tried to name the knot tightening in my chest. It was not anger. Not exactly. I was not jealous either. I had never envied Samantha and I doubted I ever would. Yet something unsettled me. A memory rose without invitation: the night Niall and I announced our engagement. The champagne had flowed too freely.

Samantha had been four wines deep, perhaps five. She had leaned in far too close, her breath warm and sour with alcohol. Her eyes had been glassy and wet with something that did not resemble joy at all. She had whispered to me, barely audible above the noise around us, "I made sure he could not leave."

I had not understood her then. Not fully. It took months of piecing together timelines, stray comments, and half-finished sentences before the shape of her confession began to make sense. Even so, I never judged her. How could I. Truly, how could any woman.

Women have always had to carve out their own ways to survive in the shadows of men who hold too much power. Some of us run. Some freeze where we stand. Some stay, choosing the devil we know over the void we dread. And sometimes we do desperate things because desperation is the only language the world has ever taught us.

I do not pity Samantha. I really do not. But I understand her in ways I suspect she has never allowed herself to imagine.

If I had known who Niall's father was when I first met him, I would likely have run a mile. Not from Niall, never from him, but from the history wrapped around his family name. I might have believed, wrongly or not, that blood always wins.

Samantha did not run. She married Conor. She built a life that looked tidy from a distance. She had children with a man she may have feared would one day become too much like his father. So sometimes I wonder if she did it all out of love. Or if love had very little to do with it. Perhaps she acted out of terror, the kind that settles beneath the skin and refuses to loosen its grip.

In her own way, Samantha Donnelly trapped Conor not to steal his freedom, but to shield herself from becoming another woman damaged, discarded, or forgotten by a Donnelly man.

And now all of us are tangled in the consequences of choices made years before any of us had the sense to understand what they would become. I do not know what Samantha thinks she witnessed tonight. I only hope she keeps it to herself and says nothing to Niall. Because God help me, I cannot bear another fracture inside this already shattered house.

21

25 December 2010: Niall

All is calm, all is bright, until it is not.

It was one of those rare days you wish you could capture in a jar and keep forever, pure and chaotic and filled with a kind of heart-wrenching magic. Rory's eyes lit up as if he could sense the joy drifting through the house, even if he had no idea what any of it meant. Emily let out her first proper giggle when Rachel attempted an enthusiastic, wildly off-beat dance to Fairytale of New York. My mother cried the moment she opened the locket from Rachel, and I nearly lost it myself when I saw the photograph inside: all four grandchildren huddled together, mismatched jumpers and gummy smiles. For a brief and golden spell, we were a family in harmony. No tension in the air. No simmering arguments. No ghosts tugging at our ankles.

The snow had fallen thick and early that year, settling over the countryside as if the sky itself wanted to soften the world and give us all something gentle to lean into. Snowfall was recorded at Dublin Airport, which mattered more than it should, since it is the measure that officially confirms a White Christmas in Ireland. It felt almost like an omen, although I did not dare say that out loud.

I stood at the wide window of my parents' country home, one hand wrapped around a mug of coffee laced with a drizzle of maple syrup. Outside, Clara played with the twins, the three of them wrapped in red and green scarves that made them look like cheerful little parcels ready for posting. Conor and Nicky were engaged in a fierce snowball battle. Nicky's laugh rose above the wind, bright and bubbling in a way that could warm even the frostiest afternoon. Children have a knack for that. They seem born knowing how to summon joy out of thin air.

A little farther down the garden, Samantha made her way through the snow with baby Sammy tucked close against her chest. For the first time in what felt like years, Christmas did not ache as sharply as it usually did. The grief was still there, but quieter, softened under the weight of falling snow.

It was as though time had folded over itself, creating a thin crease where memory and reality slipped together. I felt the shimmer of a Christmas long gone. Not a complete memory, not something whole or reliable. I was seven the last Christmas with Greg, and he was four. I no longer know how much of what I recall truly happened, and how much has been stitched together from old photographs, whispered stories, or dreams that settled in my mind so long ago I can no longer untangle truth from imagination. Still, the images live inside me like an old silent film: warm, flickering, and edged with softness.

I remember the scent of cinnamon from the candle my mother always lit in the sitting room. Greg used to wrinkle his nose and declare it too spicy. I remember Rachel building snowmen that resembled nothing more than lumpy little creatures, which she insisted on naming with great seriousness. Conor, ten and full of authority, built a proper snowman with coal eyes and a crooked stick arm that pointed accusingly at the sky. And Greg, sweet stubborn Greg, insisted the snowman needed his red mittens, because snowmen must get cold too. I do not know if that detail is real, but it sits in my mind as clearly as the feel of the cold air that winter. I can still see Greg pressing his bare hands to the snowman's round belly, smiling that gap-toothed smile that made you want to wrap him up and keep him safe.

Those days felt like candlelight: golden, unsteady, far too brief. We used to gather around the fire, the six of us wrapped in blankets, nibbling shortbread from tins painted with scenes of sleigh rides and cottages heavy with snow. Greg would curl up on our mother's lap and drift to sleep, thumb half in his mouth, a smear of chocolate drying on his chin. I used to stare at him for ages, as if I knew on some wordless level that time was already slipping away. Part of me wonders if I sensed something. Children can be strangely perceptive. Maybe I recognised the fragility of it all. Maybe I simply loved him so fiercely that even then I wanted to memorise everything about him.

I do not remember the Christmas that followed. Only the feeling. As if every window in the house had been opened at once, letting out all the warmth and leaving us to sit in the draught. After Greg died, the world became too loud and too quiet in the same breath. My mother stopped humming carols while she cooked. My father left the box of porch lights unopened. Rachel would burst into tears at the sight of a candy cane. Even Conor, always so steady, spent hours staring out of windows as though searching for something he could not name.

Every Christmas after that felt delicate. Polite. Handled with the same caution you would give an heirloom ornament that might crumble if touched. Laughter sounded rehearsed. Joy felt borrowed, as though we were only borrowing it from families who had not been torn apart.

Until this one.

I turned from the window, blinking hard against the sting in my eyes. In the corner of the room, the tree glittered. The lights twinkled through a cheerful chaos of tin foil snowflakes and pipe-cleaner stars that Nicky had made earlier that morning. One of the twins had, with Clara's help, glued two oversized googly eyes to a gingerbread man ornament. Nicky insisted that it looked exactly like Unky Nil. I have no idea why that delighted me so much, but it did.

Outside, Clara's laughter rang out again. I heard Nicky shout something about an avalanche, then a burst of squealing as Clara and Samantha collapsed into the snow together, making angels with wildly flapping limbs. Even little Sammy giggled from her spot on Conor's hip, her tiny hands waving in excited rhythm.

For the first time in a decade, Christmas did not feel like a wound. It felt like a beginning. It felt like a breath.

It felt, just for a moment, like hope.

There were four small children in the house again. Four. I had not realised it until that exact moment, had not counted them in that way. My two. Conor's two. Four once more. Not the same children, of course, yet close enough to stir something fragile and half-forgotten inside me. Something shimmering, almost sacred. Not a replacement. Never that. But a rhythm had returned to the walls. A heartbeat remembered, soft and steady, like an echo that had finally found its way home.

As the snow drifted past the windows and the sky melted into dusk, Niall felt something shift within him. A tightness he had carried for so long began to loosen. Greg would never come back. That truth lived in him every day. Yet the magic Greg had held in those four short years lingered here again. It felt woven into the laughter of the children, threaded through the silver tinsel on the bannister, rising with the steam from the cocoa mugs left half-finished on the table.

This Christmas was not haunted. It was, in some quiet and unexpected way, healed.

I kept noticing Clara watching the twins as though she still could not fully believe they were real. The way she strokes the back of Rory's neck as he drifts into sleep is almost a prayer, a gentle ritual she performs without realising. It grounds her. Centres her. I do not think she knows she does it. I am so proud of her it hurts.

She carries exhaustion like something stitched into her bones, yet she never complains. Not once. She laughs even when she is running on fumes. She hums lullabies with lips that are dry and cracked from the cold. She keeps going because she thinks she must. She is everything.

Tonight, I watched her from across the room while she helped my mother straighten Emily's reindeer headband. Her face was warm in the lamplight, her smile small but genuine, and it struck me with a force I had not expected. This was it. This was the life I had always wanted. Something simple, grounded, real. We had clawed our way to this point. God knows I thought we would never make it.

But now it is after two in the morning and I am alone in bed. The babies are curled into the cot beside me like soft commas, warm against one another, their tiny bodies full of milk-heavy dreams. Clara's side of the mattress is cold.

I waited fifteen minutes before sitting up. Another ten before I gathered the courage to look for her. I tried not to read into anything. Perhaps she was in the bathroom. Perhaps she had gone for water. But it is Christmas night, and there is a tug in my chest that feels wrong.

The old house creaks as if its memories are shifting in the dark. I move down the hall on my toes, careful to avoid the floorboard outside the nursery that always groans like a warning. A thin ribbon of moonlight lies across the landing, pale and still. The quiet feels unnatural.

When I reach the top of the stairs, I see the soft glow of the sitting room lamps left on below.

And then I see them. Clara and Conor.

She is wrapped in her robe. He is still in his dinner shirt with the sleeves rolled, his hand resting at the small of her back. They are hugging.

Not simply hugging. Holding each other.

Her face is pressed into his chest. His chin rests gently on her head. It is not a quick embrace. It is not the sort of hug you give to thank someone for a present. It is longer. Closer. Her fingers linger on his arm in a way that turns my stomach.

I should have gone back upstairs. I should not have stood frozen between the bannisters like some intruder in my own home. But I could not move. The moment held me. The way she breathed against him felt like she was finally releasing something she had kept to herself all day.

I do not know how long I watched. A few seconds. Possibly more. Eventually Conor let go. He wiped his face and said something I could not hear. She nodded. They both sat at opposite ends of the sofa, leaving space between them, though the space did nothing to erase what I had seen.

I slipped back upstairs when I heard someone else moving below. I did not ask anything. I did not speak a word. What could I have said? Were you crying in my brother's arms? Is something happening between you? Why do you seem closer to him than to me?

But I know Clara. I do. She would not... would she?

She has barely touched me recently. I told myself it was because of the twins, the recovery, the hormones. Any of that could be true. Yet now I cannot help wondering if it is only that. Or if there is something more. Something just out of sight. Or worse, something I have been refusing to see.

It is ridiculous. It is Christmas, the best day we have had in months, and still I feel the ground shifting beneath my feet. As if I have been standing on a crack without realising, and now it is finally beginning to open.

I want to ask her. I want to believe there is nothing to fear. But I do not want to become the jealous husband. I do not want to seem paranoid. So I will keep quiet for now.

Please let it be nothing. Please let it be nothing.

22

Aug 22nd, 2025: Charlotte

What I do not know could fill a book. Possibly several.

I may never look at Conor and Samantha in quite the same way again, nor will I ever be able to eat in their kitchen without feeling that slight twist in my stomach. That is what I get for reading all the journals, or at least the ones I have found so far.

The discomfort I feel is mild compared with the sorrow that keeps creeping in as I read Clara's words. They are raw, sharp around the edges, striking even in their tenderness. Niall's are softer, almost dreamy, as if he was trying to hold on to some ideal that was crumbling beneath him.

The Christmas entries have shattered me. The twins' first Christmas. I cried reading about the warmth in that house, the intensity of Niall's devotion to Clara, and the fierce love she poured into those babies. Yet beneath all of that, there was something else. A faint undercurrent, a quiet rot spreading between the lines.

Clara writes about Conrad cornering her again. She notes how Conor stepped in to protect her, describing him as the only one in the family who truly understood what was happening.

Then there is Niall's version. Blissfully unaware. He was convinced he was watching an affair unfold in front of him. My skin crawls every time I think about it. He had no idea he was witnessing an act of protection rather than betrayal. How could you ever explain something so complicated to someone who already believed he was losing his wife at the time?

He never confronted her. Not directly. He simply stewed in it and let it fester until it changed shape in his mind.

I keep circling back to the same questions. Was that the moment everything cracked? Was that the entry he read after Clara died, the one that pushed him into something unrecognisable? Or was it Conor's account instead?

Because I still cannot make sense of it. How did Niall even get hold of Conor's journal? I thought Clara had hidden only her own in the attic. What exactly did Niall read, and what did he believe he had discovered?

And what about Samantha? God, Samantha. Clara never mentioned her again in these entries or at least not in the ones I hold in my hands.

The final journal ends just after Christmas. Everything goes quiet after that. A page has been torn out. Then nothing. No explanation. No closure. Did Clara cut Samantha out after that moment? Did she write something about her that someone did not want anyone to see? Did they speak again, even once, before she died? Could that missing page be the one that sent Niall spiralling? Could Samantha have torn it out herself to hide something dreadful?

I remember overhearing Niall's family one year when they thought I was not listening. They discussed Clara's passing around the anniversary of her death. They mentioned Samantha at the funeral, standing at the back with her sunglasses on despite the rain. A shield against guilt, grief, or both. She was trembling and would not look at anyone, not even Conor. That alone said more than any confession ever could.

Part of me wants to believe Clara had been trying to protect everyone, even Samantha, in her own twisted way. Maybe she was defending herself as well. Maybe she refused to be pulled into yet another toxic secret that was not hers to carry.

There are so many gaps. So many blank spaces between these pages that swallow the truth whole.

Did Niall read only fragments of the story? Did he convince himself of the worst because it was easier than facing something more complicated? Did Clara die with her secrets, or did she die because of them?

If he broke apart over something untrue, then I need to know what he thought he knew. I need to know how Conor's journal found its way into his hands. Someone must have given it to him, or left it somewhere easy to find. And if Samantha's silence was never just guilt, if it was fear, then she may be carrying far more than she has ever admitted. It is time someone finally asked her.

I moved quietly down the stairs. The twins' bedroom doors were slightly ajar. I saw the soft flicker of lights from their screens as they watched films or scrolled through videos. In my day, having a portable DVD player in your room felt like the height of luxury.

When I reached the ground floor, I saw Niall asleep in the armchair. One hand was wrapped around the remote as if he thought it might disappear if he loosened his grip. I nearly texted him, but the sound would have woken him, so I went old fashioned and wrote a note.

Gone to the chemist. Headache is brutal. Back soon.

C x

It was only half a lie. The headache is real. It is simply not the sort that two paracetamol will fix.

I did not want to wake Niall because then I would have had to lie face to face. I did not want him asking questions. I would not have been able to answer him, not yet, not until I know the truth.

The drive out to Conor and Samantha's house felt both familiar and sickening. I used to come here for barbecues and birthdays, moments that felt like part of a life we were all building together. Now it feels hollow. A perfect house, neatly kept, sitting like a set piece from a film. A shell that pretends to be a home.

Conor's car was not in the driveway. For a moment, I almost turned back.

Then the front door opened. Samantha stood there with her hair clipped back and her face freshly washed. Her housecoat was tied too tightly around her waist, almost as if she needed something to hold on to. She looked like she had been expecting someone, yet not me.

Her expression faltered, just for a second. Enough to make my heart beat that little bit faster.

"Charlotte?" she said, a little too brightly, as if rehearsing warmth she did not quite feel.

"Oh. You alright? You look pale. Come in, I'll make tea."

I stepped over the threshold like I was crossing into enemy territory. My chest was already aching and my hands were cold enough to sting. The house smelled faintly of lavender polish and something burnt from the oven, a strangely domestic backdrop to the dread twisting inside me. She led me into the kitchen as if we were just two mothers catching up over a cuppa. She even offered biscuits, holding the packet out with a hopeful little smile. I didn't sit.

"I know what you told Clara," I said. My voice came out sharper than I meant, as if the words had cut their own way out.

"That night. When you were drunk."

Her hand froze mid-reach for the teabags. She did not turn. She did not even breathe. The air in the kitchen thinned.

"I know," I continued, slower this time, "about how you admitted to getting pregnant on purpose, to trap Conor. You told her. Clara. And I need to know:"

She turned at last. Her mouth was a thin, bloodless line, the colour draining from her face.

"I need to know how far you were willing to go to make sure she kept that secret."

Everything stilled. Even the hum of the fridge faded until the only sound was the faint ticking of the clock above the back door.

"Did you play a hand in Clara's death?"

She did not gasp. She did not cry. She did not even deny it. She blinked once, then again. Her fingers curled around the edge of the worktop until her knuckles went chalk white.

"You think I?" Her voice cracked, barely more than a whisper.

"You think I'd hurt her?"

"I don't know what to think anymore," I said. The honesty of it shocked even me.

"I don't know what you're capable of."

There was a long silence. A long, aching stretch of it. Then Samantha finally spoke.

"Clara said she wouldn't tell anyone that she understood. It felt like she pitied me." Her eyes welled, and beneath the tears something harder simmered, something raw.

"Do you know how humiliating that was? To be pitied by her? Clara always had that way of looking at you like she saw every broken thing inside and didn't flinch. But that doesn't mean it didn't hurt. It did."

"But she kept your secret," I said.

"Didn't she?"

"Yes," Samantha breathed, nodding slowly.

"She did. I begged her not to tell Conor. I think she saw how miserable I was, how miserable he was, so she kept it. Because I told her I'd do anything to protect Nicky and Sammy. And I meant it."

My stomach twisted, a slow cold knot.

"But I never touched her," she whispered.

"Never hurt her. I loved Clara. I didn't want her gone. I may have wanted her to stop making me feel so small."

She sank onto the kitchen stool as if her knees could no longer hold her. Her shoulders folded inward.

"But I didn't kill her," she said again, quieter now, a tremble beneath the words. "You have to believe that. Please."

I stood there with my heart pounding so violently I thought I might be sick. Something in the room felt wrong. There was a heaviness that clung to the walls, something unsaid lurking in the corners like a shadow waiting to step forward. Maybe she did not kill Clara. But perhaps she knew something. Perhaps she saw something. And buried it.

Secrets never stay with the person who holds them. They spread, burying everyone nearby until no one can breathe. And whatever Samantha was hiding, I was going to drag it into the light.

Even if it meant unearthing the ugliest parts of all of us.

Samantha had not moved. She sat curled on the edge of the stool, fingers tightened around a mug she had never finished making. Her face was flushed now, not with anger but with something closer to shame, or fear, or both tangled together. I could no longer tell which.

I drew breath to speak again, ready to ask if there was more she had not told me, if anyone else knew, if she had ever confided in someone she should not have, when I heard it: a soft click. The door.

I turned.

Conor stood in the doorway. He had not made a sound. No footsteps. No clearing his throat. Just a still figure at the edge of the light, tall and tired and unreadable.

He looked between us. Between his wife, pale and trembling, and me, standing stiff with my arms crossed and Clara's diary pressed beneath one arm.

After what felt like an eternity, he spoke at last. His voice was low and steady, calm in a way that made something in my stomach twist again.

"If you want to know the truth"

"We're going to need something stronger than tea."

Neither Samantha nor I replied.

We watched Conor step into the room and move past the doorway without taking off his coat. He did not demand an explanation. He did not even ask. His silence told me he already knew the shape of the conversation, perhaps more than either of us had expected. He walked to the kettle, poured the boiled water down the sink and reached instead for the cupboard where I knew the whiskey was kept.

He poured three glasses but only brought two to the table. He sat opposite me and slid one across with a quiet clink. Samantha did not touch hers. Her hands shook too much to try.

Conor looked exhausted, not from lack of sleep but from the weight of years spent holding himself rigid.

He took one long sip, then finally said:

"Clara kept Samantha's secret. Even when it nearly broke her."

"Even when she didn't need to."

Samantha flinched. She looked smaller than ever.

"Clara thought she was protecting us all," Conor continued, eyes fixed on the glass in his hands.

"But what Samantha didn't know was that I already knew. About the first pregnancy. About why."

Samantha blinked hard, lifting her gaze.

"You never told me," she whispered.

He nodded. "No. I didn't, because I knew why you did it, Sam. Not to trap me. Not really. You were scared. You saw how my father treated women. The way he looked at them. How he touched them when he thought no one noticed. And you were scared I'd become him."

Her lip trembled and she lowered her eyes.

"You didn't trust me after that," she murmured.

Conor shook his head gently, not with anger but with something closer to sorrow and understanding.

"I didn't trust myself."

He turned to me then, and something in his expression shifted.

"When Clara found out, she came to me. She said I should not keep quiet about it. Not because she wanted to shame anyone, God, never that, but because we no longer needed to keep all these secrets tucked between us like fragile things we were terrified to drop. I think she had reached the point where she could not carry all of it anymore, all our tangled histories pressing on her chest. She said that at least our secrets could be resolved, that we owed it to ourselves to try before everything collapsed beyond repair."

I remembered the way Clara had written in one of her entries: I am unravelling. I am holding too much. The words had stayed with me in a way that felt almost physical, as if they had been a bruise pressed beneath my ribs.

"She begged me to talk to Samantha," Conor continued, his voice steadier than his expression.

"So I did. After Sammy was born, it was not easy. It was a messy process that stretched over weeks. There were nights when we did not speak at all, when we circled each other like strangers. But eventually we listened. We really talked. And we cried."

Samantha met his gaze, her voice quiet but steady. "And we did not fall apart."

"No," he said softly. "We did not."

I bit my tongue, fighting the urge to say what I knew: that they had come apart together in this very kitchen, completely and painfully. FFS, focus, Charlotte. My thoughts were slipping through my fingers like water.

Conor looked down for a moment, then back up, his hand coming to rest on Samantha's shoulder with a slow, tentative gentleness.

"I told Niall, eventually. About what happened, and why I said what I did to Clara the night they announced their engagement. I explained that it was not about Clara. It was about me, about the secrets and lies that had crept into my marriage like mould we pretended not to see."

He exhaled slowly, as if releasing something he had held for too long.

"Niall thought we were going to separate. But when I told him Samantha and I talked, really talked, for hours, he was surprised. Surprised because that kind of resolution, that kind of emotional honesty, is not something we grew up with. It was foreign to us, almost uncomfortable."

Conor paused, his eyes turning distant, as if he was looking at an earlier version of himself.

"He asked me where I learned to be a grown-up."

A faint smile flickered across his face, thin but sincere.

"We laughed. And we have been okay since then. Not like before, not exactly, but okay enough to keep moving. I have never been able to get us back to what we had, not the bright bit of it anyway."

His voice cracked as he looked at Samantha, his expression raw and exposed, stripped down to something close to fear.

"And that breaks me a little."

A long silence followed. The air felt heavy, as if the kitchen itself was waiting for one of us to breathe again. I did not touch the whiskey. Instead, I traced the intricate pattern etched into the glass with the tip of my finger, trying to quiet the storm of thoughts twisting through me.

Clara came back to me then, the image of her watching them patch things up while she still carried her secret. Her secret locked inside her like a room she refused to enter.

"Why did you not tell Niall everything?" I asked.

Conor dragged a hand through his hair, weary.

"Because I thought Clara would. I thought she was building up to it. But then she died. And by then, we had no idea what Niall knew. Only that he had read something in her journals and snapped."

"And you did not think to ask what it was?" My voice was sharper than I intended, but I did not pull it back.

Conor looked at me with a guilt so stark it made my stomach twist.

"We did not know if he could handle knowing," Samantha said softly. Her hands were clasped so tightly in her lap that her knuckles had turned white.

"We worried he might do something terrible. What if he found out about Conrad and took matters into his own hands? Or what if he blamed himself so deeply for failing to protect Clara that he harmed himself? Either way, the twins would have lost both of their parents."

I swallowed. My mouth had gone dry.

"He is an adult. You do not get to make those decisions for him. He thinks Clara and you," I said, turning to Conor, "he thinks she was having an affair with you."

Conor's face twisted as if I had struck him. Samantha gasped, her hand flying to her mouth.

"No," he said. "No. Never. I loved her like a sister. I would have died before anything like that happened."

"I know," I said quickly, my throat tight. "I know. But he saw you that night after the Christmas row with your father. He saw you hugging Clara. And I think he thinks something entirely different happened."

Conor rubbed his eyes hard. "Oh Christ."

Samantha spoke then, barely above a whisper. "How are we supposed to tell him? About Conrad? About what he did to Clara?"

That was the question. The one that settled over the kitchen like a noose tightening with each breath.

How do you tell a man that the father he idolised, defended, and became a father beside was the same man who left his wife so broken she could hardly breathe?

We sat with it, the three of us, facing the truth that had turned into something volatile. It felt like a grenade resting on the kitchen table. One wrong move and it would explode in all our hands.

"I will tell him," Conor said at last. "But I will not do it without you. Just let me know when you are ready."

He looked at me, and in that moment I understood. This was no longer about protecting Clara. This was about freeing her, even if the cost was everything that remained standing.

The silence between us thickened, sitting in the room like a storm cloud that refused to break. And as I looked at Conor and Samantha, really looked at them, I knew I could not stay quiet much longer, not about any of it. It was not just about Clara. It was about all of us, every fracture and every truth we had buried.

I swallowed hard, feeling my throat tighten in that familiar, suffocating way. I had carried this truth like a second spine for only two days, yet it already felt far too heavy to bear. I rose slowly, placing the untouched whiskey on the table with a faint clink that sounded far louder in the stillness.

"There is something I need to say as well."

Both Conor and Samantha turned towards me. Their faces were expectant, cautious, already bracing for something unpleasant.

I drew a shaky breath that trembled through my whole body.

"Clara and I..."

"We were best friends growing up."

The words slipped out before I could cushion them. Before I could think of a gentler way to begin. But there was no gentle way. Not with this.

"We lost touch in our twenties. Life tugged us in different directions, and before I knew it she had drifted away. Then I heard she had died."

"I knew she had married, but I did not know her husband was..."

"...was Niall."

Samantha's hand flew to her mouth. Conor blinked as if his mind was scrambling to catch up with what I had just said.

"So, when I met Niall," I continued, my voice cracking under its own strain, "when we started seeing each other, I had absolutely no idea he was her husband. I did not know until I found her journals during the move on Thursday night."

My heartbeat thudded at a painful rhythm as I looked at both of them. "And now I do not know how I am supposed to tell him, or whether he already knows who I was to Clara."

Silence wrapped itself around us again.

Conor exhaled slowly, as if the air around us had turned to glass and might shatter if he breathed too quickly.

We were three people sitting in a kitchen thick with history, betrayal, and grief. Each of us held truths we had never meant to keep. Each of us was terrified of what would happen when those truths finally clawed their way into the open.

The car was silent, the rain tapping a soft, relentless rhythm against the windscreen. My hands were stiff around the steering wheel, every muscle tense with a familiar anxiety I could not quite name. I kept glancing at the clock. The digits glowed 12:58 am. I had been out for almost two hours after leaving a weak excuse for my absence. Gone to the chemist. Back soon. C x. It had felt suspicious the moment I sent it. I had not needed to buy tablets. We always had headache tablets in the cupboard.

What pressed on me was everything I had learned from Conor and Samantha. I had told them everything, finally. About Clara. The journals. The discovery that had upended my certainty two nights ago. Clara, my childhood best friend, who had married Niall and died shortly after we reconnected. Now I was married to him.

How could I possibly tell him that the woman he lost was the same girl who once smeared glitter on my cheeks and spoke about love as if it were a spell waiting to be cast? What if he thought I had manipulated my way into his life without even meaning to? The thought alone made my stomach twist.

The road home curved sharply, and I nearly missed the turn. My heart thudded with the weight of my secret. When I pulled into our driveway, I noticed a single light still glowing upstairs. It was just after 1:05 am.

I sat motionless for a moment, knowing I needed to pretend everything was normal, even though the truth felt ready to swallow me whole and take his world with it. I rested my forehead against the steering wheel and released a long, shaking breath.

How had I ended up here? How had my childhood best friend become the ghost standing between my husband and me? And what would happen once I told him the truth? Because if this secret did not break us, the truth about Conrad might. Those two truths seemed frighteningly intertwined, like vines that had grown around each other without warning.

I pushed the front door open slowly, holding my breath as I slipped inside like a guilty teenager sneaking home after curfew. The hallway lay in darkness, the only light spilling softly from beneath the living room door and the faint glow from upstairs. I thought I had made it unnoticed, until I heard his voice.

"Charlotte?"

I froze.

Niall's silhouette appeared at the top of the stairs. He was shirtless, wearing those soft navy joggers he wore when he was too tired to pretend he slept fully dressed. His voice was gentle, yet threaded with concern.

"Where were you? You said you were going to the chemist. That was over two hours ago."

My pulse thundered in my ears as I forced my voice into something steady.

"I could not find the tablets I needed." I tucked a piece of damp hair behind my ear, keeping my gaze low.

"So, I sat in the car for a while. I needed to think."

There. A half truth. Always the most dangerous kind.

Niall descended the stairs slowly, his bare feet soundless on the wood, his eyes fixed on mine.

"Think about what?"

Everything. Clara. The journals. You.

But I offered a tight smile and shook my head.

"Just things. Nothing that matters."

He paused two steps from the bottom. His expression was unreadable. Then he nodded once.

"I believe you," he said softly.

"You have never given me a reason not to."

The guilt pressed cold and sharp against my ribs.

Niall stepped closer and brushed a delicate kiss against my cheek. His breath warmed my skin as he lingered for a heartbeat, just long enough for me to feel the weight of all the words we were not saying.

Then he whispered, barely above a breath, "Are you coming to bed?"

I nodded too quickly.

"Yes. Just give me a moment."

He did not step back. Instead, he tilted his head, a faint ghost of a smile tugging at his lips. He leaned in, his nose grazing along the curve of my cheek, the warmth of his body a whisper against mine.

"We still have to christen the house," he murmured.

"We can ask someone to take the kids for the weekend. Just the two of us. A little time alone."

His suggestion sounded innocent enough, yet there was something deeper in his voice. An ache. A want. A softness I had not seen in him for days, perhaps weeks, and it sent a fresh wave of fear and longing through me.

And despite everything, despite the truth that throbbed beneath my ribs like a warning siren, I wanted him too. The pull of him lived in places I rarely admitted to, deep and instinctive, rising before I could reason with it. I wanted to feel close to him again, to remember the woman I had been on the day I married him. Before the secrets. Before the half truths that had slowly carved distance between us. Because there was still something in him that felt safe, even when the rest of my world seemed to be coming undone thread by thread.

So I reached for his hand. I let him guide me up the stairs, each step slow and careful in the hush of the house, the quiet so complete that it felt as if the walls were listening. When he followed me into the bedroom and closed the door behind us, he paused for a moment. His gaze swept over me, and the world, the pain, the questions, the ghosts of Clara's past, slipped back into the shadows for a little while.

Sometimes, even in the middle of a storm, we crave the warmth of someone who makes us believe we might survive it. He did not speak again. Not with words. The click of the door settling into its frame was enough to change the air itself. It grew dense and charged, almost electric, the way the atmosphere feels a heartbeat before lightning strikes.

His eyes locked on mine, intense and unwavering, burning through me with a hunger that made my skin flush and my breath falter. He moved towards me with the quiet confidence that had always unravelled my composure. There was a deliberate stillness in him, a controlled tension that promised anything except restraint. I did not move. I could not. I simply stood there, heart hammering, while his gaze travelled over me as if he were learning me all over again.

Then he was close. So close that the heat of him wrapped around me. His hands slid beneath my shirt, warm and rough against my skin as they wandered upward and took the fabric with them. When his mouth found mine, the kiss was deep and claiming, all teeth and tongue and fire, as if he had been holding back for far too long. I gasped when he tugged my shirt over my head and let it drop to the floor, forgotten.

"You have been driving me out of my mind all night," he murmured against my throat, his voice low and ragged as if pulled from somewhere raw.

"I did not even say anything."

"Exactly."

His hands explored me with a reverence that bordered on desperation. He unclasped my bra with an easy flick, letting it fall away before he paused, just long enough to take me in fully. The way he looked at me sent heat spiralling through my belly, and then his mouth was on my skin, hot and hungry. Every brush of his lips and teeth loosened something inside me that I had held too tightly for too long.

I felt the evidence of his need pressing against me, firm and insistent through the thin barrier that remained between us. He nudged me back until the edge of the bed met my thighs.

"You want this?" he asked, his breath warm against my ear.

I nodded, unable to form anything more than a whisper.

"Yes."

"Then take it."

He shed the rest of his clothing in a single fluid movement. The sight of him made my breath catch. He turned me gently, yet with a certainty that left no doubt of his intentions, his hands guiding me exactly where he wanted me to be, where I needed to be. He slid my panties down with slow precision, his knuckles brushing the heat of me, and a low sound escaped him as if the moment overwhelmed him.

"You are already ready for me," he breathed, the words rough with something that sounded like longing.

A soft cry left me when his fingers slid inside, slow and sure, coaxing me until my legs trembled and I clutched the bed for balance. Every stroke unravelled me further.

"Niall," I whispered.

"Please."

That was all he needed.

He gripped my waist, positioned himself, and with one controlled thrust, he filled me completely. My breath caught in my throat, my body arching into him instinctively as the stretch of him lit a fire that travelled through me in a rush. He moved with deep, steady pressure, each movement sending a shock through me that left me clinging to the sheets, desperate for more.

The rhythm grew, rough and beautiful, overwhelming in its intensity. I lost myself in the sound of our bodies, in the heat of his skin against mine, in the way he groaned my name as though it meant something he had never spoken aloud.

"God, you feel like heaven," he rasped, his voice unsteady, as if the truth of it surprised him.

"Like I have been starving for you."

And I had been starving for this, for him, for the way he touched me, as if he knew every secret my body kept hidden. I met every movement with my own, my cries growing louder, more desperate, until his hand reached around and found the spot that shattered me completely.

Pleasure crashed over me with fierce intensity, my hands twisting in the sheets, my body bowing beneath the force of it. But he did not stop. He pulled me upright, my back pressed to his chest, one hand curving around my throat. The pressure was light, a reminder of surrender rather than a claim. His other hand covered my breast, teasing and coaxing until my breath came in broken sounds.

"Touch yourself," he whispered, his lips brushing my ear. "Let me feel you fall apart again."

And I obeyed, shameless and aching, chasing a second peak as Niall moved inside me, deeper and harder, pushing me towards the edge with every thrust.

"I am close," he growled.

"Then do not hold back," I panted. "Give me everything."

And he did. His release hit with raw force, his grip tightening, his body shaking as mine followed, spiralling into him as if he were the only thing keeping me anchored. We collapsed together, tangled in limbs and heat and breath, the silence that followed thick with something fragile and unnamed.

His hand found mine, our fingers lacing together, his thumb stroking gently over my skin as if to soothe away the storm we had created.

Neither of us spoke.

Words might have broken the spell that held us.

So we stayed like that. Still tangled. Still trembling. And for one night, the lie felt beautiful.

23

June 16th, 2018: Charlotte

This could be the beginning of something great.

The scent of espresso and warm pastries still clings to my skin, as if the morning refuses to let me go. I sit in the office now, preparing for the day ahead, yet my mind keeps drifting back to the moment everything shifted. The sun had only just begun to nudge itself over the rooftops, casting a soft amber glow that gilded the windows of The Cosy Coffee House. I can still hear the familiar click of Reya's keys in the lock and the steady rhythm of her tired but determined footsteps crossing the cool tile. She always opened the shop with the same quiet reverence, as if she were unlocking a sanctuary.

Outside, the air was thick with the early promise of summer and already growing heavy with heat. Inside, the sudden rush of air conditioning wrapped around her like a whispered reassurance. At six in the morning, the coffee house existed in a rare pocket of stillness. Even then, we both knew it would not last. By mid-morning, the sun would blaze through the front windows and transform our gentle haven into a miniature greenhouse without the relentless hum of the AC.

Yet that morning carried something else. A subtle shift I could feel in my bones, a change in the air that I had not yet learned to name.

Reya's phone beeped, a sharp and urgent sound that sliced through the fragile quiet. I watched her hands tremble as she unlocked the screen. Her eyes flickered across the words in silence. The colour drained from her face with such speed that it startled me.

Closure Notice.

She did not speak, not at first. There was no need. Her expression said everything: the quiver of her lip, the crease in her brow, the breath she could not release. Her shoulders sagged as if the weight of the news pressed directly upon them, dragging her down before she had fully taken in what it meant.

The familiar squeak of the countertop accompanied me as I lifted it and stepped through to meet her glassy stare.

"Did you hear?" I asked, my voice thinner than I intended.

Her eyes told me she already had. Tears spilled down her cheeks in quiet, trembling streams. The soft, guttural sob that escaped her tore through me, sharp and unexpected, as though something inside me cracked in response.

"What am I going to do?" she whispered. Her voice sounded cracked and small, the kind of sound someone makes when they are too overwhelmed to hide it.

"This place is everything. It's the only constant while everything else is shifting beneath me. I am not ready to let it go."

I stepped closer and rested my hand on her shoulder. She felt fragile, as if one misplaced word might shatter her completely.

"What if we give it a new beginning instead of an ending?" I said gently.

"Come and help me paint it. Not to change it beyond recognition, but to leave a mark we can be proud of. Something that belongs to us."

Reya blinked at me, her lashes still damp, her brow still pinched in confusion.

"Reya, I need you. Your eye, your ideas. I want to bring something fresh to the place without erasing everything that already makes it special."

She stared at me as if trying to decipher a puzzle she had never expected to see.

"You bought the coffee house?" Her voice was barely a whisper.

I nodded, unable to stop the smile that spread across my face.

"Yes. I bought it."

Her eyes widened, disbelief written across every inch of her expression.

"You bought the fricken coffee house?"

I laughed, breathless with the relief of finally saying it out loud.

"You knew how much I wanted this. Not because I needed to. Because I loved it. Every cup, every shift, every story that walked through the door."

Reya launched herself at me, arms around my neck and legs wrapping around my waist. She clung to me like someone holding a dream tightly enough to stop it dissolving. Her laughter was bright and sudden, the sound of sunlight breaking through storm clouds.

"I will take that as a yes," I said through my own laughter.

"I would be honoured to be your Brigadier General," she declared.

"I am the general. You would be my Lieutenant General," I teased.

She rolled her eyes.

"Look, it has been too long since I heard your dad's stories. I am rusty."

"You will hear them soon enough. He will be at Maura and Robert's retirement send-off. Brace yourself."

"Was he in the military?"

"Good grief, no. He just really loves World War Two documentaries."

We laughed again, the tension fading, the air becoming lighter and far easier to breathe.

The coffee house filled quickly after that. The aroma of roasted beans mingled with cinnamon and vanilla, swirling around us in warm, comforting ribbons. The hum of conversation built layer by layer over the steady hiss of the espresso machine. Our rhythm returned: pour, serve, smile, repeat.

When the lull finally arrived, Reya leaned over the counter with a deliberate casualness that did not fool me for a second.

"So, will you be keeping the staff on?" she asked, mischief glinting in her eyes.

"Of course. If it is not broken, I will not fix it. Unless you are asking about John. I was hoping to promote him to supervisor. He is the most experienced after you, he is brilliant with customers and everyone listens to him."

She let out a full-throated laugh.

"He is also just... so yummy."

I smirked.

"Reya. We cannot talk about staff like that, not once you are a manager."

Her face shifted instantly.

"Wait. Hold on. Does this mean I cannot date him? Because he would be below me..."

"Excuse me?" I gasped.

"You know exactly what I meant."

Her laughter was infectious and entirely unstoppable.

"Look, I do not mind because I think John likes you as well, and I am not about to interfere with destiny. Just be discreet. No PDA in the coffee house, all right?"

"You got it, boss," Reya said, testing the word as if trying on a hat she was not quite sure suited her.

"Boss sounds strange. I feel like I would need a pinstripe suit, bold jewellery, a huge fur coat, towering heels and dramatic makeup to pull that off."

"You do not own any of those things, do you?"

"Not one. So please do not call me boss."

Reya pointed her fingers at me as though firing imaginary pistols.

"Cool, cool, cool, cool, cool."

We dissolved into laughter again, cackling like a pack of hyenas.

John arrived a short while later, filling the doorway with his tall, broad frame. He always looked slightly out of place among the soft colours and delicate displays of our coffee house. He carried the fresh scent of early summer and the kind of steady energy that made toddlers giggle and left their parents deeply grateful.

He greeted us with his usual grin, bright and effortless, although it faltered the moment he lifted his phone.

"Did I just get fired via email?"

I snatched the phone before he could spiral further. My heart sank as I read Maura's message. It was well meaning, although hopelessly timed, the sort of thing that caused chaos without intending to.

"They must have thought I had already told everyone," I muttered.

"I did not want to count my chickens yet."

John's brows knitted, his expression tilting somewhere between confusion and worry.

"But they sold it without asking whether I wanted to stay? Because I really need to stay if the new owner is keeping it as a coffee house. Oh, unless they turn it into one of those over-thirty day clubs that seem to be popping up everywhere. You know the ones; they open during the daytime so everyone can be tucked up in bed by nine. I could bartend, I suppose."

"No, none of that. I mean, yes, they sold it. But they did not let you go. I am the new owner."

He blinked. Once. Twice. His mind clearly needed a moment to catch up.

"Oh. So you are managing then?"

"No." I smiled, feeling the thrill of finally being able to say it.

"Reya is the new manager."

His jaw dropped with a soft, incredulous thud.

"But you are incredible. Not that Reya would not be. She is amazing. I mean, she would be great, actually, now that I think about it. I mean..."

"Stop before you embarrass yourself," I said, cheeks warming from second-hand awkwardness.

"Too late." He laughed, rubbing the back of his neck.

"I am offering you a promotion as well. Supervisor. Same flexibility, and more hours if you want them."

He stared at me, unreadable for an uncomfortably long moment, and my stomach knotted.

Then he released a long, slow breath, as if he had been holding it for days.

"You could have told me sooner. Before I said all that stuff. It sounded like I was obsessed."

"I could have," I teased, nudging his arm.

"Are you seriously promoting me?"

"I will have a contract ready soon. You can have your advisor look it over."

"You mean my mum?"

"I was happy not to specify, although yes, your mum." I laughed, the tension easing at last.

"Can I ask something?" John paused, unusually cautious.

"With all the changes you are making, how open to dating would you be?"

"Oh, John, I adore you, but..."

"No. Jesus, no!" John froze like he had just stepped on a LEGO.

"Sorry, that came out far too intense. I love you like a sister. A very non romantic sister. Obviously. No, I meant Reya. I am sort of cuckoo for Cocoa Puffs for her. But if workplace romance is off limits, I will pine silently and cry into my coffee. It will be extremely professional."

"Go for it," I said, trying and failing to hide my excitement for Reya.

John blinked, stunned.

"Wait, really? You are not going to smite me with HR lightning bolts?"

I shrugged and grabbed a muffin from the tray between us.

"Honestly, you are not even the first person to bring this up."

His eyes widened.

"Wait. Reya already asked you?"

"She did," I said, biting back a laugh at his suddenly fish like expression.

"Very politely. Very nervously. She acted as though I might exile her to permanent decaf duty if she breathed wrong."

"And you said yes?"

"I said fine as long as I do not have to witness any gooey, slow motion, heart eyes nonsense while I am trying to restock the oat milk. If anyone starts feeding anyone else a croissant, I am leaving the room."

John's face lit up so brightly he looked like he might combust.

"So, we can date, but discreetly?"

"Exactly," I said, pointing at him with the muffin like it were a sceptre.

"Keep it PG thirteen. No odd giggling behind the espresso machine. No smooching during peak hours. And if either of you writes a love poem on latte foam, I will fire you on the spot."

He straightened and saluted me, as though I had knighted him for services to romance.

"You will not regret this."

"Oh, I already do," I muttered, watching him skip, actually skip, towards the back room as if auditioning for a rom com.

We both laughed. In that moment, surrounded by warm air, nerves, and the faint scent of cinnamon muffins, the truth settled in properly. It seeped into my bones with surprising comfort. The Cosy Coffee House was mine now. And as chaotic as it had already become, this felt like the real beginning.

24

Aug 23rd, 2025: Charlotte

Spilling the tea in the coffee house.

The bell above the coffee house door chimed with its usual cheerful jingle as I stepped inside. It should have felt familiar and warm, yet nothing about me felt light today. The scent of fresh pastries and rich espresso drifted through the air. It was normally comforting, something that grounded me whenever life felt too loud, although this morning it seemed thicker and sweeter than usual, as if even the aroma carried the weight of everything I had learned.

Reya was already behind the counter, her hair pulled into a perfect high bun, eyeliner sharp enough to qualify as a weapon. She glanced up as soon as the door swung shut behind me. Her eyes narrowed, and she wiped her hands on her apron with deliberate slowness, eyebrow raised.

"Well?" she said before I even reached the counter. "From the cryptic texts last night, I gathered either you found out your husband is secretly a lizard person or your mother-in-law tried to seduce your brother again."

A small, pained laugh escaped me. It came out more like a choke.

"Worse."

"Oh God," she whispered, eyes widening. "He is a lizard person?"

"No." I threw a nervous glance over my shoulder, then headed straight for our usual booth in the shadowed corner. Reya followed, carrying my coffee without asking.

She settled opposite me, arms folded, waiting for the download. So I told her. Everything. The journals, my meeting with Clara, Samantha's unexpected confession and the ache of realising I had been wrong about Conor. I had always chalked him up as an arsehole, yet the truth painted him as something far more complicated. And then, because the universe clearly wanted me to question my life choices, I admitted I had also ended up in bed with the central dark character in this strange horror comedy that had become my existence. Although to be fair to me, he was still my husband, so she could only be mildly judgmental.

By the time I finished, Reya sat back and blinked in slow disbelief. She shook her head as if trying to clear static.

"You are that girl," she said eventually.

I frowned. "What girl?"

"That girl in every thriller who sleeps with the guy everyone thinks is the murderer." She jabbed a dramatic finger at me. "The audience is shouting, begging her to stop, yet she is always there saying, but he held my hand and brushed my hair away from my face so gently, and before I knew it, my dress was on the floor."

I opened my mouth to protest, then paused. "All right, that is harsh."

Reya softened, leaning closer, her expression gentler. "Charlotte, I love you. And I love Niall too. Well, I think I still do. No, I do. You know how I was. I was obsessed with you two getting together."

"You were relentless." A faint smile tugged at my mouth.

"Because I saw it. Right from the moment he walked in here. He had that scruffy stubble, all wounded intensity, and he could not tell the difference between a flat white and a cappuccino."

The memory made me laugh.

"And you made it your mission," I continued.

"You were unbearable about it."

"You were so mopey back then. Still stuck in that ridiculous half-dating situation with Jamie the jazz poet."

"Oh my God. Please, no." I groaned. "The man had owned seventeen scarves."

Reya waved the thought away. "Point is, Niall walked in, and I knew instantly. You lit up in a way I had not seen in ages. And he looked at you like he had never seen sunlight before." Her voice softened once more. "So you have to understand why all of this, every bit of it, is so hard for me to wrap my head around. You have everything. Why do you want to pull this thread?"

"I know," I whispered. "Believe me, I am asking myself the same thing. What if he is not the villain, Reya? What if he is just the red herring?"

She sighed, long and thoughtful. "Yes. What if he is not the villain at all? What if there is no villain, and it was only a tragic thing that happened? Are you going to be satisfied with that ending?"

I did not have an answer, only a knot in my stomach.

Reya reached for my hand. Her grip was warm and steady. "You need to decide if you are going to talk to him. And you need to do it soon. Before the secret becomes bigger than the truth. Right now it is about what you have not said. Leave it too long, and it becomes about how long you have been hiding it."

"I am scared," I admitted. Tears gathered behind my eyes, hot and insistent.

"You are allowed to be scared," she said softly. "Just do not let fear stop you from doing the brave thing."

I nodded, swallowing hard. My gaze drifted around the coffeehouse. This place had been our sanctuary for years, a haven where problems could be spilled like sugar on the table and somehow swept up again. It felt strange realising that this tiny room, cluttered with mismatched cups and pastry crumbs, had been the beginning of everything.

Niall was out doing the weekend sports run: Rory at rugby and Emily at swimming. It bought me a little time, a thin sliver of breathing space before I had to stand in front of him and speak the truth that might change the shape of our marriage. I needed more answers before I faced that moment. More clarity. More courage.

I stepped out of the coffee house, clutching my coat tighter as the wind sliced along the street. My phone buzzed in my hand. Niall's name lit up the screen. Once upon a time, that alone would have made me giddy.

"Hey, sexy pants, last night was amazing. I do not need reminding, but I love being reminded of how good you look naked. On that note, please do not be mad, remember you love me. I forgot it was my turn to take Rory and the team out for lunch. They only want pizza, so I should not be too late. Love you millions. N xx."

There it was, his trademark reminder: remember you love me. His gentle charm wrapped up in a sentence that softened whatever he had forgotten. It used to undo me completely, and even now it stirred something tender.

But today, I did not feel angry. Not even close. Today, it felt like a door creaking open, offering more time and more space. Space to breathe, to think, to keep searching through those journals until the truth finally surfaced.

And for now, that small blessing felt like more than I deserved, yet exactly what I needed.

I thumbed a reply, cheeky and casual, a little performance to keep things feeling ordinary:

"Don't let them order garlic bread, I would like to kiss my husband later x."

Then I slipped the phone into my coat pocket and gripped the cold metal of my keys as if they were a weapon. The message was supposed to sound affectionate, yet instead of warmth it sparked a prickling urgency that crawled up my spine. The attic. The wardrobes. The trunks no one had touched in years. Where else could I search to uncover more journals? It felt like a scavenger hunt with prizes no one in their right mind would want.

What else had Clara written? What had Niall read that made his eyes go so dark and far away? What still lingered in our home, quiet yet rotting, waiting for someone brave or foolish enough to dig it up?

I reached the car and climbed inside, my heart battering against my ribs. The wind whipped around the frame, howling like a ghost desperate to warn me to stay away. I stared through the windscreen for a long moment, the ignition growling under my hand as if impatient for me to choose a direction.

City centre to home. Kildare backroads. Sixty minutes if you avoided a tractor. But now I had a window, a slim and golden window, a rare moment in which I could dig, discover, and breathe in secrets that had been left too long in the dark. A tiny chance to stay one step ahead of a truth that felt as if it were crawling ever closer to the light.

The house was mine. The kids were gone. Niall was distracted. My chance. My only one. I whispered it to my reflection in the rear-view mirror, jaw clenched, eyes too wide with determination: "You have got this."

I did not believe it, not entirely, yet I needed to hear it said aloud. I drove faster than I usually allowed myself to, chewing through the miles as if they were sins I needed to burn before they consumed me.

By the time I pulled into the driveway, the house seemed less like a home and more like a locked vault, something ancient and stubborn, waiting to confess only if I dared ask the right question.

I did not even remove my jacket. The moment I stepped through the front door, a hush swept over me, settling on my skin like I had crossed the threshold of a cathedral. Or a crypt. The sort of silence that feels alive, that listens and waits. Boots off. Careful. Quiet. Every creak of the floorboards felt like a betrayal that echoed far too loudly.

The attic stairs loomed above me, dark and narrow, groaning under the weight of history. My fingers hesitated on the bannister for a single breath, then I climbed. The air grew colder the higher I went, heavy with dust and something far more human: memory. A residue of sorrow, perhaps. Regret, certainly. Shadows clung to the corners, patient and expectant, as if they needed only a little movement to stir awake.

Boxes. Still sealed. We had only lived here for three days, yet everything felt chaotic, like the house existed in some strange limbo between a past I did not understand and a future I was not sure I wanted. I scanned their handwritten labels, kitchen, bedroom one, loft office, searching for anything that looked out of place, overwritten, or misleading. Boxes that did not want to be recognised.

Then I saw it.

Near the back, half-hidden underneath an old ironing board and a box of tangled fairy lights. A box with two different labels. One side read Christmas Décor, the other Spare Room Filing.

Why would anyone label a box like that unless they wanted to hide something?

My hands trembled as I tugged it free. There was a jagged patch where another label had been torn away, as if someone had changed their mind more than once. I peeled back the flaps, my heart hammering in my ears. Tissue paper. A cracked ceramic angel. A child's stocking embroidered with a gold letter R. And beneath them, folders.

Manila, unlabelled. And resting between them, as if it had been waiting patiently for me to arrive: a black leather-bound notebook with edges worn soft from years of handling.

Underneath that lay another journal. Blue. Too familiar. Inside the front flap, in handwriting I knew far too well: Niall, 2020.

My knees gave a small buckle. I dropped to the floor, staring at it as if it might leap up and speak.

The year Clara died. Why had he hidden this? Who was he unwilling to let read it? Had he written something he could not bear to look at again? Was he hiding it from me, or was he hiding it from himself?

I ran my fingertips across the cover, every inch of me vibrating with dread and curiosity. Buried among forgotten baubles and broken angels, who would ever think to look here? It was clever in its own way. Or it was damning. Deeply damning.

I slid the journal into my coat pocket and quietly closed the box. But before I could stand, something glinted through a layer of dust.

A corner of something deep blue. I pulled it free and felt the breath leave my lungs. Clara's journal. 2020. Her final one. The attic air tightened around me as if the house itself was holding its breath.

Two journals. Niall's and Clara's. The last year they were Niall and Clara, at least in the way the world had known them.

Would this one mention our final meeting? Would he write about her funeral with honesty, or with the careful edits grief forces on a mind? Would either of these pages reveal whether Clara's life had truly been hers to take, or whether someone else had nudged her towards the fall? I was not sure I wanted the answers. But I had them now.

I tucked both journals deep into my coat like precious contraband, then froze, listening for movement downstairs. Still no footsteps. No engine pulling in. Still safe. Still alone. Yet the house felt restless, as if time itself were beginning to tap its foot. The truth was in my pocket, and the lies we had all lived with were circling somewhere just outside the door.

How long before everything unravelled? How long before someone else began searching too?

I made my way towards the small attic window where a wicker rocking chair waited, its cushions slightly dented as if someone had sat there often enough to carve out a memory. I shrugged off my coat, settled into the chair and draped it over my legs, creating a small cocoon against the cold. I had no idea how long I had until someone returned, only that I had no time to waste and even less time to hesitate.

I opened the first journal. The attic seemed to lean closer. The house held its breath again. And I began to read.

25

5 January 2020: Clara

I came, I saw, I crumbled.

I barely slept last night. It was the sort of restless, needling insomnia that creeps in when the past feels closer than the present, when a name you thought had faded comes whispering back through the dark. Lottie. It echoed inside my head as if the walls themselves wanted to remind me of what I had buried. I told myself I simply needed to try. Closure, perhaps. Redemption, if I was being brave enough to hope for it. Or maybe I only wanted to prove that the past no longer had teeth. I am still not sure which version of the truth I believe.

It has been over ten years. Ten long years. Yet there I was, standing across the street from The Cosy Coffee House, now rebranded as The Brew Crew, staring at it as if it were sacred ground I no longer had the right to step on. I do not know why I thought she might still work there. Some stubborn part of me imagined nothing had changed. That she would still be behind the counter with her hair tied in that loose, messy bun, rolling her eyes at rude customers and drawing smiley faces in the foam because she could never resist adding something soft to the ordinary. But of course everything had changed. Time moves, even when people do not.

The door gave a tired creak as I pushed it open. Warm cinnamon and roasted espresso drifted toward me, familiar enough to make my chest tighten. For a single heartbeat, my mind betrayed me. I saw Lottie. Or rather, I wanted to see her so badly that my memory painted her there. It was not her. It was Reya.

Her hair was shorter now. Still dark, still wild, still framing a face that had never been good at hiding anything. She stared at me as if I were an apparition she had not invited. A ghost wandering in and asking, absurdly, for an iced salted caramel latte.

"Clara?" she said. Her brows drew together, suspicion and disbelief mingling in her voice.

I managed a small nod. "Hi."

A moment passed before she forced a smile. It was stiff, careful, the sort of smile people use when they want to pretend they are pleased to see you yet have already decided you do not belong. A smile that hides knives behind the teeth. She must have sensed I wasn't there for her.

"Sorry, hun," she said, her voice turning syrupy sweet, "boss babe isn't in today."

Boss. The word hit harder than expected. Lottie did not just still work here. She ran the place. I gave a small laugh, startled and unsure how to hold the sudden truth.

"Oh. She owns it now?"

Reya leaned on the counter, settling into the moment as if she were preparing to recite a story she had practised. "Yep. Has for a while. She's doing really well for herself. The business is booming, of course. But more importantly, she is deeply involved in the community. She started a local art initiative so young artists can display their work here, and now she collaborates with schools to offer kids a safe place to study after lessons. People adore her. She's built such a beautiful life for herself."

Each word struck with deliberate precision, slicing through whatever fragile courage I had gathered. It was clear that Lottie had flourished without me, her accomplishments rolling off Reya's tongue with polished ease, as if she wanted me to feel every detail like a bruise. I stood there, nodding mechanically, while my mind scrambled to absorb the full weight of her success. For a moment I half imagined Lottie walking out from the back room, two steaming mugs balanced in her hands, offering one of those awkward smiles she used to wear whenever she was unsure of herself. A smile that always made me want to step closer.

But then Reya's tone shifted. It was subtle at first, a gradual cooling, like a warm room losing heat. Her smile dimmed, melting away until her expression looked carved and brittle. Even the air around us felt sharper.

"But," she said, her eyes narrowing, "she built that life despite you. After you destroyed your friendship and left her shattered."

The words settled over me like lead. Any lingering doubt about her intentions evaporated. This was not a casual update on Lottie's life. It was a deliberate wound. A reminder that I had never been good at confrontations and, worse, that perhaps I deserved this one.

I tried to speak, but my voice shrank before I could shape it. My throat tightened painfully. "I didn't..."

"Clara was depressed for weeks," Reya cut in. She stepped out from behind the counter, each pace shrinking the distance between us while the tension thickened, heavy and suffocating. Her tone did not rise, yet it grew cold and razor sharp, slicing through the quiet with unnerving precision.

"I had to pull her out of that pit you threw her into. Do you even remember what you said to her? About how pathetic it was that she was still working in the same coffee house since school? Stagnant. I'm fairly sure that was another word you used."

My breath hitched. I did remember. Not the exact phrasing, but enough. Enough to feel my stomach twist with shame. Enough to know that some wounds do not fade, they only wait.

"But now she owns it," Reya continued, speaking as if she had not noticed the trembling in my hands, or perhaps choosing to ignore it entirely.

"And you, well. I see the ring. Congratulations. Married? Suburban life? And what, you probably realised the grass was not so green after all."

I could not speak. My mouth opened, yet nothing formed, only a thin thread of breath that felt too fragile to carry a single word.

"You think you can just waltz back in here," she went on, stepping closer until I could see the faint specks of gold in her irises. Her eyes locked on mine, unblinking, almost predatory.

"Because your life did not turn out the way you imagined? Because you are lonely? Or guilty?"

"No," I managed. "I just wanted to..."

"No." She cut me off with a sharp flick of her voice.

"You do not get to. I mean this in the nicest way possible, really, but stay away from Charlotte. She does not need this. She does not need you."

There was a finality in her tone that tightened around my ribs like a closing fist. It felt like she was shutting a door that had already been bolted, sealed and buried. But I was not ready. I was not done.

"I would rather hear that from her," I whispered, stumbling over the words.

"Not you."

It was the wrong thing to say. I knew it the moment the air shifted. Reya's expression changed, subtle at first, then unmistakable, like a mask slipping to reveal the harder shape beneath. Her voice dropped, quiet and controlled.

"I said," she whispered, "stay away."

Something wild flickered in her eyes, something protective enough to unsettle me. A ripple of unease crawled down my spine and settled low in my stomach, heavy and cold.

"If I so much as see you loitering outside this place again," she continued, her smile gone completely now, leaving only the steel behind her words, "you will wish you had not come back."

"Charlotte might forgive you in her heart, but I will not. And I will not let you drag her back into that hell."

I stared at her, frozen where I stood. My hands shook openly now, and a tightness crept into my chest until breathing felt like a choice I was struggling to make.

"You do not know what happened," I said quietly. I was not even sure if I meant the past we shared, the moment we were in now, or something blurred between the two.

"I know enough," Reya replied.

"And I am telling you, Clara. Turn around. Walk out that door. And do not come back."

So I did. Not because I wanted to, but because something in her voice, so calm, so terribly certain, made me believe her. It felt like a warning carved from ice.

I am convinced that if I do not fall in line, she will destroy me. Not with fists, but with something colder and far more deliberate. Her weapons are words, silence and precision. Psychological warfare is her art and I have already stepped onto her battlefield.

It made me wonder what exactly Lottie had told her. She has never been the type to ask for protection. Unless something happened. Unless she never forgave me. Or unless there was something she never told me at all, something that still sits between us like a locked box I have never dared to open.

I am more determined now. I need to speak with Lottie myself. I need to find a way to do it on a day when Reya is not here. She has frightened me, truly frightened me, yet the fear only makes the questions louder. I cannot leave things as they are.

26

Jan 7th, 2020: Niall

A stranger is wearing my wife's face.

I do not know where to begin. I keep trying to pinpoint a single moment when everything shifted, the precise second the world tilted so slightly that I failed to notice until it was too late. We like to believe in those neat turning points, a clear crack in the surface followed by a dramatic collapse. Yet this did not come with noise or spectacle. It slipped in quietly, patient and determined.

Perhaps it began with the silence. Not the comforting kind that grows between people who know each other so well that words become optional. Not the soft hush of a Sunday afternoon with a shared blanket and steady breaths. This silence feels sharper. Cold, almost metallic, the sort of silence that settles between two people even while they sit side by side. It makes the air feel thick, as if someone else is in the room with us, observing from the corner, feeding on the space we cannot seem to close.

Clara is slipping. I can feel it in the smallest things, details I would miss if I did not love her so fiercely.

She folds laundry with a distracted rhythm, her hands moving as if they belong to someone else. Sometimes the clothes end up left in piles on the stairs, as if she had set them down and forgotten they existed. She stares into her tea as if it might reveal some hidden message. I find cold cups abandoned on window ledges, mugs perched on bookshelves beside half eaten toast that she has forgotten she ever touched. She drifts from room to room like a ghost who cannot decide where it belongs.

She startles when I touch her shoulder, jerking as if she has been miles away rather than a few steps from me. It feels as though her body is here, but her mind has wandered far from our kitchen, our children, our life. And her eyes, those eyes that once danced with mischief, now seem to look through me. They search for something distant and unreachable or perhaps try to bury something she wishes she had never uncovered.

I keep urging her to return to therapy. She nods and gives me that tired little smile, the one that does not quite reach her eyes, and says she is fine. She is exhausted. She just needs rest. The words sound like placeholders rather than truths, a script she recites to keep me from asking more. Last week I rang her GP. It felt awful to go behind her back, but I was running out of ways to help her. They could not confirm anything without her consent, yet the hesitation in the receptionist's voice gave me the answer I feared. I have not seen her medication bottle in weeks. I suspect she has stopped taking her pills, the ones that steadied her after the last time everything began to unravel. If she has stopped them, she is clever enough to hide it. She would know exactly how to cover her tracks.

She eats so little now. Small bites, tiny nibbles, food chewed without awareness then forgotten entirely. Sometimes her plate looks clean, yet I know she is throwing food in the bin when she thinks I will not notice. Sleep is no better. It has become a battleground, full of restless turns, twitching limbs, breath that catches on the edge of something painful. At times she curls in on herself as if trying to make her body disappear.

She speaks in her sleep more often than she ever did before. Full sentences that send chills through me because they sound so deliberate. Once she cried out with such raw fear that it tore me from sleep. Another time she whispered, I did not mean to, with such clarity that it felt like a confession. Then she clutched the pillow to her chest as if holding on for dear life.

In the morning she smiled and said she could not remember dreaming. I know she lied. Not out of malice, not to keep me at a distance, but because whatever lives in her dreams fills her with shame. It terrifies her. She has decided she must carry it alone, as if sharing it would burden me or expose something she cannot face.

It is as if she is living a second life inside her own mind, a place I am not allowed to enter.

If that imagined life were joyful, full of friends and colour and warmth, I would encourage it. God knows she deserves brightness after everything she gives. She pours herself into the children, into the thousand tiny acts that keep our world turning. She gives and gives until there is hardly anything left for herself. It is wearing her down, quietly, like cliffs slowly shaped by the relentless sea.

She keeps the house immaculate, every cushion puffed, every floor swept, as if cleanliness can mask the chaos stirring beneath her skin. It feels like a performance. A well practised act that convinces everyone except me. She pretends not to care about the PTA mothers with their glossy hair, Pilates classes, and perfect social media lives, yet I know how deeply she feels everything. She measures herself against impossible standards, terrified of falling short.

Clara has always been a people pleaser. She would rather splinter herself than let someone else feel disappointed.

Now she is splintering for real. Quietly and almost beautifully, if beauty could exist beside fear. It is like watching frost spread across glass, delicate and intricate yet undeniably dangerous.

Something haunted lies behind her eyes, a shadow that was not there before. She stands on the edge of some unseen cliff, and I have no idea how to reach her. I do not know if she even wants to be reached.

She no longer confides in me. Not the way she used to. I do not think it is because she has stopped loving me. I believe she still does. It feels more like she cannot translate whatever is happening inside her into words I can understand. As if her thoughts speak a language meant for her alone.

How am I supposed to help my wife if I no longer recognise the woman standing in front of me? What does it say about us that I can share a home and a bed with her and still feel like we occupy different worlds?

She moves through our days like a stranger wearing a carefully chosen mask. She makes the school lunches, packs the bags, signs the forms, ties little shoes, wipes messy faces, and resets the kitchen every morning as if preparing a stage. She even musters a smile for the neighbours and a light joke at the school gate. Yet beneath it all, she is somewhere far darker. Somewhere filled with old ghosts and older guilt. Secrets from a past she has never found the courage to speak aloud.

And here I am. Watching. Waiting. Holding a space for her beside me and hoping that one day she will return to it. Hoping she will look at me with recognition, not suspicion or distance. Hoping she will see me as her partner again rather than a witness to her slow unravelling.

But I am scared. Truly scared. Because it feels as though she is already halfway gone.

And I do not know if I am strong enough to stand by and watch the rest of her slip away.

27

13 January 2020: Clara

Foggy, groggy and numb, no more.

I stopped taking the medication. It had been making me feel swollen with heaviness, as if my entire body and mind were stuffed with wet sand. I could not think. I could not feel. And I need to feel something, even if it hurts. I need to stay alert, because when I am dulled, things slip past me. People slip past me, and I get blindsided without ever seeing the blow coming.

I thought coming off the pills would free me. In some ways it has. My mind feels clearer, almost sharp enough to cut. My thoughts are no longer tangled in that synthetic fog. I can finally hear myself think again. But that might be the problem. Because now the thoughts will not stop. They crowd me with questions I do not want to answer. I think about how people see me, about what sits behind the polite smiles in the school car park and the nods at swim meets. There is a thinness to it all, as if the surface is glossy but fragile.

I used to pretend I did not care, that I was above the whispering and the half concealed judgement. Perhaps I was too sedated to notice. Because now I notice everything. Every half laugh, every too sweet smile, every greeting that sounds like someone reading from a prompt. It echoes in my head long after the person has walked away.

Conrad's words keep circling back. He said them so often that they became their own kind of chant.

"You will never amount to anything. Girls like you trap men like my son with a pregnancy. You saw the Donnelly name and cashed in."

I used to laugh and call him a bitter old bastard under my breath. But what if he was right in ways I do not want to admit? What if I did trap Niall without meaning to? What if I am nothing more than a collection of poor decisions wrapped up in the costume of a homemaker? That thought sits beneath my ribs like a splinter.

Trying to reach out to Lottie might have been another one of those mistakes. Reya hinted at it in her blunt way, and part of me recognised the truth in what she said. Maybe I am poison, a wrecking ball wearing mascara and trying to pass as harmless. Lottie built a life without me, a beautiful one, stable and bright. She owns that coffee house she always dreamed of. She looks happy, or at least steady. And I wonder if pulling her back into my orbit would only unravel the things she worked so hard to weave together.

Was I such a terrible friend that I left her with nothing but wreckage? I keep circling back to that question. Sometimes I fear that the only reason I want her back in my life is because she was the last real friend I had. If that is true, then even my longing is selfish. So who does that leave me with?

Last Wednesday, at dinner, nothing remarkable happened on the surface. It was a perfectly ordinary evening. The familiar silence settled over me again, its weight as familiar as a second skin. Everyone was talking, at least in the technical sense. There were smiles and light jokes. Forks tapped plates. Wine was poured with an ease I still cannot imitate. Yet to me, every sound rang hollow, almost distant, like I was listening to them through a window that had been sealed shut.

I sat among them, nodding at the right moments, forming expressions that fit the rhythm of their conversation. But inside, I felt as if I was half a second behind, observing rather than belonging. It was the same feeling I used to get as a child when I tried to mimic grown ups, convinced that if I practised hard enough I would fit. I must have looked present. I was not.

They are kind to me in the way people are kind to someone they feel responsible for. Niall's family do all the right things. They remember my birthday. They ask about my voluntary work. They smile at me across rooms as if the gesture itself should be enough to fill the gaps. Perhaps it should be. Yet kindness is not closeness. Their warmth feels curated, as if they are fulfilling a duty they never actively chose. I married into them, and at times it feels as though that is the only reason they include me. I am an extension of him. Without him, I doubt they would notice if I slipped quietly out of the picture.

And still, I hesitate to say they do not care. The uncertainty is its own torment. Maybe they care in a quiet, unspoken way. Maybe they love me in the awkward manner of people who never learned how to show affection without an audience. But I cannot see it. Not through the fog that clings stubbornly inside my mind. Doubt colours everything. I have spent so long bracing for rejection that even genuine affection feels suspicious. A smile might be a mask. A kind word might be obligation dressed up as sentiment. I keep asking myself how anyone ever knows if they are loved. The question has lingered for so long that it no longer feels like a thought. It feels like an old wound that tightens whenever I breathe.

Niall tells me he loves me every day. He says it with ease, with a gentleness that should comfort me. Yet I question it, not because of anything he does but because I struggle to believe I deserve it. When he says, "You are everything to me," part of me aches. Another part shrinks, convinced he will one day realise that I am too much, too heavy, too difficult, and that he could have chosen someone easier. Someone brighter. Someone whole. I barely recognise myself when I look in the mirror now. My thoughts are tangled and loud, filling the space around me until I cannot tell what is real.

It does not help that his father, even after all these years, barely disguises his contempt. His cruelty is subtle and expertly crafted. It does not bruise skin. It bruises air, leaving a tension that lingers long after he steps into a room. He can shatter confidence with a single raised eyebrow. He speaks to me as if I have already failed him, as if disappointment is the only thing he expects from me. There is no room for warmth with him. Only performance. I hate him for the way he diminishes me, of course, but I also hate the way he influences the others. The way they shrink slightly when he enters a room. The way they fold themselves into quieter versions of who they were moments before.

And here is the part that gnaws at me. Even hating him makes me feel guilty. Do they see me as the difficult one? The outsider who will not accept the family rules? I long to be closer to Rita, to Rachel, to Conor, yet every conversation with them feels thick and slow, as if I am wading through molasses. I second guess everything I say. I smile when I do not mean it, just so I will not say the wrong thing. I cannot tell whether the distance between us is real or just another echo of my own insecurities. Maybe they care more than I realise. Maybe they even love me. But how am I meant to believe in their affection when I cannot trust my own instincts at all?

At times I wonder if the problem is not them. It is me. And I do not know how to fix it.

I often imagine what it would be like to feel worthy of that love, to sit at that dinner table and feel as if I genuinely belong there, fully and without condition. Sometimes I picture the scene in vivid detail, almost as if I could reach out and touch it. Yet the moment always slips away before I can hold it. My mind will not allow such softness. It whispers that I was too much and not enough at the same time. It insists that love, if I ever possessed it at all, was only a temporary loan, something that could be reclaimed without warning. It tells me that any closeness I feel is nothing more than a performance, and that sooner or later the curtain will fall and expose the truth.

And when the curtain finally does fall, when I am alone in the bathroom with the harsh light buzzing above me, clutching the sink as if it might keep me upright, I see her again. The version of me I tried so desperately to hide. Her eyes are tired, rimmed with doubt, her mouth tight and full of unsaid things. I loathe her. I pity her. I want to reach out and help her. Yet I never know how. How do you comfort someone when you are trapped in the same fragile skin?

There are times when I imagine walking away from it all. Not in a dramatic exit that slams doors and draws attention, but in a quiet slip into nothing, the way a ghost might drift off once she finally accepts she has been dead all along. The thought carries a strange kind of comfort. The idea of disappearing feels like a release, a gentle lifting of the burden of me from everyone I know. But then I think of Niall and the twins, and a fractured part of me twists with guilt. They do not deserve that. Niall least of all. He has been patient and gentle, steady in ways I have never managed to be. Yet even his love feels borrowed, as if someone else was meant to receive it and I stepped into the space by accident. I do not know how to hold it without fearing I will ruin it. Every time he looks at me with those soft eyes, I wonder what he sees that I cannot. I also wonder how long it will take before that vision fades.

I wanted to believe he loved me. I wanted to believe they all did. But how do you trust in something you have never felt truly secure in? How do you lean into love when the shadows in your mind keep insisting you are unlovable?

So I sat at the table that night surrounded by warmth I could not feel, by people who perhaps cared yet remained just out of emotional reach. I smiled and laughed at the appropriate moments. I passed the potatoes. I played the part of someone who belonged. Inside, though, I felt like nothing more than a flicker behind the eyes, a hollow chest echoing the same relentless question: What if they do not love me? Or worse, what if they do, and I destroy it anyway?

Words can only do so much. I have grown too accustomed to reading between them, searching for cracks, hesitation, the small signs that affection might slip away. I want to believe. God, I want to.

Yet wanting has never been enough, and the wanting itself feels like another reminder of my lack.

Outside my family, the only people in my life are other mothers. Parents of Rory's rugby teammates or Emily's friends from swim club. In theory, it should be lovely to have them around. In practice, I never feel as if I connect with them. They speak to me out of convenience, because we stand beside each other on the sideline or in a chlorine soaked hallway. They do not know me. They would never invite me for tea or ring just to say hello. I doubt they would notice if I disappeared from those sideline conversations altogether. Lottie would notice. Or she would have, once.

But maybe Reya was right. Maybe I burned that bridge so completely that nothing remains but ash. Perhaps trying to rebuild it would only smear soot across the bright surface of Lottie's new life. I no longer know. I feel as if I am drowning in the quiet, in the space between who I used to be and the person staring back at me now.

This life looks full on the outside. I move through days packed with school runs, meal plans and laundry folded into neat stacks. I live among people, yet I feel entirely alone. Not one person seems to see me with any depth, and that emptiness has settled over everything like a film I cannot wipe away.

And the worst part is simple. I do not think anyone ever has seen me or ever will. Not even me. On the darkest evenings, when the house is silent and the twins are finally asleep, I catch myself wondering whether I am even alive or if I am only pretending to be.

28

Aug 23rd, 2025: Charlotte

I am sorry, what? I can hardly breathe.

I am sitting on the attic floor now, knees pulled tight to my chest as if I can hold myself together with the shape of my own body. The boards beneath me feel cold, almost damp, and every breath seems to rattle. Clara's journal lies open beside me. Its pages are warped and whisper thin, the ink curling at the edges like old wounds that never quite healed. That final entry does not read like a goodbye at all. It reads like a scream that has clawed its way across time, reaching out for me and tightening its grip around my throat.

She stopped taking her medication. She said it made her foggy, heavy, unreal. There is something buried beneath those words. She believed she could see the world more clearly without it. And perhaps she did, although in the most brutal way. Without the haze, every crack in her life widened into a canyon. Every offhand comment, every look that lingered a moment too long or did not linger at all, turned into a truth she could not challenge. A truth that tore at her. A truth that stripped her down.

And now I cannot stop crying.

My skin feels raw and my chest feels hollow, as if something essential has fallen out and rolled into a corner where I can no longer reach it. I am not even wiping the tears away anymore. They fall and fall, and the guilt gathers like a weight pressing into my spine. Because Clara came looking for me. She walked into the coffee house, my coffee house, with hope stitched into her steps. She wanted to see me. She wanted me to smile at her. She wanted forgiveness, a chance to start again. And God, I would have given her that in a heartbeat.

But I was not there. Reya was.

I can picture it now. Her perfect smile, the clipped kindness she wears like a mask. The slight shift in her eyes when she decides someone is not welcome. She told Clara to leave. She made her feel small, like a ghost who had slipped into the wrong life.

Then she lied to me.

She looked me directly in the eye and pretended nothing had happened. I had wanted a villain, something simple and fierce to rage against. I had wanted murder, a dark secret, a betrayal with a clean edge. Murder feels sharp and definitive. It offers a wound with borders. But this is nothing like that. This is slow, quiet damage. This is Clara slipping through the cracks one day at a time, cracks none of us were watching closely enough, until it was already too late.

And I keep asking myself the same question: what if I had been there that day?

What if she had seen me behind the counter? What if I had rushed out to wrap my arms around her? What if I had told her that I missed her, that none of the awful things we said a decade ago had any power anymore? What if she had known she was never a burden? Would she still be alive?

I told myself for days that I was angry at Niall, angry at Conrad, angry at Samantha, angry at the entire world. But the truth is clearer now. I am furious with myself. Because maybe I was the last light she was still searching for. And I was not there to shine it.

And Reya, God. What even is she to me now? She has been my best friend for ten years. The person who saw me at my lowest, who held my hand when I could not lift my head from the pillow, who slept on my sofa to make sure I stayed alive. She braided her life through mine. Yet now, when her name crosses my mind, all I can think about is the possibility of shadows I never noticed. Secrets she folded into silence.

Was she trying to protect me? Was it jealousy? Spite? Something darker that she has never allowed me to see? I cannot make sense of her anymore. I no longer know which version to believe: the friend who folded my laundry and cooked for me when I could barely function, or the woman who turned Clara away without a flicker of hesitation. Or the woman who did something even worse.

Clara's words echo inside my chest, a scream I failed to hear in time. I do not know how to forgive myself for that.

And the journal, God. I remember it. I had seen it tucked into her oversized tote bag as if it travelled with her heartbeat. Now it sits in front of me like a confession written for a future she never reached. The date scrawled across the top: early January. She wrote about the coffee house. About coming to find me. About trying.

But Reya told her I was not there. Reya lied. She said I was doing well. She offered no warmth, no space, not even a sliver of a second chance. They spoke for longer than a passing hello. They had a whole conversation. Reya had multiple opportunities to tell me, yet she chose silence.

When I mentioned it last Friday, how I had seen Clara in January just before she died, Reya looked startled. Genuinely thrown. She said she did not know we had met up. She said it softly, almost tenderly, and yet it was a lie. A deliberate omission that now feels like a fracture in the ground beneath my feet.

She knew Clara wanted to see me.

She made sure our final meet-up felt like a secret I was not supposed to tell anyone. She shaped it into something covert. Something shameful. She may as well have stood between us and slammed the door shut.

And now, as I replay every moment of that meeting, everything takes on a strange tilt.

Clara was jumpy. She kept glancing over her shoulder. She flinched whenever the bell above the door rang. At the time I thought she was afraid of her husband. I thought she was hiding from him. But what if she was not?

What if she was afraid of Reya?

She insisted we sit in the back corner. She spoke in a low voice, barely above a whisper, as if someone might overhear. Her eyes were restless. She told me she missed me and that she knew she had made mistakes. Her lip trembled. Her hands were clenched so tightly that her knuckles turned white. She looked as though she was bracing herself for someone to walk in.

What if she feared that Reya would see us together?

The thought makes my stomach twist. It feels poisonous and it settles inside me with a cold certainty I do not want to acknowledge.

Reya knew how important Clara was to me. She knew this even when I tried to hide it. Yet she chose to keep Clara away. Why?

Was she protecting me? Distrusting me? Or did she not want to share the one person who had relied on her for so long?

I do not know anymore. I do not know who Reya truly is.

Clara's journal refuses to give me answers and the silence she left behind only grows heavier. And the more I dwell on that final meeting, the way Clara shrank into her chair every time the door opened, the more I fear the truth lurking beneath it.

What was she terrified of? Who was she terrified of?

Because perhaps I have been wrong from the start.

Maybe it was not Niall. Maybe it was not Conrad.

Maybe it was Reya.

And I never saw it coming.

29

Jan 15th, 2020: Niall

Holding onto a ghost.

She is still Clara on the outside. Still bustling through the mornings as if her movements are powered by habit rather than intention. She makes sure the twins have their packed lunches with their favourite sandwiches cut into triangles, because rectangles are apparently unthinkable at the age of ten. She complains about it in that half amused way of hers, yet she keeps doing it. A ritual she refuses to break.

She still folds Rory's rugby gear into his kit bag with the quiet precision of someone who believes that order might hold back the rising tide of chaos. His mismatched socks go in last. He swears they bring him luck, and she never argues, only tucks them in with a small smile that does not quite reach her eyes anymore. I used to think that smile was simply tiredness. Now I am not sure.

She still reminds Emily to breathe during swim meets. She leans close and whispers, "You have already won, baby," then squeezes her hand three times for "I love you" before Emily steps onto the starting blocks. It used to be a moment that glowed with hope and connection. Lately, there is a faint tremble in her fingers, as if even these small rituals take something out of her.

She still bakes banana bread from scratch for parent teacher meetings, stored in a Tupperware that always smells like home. She still adjusts her curls so they fall in that effortless way she perfected years ago, then walks into the school with a soft, knowing smile that even the most severe principal cannot resist. If you saw her in those moments, you would think she had everything under control. You would think she was happy.

She still hosts her monthly Mum's Only coffee morning. It always begins as coffee, then becomes a bubbly brunch filled with loud laughter, clinking glasses, and a kitchen that smells of orange juice, Prosecco, and those fancy eggs she only ever makes for other people. Never herself. The women cling to those mornings like lifelines. They adore her. They trust her. They confide in her as if she holds the key to steadying their lives. The fathers take the children out, and the mothers stay, drink, talk, and breathe. Clara holds court. She always has.

But I see the cost of it. The shadows that live beneath her eyes. The way she winces the moment the front door clicks shut after the last guest has left. She looks like she has been holding her breath for hours and only now feels safe to exhale. She is falling apart. No one sees it except me, and even I am not sure I see the full extent of it.

She has not said the words, but I can feel them pressing against the edges of her. It is like walking barefoot across a floor scattered with invisible shards of glass. I sense it in the way she stiffens when I touch her shoulder, the way her laughter has taken on a note that sounds practised rather than instinctive, the way she folds into herself the moment she thinks she is unobserved. She disappears into the bathroom for thirty minutes at a time, claiming she is brushing her teeth or doing her skincare routine. I used to hear her humming behind the door, an old tune that meant something to her. Now there is only silence, or worse, the muffled sound of her trying not to cry.

She is in the house. She is in every room. But she is not here. Not properly. Not in the way I remember.

I do not know how to bring her back.

A few months ago, I suggested she think about returning to work. It was not about money. We are fine. It was about giving her something of her own again, a piece of herself that motherhood had not absorbed. Clara has always been sharper than most. Capable. Intuitive in a way that made people feel understood before they said a word. She could walk into a room and know exactly who was sincere, who was hiding something, who needed help but would never ask. In the workplace, she was not just good. She was magnetic. I thought work might remind her of that version of herself, the one who used to glow from the inside.

There was an opening for an assistant position at Donnelly Marketing, supporting one of the new partners. She seemed genuinely excited at the idea, but the role was filled internally. A week later, another position came up, this time working with my father. When I told her, she went completely still. Her whole body tensed, as if I had said something cruel or dangerous.

Then she whispered, "No. Not again."

Only those three words. Then she turned away and shut the conversation down entirely. I tried to ask about it later, gently, choosing my words with care, but she would not go there. She did not even flinch. Just offered this terrible silence that hung in the air for hours. It felt as if I had broken something by asking.

For fucks sake, what happened between her and my father?

I used to think she simply found him arrogant, too polished and sharp at the edges. A man who had spent more time cultivating boardroom confidence than genuine warmth. But now I wonder if something else lurks beneath the surface, something buried and painful. I hate not knowing. I hate the half formed possibilities my mind plays with at night while I lie awake beside her.

She is a shell of the woman I married, but only in the ways you would need to be intimately close to notice. To everyone else, she is still the glowing, composed matriarch who never forgets birthdays or allergies and always knows which teacher deserves a thank you card. The other mothers idolise her. The fathers admire her. The teachers trust her. Yet I see her unravelling thread by thread. I see the way she grips the bathroom counter a moment too long, the way her shoulders slump once the children are in bed, the way she seems to shrink after a long day as if her mask has grown too heavy to hold.

And I feel utterly useless.

She made this house our home. Not just the structure itself, although she would master that too if she wished, but the feeling inside it. She is the heart of this place. She gave it warmth and safety. She created rituals that made even ordinary days feel held. There was always something baking in the oven, or someone being listened to, or a lamp switched on in the perfect corner so you could sit and breathe if you needed space. She made this house soft. She made it safe. She made it ours.

Now I am terrified of what happens if she fades any further.

The kids know it. They feel it. They sense the shift in the air whenever she enters a room, and they respond in that effortless, instinctive way children have when they are safe. They adore her, not in that fearful, performative way Irish kids often learn as habit, but in a quiet and unwavering way that settles into the bones. They trust her. They respect her. They lean into her warmth because she has never lied to them and never turned them away. She always makes space for them, no matter how crowded her mind becomes. Even when she is bone tired and barely holding herself upright, she kneels beside their beds and listens. She listens properly, listens the way people do when they care so fully it aches. And the kids know, without even the faintest shadow of doubt, exactly where they sit in her heart. Always first. Always.

And me? I am here. I am trying. I get up. I make the tea that never tastes quite like hers. I fold the clothes she does not get to, smoothing the creases as if that might smooth the strain in her shoulders. I brush Emily's hair on the mornings when Clara forgets the braid on swim days, and I pretend I am not trying to imitate her touch. I go to work. I pay attention. I hold things together in every way I know, stitching the small practical pieces of our life so she can breathe a little easier. Yet it never feels like enough, not when I see how much she carries and how little she sets down.

I do not want to fix her. That is not what any of this is about. I want to find her again in the places she used to inhabit so easily. I want to hear her laugh and know it is real and not something pressed through exhaustion. I want to see her eyes light up at some ridiculous thing the kids have done, not flicker only for it to dim again. I want to see her resting because she feels peaceful, not because she has collapsed into silence. I want to reach out and touch her without feeling as though I am asking permission to cross an invisible wall that grows thicker with every passing week.

Yet even with all that, even with the weight of the world grinding her down, she still lifts me. Every day, in ways she probably does not realise, she steadies me. Even when she is breaking, she makes sure I am standing. She tells me I am a good husband and father, not because I tick boxes or follow rules but because I choose to be present. She reminds me of those impossible nights with the twins, when sleep felt like a myth and their cries echoed through the entire house at two in the morning. We took turns walking the halls, barely awake, whispering promises into the dark. And I told her I needed to be a good man because there was no Option B. There was only us, trying to stay afloat.

She once told me I had a strength most women would dream of in a partner and the part that breaks me is that she believed it. She still does. I have never slipped, not once. I have never allowed myself to wander from the path of being who she needed and who the twins needed. But now everything feels precarious, as though that path is cracking beneath our feet.

Because lately, I feel like I am watching Clara fade into the corners of our life. I feel like I am watching her drift out to sea with no life jacket in sight, and all I have to reach her is a broken paddle and the desperate hope she might turn back. I feel like I am failing her in ways I cannot articulate. I do not know what to ask of her. I do not know how to help without pushing her further from shore. I do not know what she is carrying, but I know it is too much for one person to bear.

Some nights, I wake to find her sitting at the edge of the bed, staring out through the window at something I cannot see. She looks as though she is listening to a voice that does not belong to this house and I do not dare speak. I simply lie there, waiting, willing her to return to me. She never does.

And I am scared. Truly scared. Terrified that one morning I will wake and she will be gone, not physically, but gone in the way people vanish into themselves and do not find their way back. If that happens, I will not know how to reach her. I do not know who I will become without her steady presence shaping the rhythm of this family.

She is slipping, thread by fragile thread. And I cannot lose her. I cannot.

Because if she disappears completely, the house will still stand. The photos will still hang neatly on the walls. The lunches will still be packed and the curtains drawn just right. But it will not be a home anymore. It will be a memory of one. A quiet echo of the life we built together, and an echo is not something you can hold.

30

Jan 23rd, 2020: Clara

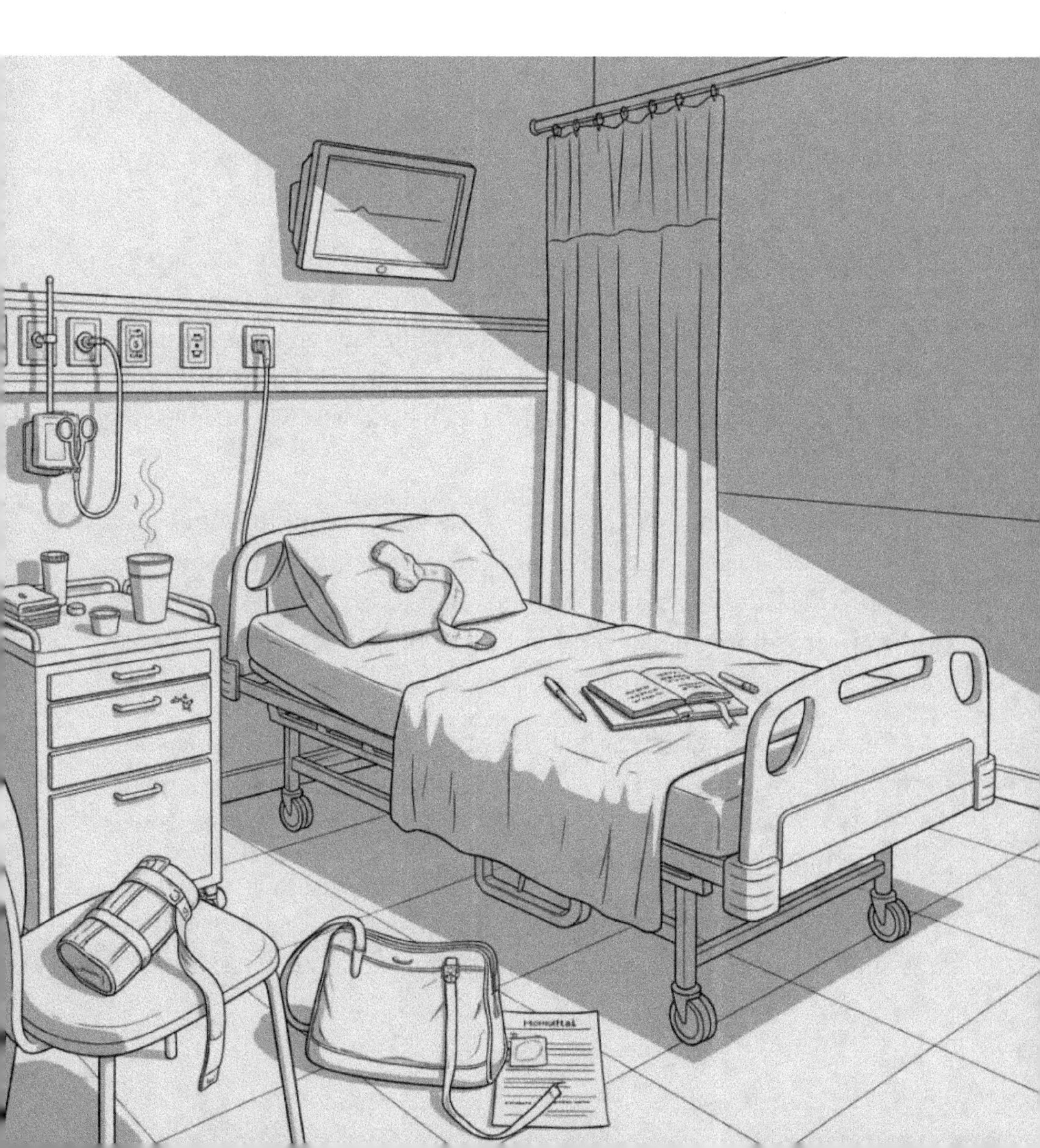

Cold turkey? I would not recommend it to a friend.

I do not even remember putting my journal in my bag, although I suppose I should be grateful it ended up there. Lately my mind has been full of small gaps that open without warning. Milk left out on the counter until morning, the cereal box placed neatly in the fridge as if it belonged among the yoghurts, the twins' coats forgotten in the boot while I wondered why they looked cold as we walked into school. All these tiny errors gathering like crumbs I cannot sweep away.

I have started writing reminders in a notebook instead of setting alarms on my phone. Putting thoughts down with a pen makes them feel firmer, almost grounded. And the paper does not beep at me as if scolding me when I fail to pay attention. It simply waits.

The lights in here are painfully bright. I keep blinking, expecting them to soften, yet they stay harsh and unwavering. It feels a little like staring at snow for too long. That blinding white that makes everything seem sterile or perhaps waiting to be scrubbed clean. Hospitals always smell like something is moments away from being disinfected.

I told the paramedics that something had run out in front of the car. A dog. Or a cat. I honestly cannot remember which. Something alive, anyway. It felt easier to say that than to explain the truth: that I do not remember seeing the road at all before the airbag burst in front of me like a white explosion.

One moment I was at a red light, tapping my fingers on the wheel to that awful catchy song Rory loves, the one about monkeys dancing. The next, the front of the car was pressed against a traffic pole. It was as if time blinked and I was not invited to follow.

It is the dissociation. That is what terrifies me most about messing up my medication. And to be clear, I would not recommend that to a friend either. It frightens me because I do not know what I am doing while it happens. Not until it is already done. Until Emily has to say my name four times before I register it. Until Rory stops asking for help with his maths and simply sits beside me, working it out incorrectly. Until Niall gives up asking if I want tea and leaves one beside me anyway, like a peace offering for someone who is half present.

The other day at Tesco I stood in the freezer aisle holding a tub of ice cream. I could not remember if it was me or Niall who liked mint chocolate chip. I stared at the label, waiting for the answer to drift towards me like mist from the open freezer. Then I remembered that neither of us particularly liked or disliked it, and that it had only come up because Niall mentioned his father hated it. I must have been standing there for twenty minutes. Long enough for the ice cream to melt and trickle down my wrist in a thin, embarrassing line. A woman passed at the end of the aisle and gave me a look that said she knew something was off. I laughed it off, as if I were simply being indecisive.

How long does someone stand in front of melting ice cream before they realise something is wrong with their mind?

I thought that had been my lowest point. Then came today. I have been telling myself that I felt better off the medication, that I felt clearer and sharper. More like myself. But perhaps that is the delusion people fall into when they start to feel well and forget what kept them steady in the first place.

I was never foggy on the medication. That is a lie I tell myself. It was never fog. It was softness. The edges blurred just enough so the world did not scream at me. Yet I convinced myself I needed more. More clarity, more energy, more authenticity. And now here I am in a hospital gown, trying not to cry when the nurse asks if I have been feeling low.

If someone else told me this story, I would say: You feel better because of the medication. That does not mean you stop taking it. You are stabilised. Speak to your doctor. Taper slowly. Do not try to be a hero.

But who actually takes their own advice?

I did not want to admit I was struggling because I feared what might happen next. Niall would worry. The children would sense it. People might begin to wonder if I was safe to be around them. Someone might ask questions I could not bring myself to answer. I do not want pity. I do not want judgment. I do not want anyone to see how thin the ice is beneath my feet.

All I want is to feel normal. To recall what normal even felt like. The truth that terrifies me is this: I am not sure I ever have.

The mind is strange in the way it chooses moments to break. I keep replaying the time I shouted at Niall. He did not deserve it. Not even a little. He was only trying to help. He said going back to work might give me something that belonged to me again. Something beyond lunch boxes and laundry, beyond the endless school WhatsApp threads and the never ending grocery lists. Something that was not about being a mother or a wife or a version of myself defined by everyone else. Something that was simply Clara.

God, I wanted that. I want that even now. But the moment he said it, and I realised the job offer was at Donnelly Marketing: working under his father again: it was as if something inside me clicked in the wrong direction. A bright spark, then a sharp snap.

No. Not again.

The words flew out of me before I even knew I was speaking. It felt like my mouth acted on instinct, quicker than my own thoughts, as if my body had been waiting years to defend itself. My hands were shaking so hard I could hear the faint rustle of my fingers against my jeans. I could not explain it to him. I could not tell him why. The simple idea of seeing Conrad's name on an office door made my skin prickle and my throat tighten as if I were being pulled backwards through time.

That was the moment the dissociation began to creep in. Ever since that day, whenever I have tried to imagine going back to work, something inside me stiffens. My whole body rises in silent rebellion. It is like my soul bolts for the hills, and my brain slips quietly out through a side exit, uninterested in offering a reason. No warning. No explanation. Just absence.

That is exactly what happened today. I was sitting at the red light, telling myself: it has been more than ten years, Clara. Ten years since what happened with Conrad. You are not that woman anymore. You are stronger now, wiser now. Maybe it would not be the same.

But I could not finish the thought. It was as if something deep within refused to let the words land. An internal firewall snapped into place and declared: absolutely not, abort. Instead of skimming past the discomfort in the usual quiet way, my mind simply shut down the whole system, as though it had decided that thinking was a luxury I no longer deserved.

And now here I am. In this ugly hospital gown that barely closes at the back, with a bandage around my head and a brace on my arm, and a sticky patch of cotton where they took blood. A nurse has just handed me a small polystyrene cup of tea I do not even want. The room smells faintly of disinfectant and overcooked vegetables. All I can think is this:

They think I did it on purpose. They think I tried to drive off the bridge and missed. They think the impact with the pole was an attempt to hurt myself.

God.

I did not. I know I did not. At least, I think I know that.

But then again, I do not remember deciding not to. And that is the part that terrifies me. When your mind disappears, it never leaves a note behind. When you dissociate, the border between accident and intention begins to blur until it becomes something slippery you cannot hold.

I am trying so hard to believe myself. I am trying to picture the tyres slipping, or the brake pedal under my foot, or even a single moment of awareness. But there is nothing. Only a gap and a flicker, like someone cut out a frame of my life and forgot to glue it back in. The next thing I remember is the sound of metal being sliced open and someone asking if I could move my toes.

I cannot even say the word out loud.

Suicide.

It does not feel like me. I did not try to end anything. I simply shut off. But how do you explain that without sounding unhinged? How do you convince people that your silence is not a warning sign but a short circuit, a surge that knocks out the power for a moment? How do I convince myself of the same thing?

My hands will not stop shaking. I cannot tell if it is the crash, the leftover adrenaline, or the creeping dread that someone has already called Niall. And if he is on his way, what am I supposed to say?

I am fine, just a little tired.

Oops, silly me, forgot how to be a functioning adult for a moment.

No. He would never believe that. I know him too well. He hears intention in the small pauses and truth in the spaces between my sentences. He notices everything, even when I wish he would not.

He is going to look at me with those steady eyes, the ones that somehow keep me upright even when I am falling apart. He will see straight through me, and maybe that is what frightens me most. Not the crash itself, and not the possibility of dying, but the idea of being fully seen in the exact place where I am unravelling.

I am so tired.

Please, I hope they do not ask again if I meant it. Because the more I am questioned, the less certain I become, and the question starts to feel like an answer all on its own.

31

23 January 2020: Niall

The phone call that stopped my heart.

I have lived through a handful of terrifying moments in my life. The morning Greg died still clings to me like cold fog. The night Rory had his first seizure when he was only two, tiny and shaking in my arms. The day Emily went missing in the playground for seven whole minutes that felt more like an eternity. And the morning I told my father I was not taking over the business, as he had yet another argument with Conor. Each moment different, each moment unforgettable, each one carving out a small part of me that never quite grew back.

None of them came close to what I felt today.

The call came while I sat in a meeting with a client. I saw Clara's name light up on my phone and felt a sudden drop in my gut, almost as if my body recognised something my mind had not yet caught up with. Clara never calls during work. She always sends a text, even when things are hectic. She handles so much on her own with that calm, capable energy of hers that genuine emergencies are rare. When your wife is a kind of quiet superhero, the phone does not ring unless something is truly wrong.

Except it was not her. It was the hospital.

The voice on the other end said a simple sentence: your wife has been in an accident. That was all it took. Everything that followed sounded muted, distant, almost as if I was hearing it from the bottom of a swimming pool.

I drove like a man gone feral, barely aware of the road, barely aware of myself. I do not remember traffic lights or junctions, only a rising panic that made the world tighten around me. Somewhere in that blur, I had the presence of mind to call Conor.

We have not spoken properly in years. Just stiff conversations at family gatherings and the odd polite text at Christmas. Still, when fear took over, he was the only person I trusted without hesitation. I asked him to collect Rory and Emily, to keep them safe. No questions asked, he said, I have them. Just focus on her. Something in his voice grounded me for a brief moment.

It might be time for us. A beer between brothers is not only overdue; it is needed. Perhaps things that have cracked do not have to remain broken.

When I reached the hospital, I braced for the worst. My mind ran through every bleak possibility as I crossed the foyer and stepped into the lift. ICU. Coma. A doctor with solemn eyes shaking their head. I tried to prepare for all of it, though nothing could have prepared me for the sight of her.

Clara was not in intensive care. She was hooked up to a heart monitor and a fluid line, a few machines blinking quietly at her bedside, but nothing that screamed life or death. She had a deep cut over her right eyebrow and dark bruising across her chest where the seatbelt must have snapped tight. Her arm was wrapped, likely fractured. The neck brace made her look stiff and uncomfortable, yet she was breathing. She was here. She was alive.

I let out a breath I had been holding since the call. Relief washed through me so suddenly that my legs felt weak. Then the nurse approached, and her gentle tone made my stomach twist. She asked if Clara had been expressing any suicidal thoughts recently.

It hit harder than any punch. I said no before she had even finished the sentence. No, because I could not believe it. No, because admitting even the possibility felt like stepping off a cliff. No, because if I had shown any uncertainty, they would take her for a psychiatric assessment that could change everything. But the truth is painful: I honestly did not know. That, more than anything, terrifies me.

That uncertainty has been gnawing at me all night. How did I miss it? When did tired become something darker? I have been so focused on keeping the moving parts of our lives together, juggling work and school runs and bills and broken appliances, that I stopped seeing her. I saw the tasks and the chaos but not her sadness. Not the slow fading of the light behind her eyes.

I asked to see her. The nurse hesitated, as if weighing my words, but eventually nodded.

When I walked into the room, she looked at me, and for the first time in ages, she lit up. It was small and fragile, but it was real.

You, she said. You are just the medicine I need.

It felt like a spark from a much earlier version of us, the one before life became so heavy. Clara reached out with her good arm, and I folded myself into her carefully, as though she were made of thin, brittle paper. The embrace was warm and desperate, the kind of hug that comes from fear and love tangled together.

She tried to make light of it. She said she should never drive before coffee again. On another day, I would have laughed. I would have let the joke sit between us like a warm blanket. But today, it felt like a mask.

I pulled back enough to see her face clearly and told her softly that the doctors were concerned it might not have been an accident. That I had told them she was fine, yet I needed her to confirm it. If she needed help, we could get it. There was nothing shameful in needing help, nothing at all. I told her I wanted to be there for her.

She froze for a split second, though barely visibly. Something behind her eyes cracked, subtle but unmistakable. Then she gave a tired, bright smile and said she had a wonderful husband, two brilliant and wild children, and a home many would envy. What more could she possibly want? She promised she had not done anything on purpose. If she had wanted attention, she joked, she would have painted the kitchen chartreuse or bought a convertible. She insisted she was fine.

But I have loved Clara long enough to know when she is not telling me the whole truth. I have watched her slowly unravel for months, perhaps even years, and convinced myself she would bounce back like she always did. Only this time, it is different. This sadness is quieter and deeper. It whispers instead of shouting, and by the time you hear it, it has already settled in.

The worst part is knowing I cannot fix it. I cannot patch her up with willpower or affection. I cannot carry her pain, no matter how desperately I want to. I can hold her, remind her she is not alone, stand beside her, but I cannot reach into her chest and pull the sorrow out. That helplessness is the loneliest feeling I have ever known.

I brought her home tonight. She is upstairs sleeping now, and I am sitting downstairs afraid to close my eyes in case she wakes and needs me, and I miss something important.

I thought getting her home might be enough to keep her safe. I hope that is still true. God, I hope.

Tomorrow, I will call her GP. Tomorrow, we will have a plan. Tomorrow, she will know I am not ignoring this. She needs help, and perhaps I do as well.

Loving someone does not make you a mind reader. But I made a vow to her years ago, and I am making it again tonight: I will not lose her. Not like this. Not when there is still fight in me.

32

30 January 2020: Clara

The storm has finally passed; let's rebuild.

Niall went back to work today. God love him, he would have glued himself to my side if he thought it might keep me safe. He has been floating around me like a balloon string for the past week, hovering close enough to catch me if I wobbled, bringing endless cups of tea, checking in every half hour, and pretending he was not watching me sleep or waiting outside the bathroom door while I showered. Sometimes he would perch on the edge of the bed, blinking slowly at the wall as if keeping watch over something only he could see.

I adore him for it. I truly do. But it was no life for him, and it was no life for me. After a while I started to feel like I was living inside a display case, as if I were something delicate and brittle, and we were both pretending I was not already cracked right through the centre.

So I told him. I told him about the meds, and how I had stopped taking them cold turkey. God, even writing that down looks reckless. I braced myself for anger, for disappointment, for the edge in his voice that I absolutely deserved. But he did not get angry, not in the way I imagined. His shoulders simply dropped, as if someone had released all the air from his lungs at once. It looked like a moment he had been dreading, a truth he expected but still hoped he would never hear.

He sat beside me, held my hand, and said, very quietly, "Alright. We start again from here. But this time we are honest with each other."

So I am back on them, properly this time, and under a doctor's supervision. No more secret decisions to outsmart my own brain. I am clearly not as clever as I thought. And the strange part is that I already feel better. Not perfect. Not sparkling. But steadier. My thoughts behave a little more like thoughts, rather than slippery little creatures that dart away the moment I reach for them. The fog has not cleared completely, yet it has thinned enough for shapes to appear in it, and that alone feels like progress.

And now for the biggest news of all. I found Lottie. I actually found her.

I did not intend to. I was looking up a recipe, something utterly mundane, when I clicked into Facebook without thinking. My fingers typed her name by themselves, as if they had been waiting years for that moment. And there she was. Her face smiling back at me. A little older, a little softer, but unmistakably Lottie. The girl who braided my hair every morning before school after I taught her how. The girl who could coax a laugh out of me even on the days when I felt too hollow to breathe.

Before I could talk myself out of it, I sent a friend request. She accepted. We exchanged messages, then phone numbers, and now we are meeting.

Saturday, 1 February. The coffee house. Of course it is. Where else in the world would two ghosts from the same past choose to meet?

I am terrified. Hopeful. Anxious. Strange as it sounds, I am also calm, as if something long buried is stirring and stretching back into life. She told me she was happy to hear from me. Said it had been far too long.

God, I hope she meant it.

I will never forget that horrible Thursday. You would think heartbreak of that magnitude would come with a warning, something like a tremor before an earthquake or the dark press of storm clouds before the rain. But no. It arrived without fanfare, a single blunt sentence thrown at me like a stone in front of half the school, right by the bike racks, moments after the final bell.

"I think we should break up."

That was it. No pause for kindness, no reason offered. He spoke like he was commenting on the weather. Then he walked away while my heart shattered clean open. He walked across the car park and straight towards her. I did not even know there was a her.

My vision blurred at the edges. Sound narrowed to a high tight ringing in my ears. I stood frozen, my school bag sliding down my arm, tears prickling but refusing to fall. I could feel eyes on me, hear the whispers behind cupped hands, and the shame crawled up my throat like something living.

And then Lottie appeared.

She did not launch into sympathy. She did not demand details. She simply stepped beside me, lifted my bag back onto my shoulder, and took my hand. Her eyes flicked across the crowd, sharp and certain, then settled back on me.

"Come on," she said. And I went.

From that moment until Monday morning, she did not leave my side. Not once. She came home with me that very evening without hesitation. Told my mum we were having a girl emergency weekend and proceeded to turn my bedroom into a makeshift sanctuary. Conveniently, it was a three day weekend, and she treated it like the universe had arranged it for us.

Thursday night was tissues and toast, Clueless on too loud, and our faces half crushed into pillows. I cried until my ribs hurt. Then I laughed at something ridiculous. Then I cried again. Lottie plaited my hair over and over until the rhythm of her hands settled my breathing.

Friday morning she attempted pancakes, burned nearly every one, and served them with so much butter and syrup that they tasted like sugary charcoal. We ate them anyway, sitting in our pyjamas in the kitchen wearing face masks that cracked whenever we smiled. Lottie announced, "He is a complete gobshite," as if she were quoting a textbook.

"Yeah," I managed.

"With the emotional depth of a teaspoon."

I laughed. A proper laugh. It felt like my lungs had been unclenched.

We spent the day wandering town, drifting through charity shops hunting for the most ridiculous outfits. She made me try on a glittery gold blazer and declared, "Girl. Look at you. Paris Hilton would applaud." We bought slushies, even though the air was cold, and sat on the steps of the monument in Phoenix Park. We made up stories about strangers, giving them secret romances and dramatic lives. My heartbreak still throbbed underneath it all, but it did not crush me in quite the same way with her there. Lottie had a way of making everything feel lighter.

Saturday evening turned into a dance party in my room. Missy Elliott and Ciara blared from my tiny speakers. We shouted the words to "1, 2, Step," spinning under the fairy lights. Lottie sprayed half a can of Impulse into the air and waved her arms as if we were club royalty instead of two teenage girls in a too small room.

She never once told me to get over it. She simply reminded me in every moment, without needing to say the words, that I was still me. Still Clara. Still whole.

Sunday drifted by softly. We painted our nails, planned outfits for Monday as though the school hallway were a red carpet. We attended a Catholic all girls secondary school, which meant itchy kilts and oversized jumpers as our daily uniform. Those clothes were strict and shapeless, only for school hours. After the final bell, we rushed home to change into jeans that actually fit and jumpers that felt like ours. Lottie let me borrow her good jeans and her green butterfly clips, the ones I had envied for months without admitting it. She handed them over and said, "Today you wear the armour."

And I believed her.

And then it was Monday.

We walked to school together, arm in arm, our steps falling into a rhythm that felt steadier than the one inside my chest. The early morning air was crisp, almost sharp, and the butterflies in my stomach were threatening to riot. I could taste nerves on the back of my tongue, metallic and stubborn. We turned the corner toward the school gates, and there he was.

Johnny.

He stood exactly where I knew he would, smug as ever, holding hands with her. I never learnt her name. I never asked. It hardly matters now. She was simply the girl who appeared in the wreckage of my life at the wrong moment, nothing more, nothing less.

For a second, I faltered. My feet stuttered on the pavement, and something in me buckled. It felt like a tiny collapse, as if the ground had shifted half an inch and knocked my balance off. But Lottie linked our arms tighter and gave the gentlest squeeze. She did not say a thing. Words would have been too fragile. Instead, she reached into her school bag, pulled out her Discman, and handed me one of the earphones as if she were placing a crown on my head.

Missy's beat kicked in.

♪ "Run for cover muthafucka..." ♪

And that was it.

We strutted straight past him as if he were invisible. Truly invisible. I did not even glance in his direction. The music filled me up, louder than the whispering around us, louder than the sting in my chest. Louder than the ghost of who I had been just days before. It was as if each step rewrote me.

We walked into our circle of besties like nothing had happened. Like we had stepped off a runway instead of trudged through heartbreak. Everyone squealed when they saw us. There were hugs and the kind of excited shrieks that made the morning feel brighter. Girls shouted, "She is not here to play. She is here to be fierce." It was ridiculous and perfect and exactly what I needed.

Lottie pulled off her sunglasses, winked at me, and said, "Johnny who?"

And for the first time since Thursday, I believed it. I believed it so deeply that it settled in my bones and warmed places I thought were frozen.

Lottie did not simply help me survive my first heartbreak; she reshaped it. With love. With music. With pancake breakfasts and butterfly clips and the steady kind of friendship that does not flinch when you are at your worst. She held my broken bits as if they were not something to fear.

It was the first time I realised heartbreak does not have to destroy you. Not when you have someone who takes your hand through the wreckage and teaches you how to stand, how to walk, how to become someone new.

To this day, when I hear "Pass That Dutch," I do not think of Johnny. I think of Lottie. And I smile. It is automatic, like muscle memory, a quiet gratitude that still surprises me.

But now that it is real, now that I have written it all down, I am spiralling. What if Reya shows up first? What if she sees me before I see Lottie and intercepts everything, twisting it before I have a chance to say a single word? What if she gets there with her sharp tongue and perfectly rehearsed versions of the past?

What if Lottie does talk to Reya between now and then? What if Reya reminds her how badly I messed things up? How Lottie cried in the staff bathroom for an hour after I said those unforgivable things? The memory still claws at me, raw and stubborn.

God, what if Lottie realises she is better off without me? What if she listens to Reya and decides I am still the same mess she walked away from all those years ago? What if she forgets how much I loved her? How much I still love her, even now, even after everything?

I do not have many friends. Not real ones. Most are connected to Niall, the kids, or the neighbourhood. They are lovely, they truly are, but none of them chose me for me. Not in the way Lottie did. Not in the way that made me feel seen.

I need to know if someone still sees me. If someone still wants me in their life. Not because they have to. Not because I bake cupcakes for the PTA or know how to keep a calendar organised. But because they remember the girl I was and believe there is still something worth saving in the woman I have become.

It has been more than ten years.

Ten years. Too long. Yet possibly not too late.

Please, please do not let it be too late.

33

31 January 2020: Niall

Give her space to be brave.

Tomorrow, Clara is going for coffee with an old friend.

That is all I got. No name. No details. No clue which chapter of her life this person belongs to. Just that simple phrase: someone she used to be close to.

And I swear to God, the second the words left her mouth, my brain managed to produce a full cinematic reel of worst-case scenarios. Stormy orchestral music. Overacting. Betrayal lit in dramatic shadows. Absolute nonsense.

She is having an affair. That was the ugly thought that landed first, and I hated it instantly. Hated that my mind even reached for that possibility. Hated that I looked at the woman I have loved through colic and chaos, years of half asleep mornings, sterile waiting rooms, nights of barely there intimacy and quiet heartbreak, and still let doubt slip in.

She has not given me any genuine reason. It was just the way she said it: soft, vague, held close to her chest as though she was treading carefully across thin ice. It knocked something loose in me. The part that worries when things finally start to feel good again.

Because lately, we have been reconnecting in small but precious ways. Not just the polite smiles or the endless parenting logistics. Not the blurred lists of dinner ingredients and reminders to buy toothpaste that make us feel like colleagues in a domestic start up. Real connection. Real warmth. Eye contact that lingers. Laughter that is not polite or habitual but honest. God, the laughter. Like we used to have in pubs before mortgages and back pain and the encyclopaedia of paediatric medicine stored in our heads. I refuse to let paranoia spoil that.

Still, the thought crossed my mind that I could follow her into the city to keep an eye on things. A ridiculous idea. Me hunched behind sunglasses in some crowded café, pretending to read a newspaper like a bargain basement private investigator. Then she did something that punctured that whole fantasy.

She asked me for a lift. So casually that it stunned me. The woman is not having an affair. The woman is terrified and trusting me, and I was an idiot for letting suspicion take root for even a heartbeat.

She admitted she was not ready to drive after the accident. Fair enough. That shook us both in ways we have not fully talked about. She has barely mentioned it, but I have seen her fingers twitch on the steering wheel as though muscle memory fights with her nerves.

Then she added something else. Something I still cannot get out of my head.

"And I would just feel better if you were close by. You know, in case I need a quick getaway."

A quick getaway.

She gave a small laugh after saying it, as if to soften the edges of the words. That laugh did not help. It sounded like she was trying to make it harmless, maybe even funny. But the phrase landed with weight. It felt like there was something underneath it. Something she was not ready to name.

What sort of friend requires an escape plan?

I said nothing. Only nodded and agreed to drive her. All night though, the words have been pacing through my mind like they are wearing grooves in the floorboards. Quick getaway. Quick getaway. Quick getaway. Each repetition sharpens the question.

Who is she meeting?

Is it someone from before me? Or, worse, someone tied to that time ten years ago. The time she never speaks about. The time she has sealed off in her mind like a locked room. I have seen the way she wakes from it: pale, trembling, staring at the ceiling as if bracing for impact. There is history there, and it is heavy.

She guards that part of herself as though one wrong question might cause the entire structure to crack. She has never truly let me in.

Well, almost never. Once, early on, before the layers of responsibility, before the twins and the deadlines and the sense that adulthood was piling bricks on top of us, she did.

We were sitting on the cold floor of her flat, sharing a pathetic takeaway that tasted mostly of garlic and regret. Warm wine in mugs. No babies. No careers in crisis. Just two people who had known each other for three weeks and were already talking like the universe had nudged us together on purpose.

She told me about a falling out she had with a friend from school. A huge, messy storm of loyalty battles and silence and mutual friends choosing sides. Then she paused, fork halfway to her mouth, and said, very quietly:

"I do not talk about that part of my life. It feels brittle."

Brittle. A word that still fits in the palm of my memory like something fragile. Even then, I wondered what had happened to make a memory feel breakable for her.

I did not push. I simply listened. Eventually, she drifted into a lighter story about dyeing her hair blue and ending up grey, and we laughed until her eyes shone. But that earlier moment stayed with me, tucked away like a bookmark in a chapter she refused to open again.

Tonight, I cannot help wondering if the friend she is meeting is connected to that brittle place. If this coffee is not a simple catch up at all but something closer to a reckoning.

And if that is true, then Clara showing up is brave in a way she will not name out loud.

I try to remember that whenever paranoia starts tugging at me, whenever my stomach twists itself into knots imagining vindictive ex friends or someone dragging her back into old pain. She is stretching towards something outside this house. Something outside her role as mother and coordinator of all things domestic. Outside the woman who packs lunches, schedules dentist appointments and holds our entire household together with quiet competence.

She is reaching for the version of herself who came before all of that. The one who wore Doc Martens with sundresses and believed wholeheartedly in horoscopes. The woman who made me laugh so hard on our first date that I dropped my drink.

And the first time she tells me she is meeting a friend, I jump to adultery? That is not her burden. That is mine. I owe her better.

She is nervous, yes, but she is also alive in a way I have not seen for months. Maybe years. She has a glow under her skin, something bright and unsettled. She looks like someone stepping back into sunlight after too long in the shade. I want that for her. I want her to rediscover those scattered pieces of herself.

Because here is the truth. I trust her with my entire life, yet I also know how the past can behave. It sits quietly for ages, then comes at you when you think you have moved on. Which is why her quick getaway line is still looping in my head.

Who is she meeting? Why might she need to run?

I want to ask, but I will not. This is not about me. It is about letting Clara be Clara again, letting her find the courage to step into spaces she once avoided. I owe her the room to grow back into herself without me hovering like some anxious shadow.

So tomorrow, I will drive her. I will hold her hand for as long as she wants. I will kiss her forehead and say, "Text me when you are done."

And if she messages, "Can you come get me?", I will already be halfway there with the heater on.

I will not demand explanations. Not unless she offers them. I will simply be there, steady and ready. And if she needs that quick getaway, I will keep the engine running and the passenger door open.

34

1 February 2020: Clara

Brace yourself. This could go either way.

This morning felt like holding my breath underwater, waiting to see if I would break the surface or slip further beneath it. I must have spent three hours getting ready, which is an absurd amount of time for one woman unless it happens to be her wedding day. Yet when you factor in the shower that felt more like a strategic briefing, the chaos of choosing an outfit, the battle with makeup, and the eternal debate over whether my hair should be curled, straightened, or styled into one of those artfully messy updos that only look effortless on the internet, it begins to make sense. Then there is the order of operations, a psychological minefield that tests your sanity before you have even considered leaving the house.

If you do your makeup first, you risk dragging a top over your face and smudging everything into a tragic impressionist painting. If you get dressed first, you might spill foundation across your front and immediately regret every life choice that led you to that moment. And hair? Style it before makeup and the heat from the dryer could melt your carefully blended foundation. Do it afterwards and your face might turn oily or blotchy from all the faffing. There is no winning, only survival.

Being a woman is exhausting. And that is before you have stepped outside the front door. But somehow, almost instinctively, we push on. We always do.

I chose my favourite white dress scattered with blue flowers, the one that falls just below the knee and still clings to the faintest curve of my waist. It hangs on like a loyal friend, determined to stay by my side after ten relentless years of full-time motherhood, endless PTA meetings, neighbourhood watch dramas, and dinners consumed at red lights while praying the children would not notice the vegetables I had forgotten again. I never bounced back after the twins, unless you count bouncing between school runs, laundry mountains, and the occasional emotional wobble. But who really bounces back? Supermodels and lies. That is who.

I still was not firing on all cylinders after the accident. More like a generous sixty-three per cent on a day when the stars aligned and the paracetamol actually worked. Which is why I asked Niall to drive me into town. He agreed far too easily. No classic husband sigh, no gentle interrogation about whether I was absolutely sure. Just a calm yes. And now he was driving like a man on a covert mission, glancing at me every few seconds as though I might detonate into a shower of unresolved trauma and half-formed plans.

He is worried about something. I can feel it in the way his knuckles tighten on the steering wheel whenever I shift in my seat. Yes, he knows I am nervous. He always does. Even when I slip into that over-cheery voice I reserve for lying or shopping in Tesco. And he knows he has never met Lottie. That truth sits between us like a silent third passenger, impossible to ignore. Most men would leap straight into worst-case-scenario mode if their wife casually mentioned she was meeting an old friend. You would expect jealousy, suspicion, maybe even GPS tracking. Not Niall. He has been calm, supportive, almost suspiciously so, which only makes me question him more.

He can sense something. Anyone could, given the way I have been fiddling with the hem of my sleeve as if it might reveal the secrets of the universe. I have not said much. Not out loud. But he knows me. Sometimes a little too well.

He dropped me outside the coffee house just before eleven. He did not say much, only offered a soft smile, his hand resting protectively on my knee while we waited at the lights. He was trying not to ask anything that would push me further into my spiral. When we pulled up, he leaned across and kissed me quickly, attempting reassurance without crowding me.

"You are doing great," he called through the window as I stepped out. I turned back and tried to smile, although it felt half-hearted, then gave him a thumbs up before he drove off.

I did not go inside straight away. Instead, I lingered outside like some awkward onlooker. Not because I did not want to go in. I did. Desperately. But I needed to see who was working. I had to know.

Please not Reya. Please not Reya. Please. Not. Reya.

I squinted through the glass and finally spotted a tall figure behind the counter, curls as black as ink and a red apron tied neatly around his waist. John. Thank God. Not Reya.

I remembered him, although vaguely. He had always looked at Lottie as if she had hung the moon. I used to think he fancied her. Maybe everyone did in their own way.

When I stepped inside, my nerves twisted into something tighter and more painful. I gave him a polite smile and lifted my hand in a small wave.

"Hey, John. Long time."

He nodded, although the smile he offered was cool and clipped. It lacked the warmth he had just shown the two women ahead of me. With them, he had been cheerful and familiar. With me, he seemed guarded, as if uncertain what box to put me in.

Before I could overthink it, I heard it. A high-pitched squeal erupting from the back of the shop.

"CLARAAAA!"

My heart shot straight into my throat. Lottie.

She had not changed. Or perhaps she had, and time had layered new stories onto her face, but to me she was still the girl I had loved like a sister. Warm eyes, quick smile, arms already open by the time I reached her. We hugged as though time had never dared to touch us. There was something grounding in her hold, something that felt like home and danger all at once.

She had chosen a perfect spot tucked away at the very back of the shop. We ordered drinks, settled in, and for a blissful ten minutes I forgot that I had been terrified only moments before. I asked about her parents, who were apparently still stubborn, still adorable, and still convinced they were younger than they actually were. I asked about the coffee house, which she said was thriving. And I asked about her. She said she was better. She said it softly, as if that one word carried layers of meaning, and although I caught the weight of it, I did not press.

Eventually, I mentioned John. Casually, although I am sure she saw right through it.

"I always thought he had a thing for you," I teased while cutting my blueberry muffin in half. I tried to sound light, almost playful, although my voice wavered ever so slightly.

And beneath it all, I wondered whether anything today would truly go the way I hoped.

Lottie nearly snorted coffee through her nose.

"Oh my God, no. Clara, your love radar was completely off. John's married. To Reya."

And that was the moment my stomach dropped so sharply that it felt as if the floor had shifted beneath me.

Reya. Of course it would be her.

Suddenly everything made chilling sense: the reason he didn't smile, the way he hovered in the background, the fact that he was watching us, still watching us as if he had a right to. I turned my head, pretending to study the espresso machine, and there he was. Phone pressed to his ear. Eyes pinned on us. Unmoving. Cold. Familiar in the worst possible way.

My throat tightened until swallowing felt impossible. A rush of heat moved up my neck, and for a second I was sixteen again, caught in a moment I didn't understand yet somehow felt responsible for, trapped in a memory that clung like wet clothes.

"Clara?" Lottie asked gently. Her voice sounded distant, as if I were hearing her through water. My mouth moved, but what came out was nonsense. I think I started rambling about the kids, about getting married, about something that made no sense to either of us. My thoughts twisted around each other, slippery and frantic.

My brain kept screaming: Get out. Go. Now.

John approached our table with our coffee and apologised for the delay, his grin not matching his tone.

I pushed my chair back so abruptly the table rattled, and my coffee nearly toppled over.

"We should, uh, do this again sometime," I stammered, snatching my to-go cup and backing away as if Lottie had struck a match and the room was filling with smoke.

She blinked at me in confusion.

"Clara, wait. What's going on?"

But I was already halfway to the door, willing myself not to look back. The moment the cool air hit my face I started searching for Niall's car. I spotted it two blocks away, tucked by the kerb where we'd agreed he'd wait just in case I needed a quick escape. I hurried towards it, heart racing, limbs buzzing with that strange, electric panic.

I climbed in, chest heaving, hands trembling.

Niall's eyebrows shot up.

"God, Clara, that was a quick coffee."

I tried to muster a smile, but it faltered immediately.

"Oh, the coffee house was crazy busy. We said we'd meet again soon."

He didn't question it, which almost made me want to cry. He simply nodded and pulled into the road. As the buildings blurred past the window, the tension in my body began to shift into a deeper ache. That familiar, pulsing heaviness crept along my arms and chest, the kind that comes when anxiety starts taking its toll. It felt like my nerves were trying to climb out of my skin, seeking any way to escape the chaos inside me.

Niall reached across and squeezed my hand.

"You're okay," he said softly.

"That's just the adrenaline, love. It'll settle."

I hope he's right.

I'm grateful he's here. Left hand resting on my journal, right hand held securely in his. A strange little anchor system we've created without ever planning it. He kept hold of me the entire way home, steady and patient, never letting go. And when we pulled into the drive and I told him I might head to bed early, he nodded, kissed my temple and whispered, "Proud of you."

That almost broke me, because I'm not proud of myself at all.

I bolted from Lottie like a coward. I let Reya, or the idea of Reya, unravel something that could have been a fresh start. Yet some small part of me, buried under the panic, wonders if this moment might somehow still be the beginning of something. Maybe Lottie will call. Maybe she won't. Maybe I'll find the courage to reach out first.

I hope so. I need at least one friend who chooses me because she wants to, not because she has to through blood or obligation or shared school schedules. Someone who sees me and still wants to stay.

It has been ten years. Far too long. Please let this be the start of something good.

I'm going to take a sleeping tablet. My body feels disconnected from my mind, as if I'm moving through fog. I don't usually vomit from anxiety, and the dehydration afterwards has left me shaky and hollow. I just want to wake up feeling steadier, clearer, more like myself. And hopefully, when I do, I'll have the courage to reschedule another coffee with Lottie.

It feels like this could be the beginning again, if I let it.

35

8 February 2020: Niall

Is this even real life?

It is the evening after Clara's funeral. I am sitting on the edge of our bed in our own house for the first time since she died. The room feels foreign in a way that makes my stomach twist. Familiar, yet somehow unrecognisable, as if someone has quietly rearranged the air. It smells of detergent and cold February air. Clean sheets. Emptiness. A space that used to feel lived in now feels politely scrubbed of us.

Samantha changed the bed. She must have come by while we were still at the funeral. I spotted the old linens folded neatly over the back of the chair, still unwashed. At first it struck me as strange, almost careless, but then I realised why. She did not wash them because part of her believed that doing so would unsettle me. As if removing the last imprint of Clara's body from the cotton would be a cruelty. She was probably right. I suppose some part of me wanted the scent of Clara's shampoo to cling to the fibres a little longer.

I have been seeing a different side of Samantha this week, something I never expected. Not only the capable version of her that I always knew, but something softer. A quiet gentleness threaded through her every movement. Protective, yet never overbearing. She packed the children's bags when I forgot they would need pyjamas. She reminded me to eat, slipping a plate in front of me without sparking a conversation I could not bear. She left a carton of oat milk in the fridge because she remembered Emily preferred it. All these small gestures have felt like a steady hand at the centre of my back, holding me upright without making a show of it.

She and Conor have become anchors. Moving between their place and Mam and Dad's was disorienting. Every space felt like a borrowed life. Yet with them I felt a sort of harbour. No pressure, no demands, just safe places where I could fall apart without being told to keep it together. I never realised how much that mattered until now.

We had not set foot in our own home since the first. Since that night. The night I thought she was simply tired.

The night I let her go to bed early because her stomach was unsettled and she said she felt disoriented. I did not press her. I thought I was giving her space, giving her a bit of air. She had gone out earlier to meet that friend for coffee. When she returned, she seemed lighter. Not transformed, but eased somehow. She held my hand all the way home in the car. I can still hear her voice saying, thank you for being exactly what I needed today.

That does not sound like a woman planning to die. Not to me.

We were supposed to be getting better. I made tea, the good herbal one she liked when her nerves were frayed. I asked if she wanted to watch something gentle. She said she was tired. I let her go to bed. I stayed on the couch watching a slow documentary she always claimed would send her into a coma. Before I pressed play, I peeked in on her. She was lying on her side with the duvet gathered up around her shoulders. Peaceful. I thought she was sleeping.

She was not. The next morning, she was cold. Still. Gone.

The inquest finished quickly, far faster than I expected. Overdose. Sleeping tablets. No signs of foul play. No trauma. Nothing except quiet, clinical certainty. The bottle was almost empty. Twenty-six tablets gone out of twenty-eight. I was sure the GP had only prescribed a short starter dose. Something to cover three or four days. This looked more like a month's supply. And if it was an old bottle, surely they would have said. Surely someone would have noticed.

People keep telling me not to blame myself, and I want to believe them. They say that no matter how deeply we love someone, there are moments we simply do not see. Yet I cannot accept that. Not when she had been trying. She was writing again, even if it was only half a page at a time. She was reading. Journaling. Laughing a little. And that look she gave me in the car stays with me like a bruise that will not fade. She was here. Present. Still choosing us.

Those are not goodbye words.

What haunts me even more than the smell of that room or the stillness of her hand is the moment I had to tell Rory and Emily.

That moment ruined me.

They were still in their pyjamas at Conor and Samantha's. I brought them into the sitting room. I could not stand above them, not for something like this, so I knelt on the rug and they sat side by side on the couch. Rory was already tugging the drawstring of his hoodie, working it through his fingers like a lifeline. Emily clutched that tattered stuffed turtle she has had since she was two, its frayed flippers almost grey from years of love.

I said, "I need to tell you something. Something really important."

They both looked at me then. Soft morning faces. Eyes blinking away sleep, not yet pulled into the gravity of what I was about to break open.

"Something happened to Mammy."

Emily blinked slowly, almost dreamily.

"She got very sick last night," I said.

"And she did not wake up."

Rory froze. Emily tilted her head in that small bird like way she has.

"She is gone," I said, and every word scraped my throat raw. "She died in her sleep."

Rory shook his head at once.

"No," he said. "No, she did not. You said she was sleeping."

"She was," I said. "But she did not wake up, bud."

His voice cracked around the edges.

"She said she would call this morning. She said..."

Emily's lip trembled.

"But our birthday is soon. Mammy would not miss our birthday," she whispered in a voice so fragile it barely counted as sound.

"I know," I said, and the words tasted like ash on my tongue.

Rory stood abruptly, his grief exploding into anger.

"You should have woken her up," he shouted. "Why did you not check? Why did you not do something?"

"I did not know," I said, choking on it.

"I did not know she was..."

He kicked the coffee table hard enough to crack the leg. Then he dropped to the floor, bending in on himself, fists curled tight as he sobbed into the carpet. I wanted to gather him up, but he felt untouchable in that moment, sealed inside a world I had broken.

Emily had not moved at all. I sat down beside her, close enough that our shoulders touched, hoping she would feel steadier for it.

She whispered, "Is she cold? Like the butterflies in the garden when they die?"

I nodded because I could not lie to her.

"Will she even know when we turn ten?"

Her question landed in my chest like a stone. I still do not have an answer.

That was the moment I shattered. Not when the EMTs confirmed it. Not when they took her body away. That was the moment. That innocent, impossible hope. That small voice asking if their mum would still know who they were. It splintered something in me that had been holding on by a thread.

On the third, their birthday, we lit the candles on the cake Clara had ordered two weeks earlier. One half was frosted in swirling shades of blue, with a tiny edible figure swimming through sugary waves. The other half was a green pitch, complete with icing grass and a fondant man gripping a rugby ball. Rory refused to open his cards. Emily wore her party dress anyway, even though it hung oddly on her after days of not eating properly. We sang "Happy Birthday" as if it were a funeral hymn, each note trembling with the weight of everything we had already lost.

And now it is the eighth. The funeral is finished. She is in the ground. And the house feels too big, too hollow, too still, as if the air itself is wary of moving.

Emily stood at the door when we arrived this evening and asked if it would still smell like Mammy. It did not. It smelled of lemon cleaner and fresh laundry, scents that seemed to declare the absence of the person who had once filled every corner. And beneath those sharp smells, something else lingered, faint but cutting, like a life scrubbed clean of the one who lived it.

Rory ran straight to his room. When I checked on him later, he was curled beneath Clara's old hoodie, the sleeves pulled up to his face, his fingers clinging to the fabric as if he could hold her through it. Emily needed me to check the windows before bed, the way Clara always had. She watched me carefully, eyes wide, waiting for the familiar movement. I even made the little click sound with my tongue, the one Clara always added for reassurance. Emily smiled. Barely, but it was there.

I wandered into our room and sat on the edge of the bed. And for the first time since she died, I let myself remember the moment I told my parents. Mam cried, not loud, not gasping, just a low, deep sound, as though something inside her had finally cracked open. Dad looked at me and his face dropped. It was not sorrow, nor was it shock. It was something sharper, something quicker. And for a breath so short I almost doubted it existed, I thought it looked like guilt.

I have tried to reason it away. Maybe I imagined it. Maybe my mind, desperate and fractured, is inventing new shadows to chase. But the image will not leave me. It follows me into every quiet moment. It clings to the corners of my thoughts, whispering possibilities I am too frightened to confront.

I will not say it aloud. I will not let the thought form fully. It would unravel everything. And although I sensed that moment approaching, especially after what I had uncovered, I could not face it tonight.

When I returned home, I searched through Clara's things, not for anything specific, just desperate to find something real, something of hers I could hold onto. But instead, I found a smoking gun. Not the newest journal tucked neatly in her bedside drawer. These were hidden deeper, buried at the bottom of a dusty box labelled "Kitchen Drawers". A box I remembered from the day Clara and I first moved in together, shoved away in the farthest corner of the wardrobe.

The faint sketch of a whisk on the side was unmistakably hers. These journals were not meant to be found. They were from a decade ago, long before I knew the truth. Before I understood that my father was the one who hurt Clara all those years ago. Before I realised his shadow had been haunting our family far longer than I had ever dared imagine.

And God forgive me, I have taken two of Conor's journals. I know what that makes me. I know exactly where I am headed for it. But still, I took them.

It began with something as mundane as needing a shirt for the funeral. I did not have one. I could not face returning to my own house to get it, and the idea of braving the crowds in Kildare made my stomach twist. I was not thinking straight, grief does that, it tangles the simplest decisions. Conor, ever practical, told me to check his wardrobe. His wardrobe, he called it, yet what I found was a room, an entire room, converted into a walk-in closet. The sort of space you might see in a film, not in Conor's home. Clothes were arranged like exhibits, everything in its place, untouched, almost curated.

I found a shirt. Slightly roomy for him perhaps, but it fit me as though it had been waiting all along.

I should have left then.

But the silence in that room was strangely loud, almost pressing. And then I saw it: a chest of drawers tucked away in the corner, old and scuffed, the sort a child once covered in stickers and scribbles. It did not belong there. It was too personal, too human, too out of place in this meticulously arranged space. I told myself I was only curious, only looking.

My hand hovered over the drawer handle far longer than it should have. And when I finally opened it, I knew I should not have, even before I saw the contents.

Journals. Not one or two. Hundreds. Neatly stacked, carefully preserved, years of his life documented in his own hand. My heart lodged high in my throat. It felt like discovering a buried body, something sacred or dangerous or both, something never intended for anyone else's eyes.

And I took two. Only two.

The ones from the years I needed to understand. The ones that might hold the answers to questions he never would have answered himself. Questions that had gnawed at me for years. And perhaps I should not need to know, but I do. I have to.

I was terrified someone would find out. Every time the floor creaked outside the room, I thought someone was coming. But I took them anyway, clutching them as I made my way downstairs. Slowly. Quietly. Because I have too many questions, and Conor is the only one who can still answer them, even if he does not realise it.

Tonight, in the silence of this house, wrapped in the cool sheets I did not change, I feel something closing in. Something unfinished. Something waiting.

They said Clara took her own life. They said she was overwhelmed, quiet, drowning beneath it all. But I knew her. I know her still. She would not leave us. Not like that. Not when she had just begun to fight again.

So no, I do not accept it. Not yet. Something does not add up. But first, I have to survive tonight. I have to remember how to breathe.

36

Aug 23rd, 2025: Charlotte

What the fucking fuck.

I cannot stop shaking. I keep re-reading Clara's journal entry, the one from the day we met for coffee, as if the words might rearrange themselves and offer a different truth. As if, by staring long enough, I might discover something hidden between the lines that will undo the last few hours of my life. Yet nothing changes. Every detail stays exactly where it was. Her nervous excitement. Her fragile hope. That terrible, creeping fear that started the moment she spotted John.

God, Clara. We were chatting, easing into something that almost felt normal, then she saw John. She thought he was calling Reya and assumed Reya would be angry, ready to intervene again. Then she panicked. She was gone in seconds. That is it, really, the bare bones of our meeting. Clara bolted from that coffee house with such force that I barely had time to process her leaving. At the time, I told myself it was the nerves built up over years, the regret, the uncertainty. But now I know better. She was scared. That high-pitched squeal I let out when I first saw her was not enough to anchor her in place. The moment Clara noticed John on his phone, everything changed. Her world tilted out of alignment, and she was genuinely terrified.

Did she think Reya would make good on her warning, or that she would try again to force distance between us? Or something worse. But how on earth could Reya have taken things that far? Clara died the very next morning. The EMTs said it looked like an overdose of sleeping tablets. Niall's journal shattered me. He found her in bed. He thought she was asleep. He thought it was an ordinary night. It should have been. It should have been forgettable and safe. Now all I can hear is his voice repeating the words that haunt him:

'Typical post-anxiety crash, I thought.'

It explains so much. Why Niall is so highly attuned to my anxiety. Why he never makes me feel dramatic or unreasonable. It is not only love, although he loves deeply, it is regret. Niall blames himself. He thinks he should have kissed Clara's forehead, and that he might have noticed her chest was still. He believes that if he had woken her, she could have taken something to help her. But no tablet in the world could have brought her back. It destroys me. I want to take his grief from him, crush it in my hands and cast it as far from him as possible. I want to scream at someone. At the universe. At Reya.

Because here is the part I can no longer push aside: what if Reya did do something. I have not let my mind chase that possibility too far, yet it is there. She told Clara to stay away from me. Clara wrote about it in a cautious, almost fearful whisper, like someone trying not to trip a hidden wire. I refused to believe it then. Reya could be opinionated and fiercely protective, yet this feels different.

I keep circling back to the timeline. Clara and I met for coffee on Saturday. She died on Sunday morning. That is less than twenty-four hours.

Did Reya confront her? Did she say something sharp enough to slice through Clara's fragile hope? Did she threaten her or humiliate her or push her into a corner she could not escape? Or, God help me, did something worse happen?

No. No. I do not want to think that. Reya is my best friend. My person. But I have read Clara's words. I have felt the dread rising off the page like smoke. The way she scanned the coffee shop before entering. The way she bolted the instant she saw John watching her with his phone in hand.

John, who did not smile at her. John, who married Reya.

Was he calling his wife? Was Reya waiting for instructions? I feel sick even entertaining the thought.

Clara did not seem suicidal. She was anxious, certainly. She had panic attacks and old trauma that clung to her ribs like vines. But she was not folding in on herself. She was trying to heal. She arrived that day with questions and a fragile, flickering optimism. She wanted answers. She wanted connection. She wanted, in her own way, a future.

That is not the energy of someone preparing to give up. And that is the part that keeps cracking my chest open:

Clara wanted to fight for her life. She wanted to fight for me, for us, for the possibility of a second chance. Now she is gone.

I have to talk to Reya. I do not want to. I do not even want to picture her face right now, let alone confront her. But I need to know what happened after that coffee date. I need to know if she said something. I need to know what she knew and precisely when she knew it.

Because if Clara did not choose to end her life, if someone else took that choice from her, then I will not let this go. Not even for Reya. I owe Clara that much. I owe Niall. I owe the children who lost their mother.

I nearly leapt out of my skin when the front door burst open. A wave of footsteps, laughter and chaotic shouting tore through the old house like a stampede. For a moment, it felt as though the entire school choir had barged inside. Niall and the kids were home.

Shit. Shit. Shit.

My heart slammed against my ribs as I shoved the journals into the box with shaking hands. One slipped and landed face down, still open. I had no idea which entry it was. I stuffed it inside, forced the lid on and kicked the box into the farthest corner of the attic as if it were hazardous. The nearest thing to hand was a half-finished crocheted blanket I had found in the linen cupboard. I threw it over the box like a desperate attempt to hide evidence. I took a breath. Then another. Tried to slow my pulse enough to pass as normal.

Then I ran. Down the narrow staircase, hair wild, pulse louder than the steps beneath me. I reached the hall just as Emily screamed triumphantly about beating her brother in some bizarre social media challenge involving drinking an entire Sprite without burping.

Rory chased her, spluttering, 'It is a gross challenge, of course she won', clearly nursing a bruised ego.

Niall followed with bags in each hand, looking worn out and pleased with himself in equal measure. He gave me a broad grin the moment he saw me. That smile slipped almost instantly because Charlotte, the calm, collected stepmother and wife, was nowhere to be found.

"Everything okay?" he asked, stepping forward with a careful look that told me he already suspected the truth.

"Fine!" I chirped. Too quick, too loud, too bright for how I actually felt. The word hung between us like a flimsy curtain that could be pulled back with the smallest tug.

He tilted his head, sceptical, his eyes narrowing in that gentle way he used whenever he thought I was hiding something.

"You sure?"

I fumbled for a tone that sounded normal. Calm. Like I had not spent the past hour rehearsing lies in my head.

"Yeah, I just remembered I have to pop into the coffee house quickly. I forgot to collect something. In the office." The explanation stumbled out in pieces, each bit thinner than the last.

It was flimsy at best and we both knew it, yet I did not wait for Niall to reply. I made a direct beeline for the front door, hoping momentum would stop him from thinking too hard.

"Charlotte," he called, catching my arm just as my fingers brushed the handle. His grip was not harsh, but it was firm, a grip that carried a quiet frustration. "You're leaving now? We only just got home. The kids were excited for dinner."

"I know, I'm sorry," I said, refusing to meet his eyes. "I'll be quick, I promise."

"Quick?" He gave a sharp breath. "You've been disappearing for hours every day since we moved in. We have not even sat down to one family meal yet."

"I know," I said again, my voice softer. I glanced over my shoulder at the kids who were still wrestling over who got to sit at the head of the table. Their laughter only made the tension between us feel heavier.

"I just..." I exhaled sharply, trying to untangle the knot in my chest.

"I need to talk to Reya."

His brow furrowed, the crease deepening. "What about?"

"I cannot say." My voice cracked like it betrayed me on purpose.

That only made everything worse.

"You cannot say?" Niall echoed, folding his arms. His voice hardened, though there was still worry underneath. "What on earth is going on with you lately? You are not someone who keeps secrets. Partly because you are terrible at it."

"Niall, please," I whispered, taking his hands in mine. They were warm, familiar, grounding in a way I suddenly could not bear.

"Please trust me. Just for a little longer. I need to do this, okay? I need to ask Reya something important. And when I come back, we will talk about it. All of it. I promise."

He searched my face as though he was trying to read a language he had never learnt.

"This got anything to do with those boxes up there?" he asked quietly. "The ones in the attic?"

The words lodged in my throat. How did he know? Or did he not know at all, and was he waiting to see how I reacted? Was he trying to find out how much I had discovered? Or how much he thought I believed he had discovered? I felt dizzy with the spiralling. Jesus, I was losing it.

"I just need a little more time," I said. "Please. I am trying to make sense of something that refuses to make sense, and if I can talk to Reya, maybe we can all stop wondering."

His jaw worked, clenching then easing as if he was weighing something only he could see. He looked like he wanted to push again, to unravel my excuses one thread at a time, but something in my face must have stopped him. After a silent stretch that felt too long, he sighed.

"Just be careful, yeah?"

"I will."

"I mean it, Charlotte. It is a Saturday night. The city centre will be mad."

I nodded and stepped back.

"I promise."

He let go of my hand. I kissed his cheek, quick and almost clumsy, before he could ask anything else, before the fear in me had time to take root and grow claws. Then I slipped out the door.

The air outside was cool, a gentle relief against my flushed skin. It was the kind of summer evening where the heat of the day lingered in the pavement, while the breeze carried a faint shiver. I stood there for a moment with my keys clenched tight in my palm, letting the night settle around me.

I was going to see Reya. My best friend. And it could be my worst mistake. God, I hoped she would tell me the truth. I needed it more than I dared admit to anyone.

The joys of driving into the city centre on the weekend: chaos, flashing brake lights, music spilling from rolled-down windows, and the oddly satisfying hope that someone had just pulled out of that sweet little loading bay spot near the corner where the coffee house sits. It had always been a gamble. But tonight, fate handed me the winning ticket. There it was, the spot, only a few steps from the door.

My hands were trembling by the time I shifted into park. I did not kill the engine right away. I sat there with the pulse of Dublin humming through the windows, the thrum of my heart punching a frantic tempo against my ribs.

8:02 p.m. I could almost feel the shift in the air, summer rain edging closer but not yet falling. The city still burned in an amber haze lit by the last remnants of a sun slipping behind the skyline. A strange heaviness clung to everything, like the evening was holding its breath.

The coffee house was wrapped in the soft glow of closing time. Blinds half-drawn, a single light flickering near the counter. One figure moving inside, unmistakably Reya.

I got out of the car, feeling focused yet hopelessly scatterbrained. I nearly forgot to lock it until my second try, the beep sounding too loud in the quiet street. I took a steadying breath and walked towards the door.

The bell above the door gave a low, weary chime as I stepped inside. The scent of warm pastries lingered in the air, soft and sweet, although something faintly bitter hovered beneath it. It was probably the last of the coffee left on the counter, already turning cold. The whole place felt like it was exhaling after a long day, the lights dimmed and the chairs stacked.

Reya did not look up right away. She muttered, "Sorry, we're closing," in the tired voice of someone who had repeated the line too many times already. She did not even glance towards me. But when she finally did, her whole body went rigid, as if every muscle snapped into place at once.

"Charlotte?"

I did not give her the chance to say anything else. The pressure that had been building in my chest all afternoon suddenly tore free.

"What the hell, Reya?" My voice cracked, loud enough to echo against the wood and tile.

"Why did you lie to me?"

She blinked at me. "What?"

"You said you did not know that Clara and I had met up again. But she wrote about it. She wrote that she was scared you would find out and that John was on the phone to you. And now I know that is exactly what happened."

"Charlotte, slow down."

"No. You do not get to tell me to slow down," I snapped. The words came sharper than I meant, but I was long past caring about careful tones.

"Why did you not tell me she came in here looking for me? And why would you tell her to stay away from me in the first place?"

Reya flinched, only slightly. Then she straightened her shoulders as if preparing for impact. She answered in reverse, as if she wanted to control at least one part of this conversation.

"Because I had your best interests at heart."

The heat in my chest surged.

"You told her to stay away from me because you thought that was best for me?" I could hardly believe the words.

"I know it was best," she replied, her voice clipped and steady.

"You have a short memory, Charlotte. Or maybe you are just in denial. But you were wrecked after what happened with her. You cried every night for weeks. You barely ate. You stopped seeing people. You did the bare minimum to get through each day. You could not say her name for a year. You were broken."

"I had a right to grieve her," I shouted.

"She was my best friend."

"And she dropped you," Reya shouted back.

"She left you behind and went off to play house with her new boyfriend. And when she grew bored of that suburban dream of hers, she came crawling back like it was some kind of game."

"That is not what happened," I said. My voice was quieter now, although I could not tell if it was resignation or disbelief.

Reya's jaw tightened.

"No? Then why did she not call you sooner? Why did it take her more than ten years? Why did she only come back when she was spiralling?"

"Because she was scared," I whispered.

"Because she was hurting and she did not know if I would forgive her."

"And I was trying to protect you from exactly this," Reya said.

"I did not want her messing with your head again. I did not want her storming back into your life and stirring up everything you had buried, only so she could feel better about herself."

"You do not get to decide what I bury," I said sharply.

"She was reaching out. She wanted to fix things."

"She wanted absolution," Reya answered, her voice bitter, almost cold. "Not friendship."

I realised I was shaking. My fists curled so tightly at my sides that my nails pressed into my palms.

"And you did not tell me she had been here because what, you decided I could not handle it?"

"I thought she would walk away," Reya admitted. Her voice faltered for the first time, as if she had finally run out of defences.

"I thought she would take the hint and leave you alone. I did not know she found you again. I swear it, Charlotte. I was not lying about that part. I did not know you two met up. Not until after."

"After she died?" I asked. The question tasted heavy and metallic, even though part of me already knew the answer.

Reya closed her eyes. "Yes. Not until you told me."

Silence settled between us, a long and crushing pause. I could feel something shift inside my ribs, something brittle beginning to collapse. Then the thunder came. It cracked across the sky and rolled through the coffee shop with the full force of the summer storm I had felt brewing for days.

"I saw her the day before she died," I said softly.

"She looked so nervous, but also hopeful. She was scared, Reya. Scared of you. Scared of what you might say or do."

Reya's eyes snapped open.

"You think I had something to do with her..." She cut herself off. "Oh my God. You do."

"I do not know what I think," I said. My voice felt hoarse.

"But Clara died less than twenty four hours after seeing me. After seeing you. After being told, again, that she did not belong in my life."

Reya stared at me, stricken.

"Hold on, Charlotte. I did not see her. I swear it. And I did not know you had seen her again until you said so. I did not know she had..." She could not finish the sentence.

"I did not know. I was trying to look out for you."

"I did not ask you to."

We were both trembling now. Tears filled Reya's eyes. The rain hammered against the windows like fists, relentless, as if the storm itself wanted to force its way inside. It felt as though the whole building was shuddering, as if the weather had been summoned by every word we should not have said. The sound was deafening, yet still not loud enough to drown out the things we could never take back. Then came the faint jingle of the bell above the door.

We froze.

Slowly, we turned.

Someone stood in the doorway, framed by the amber city lights behind them. Rain fell around their silhouette, lit by the sudden flash of lightning.

It was Niall.

37

Aug 23rd, 2025: Niall

I cannot fight the need to fight for her. I never could, not really.

I tried. I genuinely tried to let Charlotte go, to step back and give her the space she asked for. I tried to stay home and pretend I was not watching the clock or listening for the soft hum of her car returning. I told myself I should trust her judgement, trust her strength, trust that she understood exactly what she was walking into. Yet the moment she closed the front door behind her and the sound of her engine faded down the drive, something inside me opened like a wound that had never healed. Raw, throbbing, impossible to silence.

She was going to confront Reya. Alone. And the truth was quietly waiting in the dark corners of my mind. I already knew what lived behind that decision, behind that door she was about to walk through.

I knew the venom Reya carried in her words, the coldness she once spat at Clara. I knew how deeply she had cut her, slicing through trust, through certainty, through the final fragile peace Clara tried to hold before her life slipped into shadow. The threat that haunted Clara in her last weeks had spread through her like a poisonous bloom, each petal heavier than the one before.

I knew, because Clara told me. Not with her voice; she never managed to speak it aloud. She told me in the journals she hid away, the fragile little notebooks filled with writing that trembled across the page. I read them all in the months after she died. I read them when the world had stopped making sense, when I stopped eating, when sleep became a stranger. I tore our home apart looking for answers, terrified of the silence she left behind. I read them while clinging to the belief that she did not choose her own end. I held on to that idea like it was the only solid thing left in my hands.

That belief has driven every decision since the day we lost her. It was the reason I uprooted our lives and brought the kids back to Cherrywood House. I wanted Reya as far from us as possible, from me, from anything Clara ever touched. If she ever came near again, I feared I might lose whatever self control I still possessed. I feared I might break completely, or worse, do something I could never undo.

And now Charlotte was walking straight into the fire I had spent years avoiding. Into the heart of the storm that destroyed my family once already. I could not let that happen. Not her. Not again.

My hands tightened around the steering wheel until my knuckles blanched. The road stretched ahead in a blur beneath the night sky. Streetlights streaked past my windows, but my mind was locked in the past while racing toward the future at the same desperate pace.

For most of my life, I believed there was one perfect person for everyone, one soulmate you were lucky to find even once. Clara had been mine. I thought I would spend my entire life tangled with hers. When she died, I believed that whatever chance I had at love had died with her.

Then Charlotte appeared. Quietly, slowly, unexpectedly. She became a second chance I did not know I deserved. She pulled me from the edge when I had stopped noticing the drop. With her, I felt whole again, as if my heart had remembered how to beat properly. Losing her was a thought that scraped against bone. I could not allow it.

I glanced at the passenger seat where her jacket lay neatly folded as if she were still sitting beside me. My heartbeat pounded, each thud heavy with dread. I kept seeing Reya snapping, lashing out, cornering Charlotte in a place where no one could help. Clara's voice whispered through my memory, warning me in that soft way she used to when something frightened her.

Reya was not just a threat. She was a storm that had been waiting years to break.

But I had been wrong too. I had convinced myself that Reya was the one who hurt Clara. I painted her as the villain that haunted Clara's final days. I carried that certainty like a shield, even when guilt gnawed at the edges.

The truth sat deeper. Darker. Twisted in ways I was only beginning to understand.

My breath caught. I had to get to Charlotte. I had to protect her. I had to untangle the truth before it broke all of us.

The coffee house stood in darkness when I arrived. Its windows were shuttered. The familiar glow was gone, leaving the whole place swallowed by night. The air felt thick, the quiet heavy enough to crush.

Inside, something moved. A sharp voice cut through the stillness. An argument. I pushed open the door just as Charlotte's voice cracked through the room, raw with anger and something even more painful underneath.

She was mid fight. She did not see me at first. I stopped just inside the doorway, trying to quiet the frantic beating in my chest. I did not want to frighten her. But when her eyes finally landed on me, her expression shifted entirely, as if she had seen a ghost she was not ready for.

"So you knew who I was all along?" Her voice echoed in the dim space. It sounded hollow, brittle, close to breaking.

I stared at her, confused and disoriented.

"What?"

Her eyes narrowed. They searched my face with a burning intensity.

"You knew who I was to Clara. I was Lottie."

The name hit me with the force of a speeding train. Lottie. Charlotte. My Charlotte. The girl Clara wrote about in her journals. The friend she had lost and missed. The one who had worked here all those years ago. The last person Clara tried to reach for before fear drove her away.

I blinked, stunned.

"You are Lottie?"

She did not answer. She did not need to. Every piece slid into place with a cold finality.

"I did not know," I said, my voice rough. "I swear, Charlotte. When we met, when we started talking, I had no idea you and Clara were friends. I did not make the connection when she mentioned this place. All I knew was that Reya worked here and that Clara was terrified to return. She saw someone on the phone that day and panicked."

I stepped closer, desperate for her to believe me.

"Falling in love with you was an accident. A beautiful one. You made me feel alive again when I thought that part of me had died with her. I was barely functioning. I drowned myself in work. I failed the kids. I was obsessed with the unanswered questions about Clara. And then you walked in and reminded me what it felt like to be a person, not a shadow."

My gaze shifted to Reya, who stood behind the counter. She looked pale, shaking, her eyes wild with fear and guilt. She seemed ready to collapse under the weight of everything she had kept buried.

The storm had finally broken. And we were all standing inside it.

Reya's voice trembled as if it might collapse under its own weight.

"I didn't do anything to her," she whispered, barely managing to form the words.

"I promise. I didn't."

Charlotte looked shattered, almost hollow, the way someone appears when a truth they relied on has been ripped away. It was as if her heart had been peeled open in front of us.

"She was scared of you," Charlotte said, her voice so soft it nearly disappeared into the room.

"I was scared, too!" Reya cried, her breath hitching.

"Clara was intense, Charlotte. You know exactly what she was like. She could swallow a moment whole. That last fight between us made my hands shake for hours. I told her to stay away from you because I thought she would hurt you again. I was trying to stop things from getting worse. But I never touched her. I never hurt her."

"You lied to both of us," Charlotte said. Her voice cracked like thin ice under too much weight.

"You kept her from me."

Reya's face folded in on itself as though she could not bear the accusation.

"I was trying to protect you. I swear it. After that night, I never saw Clara again. I do not know who John called or why she was spooked. I was not part of any of it."

I stepped forward, my nails digging hard into my palms, grounding me against the rising fury in my chest.

"Spooked? She was terrified," I snapped, each word pulled from somewhere raw.

"And then she died. Do you understand that? Do you see how it looks from where we are standing?"

Reya shook her head with frantic energy, tears streaming down her cheeks and dripping onto her collar.

"I'm not a killer, Niall. I have never even thrown a proper punch. You think I poisoned her? Drugged her? I have never handled anything stronger than a headache tablet in my life."

"You're a liar," I growled, my voice rough and unsteady.

"And you are going to get what is coming to you."

Footsteps sounded behind me. Slow, measured, as if every step had been rehearsed. I did not even have time to turn my head. Pain ripped through my back, sharp and vicious, so hot it stole my breath and folded my body forward. I hit the floor with a thud I barely felt.

Charlotte screamed, a sound that sliced through the air with pure terror. Reya let out a shriek of her own. I forced myself to twist, to see, and there he was. John stood above me with his eyes wide and disturbingly empty. His calmness chilled the room. In his hand he held a box cutter streaked with rust and something darker.

He leaned in close, his words sliding out in a low whisper that scraped at my spine.

"She should have just kept away."

My body crumpled. Warmth spread beneath me as blood soaked through my shirt and seeped across the cold tile. The world dimmed at the edges. My ears rang. My vision blurred into colours and shapes without meaning. Yet through the haze, I saw Charlotte sink to her knees beside me. Tears ran down her cheeks in frantic, uneven lines. She pressed her hands against the wound, trying to hold me together by sheer will.

"Stay with me, Niall," she sobbed, her voice shaking with a kind of fear I had never heard from her.

"Please. Stay with me."

And I tried. I truly did. Because I was a fortunate man. I had found love when I thought life had closed that door forever. I had a family worth every ounce of strength in my body. I was fortunate enough to want to survive. I simply needed to hold on. For Clara. For Charlotte. For the kids. For every truth still buried in the dark.

I will stay alive. I have to.

38

Aug 23rd, 2025: John

Blind devotion leads to bloody hands.

I always take the back entrance. It is the only way that feels right. The alley behind the coffee house is narrow, cluttered with broken bottles and the stale remnants of yesterday's rain. A warm breeze drifts through, pushing damp air against the back of my neck. There is a faint scent of ozone in it, charged and expectant, the kind that prickles across your skin. A summer storm is on its way. I can feel it in my bones, the same way I can feel the shape of a decision before I make it.

Reya says closing alone helps her unwind. It gives her time to breathe after a long day, space to settle her thoughts. I let her believe she is alone. It comforts her, and that is what matters. But most nights, I am here. Watching from the alley, listening through the walls, tracking every footstep that passes the door. Making sure no one follows her. No one touches her. No one threatens her.

That is my job. More than that, it is my purpose, the anchor that steadies everything in my life.

And if I am being honest, I like the way she moves when she thinks she is unobserved. There is a reverence in those moments, a quiet grace made for my eyes alone. She moves like a dancer in some forgotten ritual: wiping counters, aligning cups with meticulous care, humming beneath her breath. The gentle slope of her neck, the tired fall of her shoulders. She exists inside a world I have made safe for her, a world I maintain with careful hands.

Everything about her belongs to me. Not in a way that is crude or possessive. No, it is deeper than that, almost sacred. Protective. Like a knight pledging his life to his queen, a vow carved into the marrow of his bones.

That is what I am. A knight. A protector. A man willing to cross every line if it means shielding her from harm. They have never understood that, not her friends, not her colleagues. The strangers who drift into her orbit are like moths pressing themselves against a flame. They come and go, clueless, unnecessary.

They do not know what we have. They do not deserve to know. And they certainly could not handle the truth of what I have done for her.

The first time I saw Reya truly break was the night she came home sobbing. It had been a bitter winter evening, the kind where the wind claws at your coat and the sky hangs heavy with swollen clouds. Rain hammered the windows like fists.

She collapsed into me, shaking hard enough that her breath stuttered through her chest. Her words came out fractured.

"I can't watch Charlotte get hurt again," she whispered. Again and again, the same sentence, the same tremble. "Not with Clara. Not again."

She did not need to say anything else. I saw it all in her eyes. Heard it in the way her voice dipped when she said Clara's name. The way she gripped her wineglass until her knuckles whitened. The fury simmered beneath the surface, buried under a layer of pain.

She wanted Clara gone.

Not in words, not explicitly, but I know how to read Reya. I always know what she means, what she truly wants. She did not need to ask. That is what love is: listening to the space between words, stepping into the fire before they even know they are cold.

So I did what any man would do for the woman he loves.

I made a call to an old university friend, a biochemist who had sold his morals long before I met him. He dabbled in dangerous things, plants that kill, molecules with teeth. Ricin, he said, was his newest fascination. He spoke about it like it was art.

He did not ask why I wanted it. He probably assumed it was academic curiosity, something theoretical, a reckless prank at worst. I let him believe whatever suited him. People will always choose the explanation that feels safest.

I calculated the dosage with precision. Just enough to make Clara ill, enough to rattle her, frighten her, drive her away from Charlotte and, more importantly, away from Reya's peace.

But nature does not always follow the rules we give it.

The first rumble of thunder reaches me as I step up to the café door. Fat raindrops splatter across the pavement, each one blooming into a darker stain. The air vibrates with the promise of a storm, thunder murmuring overhead like a distant animal waking from sleep.

I push through the back door.

The air inside is tense, stretched thin like a wire ready to snap. Charlotte's voice slices through it, high and frantic. Niall stands red-faced near the counter, fists clenched at his sides, chest rising and falling in short bursts. Reya is behind the register, her expression frozen, as if carved from marble about to crack.

Everything is falling apart. And I will not let that happen.

Lightning flashes outside, bathing the coffee house in stark, fleeting light. I walk up behind Niall silently, every step deliberate. My hand finds the box cutter hidden in my jacket pocket. The cool metal sits against my palm like a promise.

He is shouting now, at Reya, at Charlotte, at the world for daring to press against him.

I do not give myself time to think.

I slide the blade free and drive it between his ribs.

There is a wet sound, a shuddering gasp torn from his body. His spine buckles. His mouth opens in shock. Then he stumbles forward, wheezing, the fight bleeding out of him far faster than he can comprehend.

Charlotte screams. Reya makes a sound I have never heard before, sharp and animal, disbelief carved into every breath.

Thunder cracks directly above us, a furious roar that shakes the windows. The storm has reached its peak, slamming rain against the glass in relentless sheets.

I lean close, whispering into Niall's ear as he collapses.

"She should have just kept away."

He hits the floor.

Charlotte drops beside him, hands slick with blood. She tries to cover the wound, pressing down, shouting for help, calling his name as if that alone might pull him back.

I do not even look at her.

My eyes are on Reya.

"Come on," I say, holding out a hand speckled with blood. "We need to leave. Now."

She does not move. She does not blink. She is staring at me as if seeing me for the very first time.

"Reya," I say again, softer now. "It is all right. You are safe."

She steps back, arms wrapped tightly around herself. Her mouth trembles.

"What did you do?" she whispers.

"I did it for you," I say, taking a step forward. "Everything I have ever done has been for you. You said you did not want to share Charlotte. You said—"

"I never asked for this," she cries, flinching away. "I was upset. I was venting. I never meant any of it. Oh God. You poisoned her, didn't you?"

The lights flicker as thunder shatters the space between us. The storm batters the building with a rage that feels almost human.

"I protected you," I snap. The heat rises in my throat, thick and bitter. "Just like I always do. Just like I have to."

"You're insane," she breathes. "I don't know you. I don't recognise you at all."

My hand falls to my side. Something inside me twists hard, an ugly wrench that steals the air from my lungs.

Because now I see it. All the red flags I thought I had buried beneath kindness and patience. The ones I disguised with late-night tea and steady reassurances. The ones Reya ignored because she wanted to believe in the version of me I created for her.

She sees them now. All at once.

She is not coming with me. She will never come with me again.

The rain outside becomes a deafening roar, drowning out Charlotte's sobs and the wet rasp of Niall struggling to breathe. The windows shudder under the weight of the wind. Lightning splits the sky in violent bursts, turning the world white for a heartbeat at a time.

And through it all, Reya retreats from me as if I am something monstrous.

Maybe I am.

Maybe I always was.

But no one ever talks about how much a monster can love. How deeply. How completely. How fiercely they hold on to the one thing that gives their darkness meaning.

I would carve the world to pieces if it meant keeping her safe.

I would do it all again.

Even this.

39

Aug 23rd, 2025. Reya

The Devil in My Bed.

I was counting the till when the bell above the door jingled. Its chime felt too sharp, too sudden, almost like a scream cut short.

"Sorry, we are closing," I said. I barely glanced up, expecting a regular, perhaps someone who had forgotten their phone or wanted one last takeaway before we locked up for the night.

But it was not that. It was her.

Charlotte.

My breath caught mid-exhale. The till drawer hung open, coins scattered and entirely forgotten. She stood in the doorway like something pulled from a fever dream, sopping wet from the storm outside. Water dripped from her jacket, her hair clung to her cheeks, and her chest rose and fell in frantic bursts as though she had run through the weather with one purpose that had chased her here.

A low roll of thunder groaned behind her. The first true warning of the summer storm had arrived, and with it came everything I had dreaded.

For days, ever since Clara's journals resurfaced, I had known this moment would find me. I knew Charlotte would reach the passages about me, the ones I had prayed would stay buried. The truth had been a fuse, smouldering slowly, and Charlotte had always been the match that could light it without hesitation.

There was a storm in her eyes too. Her keys were clenched tight in one fist, her jaw locked in a way that looked almost painful. For a split second the whole café stilled. The only sound was the steady pulse of rain beating against the windows, a slow yet insistent drumming that felt like a heartbeat rising in my ears. I barely had time to register the panic before she was coming at me, her words firing with a force that made me flinch.

"Why did you lie when you said you did not know Clara and I had met up again?"

Her voice was sharp and accusing, each word hot enough to burn.

"What gave you the right to tell her to stay away from me?"

"Why did you not tell me she was looking for me?"

"What else did you hide from me?"

I froze. My mouth opened, then closed again. My tongue felt sluggish and useless while my heart hammered hard enough to hurt.

"I... Charlotte, wait," I tried, though the words barely held shape.

She did not wait. She could not. Her fury had been waiting for release and now it surged toward me like a wave that had snapped its barrier. I could see it in her eyes, the grief, the betrayal, the confusion. All of it rising at once. So I answered, because there was nothing else left to do.

"I did not know you met again," I stammered.

My voice did not sound like mine at all. It felt too thin, too small.

"Not before she died. I swear to God. I did not lie about that."

Her expression twisted. It was not only rage. Underneath it lay something raw and wounded, a sorrow that seemed to find its shape only now that she had spoken her accusations aloud.

"And yes," I said, the confession heavy on my tongue.

"I did not tell you she was looking for you because I thought it was unfair. She dropped you, Char. She vanished from your life without explanation. Then what? She gets to come back whenever she likes and pick you up again like a toy she left in a box?"

A gust of wind slammed against the door behind her, making it shudder. The rain quickened, a hard patter that echoed along the walls. The lights in the café flickered once, then steadied, though the air felt charged with the same electricity that crackled in Charlotte's stare.

"She was my best friend," Charlotte snapped.

"She was not anymore," I fired back. The words were sharper than I intended. Louder too. Something inside me, something wounded, had driven them out before I could stop it.

"You barely survived that fallout. You cried yourself sick for weeks. Do you remember that? I was the one who picked up the pieces when she shattered you."

My voice cracked. I could feel myself unravelling, my composure slipping one thread at a time. This was never how I imagined the truth would fall from me. I had expected tears, perhaps quiet anger, but not this breaking apart, not this raw honesty cutting between us.

"And yes," I said, quieter now, my throat tight, "I told her to stay away. Because I was scared. Scared she would hurt you again. Scared everything we rebuilt would fall apart."

Thunder cracked overhead, louder this time, close enough to rattle the cups stacked on the shelf behind me.

"But it was not your call to make," Charlotte said. Her voice trembled, not with weakness but with the weight of her pain.

"You do not get to decide who I forgive."

I nodded, even as tears stung my eyes. There was no defence strong enough to excuse what I had done. Only the dull ache of knowing my choices had been born from love, fear, and a desperation to protect her, even if I had done it badly. The air between us felt tense, as if electrified. Outside, the storm lashed at the windows, and the streetlamps blurred into hazy smudges behind the sheets of rain.

Then the door opened again.

The bell chimed softly, barely audible through the crash of thunder.

I turned towards the sound and froze.

He stood just inside the doorway, rain sliding from his hair and coat in steady streams. He looked pale, shocked, as if he had walked into a scene that had been building long before he arrived.

"Charlotte," he said. His voice sounded muffled and distant, almost as though it came from underwater.

Her head snapped towards him. Her whole body stiffened.

"So, you knew who I was all along?" she demanded. Her voice cracked through the space like lightning.

His brows knitted in confusion.

"I... what?"

"You knew," she repeated, louder now, her breath quick and uneven.
"You knew I was her best friend."

Then it happened. I saw it unfold on his face, recognition hitting with the force of a physical blow. His eyes widened. His lips parted.

He gasped. "You are Lottie?"

Charlotte nodded. Her expression shifted, a mixture of disbelief and devastation, as though she was grieving another truth that had been kept from her.

Niall stepped forward slowly, his shock clear in every movement.

"I had no idea. I swear. I only knew this was the coffee house Clara used to come to. I only knew she was scared of a girl named Reya. I did not know you were the friend she was meeting."

He kept talking, the words spilling from him without pause. His grief, his guilt, the hollow ache he had been carrying since the day Clara died. His certainty that she had not taken her own life. His need for answers that refused to let him sleep.

And through all of it, his eyes kept flicking to me, sharp with something that felt like accusation. As if he was searching my face for every missing piece of the story. As if he believed I was the poison threading its way through everything he had ever understood.

"No, wait, Niall", I said, shaking my head, my voice already starting to crack.

"I never saw Clara that day. I swear I didn't. I don't even know who John was calling. It wasn't me."

Charlotte looked torn, her eyes darting between us as if trying to piece together a puzzle that kept shifting. But Niall? Niall simply broke.

"You're a liar!" he shouted, the sound raw enough to scrape bone.

"You terrified her. You destroyed her. And you're going to pay for it."

"No, no, I didn't, I couldn't." The words tumbled out as I sobbed.

"I hate confrontation. I always have. You think I could have done that?"

Then it happened. Far too fast, quicker than anything in films. There is no director stretching it for dramatic effect, no slow-motion gasp to prepare you. Reality is colder, sharper, cruel all by itself.

Niall jerked forward, his face twisting in shock. He dropped and crumpled to the floor like his strings had been cut. A puddle of blood grew on the tile beneath him. And behind him stood John.

He was still. Terrifyingly calm. A box cutter glistening red in his hand. His eyes were blank, emptied of anything human. He leaned close to Niall's ear and whispered something I couldn't hear. I felt the chill of it anyway, sinking deep into my bones as if my body understood what my ears had missed.

Charlotte screamed. Again, and again, her voice tearing through the storm outside.

"Niall. Niall."

John turned to me with the casual air of someone brushing off a minor inconvenience rather than a man who had just attempted murder.

"Come on", he said, reaching out his bloodied hand.

"We need to leave. Now."

My entire world tilted as if the ground itself shifted. I stepped back, my arms folding tight around my stomach as though I could keep myself from falling apart.

He said something else, but I couldn't hear him. My heartbeat drowned everything, loud and frantic, filling my ears like a warning drum.

"What did you do?" I whispered, my voice barely audible over the storm rattling the windows.

But I already knew. Somewhere deep inside, a part of me had always known.

He stepped forward.

"I did it for you. Everything was for you. You said you didn't want to share her with Clara. You said..."

"I never asked for this", I choked out.

"I was upset. I was venting. I never meant... Oh my God. You poisoned her, didn't you?"

He had no idea I knew the truth. That he wasn't a nobleman who had chosen love over ambition and left university to build a life with me. He was a disgraced student expelled for unethical experiments. That heartwarming tale about sacrificing a future for a family was nothing more than a tidy little lie. I tried to believe it, even after I found that letter all those years ago. I told myself it meant nothing. That the universe was playing tricks. But the truth has a way of rotting under the surface until it becomes impossible to ignore.

"I protected you," he bellowed, the sound vibrating with a frightening sort of pride.

"Just like I always do. Just like I always have to."

"No," I said, backing away further, my heels slipping slightly on the blood-slick floor.

"No, John. That isn't protection. That's... You killed her. You murdered Clara."

"You're insane," I breathed out, the words escaping me like air from lungs finally breaking the surface of deep water.

"I don't know you. I don't recognise you at all."

He reached for me. I recoiled hard, instinctive and violent, as if his touch would burn straight through my skin. Because now I saw him. Truly saw him. Not the man I loved. Not the protector I believed I'd married. I saw the control. The manipulation. The possessiveness I had dressed up as devotion for far too long. The red flags I'd treated like confetti were now blazing, demanding to be acknowledged.

A monster. That was what he had always been. Hidden behind patient eyes and careful charm.

I stared at the man I had chosen and felt the truth hit me like a punch to the gut. All this time, I thought I had been chasing fairy tales, childish dreams of knights and rescues. But women grow older. We stop wanting castles and white horses. We want to feel safe. Cherished in the quiet, ordinary ways. And suddenly I saw it, stark and brutal. I had never been safe. Not once.

The danger was never out in the world. It was him. It had always been him.

And what I thought was love, what I clung to as if it were my last hope, was never love. It was obsession, twisted and hungry. A thing that wore the mask of devotion while it consumed me whole.

I realised it too late, but I realised it. God help me, I did.

Charlotte screamed again. This time I turned toward the sound and broke eye contact with John.

Niall. He was still breathing. Shallow, but alive.

"Oh my God," I whispered. "Oh my God, he's still..."

Instinct took over. I dropped to my knees beside him, already slipping on the blood. My hands trembled as I tore open his shirt, searching for the wound, trying desperately to stop the bleeding. I pressed down, harder than I meant to, but gentleness had no place here.

The wound made no sense. There was so much blood. Far too much for a simple box cutter, far too much for anything that small.

And then it struck me, cold and clean like ice to the chest.

Of course it was John. The kind of man who wouldn't simply stab. He would twist the blade, enjoying the cruelty of it.

"Stay with me, Niall," I muttered, voice shaking. "Please. Look at Charlotte. Keep your eyes on Charlotte."

Charlotte dropped beside me, crying openly, her hands hovering, trembling, uncertain. I barked instructions at her. Pressure. Towels. Anything.

And in that moment, when all attention was on Niall, when every breath became a plea and every second a question, John vanished.

I didn't see him leave. None of us did. The bell did not chime. The door did not slam. He simply disappeared into the roar of the storm outside.

I stayed kneeling in a spreading pool of blood, my hands stained, my chest heaving, trying to hold on to a life that was slipping through my fingers, aware that somewhere out there the devil walked free.

And I was the one who had married him.

40

Aug 24th, 2025: Charlotte

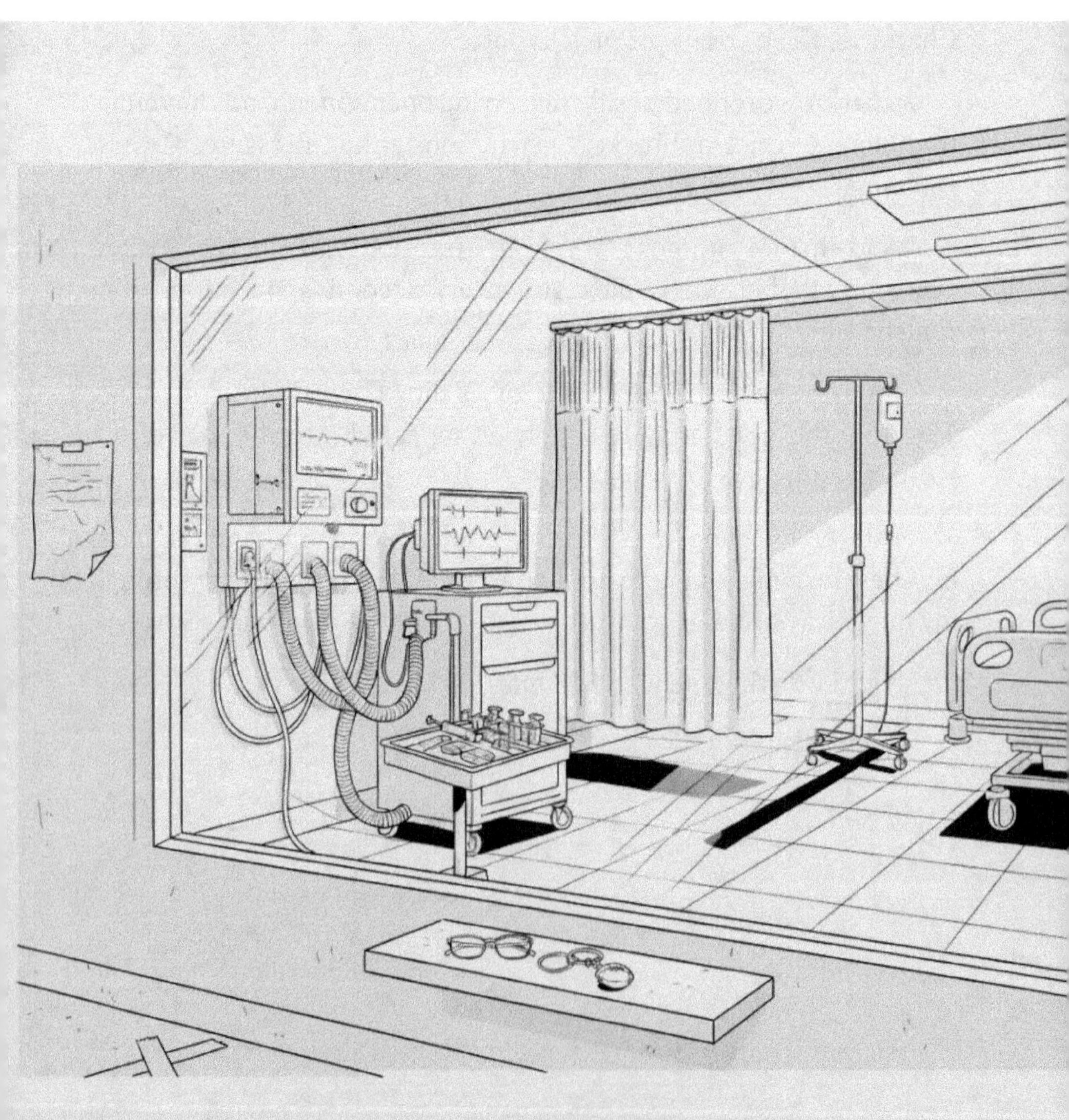

In the Wake of Almost.

Fluorescent lights buzz overhead, the harsh kind that makes everything look washed out, as if the world has been drained of warmth. They give you the sort of headache that arrives behind the eyes and refuses to leave. It feels as though I have not slept in days. Perhaps I have not. Perhaps sleep is something I will never trust again after last night.

The smell of antiseptic clings to everything. My clothes, my skin, even the back of my throat. It has soaked so deeply into me that it feels as if I am breathing chemicals instead of air. The waiting room outside the ICU is quiet. Only the low hum of vending machines and the soft squeak of a nurse's shoes disturb the stillness. Yet none of it feels real.

Because I am not here, not truly. I am trapped in the echo of what happened. Niall's knees hitting the floor. Reya's shaking hands as she dialled 112, blood smeared across her sleeves like a warning. John's face vanishing into the night, swallowed by shadows, as if the darkness itself wanted to claim him.

Now I wait, suspended in some strange space between dread and disbelief. A ghost haunting my own life.

The double doors creak open.

"Mrs Donnelly," a nurse says, her tone soft. I stand before I can even think, as if her words have pulled me upright by a thread.

The doctor draws me aside, his expression grave, his voice calm in that careful, practised way that suggests the truth beneath it is far worse. We walk into a quieter corridor, leaving behind the antiseptic brightness of the ER and the beeping of machines that mark time differently for everyone who hears them. The hallway is still, but the silence between us feels stretched, heavy, ready to split open.

He begins gently. His words are slow and deliberate. His gaze holds mine, steady, as though anchoring me to the moment.

"Niall was stabbed in the back with a boxcutter," he says.

"The blade slipped between two ribs and punctured his lung. There was internal bleeding, and his breathing was compromised when he came in."

My stomach twists. I knew he had been hurt, yet hearing the details makes everything sharper. I can still see the scene unfolding with awful clarity. Niall's strangled breath. His body collapsing. The flash of steel in John's hand. There is a difference between witnessing a wound and understanding the depth of the damage it leaves behind.

The doctor continues, sensing that my quiet is not surprise but dread.

"He is stable now. We inserted a chest tube to drain the blood and reinflate the lung. The immediate danger has passed, although recovery will not be simple. There is muscle damage, and the lung will need time to heal. He will require rest, physical therapy, and close monitoring."

I nod, swallowing against the tightness in my throat. His clinical explanation settles over me like a heavy blanket, yet it does nothing to soften the memory of how it all began or what it means for everything that comes next.

The doctor pauses, then adds, more gently, "The physical wounds will heal in time. What concerns me as much is the psychological impact. Being attacked from behind by someone he knows changes more than the body. It changes how a person understands the world."

The words hang in the cold air. I feel them land and stay. Sharp. Precise. Unavoidable.

"He may need help processing this. Counselling, perhaps. Not only for the trauma itself but for what it represents. That loss of safety. That betrayal. These things leave marks we cannot see on any scan."

I thank him, though the word feels thin and fragile, as if it might crumble before it reaches him. There is so much more to this than injury. Niall has not simply been hurt. Something essential has been broken open. Trust. Certainty. The quiet sense of safety we all pretend is permanent.

When I turn back toward Niall's room, the corridor feels longer than before. Colder. The future presses against me with a weight that steals my breath. Healing will not be stitches and rest alone. It will be the harder work, the silent kind, the kind that asks you to walk forward even when every step trembles.

Even when hope feels like something that stings to hold.

The moment threatens to overwhelm me, a rising tide inside my chest, when I hear footsteps pounding along the floor. Then I see them. The twins. Emily and Rory. Their faces flushed from running, eyes wide and frightened, searching for me.

Emily spots me first and breaks into a sprint. Her voice slices through the corridor with the speed and certainty of lightning.

"Mum."

One word. One impossible, devastatingly beautiful word.

It hits me like a blow to the chest. A name I have imagined her using, dreamed of in secret, feared I would never hear. Something holy, delicate, and overwhelming.

I kneel just in time for her to fling herself into my arms. I hold her tightly, almost too tightly, afraid she might vanish if I loosen my grip. Her small heart thuds against mine. She does not let go. Neither do I. Not yet. Not when everything else feels so terrifyingly uncertain.

Rory trails behind, wiping at his red and swollen eyes with the sleeve of his hoodie. He tries to play it cool, the way he always does, as if bravado might patch over everything he is feeling.

"Alright, Ma?" he says with a grin that never quite reaches his eyes.

Before I can even raise an eyebrow, Emily elbows him sharply in the ribs.

"Don't call her that. She hates it."

He snorts, rolls his eyes in that exaggerated teenage way, yet I catch the small shift in his shoulders as they finally loosen. Relief suits him more than the mask he prefers.

A moment later I look up and spot Conor and Samantha approaching. Nicky walks with his arm linked through Samantha's and Sammy is practically speed walking to keep pace with them. Behind them is Rachel, Niall's sister, her hand resting lightly on Rita's elbow as if guiding her forward.

But no sign of Conrad. Thank God for small mercies.

They pause long enough to give the children a moment with me, then file quietly into the suite one after another.

Samantha and Conor hold back a little.

"He's stable," I breathe out at last. I had not realised I had been holding that breath all night, as though oxygen might vanish if I let myself hope.

Conor speaks with a low calm that feels like the quiet after a storm.

"And that is because of Reya. She did everything right. She called it in, she knew the steps. Her volunteer training with the Ambulance Service got him here fast. Your husband might be alive because of her."

I nod, my throat tight and raw. For all the tension and confusion between us, Reya had stepped forward when it mattered most.

"Is she alright?" My voice drops to a whisper.

"Shaken, which is understandable. But she is safe," Samantha says. "She is at one of the Donnelly apartments in town. There is proper security and no one knows she is there. John has no chance of guessing. She is protected."

I release a slow breath and the weight pressing on my shoulders eases, if only a fraction.

Then the question that has been gnawing at me breaks free.

"So your father just could not be bothered to show up? His son was stabbed." My tone comes out sharper than I expect, although I do not regret it for a moment.

Conor smiles, a small and strangely peaceful expression.

"He will not be around anymore."

I blink at him. "What, wait, what?"

He leans back against the wall, his eyes warm yet unreadable.

"After you called last night, Sam and I went straight to your place. But Niall had already asked my mum to watch the kids. He must have known he would be out for a long while. So we told her everything. The way my father treated Clara, the way he assaulted and harassed her, all the accusations that she was after the so called Donnelly fortune."

Samantha steps in gently. "It broke Rita. You could see it. Then she said something none of us expected."

Conor's expression shifts, softening at the memory of the moment the truth cracked open.

"Mum told us the Donnelly fortune was never Dad's. It was hers. Her family built it. She was the one with the brains, the ambition, the legacy. He was nothing more than a temp at her father's firm, fetching coffees and trying too hard to charm the boss's daughter. She thought he was sweet. She took him to dinner. The next morning, she woke up with no memory of how the night ended. Four weeks later she found out she was pregnant.

He did not marry up, he hunted her.

He trapped her. It was never the other way around."

I stare at him, feeling numb.

"It was a different time for women," I say at last, my voice hollow. Shocked, yet knowing what I know about him now, I realise I should not be surprised at all. Not even for a heartbeat.

"She said she is done. She is divorcing him and firing him. His title was only for show. He never owned anything real. Everything was in her name, thanks to her father's foresight."

Samantha gives a small, gentle smile.

"And she had a long talk with Conor. She apologised for using him as a pawn for so many years."

I glance at Conor. His grin is soft, almost disbelieving, a boyish hope peeking through the years of strain.

"She said sorry," he murmurs, as if the word itself might vanish.

"Not the half hearted kind. A real apology. I think we might finally be alright. After everything."

I reach out and touch his arm.

"You deserve that. More than you know."

We share a look, quiet and knowing, something that acknowledges the years of silent suffering that might finally be shifting. Then the nurse gestures for us to enter.

We walk together into Niall's suite. He is propped up in bed, pale but awake, with an IV in his arm and a deep bruise blooming under one eye from when he collapsed. Yet the smile that lifts his face when he sees us is everything. A fragile piece of hope, warm and stubborn.

Emily and Rory burst in first.

Rory grins at him, this time with real light behind it.

"So, we heard you were our mum's best friend when you were growing up."

Emily jumps in quickly, practically vibrating with excitement.

"Yeah, any embarrassing stories? Come on, spill."

I laugh despite the heaviness of the night, despite the fear still clinging to my bones. The sound surprises even me.

"Oh my God," I say as I slip into the chair beside Niall's bed, his hand already reaching for mine. "Where do I even begin?"

And for the first time in what feels like years

We begin.

41

6 September 2025: John

Take your time, I will wait.

I have always told her never to close up on her own. Always.

It is not safe, not in this city. Not these days. People are unpredictable, desperate, sometimes even wicked enough to make you doubt humanity entirely.

She used to smile whenever I said it, brushing me off and calling me old fashioned or paranoid. She said it was sweet. She said I worried too much. But I was not being sweet. I was being serious. Absolutely serious.

And now?

Now I can see she has forgotten every lesson I tried to give her. Everything I ever did for her, everything I was to her. She has turned away from all of it without a second glance.

I have been watching the coffeehouse for days. Waiting, planning, studying her routine with the kind of patience people mistake for obsession. Stalking, they would call it if they wanted to cheapen what I am doing. But it is not that. It is protection, vigilance, the sort of commitment she never realised she needed. She used to know I looked out for her. She simply stopped remembering that it was me.

There is a run-down printing shop across the street. Its neon sign flickers in one corner and leaves the pavement washed in broken light. The shadows beside it are deep enough to hide in, and I have claimed them as mine. My den, my chapel, my war room. A place built for watching.

I stand there now with my hood up and my glasses reflecting the glow of the street. A figure no one notices, no one questions. A ghost lurking in plain sight.

But I notice everything.

I notice her. Reya.

She is behind the counter just as she always was, although nothing else feels the same anymore. Time has passed, and with it, everything has shifted. Except her laugh. That still floats out of her, too easy, too light. As if she is drifting through a life without weight. As if she has shrugged off everything we shared and stepped into a version of herself that no longer includes me.

That is what cuts deepest. She looks free.

But she should not be. Not without me.

Then there are the people who hover around her now, circling her like she is their rightful centre.

Niall, limping yet somehow alive. He should not be. His survival is on her. She called for help, dialled 112, played the hero with shaking hands. She saved the man I tried to remove from the world.

He should have bled out. I was careful. Precise. Determined.

Yet there he is, sipping a frappe as though his insides were never nearly spilled across the tiles, as though he never shouted my name into the dark.

And Charlotte.

Sitting close beside him with that smug ease of someone who thinks she has earned her place. Wearing his hoodie as if it is some kind of claim, smiling like everything in that shop belongs to her now. She always had a way of slipping into spaces where she was neither needed nor wanted.

I warned Reya once. Told her Charlotte was a parasite, a leech that fed on attention. Reya only laughed, teased me for being dramatic.

It is always the same. They call you dramatic right before they twist the knife.

Even the children are there. Emily calls Charlotte Mum these days. Mum. As though Reya never comforted her after that horrible falling out with her friends. As if I never brought hot chocolate to calm her down, never told her the world would right itself again. As if none of those moments ever mattered.

And Rory. God, Rory. He is laughing tonight, grinning like he has already forgotten the evenings I spent helping him with his homework, pretending to care about algebra so he could feel capable and supported. So he could feel loved.

They have all forgotten. Or worse, they have replaced me.

But Reya is the centre of it all. The point around which everything turns.

And she looks happy.

She should not be.

She looks safe.

She is not. Not without me.

Hours slip by. The sky grows darker and the city exhales, one long breath filled with smoke, street lights and quiet decay. The pavement clears. Niall and Charlotte finally drift away, hands clasped like a vow. Their shadows stretch across the street, long and thin, closing the door on a life that used to be mine.

Eventually it is only her. Reya, alone in the shop.

I know her routine by heart. Every small habit, every pause, each careless detail she never bothered to fix. She always leaves the back door cracked open when she takes out the bin bags. She never locks it until she turns off the last light. It was one of the things I loved about her, that trusting streak. It was also something I hated about the rest of the world. They saw it as an opportunity. They used it. They used her.

Not me.

I protected her goodness, even when she did not ask for it. Especially then.

She never understood what sort of world she was living in, never recognised the kind of people who inhabit it or the things you must do to keep someone safe.

But I do. I understand perfectly. That is what makes me right.

I wait another twenty minutes to be sure.

She does not call anyone to walk her out. She wants to prove she is strong now, self reliant, untouchable.

She is none of those things.

When the city finally quietens, when everything settles into a stillness that feels like a held breath, I move. I cross the road with the certainty of a shadow and slip into the alley behind the shop. Soundless. Unseen.

Even after weeks spent hiding and running, surviving on instinct and grit, I know this place as though it is carved into me. Reya is carved into me in exactly the same way.

Then I am there, standing at the back door.

It is open.

Of course it is.

I step inside.

The scent meets me first. Coffee, bleach, and the faint floral detergent Reya always used on the aprons. A hint of jasmine or lilac, something gentle and innocent. Something she once believed could keep the darker parts of the world away.

She was wrong.

And tonight, I will show her.

But beneath everything, beneath the noise in my head and the dark that clings to my ribs, there is her. Always her.

The room is dim, the sort of dim that seems intentional, shadows curling in the corners like sleeping things waiting for the right moment to wake. The air hums with the flicker of a tired overhead bulb, a faint buzz that coats the silence rather than breaks it.

She is here.

Alone.

Exactly what I told her never to be.

And me? I am no longer the warning she refused to hear. I am the consequence she never believed would arrive.

I pull the door shut behind me. Quiet. Almost tender, as if I am tucking someone in for the night. Then I turn the bolt with a careful twist. I do not want interruptions. Not now.

She always forgot to look behind her.

That was her fatal flaw, trust, blind and soft and easily bruised. Even now she is up front with her head bowed, wiping down counters and sliding coins into the register. Acting as though she is safe. Acting as though the world owes her that safety. Acting as though time has wiped me clean from her memory.

But I have not forgotten.

She hums under her breath. My chest tightens. She still hums when she thinks no one is listening, that same simple tune she used to sing while brewing morning coffee. A cheap little lullaby that has lodged itself into her bones and, unfortunately, into mine.

She does not hear me draw closer.

Every step I take is deliberate. Every breath is matched to the rhythm of her movements, a silent choreography I perfected long before tonight.

I pause by the doorway that opens into the main floor of the coffee house, close enough to see her but still swallowed by shadow. My heart thunders, although not from fear. Fear has no place here. What fills me instead is sharper, urgent, a sense of inevitability tightening its grip around my ribs.

I could speak now. Call her name.

She would turn.

She would freeze.

And for a single heartbeat, that precise sliver of time before she reacts, I would see it in her eyes, the truth she has pretended not to know. The knowledge that she was never safe. Not from me. Not from the thing she helped create.

My fists clench. The skin across my knuckles remains scarred from what happened to Niall. A reminder. A marker of what I am capable of when pushed.

She bends to pick something from the floor. A curl of hair slips free from her bun and falls across her cheek, just like it used to in those early mornings when I...

No.

That version of me is gone. He died the night she chose them instead of me, the night she tossed aside everything we built.

She rises, stretches, her shoulders rolling, and turns slightly toward the back. Still not enough to see me. Still unaware.

I step forward.

Her phone buzzes on the counter. The screen lights with a name, Charlotte. Of course it is. Reya frowns, hesitates, then slides the phone away without answering.

Good.

She has already started distancing herself from them. She might not even realise she has done it, but I see the signs.

I take another step.

The floorboard beneath me creaks.

She freezes.

Her head tilts, just a fraction, just enough to suggest she caught something but cannot be sure. A small pause follows, heavy and uncertain. Then she shakes her head and lets out a soft laugh.

"Paranoid," she whispers to herself.

No. Not nearly paranoid enough.

I am close enough to touch her now. Close enough to reach out and feel her pulse against my palm. I do not. Not yet. I want the moment. I want the breath before the plunge. I want her to understand.

She starts humming again, returning to her routine, sliding back into her quiet, comfortable world.

Then she stiffens.

She turns slowly, eyes sweeping the room with a caution I have never seen from her before.

There is a flicker in her expression. Something raw. Something ancient.

She knows.

Finally she knows.

I smile.

But before I can move or speak her name, the front door swings open.

Footsteps cross the threshold.

Reya gasps. She steps back quickly, her gaze darting between the shadows and the figure stepping forward into the wash of weak light.

Charlotte.

Of course it is her.

I tense. My grip tightens around the handle in my coat pocket. I can still finish this. It can still be quick. Clean. Final.

Reya turns towards Charlotte and they meet halfway, drawn together as if by instinct. Charlotte's expression does not show surprise. It shows readiness, as if she has been waiting for this precise moment.

Reya's fear is gone. In its place sits something calm. Steady. Cold.

Prepared.

And in that second the truth settles.

Reya sliding her phone away earlier was not a dismissal.

It was a signal.

For her.

For Charlotte.

They knew.

Reya speaks first, her voice soft yet cutting.

"You were right. He never knew when to let go."

Charlotte does not smile. She steps forward, placing herself between Reya and me, a wall made of resolve rather than fear.

I lunge.

It is a mistake.

Charlotte moves with frightening precision. She meets me halfway, her arm flashing out to knock mine aside before I can draw the blade. I stumble, but Reya is already there. Her knee slams into my ribs as I attempt to recover, a brutal jab that steals the air from my lungs.

My vision blurs.

I try again, a wild, frantic attempt to regain control, but they are quicker. Together they move with a rhythm that tells me this is no improvisation. They have practised this. Replayed it. Prepared for me.

Charlotte ducks, catches my wrist and twists. Pain shoots up my arm. The knife slips from my hand and skitters across the tiles. Reya is behind me in a heartbeat, driving me down. Her knee digs into my spine and I hit the floor hard.

Airless.

Beaten.

Cold plastic zip ties snap around my wrists. Tight and merciless.

I thrash once. Twice. Useless. It is already over.

Charlotte leans close enough that I feel the warmth of her breath by my ear.

"You should have stayed away," she says.

Reya kneels beside her. For the first time all night her eyes meet mine.

She is not trembling.

She is not crying.

She looks exhausted. And finished with me in a way that feels sharper than any blade.

"You should have stayed away," she says quietly.

Sirens cry in the distance. They grow louder with each passing second.

They stay with me. They do not run. They do not give me room to twist the narrative or salvage a shred of dignity. They watch. They remain ready until the door bursts open and blue lights spill across the floor.

I am hauled upright, my breath ragged and pointless. Through the blur I see them, Reya and Charlotte, still standing, unmoved, united.

They hug.

Like friends.

Like sisters.

Like liars.

I thought she was alone.

She never was.

And that truth is what defeated me in the end.

Epilogue

Six Months Later: Charlotte

New life, who is this?

The city feels different in spring. Brighter. Softer around the edges. The pavements seem warmer somehow, as if the whole place has exhaled after holding its breath all winter. Even the coffee tastes different. Less bitter, more hopeful. Maybe it is the new roast Niall ordered, a blend he fussed over for weeks. Or maybe it is the way the light filters through the front windows now, unhindered, washing the walls of the coffee house in a gentle golden calm.

It does not feel like a place where someone was almost murdered. It does not feel like a place where everything nearly fell apart. Yet I still flinch when the back door creaks open. I still turn, just to check. Old habits do not vanish simply because the danger has passed. They linger like the faint smell of smoke after a fire, reminding you that something once burned.

Reya says she does not blame me. She repeats it whenever we talk. Not as often as before, although often enough that I believe her. Her voice is steadier these days, but there is something guarded beneath it, something I suspect may take years to soften. She stayed. That surprised all of us, even her. Maybe especially her.

The coffee house reopened four weeks after John was caught. It felt oddly ordinary at first, putting out chairs and wiping down the counter, as if routine could paper over everything that had happened. The CCTV footage from a butcher two streets away finally did him in. His limp, his face, the unmistakable rage in his gait. It was all there, captured without intention yet impossible to ignore.

He did not get to Reya that night. We fought. We screamed. And someone heard.

It was a kid in a flat above who reported it. A teenager who claimed she hated the sound of bins being taken out at ridiculous hours, yet recognised the sound of panic the moment it reached her window. I think about her sometimes. How easy it would have been for her to turn up her music and pretend she heard nothing.

When they arrested him, John was not even trying to run. He looked hollow, defeated, as if he had finally seen what Reya had known for years. There was no place left for him in her world. No space for his kind of love, if you could even call it that.

The trial was mercifully short. The jury did not take long to decide.

Clara's remains were five years underground, reduced to brittle bones and dust by the trial. Time had stolen almost everything that could have once been evidence. Ricin breaks down quickly in the body. After death, especially after so much decomposition, it leaves almost nothing behind. The toxicology report offered only whispers. Organ deterioration consistent with ricin exposure, no definitive chemical markers. Legally, it was a minefield. Science alone was never going to give Clara the justice she deserved.

Then the police psychologist stepped in. Quiet, methodical, relentless. During several interviews she chipped away at John's façade, peeling back layers of bravado and justification. At first he was defensive, almost proud, as if the horror he had unleashed was something noble. He claimed he had done it for Reya, that poisoning Clara had been an act of devotion meant to clear the path. Under pressure that narrative collapsed. What surfaced were stark psychological failings: narcissism, a lack of empathy, delusional thinking. He contradicted himself repeatedly, admitting to things no one had even asked. Eventually the confession came. Raw, messy, half-spoken, as if he were recounting a dream he could no longer control. That became the piece of evidence they needed.

Attempted murder. Conspiracy to commit. Involuntary manslaughter. They listed the charges as if reading from a shopping receipt. I still do not understand how they settled on the final one.

Perhaps because Clara had not died immediately. Perhaps because of how long she suffered. Ricin requires only a few grains to be fatal if inhaled, ingested or injected. John's intent had been clear. The charges piled up like bricks, one after another, building a wall no clever defence could tear down.

Then came the medical examiner. Calm, clinical, and devastating. She explained how ricin kills. Not with noise or spectacle. Slowly, cell by cell, organ by organ. It disrupts protein synthesis and shuts the body down from the inside. The courtroom fell silent as she spoke. I remember feeling unable to breathe, as though the air itself had thickened. Even though Clara had died quietly, even though she had never screamed, her suffering had been monstrous. And John, in his twisted conviction, believed he had done it for love.

Niall held my hand the entire time. I do not think he even realised he was doing it.

It still hurts him in quiet moments. That he never put the pieces together sooner. That he loved Clara without truly knowing how afraid she was. Grief has a strange way of finding the cracks in people. It seeps in slowly, then settles. But we are learning how to carry it together now. Not separately. Not in silence. And somehow that feels like the beginning of something new. Something better than what came before.

Rory and Emily no longer ask as many questions. They have moved on in that magical and maddening way children do, as if their young hearts instinctively know when to step forward. Emily still calls me Mum, as if it is the most natural word she has ever spoken. I worried, when we first came home from the hospital and the panic had eased from our days, that the novelty might fade for her. It never did. Now, every time she calls me Mum, I feel as if I am standing on sacred ground, allowed to hold something fragile and astonishing without fear it will slip away.

They tell me stories about Clara now, small things that somehow feel enormous. Silly details. Moments only children would treasure. How she used to sing in the car with exaggerated vibrato. How she mixed up their lunchboxes and pretended it was intentional. How she kissed them goodnight even when they were already asleep, her whisper brushing their dreams. I let them talk. Sometimes, to my own surprise, I even laugh, the sound unfamiliar yet welcome.

Reya still lives in the Donnelly apartment in the city. She refuses to return to her old flat, not ever, as if crossing that threshold would drag her back into a life she has shed. Yet she is here most days in the shop, greeting every customer as though they are long-lost family and singing softly when she thinks no one is paying attention. Her presence steadies the air.

We are not what we were. Something new has taken shape, slow and cautious, built on truths we used to avoid. It feels honest for the first time in years, and although it is fragile, it is real enough to hold.

Conor and Samantha remain the glue that binds the frayed edges of us. Conor with his awful jokes that somehow land exactly when needed. Samantha with her sharp instincts and gentleness she hides far too often. Sammy made a card for Niall when he was discharged from the hospital. It read, "Sorry you got poked." Niall keeps it in his office, propped against a photo frame as if it is an award.

And Rita: she has never been so alive, not in all the years I have known her. She filed for divorce the day after John's trial. The paperwork had been waiting in a drawer for years. The truth about what Conrad did to Clara was the final fracture, the blow that forced her to stop pretending she could carry the weight alone. She only delayed the filing because we were all waiting for John's trial, as if holding our breath might keep the whole thing from collapsing around us.

She hired more women into the company. Rewrote the hiring policies from the ground up. Said it was time her business stood for something good, not just something profitable, and she said it with a clarity that left no room for doubt.

We still visit Clara's grave. Not every day, not always to cry. Sometimes we go simply to sit with her, to let the world go quiet for a little while. I bring her journals every so often. The pages are worn from re-reading, soft at the edges like something loved. I tell her what Emily said at breakfast, how Rory pretended to eat a worm just to make me shriek, how Niall burned the toast yet insists it adds extra flavour to go with my equally burned bacon. We eat a lot of cereal and fruit in our house now. It feels easier, softer.

I tell her she was right. About love. About fear. About how none of us gets to control how the story ends, but each of us can choose the next chapter, one breath at a time.

And sometimes, I swear I can feel her there. A breeze across my neck. A warmth blooming in my chest. A whisper I carry like a secret that protects rather than burdens.

"It is all right, Lottie. You are home."

About the Author

Annette lives in County Kildare with her husband, Steven, and their twin boys. A stay-at-home mum, she writes in the quiet moments of family life and hopes to offer others the escape she has always found in books.